THE REVENANT

JAMES HARPER

This is a work of fiction. Names, characters, organisations, places, events and incidents are either products of the author's imagination or are used fictitiously. Any resemblance to actual persons, living or dead, or actual events is purely coincidental.

Copyright © 2024 James Harper

All rights reserved

No part of this publication may be reproduced, or stored in a retrieval system, or transmitted, in any form or by any means, electronic, mechanical, photocopying, recording, or otherwise, without express written permission of the publisher.

www.jamesharperbooks.com

ISBN: 9798327661806

PROLOGUE

He closed his eyes. Breathed the smell of old leather deep into his lungs as he sank into the driver's seat of the 1959 Jaguar XK150 Drophead Coupe. Wishing he could peel off the blue latex gloves, feel the polished wood of the steering wheel in his hands. Imagining Jessica beside him. Top down, the wind whipping their hair—hers in a ponytail or a polka-dot headscarf—the wheel solid in his hands and forget your power steering upgrade kit as he put the car through its paces on the winding country lanes.

It wasn't ever going to happen. And not only because she'd been dead thirty years.

The sixty-year-old engine started first time, exhaust fumes sucked out into the night air through the open garage doors behind him. Clutch in, slotting the gear stick into reverse. Trying to remember the last time he'd driven a manual car, let alone one this old.

Handbrake off, easing the clutch up, the car creeping backwards . . .

Then his foot slipped off the polished-metal pedal. The old Jag lurched backwards, a gut and wallet-wrenching scrape of lovingly-restored metal on unyielding wood as the rear wing clipped the door frame, and God knows how many thousand pounds went down the toilet in the process.

Shit.

He tried again, now that he had a better feel for the aggressiveness of the clutch. Pulled cautiously forward, straightened up, then backed all the way out without further incident. In the stillness of the night the crunch of tyres on gravel sounded as if an armoured brigade on manoeuvres had just passed through sleepy Ampfield village.

Then back into the garage, heart sprinting in his chest, the blood roaring in his ears.

Killing a man does that to a person not accustomed to it.

He threw the coiled clothesline up and over an exposed ceiling rafter, placed a small step ladder beneath the rope, then went through the side door and into the house. Roy Lynch sat slumped on a hard, wooden chair in the kitchen exactly where he'd left him. Chin hanging down, a viscous string of drool joining it to his chest, liver-spotted hands hanging limply at his sides.

The laptop was already powered-up on the kitchen table, a blank document waiting ready for him to pen Lynch's suicide note once the suicide itself was out of the way.

He put a hand under Lynch's armpit, sweaty with fear, the rank odour coming off him competing with the sharp smell of an old man's urine in his nose. Steering Lynch through the door like an aged relative unsteady on their pins—*careful of the step now*—and over to where the noose hung down from the rafter. Over his head and under his chin. Sliding it tight. And all the while Lynch standing staring uncomprehendingly at the shelves filled with half-empty cans of paint and boxes of screws and nails. Like an impatient small boy allowing his mother to button his coat for him before he could get outside and run wild.

And when everything was in place, they waited together until the time was right.

He had the burner phone out and ready for when it was.

This wasn't for his pleasure alone, after all.

A video to capture the pitiful, squalid death of a man who'd had it coming for a very long time.

Lynch's body twisted and thrashed, legs kicking wildly as the rope cut into his scrawny turkey neck, a final dance choreographed by a madman. And all in vain, adrenaline staging a hopeless rearguard action against the lack of oxygen. Above it all, an obscene choking melding with a high keening wail. The sound of a lifetime's evil hissing out of his body like pus oozing from a lanced boil.

Good riddance and the world a better place for his passing.

Only when the last pathetic kicks had subsided and the desperate *nngh, nngh, nngh* choking quietened to leave a silence interrupted only by the hum of a chest freezer against the back wall, did he hit the red icon and stop the recording.

He stayed for a minute longer as the violent swinging back and forth calmed to a gentle swaying. His own pulse slowing in perfect harmony, soothing and hypnotic, enough to make him want to set him swinging again when at last Lynch's lifeless body was still.

But *tempus fugit* and all that. The suicide note called.

Something classy. As befits a man who owns a 1959 Jaguar XK150, nasty scrape on the rear wheel arch or not.

Except it was more than a final farewell. Killing two birds with one stone.

Payback for another betrayer every bit as culpable as Lynch.

Selfish, lying bitch.

1

'Good walk, Max?'

Detective Superintendent Marcus Horwood had a way of making it sound as if Angel had just got back from a stroll around Mayflower Park in his lunch hour. He'd seen him do something similar at press conferences many times over the years. Transform a major crime wave by a vicious gang into a few high-spirited kids larking around. It was a useful skill to have for a man tasked with reassuring a nervous public, but even so.

'Very good, thank you, sir. Very relaxing.'

Horwood narrowed his eyes at him. The look suggested maybe it was too early for Angel to come back to work, after all. Too many hours in the hot sun without a hat and all that *mad dogs and Englishmen* stuff.

'*Relaxing*? How many miles did you say it was?'

'Four hundred and ninety-two, sir. The *Camino Frances* from St Jean Pied de Port in France to Santiago de Compostela in Spain.'

Horwood snorted, sounding as if he'd rather spend his time cleaning public urinals in a notorious gay hang-out.

'That's not what I call relaxing.'

Angel could believe it. Two laps around his immaculate, paper-free desk and Horwood would be red-faced and looking for a well-earned sit down with a restorative G&T.

'There was a rest day in León at the halfway stage.'

Horwood acted like he hadn't heard, his tone changing from incredulous to wistful.

'I always fancied going there myself. Not doing the walk, of course. I hope you treated yourself to a nice hotel at the end of it.'

'I did, sir. Hotel San Miguel in the old town.'

Horwood nodded appreciatively, a *case successfully solved* press-conference smile on his thin lips.

'Any hotel named after a beer can't be all bad.'

Angel could have pointed out that the saint came first, then the plaza, then the hotel, and finally the beer. It wasn't worth the effort. He waited patiently as Horwood studied him, eyes narrowed once again under his bushy brows. Knowing what was coming. Horwood didn't disappoint.

He swept his arm around his expansive corner office with its view across West Quay Road and the container yards beyond it, to where floating cities full of tourists preparing to over-eat their way around the world were moored at the Mayflower and Horizon cruise terminals on the River Test.

'All that time to yourself. It didn't make you reconsider all this?'

Angel looked around the room Horwood had just indicated.

'I didn't realise the option to move my desk in here with you was on offer, sir.'

Horwood looked at him as if already it felt as if Angel had only been away six minutes, not six weeks.

'You know what I meant, Max.'

'No, sir, it hasn't made me reconsider. Lots of time to think and reflect, but I'm looking forward to getting back into the thick of it.'

'You can spend too much time thinking, eh?'

'Exactly, sir.'

Wondering not for the first time how a man who advised against over-thinking life's problems had risen so high in the CID ranks as he had.

Horwood pushed back from his desk, went to stand in front of a filing cabinet. He dipped until he could see himself in the small mirror sitting on top of it, adjusted his tie which had needed no adjusting in the first place. Then went to stand in front of the window, hands clasped behind his back, at-ease style, looking out towards the cruise ships.

Angel got up and went to join him, his own hands thrust deep into his pockets. The move to the window signalled a more relaxed mood than facing each other across the wide-open expanse of the superintendent's desk.

'You do know Stuart Beckford won't be coming back any time soon, don't you?' Horwood said, making a point of not looking at Angel. 'If at all.'

'I do, sir.'

He also knew what that implied. They'd be getting to that soon enough. But not quite yet it seemed.

'Have you spoken to him recently?'

'Not since I've been back, no.'

Horwood shook his head, still looking out of the window. A scowl on his face as if they'd built an eyesore overnight that he hadn't noticed until now.

'A bad business.'

Saying, *it is, sir* seemed superfluous, so Angel held his tongue. Willing Horwood to move on. Which he did soon enough, hands unclasped from behind his back, rubbing them briskly together. The gesture a throwback from the old days.

From when he actually did some real police work instead of pushing paper around his desk and thinking about his index-linked pension and the nineteenth hole.

His voice had an overly enthusiastic edge to it when he spoke. One that set alarm bells ringing in the back of Angel's mind.

'We've got a new DS for you.'

Angel smiled to himself at the way Horwood made it sound as if they'd all chipped in and bought him a new executive chair while he'd been away, rather than assign him a replacement Detective Sergeant. He waited for the rest of it.

Horwood cleared his throat, never a good sound coming from a superior officer's mouth.

'She's from the Met.'

'Okay.'

'Don't say it like that, Max.'

'Like what, sir?'

'So that it sounds like, *someone has to be.*'

'No, sir.'

Horwood studied Angel a long moment as if expecting more. Something insubordinate but delivered in a way that could be passed off as innocent. He carried on when it didn't materialise, after a second clearing of his throat.

'Her name's Catalina Kincade. She was, until an unfortunate incident very recently, Detective *Inspector* Catalina Kincade.'

Angel knew that saying *okay* again was not the way to go. Nor was a disingenuous question about whether she'd asked for the reduction in rank for personal reasons advised.

'She's been demoted.' A statement.

'She has.'

'And you're going to let her tell me all about it herself.' Another statement.

'I am.'

Angel couldn't remember the last time he'd seen a person look so pleased with themselves about the two short words they'd just uttered.

'Will that be all, sir?'

Horwood turned away from the window, moved towards the door. Hand extended for Angel to go with him. Again, Angel smiled to himself although it was no laughing matter. Whoever Horwood had sicced on him had left the superintendent feeling he needed to compensate in some small way. Escorting him personally from the room rather than a curt, *dismissed* barked from behind his desk.

'DCI Finch has got something for you to ease you back into the swing of things,' Horwood said, his hand on Angel's elbow propelling him through the now-open door. 'Nothing too taxing. An apparent suicide. It only came in yesterday. Good to have you back, Max.'

'Good to be back, sir,' Angel said to the already-closed door.

2

Angel took the stairs down a floor rather than wait for the lift, the slight niggle in his left knee that had developed on day thirty-six of the walk between Palas de Rei and Arzúa reminding him of its continued presence—and that he wasn't getting any younger. He went along the corridor to where DCI Olivia Finch's door sat wide open, knocked and went in without waiting to be invited.

Finch looked up, pulled off her reading glasses and laid them on top of the papers she'd been reading when she saw who it was. Angel took it as an indicator of the mutual respect and liking that existed between them. The majority of his colleagues would be viewed over them as they perched disapprovingly on the end of her nose. In contrast to Superintendent Horwood's agoraphobia-inducing desk, hers was reassuringly cluttered and chaotic.

Maybe not so reassuring for a member of the public who might wander in.

'How was the trip?' she said, standing and extending her hand towards him. He shook it, then found himself by some dexterous sleight of hand holding her empty mug as she gestured towards the coffee machine sitting on a filing cabinet against the wall—a much more useful addition than the Super's mirror.

Angel immediately revised his assessment about the glasses—she hadn't wanted them to steam up when she sipped her coffee—and thought about the question as he poured them both a cup. One word seemed to fit the bill more than any other.

'Cathartic.'

'That sounds like how I'd feel at the end of it. Or is that arthritic?'

He smiled with her as she came around the desk and parked herself on the edge of it. At thirty-nine, three years younger than him, she was every bit as fit as he was.

'Superintendent Horwood says he wants to come with me next time.'

Finch stopped blowing on her coffee, gave him a look.

'Really? Apart from the fact that you'd have to carry him for four hundred and ninety-one of those miles, is there going to be a next time?'

'That depends on whether anything happens that makes me feel like I need there to be.'

'Let's hope not. Did it work? Did it restore your faith?'

'In what, ma'am? The human race?' Hiding his face behind his cup as he said it.

She took a deep breath, looking, as had Horwood, that it didn't feel like six weeks.

'Don't be an arse your whole life, Max. And I've told you before, don't call me ma'am.'

Angel nodded, the *no ma'am* remaining safely inside his head. Thinking back to when he'd first joined and a sergeant called Gibson had told him how *ma'am* should be pronounced with a short *a* so that it rhymed with *ham*, not *harm*.

She cleared her throat, again as Horwood had. Practising for greater things.

'Did—'

'The Super tell me about the new DS you've arranged for me? Yes, he did.'

She raised an eyebrow at him. He nodded.

'He mentioned that until recently she was known as Detective *Inspector* Kincade.'

'Mentioned?'

Already Angel felt as if he hadn't been away. They always had been and always would be on the same page. It was scary at times.

'*Mentioned*, yes, not *explained*.' He smiled suddenly, Finch's brow creasing in response. 'I get the feeling you're about to demonstrate exactly the sort of potential top-floor material you are, ma'am. You're going to let DS Kincade tell me how she made the move from inspector down to sergeant herself.'

Finch made a point of turning around and shuffling through the piles of papers on her desk instead of trying to answer the accusation. She turned back to him again once she'd found the file she was looking for—it had been on the top of the pile the whole time.

'I'll introduce you in a minute. Let me show you this first . . . what are you doing?' He'd pulled out his phone while she searched through the papers on her desk. 'You can show me your holiday snaps later.'

'I was actually looking for the results of DS Kincade's misconduct hearing.'

'You can do that later, too. Take a look at this.' Holding the file out towards him.

'The apparent suicide?'

'Horwood told you already?'

'No details.'

Angel took the file from her outstretched hand, glanced at the front cover. Then immediately back at Finch's face, the reason for the word apparent, aka suspicious now clear.

In a perfect world, a detective would attend the scene of every unattended death, whether it was initially reported as a murder, suicide, accident or due to natural causes to ensure that any potential crime scene was not contaminated. This would help avoid the *CSI Effect*—the impact that crime dramas and forensic investigation TV programmes have on the general public. Suddenly everyone's an expert. The problem is that criminals watch the same TV programmes as everyone else, gaining an insight into the investigative process as well as the value of trace evidence.

In the real world, resource constraints mean it isn't feasible for a detective to attend in every case.

The name on the file in Angel's hand meant that on this occasion they couldn't afford not to.

'Roy Lynch,' he said.

'Uh-huh.'

'I haven't heard that name for a while. I thought he'd retired.'

'He had. But one of his sons is still active.'

Until ten years previously, Roy Lynch had been a minor player bringing in Colombian cocaine via the Caribbean through the Southampton docks, the UK's second largest container terminal. Having made his dirty money and managing to both stay alive and avoid prosecution, he'd gone out on a high, retired and assumed the self-appointed role of country squire. One of his two sons, Gavin, was still in the life. Like their father, he had avoided the unwanted attentions of both the National Crime Agency and the increasing number of Albanian and other Eastern European gangs who were busy turning the south of England into a European crime mecca.

Until now. Perhaps.

Angel held the file up.

'You think this is a warning to Gavin Lynch?'

'Could be.'

'Why not go after him directly?'

'The old man's easier to get at.'

She had a point. He went back to the file, flicked through a number of crime scene photographs. Pulled out a graphic shot of Lynch hanging by his neck from a rafter, the grotesque bulging eyes and protruding swollen tongue a result of increased blood pressure in the head—the noose seals the jugular veins preventing blood from leaving the head while the vertebral arteries continue pumping it in.

He took a closer look, saw a dark stain that extended from his groin all the way down his trouser legs. Although not as obvious as it would have been before it dried, it was still visible.

'He's wet himself.'

She leaned in and looked for herself as if she hadn't noticed. Except her words made it clear that she had, and that it was the reason the case had been passed to the Major Investigation Team.

'That's one possible anomaly.'

The human bladder releases its contents at death in roughly a third of all cases. That leaves two-thirds of the cases when, if it happens at all, it happens before death. For example, when a person sees the news of their death in another man's eyes, hears the sound of shovels in the dirt.

'There are others,' she said, 'which is why it's being treated as suspicious. The SOCOs are at the scene now.'

'Any reason he would kill himself?'

She extended her hand towards him—*that's your job to find out.* Then sipped at her coffee, as if her throat required lubrication to help release the words that had become stuck there.

'His wife died recently.'

Their eyes met briefly. Then the moment was past.

'How recently?'

'A few months.' She pointed at the file. 'It'll be in there.'

It was a pointless discussion and they both knew it. Men like Roy Lynch do not waste away and die of a broken heart. Nor do they kill themselves as a result of one.

'Did he leave a note?'

It seemed a reasonable question to him. For some reason it made her smile.

'On his laptop. It's not your average suicide note written by your average retired drug dealer. Anyone would think he was expecting the case to be assigned to you. It's in the file.'

He flicked through it, found Roy Lynch's last words to the world he was departing typed out onto a sheet of paper easily enough.

We are in the power of no calamity, while death is in our own.

As expected, the knowing smile was still in her eyes when he looked at her.

She said, 'It's a quote by—'

'Thomas Browne, I know. A fifteenth-century physician and writer. Basically, nothing can hurt you if you're prepared to kill yourself.'

'Trust you to know it. I hope you weren't thinking thoughts like that on your walk.'

It didn't deserve an answer and he didn't grace it with one. Instead, he said something equally obvious to anyone who'd spent more than five minutes in the job rubbing shoulders with the nation's underclass.

'It's not the sort of thing faked by your average murderer trying to make it look like suicide, either.'

'True.'

She took the sheet of paper out of his hands, read the line silently to herself.

'It's got a nice poetic feel to it. Makes killing yourself sound almost noble.'

Angel still had the crime scene photograph of Roy Lynch swinging from a blue clothesline in his hand. There was nothing noble about that. To be slowly strangled to death while you claw desperately at your own neck as the reality of what you've done hits you like a too-late epiphany.

Finch handed him the suicide note and took a step towards the door. Angel put everything back in the file and followed her.

'Have the next-of-kin been notified?'

'I did it myself yesterday afternoon. Alistair Lynch. Took a statement at the same time. I thought I'd spare you that dubious pleasure as your first job back.'

'Much appreciated, ma'am.'

She shook her head at the word.

'And that's how he thanks me. By calling me ma'am. Like I'm seventy with a blue rinse. Anyway, the post-mortem's scheduled for four o'clock this afternoon. You might want to take your new DS along.'

'Remind me never to ask you for ideas about what to do on a first date, okay?'

Finch stifled a laugh.

'She's waiting in your office. She might as well use Stuart Beckford's desk for now. Have you talked to him since you've been back?'

Although he'd chosen not to hide behind an easy excuse when Superintendent Horwood asked the same question, he did so now.

'I only got back yesterday.'

She paused at the door. The disapproving look on her face fitted perfectly with the weary note in her voice.

'When was the last time you accepted an answer like that from a suspect during an interview?'

'No, I haven't spoken to him.'

'You should.'

'I know.'

'He feels guilty. Blames himself.'

'I know that, too.'

'So where's the legendary forgiveness?'

'There's nothing to forgive.'

'Then bloody well talk to him you stubborn . . .'

She paused, searching for the appropriate word. He filled the lull before she found it or resorted to something simpler and not befitting her rank or gender.

'Words fail you, ma'am?'

'Too bloody right they do. God help DS Kincade.'

3

THE INTRODUCTION WAS NOT A LENGTHY AFFAIR. INDECENTLY short was a better way to describe it.

Detective Sergeant Catalina Kincade was sitting in what had been DS Stuart Beckford's chair texting on her mobile phone. She jumped up when Finch and Angel entered the room, dropping the phone on the desk, the text unfinished and unsent.

'Cat Kincade, Max Angel,' Finch said, her mobile ringing as they shook hands. She pulled it out, glanced at the screen. 'I've got to take this. I'll leave you to get to know each other.'

Angel suddenly felt a huge wave of sympathy for his cat, Leonard, wash over him. Six months back when his world was a very different place, his sister, Grace, had asked him to look after her own cat, whose name he couldn't remember, while she was on holiday for a week.

Angel now felt as Leonard must have done. Forced together with an equal in all the ways that counted, but an intruder in his domain, nonetheless, with all the uncertainty that entailed. The only things missing were the arched back and erect tail.

There was a brief moment of awkwardness in the wake of

DCI Finch's interrupted introduction before Kincade broke the ice with a flick of her head in the direction of Finch's departure.

'You think the boss arranged for someone to call her at that exact moment?'

He smiled with her, the same thought having gone through his own mind.

'Definitely.' The awkwardness was immediately back. He met it head-on. 'I'm trying to decide which one of us feels more uncomfortable.'

'That's got to be me. I knew it was a mistake to put two heads on this morning.'

'I know how you feel.'

It wasn't said simply to put her at ease. The looks and hesitant greetings he'd got walking through the operations room had made him feel like a leper returning from the colony with a faked all-clear letter in his hand.

She cocked her head to the side, considered him a long moment.

'You know, I think I believe you.' She twisted towards the desk she'd been sitting at, waved her hand at it. 'This doesn't help. I know DS Beckford is off with something nobody wants to talk about. It makes me wonder how bad can it be.'

About as bad as it gets, he thought and didn't say.

'Don't worry. You won't catch it off his chair. Stress.'

Immediately, he saw her thinking.

Stress isn't an explanation, it's an outcome.

He waved the file on Roy Lynch's suicide at her to avoid further questions, already halfway to the door.

'Are you off?' she said. 'I hope it wasn't anything I said.'

'*We're* off. To find out whether Roy Lynch did the world a massive favour—'

'Or someone did it for him.'

. . .

Angel drove. He wasn't sure he'd trust anyone else to drive ever again. And it would be a cold day in hell before he got into the back seat of a car. Besides, it gave Kincade a chance to look over the file.

Except she had different ideas. The file remained closed on her lap as she finished the text Angel and Finch had interrupted. She caught him glancing sideways at her.

'My oldest daughter. Isla. She's eight. She's worried about me on my first day in my new job. She wants to know if my new colleagues are nice.'

Angel held his tongue about the wisdom of allowing an eight-year-old a smart phone with its potential to unleash all of the world's evils on a child. He made a joke of it, instead.

'Difficult one. What are you going to tell her?'

'The truth, of course. Too early to say.'

He'd have said it with a wry smile on his lips, but each to their own.

'How many kids have you got?'

'Two. Isla and Daisy. She's six.'

'Have they moved down here with you?'

She finished tapping out the text, hit *send* and pocketed the phone.

'They're staying with their father until I get things sorted out. We're separated, but we manage to behave like reasonable human beings towards each other. Most of the time.'

He'd have expected her to follow protocol. *How about you?* He didn't volunteer anything when she didn't. Instead, he gave her a brief background on Roy Lynch as she flicked through the file, then left her to read it.

It took them twenty-five minutes to drive the eight miles to the village of Ampfield. They passed The White Horse pub on their right, then went left at the Ampfield Memorial down Knapp Lane, the sort of quiet country road favoured by couples looking to exchange bodily fluids in the open air. A quarter mile further on, he stopped at a pair of stone gate posts, a uniformed constable standing guard in front of a strip of crime scene tape strung between them. The gates themselves were an intricate wrought-iron design and needed a lick of paint. They were fully open. From the grass growing at their base, it looked as if they stayed that way. The lack of an intercom on the gate posts suggested visitors—welcome or otherwise—simply drove in through the open gates.

'Better park on the verge, sir,' the constable said after Angel flashed his warrant card and gave their names. 'There isn't room for any more vehicles inside.'

Angel did so, then they dipped under the tape as the officer held it up for them. They crunched their way down a short tree-lined gravel drive with well-kept lawns on either side. Somewhere off in the distance a dog barked, a pair of crows responding. Kincade let out a low whistle as they got to the end of the drive.

'Nice house.'

He couldn't disagree, unable to tell from her tone of voice whether she suffered from the same pangs of envy that he felt when faced with evidence that the wages of sin weren't actually so bad, after all.

'What idiot said crime doesn't pay, eh?'

An ostentatious circular fountain took pride of place in the middle of the immaculate gravel drive in front of the house, a number of vehicles belonging to the crime scene technicians parked around it. There was also a white Tesla Model 3 parked closest to the front door spoiling the overall feel of old-world charm.

At the right-hand side of the house the doors to the attached garage stood wide open, a proper car parked in front of them—a dark blue, vintage Jaguar XK150. He headed towards it to take a closer look, Kincade trailing after him.

'What's it worth?' she said.

'Anything up to a hundred and fifty thousand.' If it hadn't been part of a crime scene, he'd have run his fingertips over the gleaming paintwork. As it was, he walked slowly around it, then pointed at a long scrape on the rear wheel arch, a pained expression on his face as if the damage had been inflicted on his own arm. 'That'll knock a fair bit off. Should be more careful backing out of the garage.'

They stopped in front of the open doors to put on all-in-one paper crime scene suits, plastic overshoes and latex gloves, didn't go inside yet. He looked from the Jag to the Tesla outside the front door.

'The Tesla's got to be his everyday vehicle. I'm guessing the Jag lived in the garage and only came out on sunny days with no chance of rain.'

'And when he needed to make room to hang himself.'

He corrected her.

'When *somebody* did.'

In different parts of the garage three Scene Of Crime Officers stooped and crawled on hands and knees, scraping and collecting, bagging and tagging anything they found, dusting for fingerprints. Angel called the nearest SOCO over, pointed at the scrape on the Jag's wheel arch.

'Can you tell if that's recent?'

The SOCO led him over to the left-hand side of the white-painted garage door frame. Pointed at a matching deposit of blue paint at the same height as the scrape on the car.

'From an initial look I'd say, yes.'

'What do you think?' Angel said to Kincade.

She crossed her left arm over her body, rested her right

elbow on it, the knuckle of her index finger pushed into her top lip. Thought about it.

'Maybe he got drunk before hanging himself, crashed into the door frame as a result. You wouldn't necessarily need to be drunk. I'm guessing your legs go a little wobbly when you're thinking of topping yourself. If he was murdered, the killer moved the car and wasn't used to it. It's an old car. Probably takes some getting used to.'

'And unless he's a stone-cold killer, he would've been wired at the prospect of what he was about to do. That's not going to help your clutch control.'

He glanced at the Jag's door handle, then looked inside at the steering wheel and gear stick. All showed the signs of having already been dusted with fingerprint powder, as did the interior door handle and every other surface a person getting in and out and moving the vehicle would've touched. Trouble was, all they were likely to identify would be the mechanic who serviced the car, the neighbour's son who cleaned it to earn some pocket money, and a whole host of other people apart from a potential killer who would've worn gloves.

They moved away from the Jag, stood looking into the garage. The body had already been removed. A three-step stepladder lay on its side in the middle of the floor directly underneath an exposed rafter. Kincade fished a photograph of Lynch hanging from that same rafter out of the file, held it out at arm's length in front of them. It showed the rope going up and over the rafter then disappearing off to the right-hand side where it was tied to a vertical strut on some industrial-grade metal shelving bolted to the side wall.

He looked from the stepladder to the rafter to the metal strut, the photo of Lynch superimposed on it all. Subconsciously calculating heights and distances and the mechanics of actually getting the rope around your own neck and hanging yourself. The results from the forensic lab would make things clearer.

The door into the house was on the other side of the room, at the back. Even from where they were standing it was possible to see that the door and the frame had suffered some damage. Angel called the same SOCO over as they approached it.

'What happened to the door?'

'It was locked from the inside of the garage. The key was still in the lock. When the cleaner turned up and couldn't find Lynch and then couldn't open the door to the garage, she called her husband. He kicked the door down.'

'She doesn't have a key to the garage front doors?'

The SOCO shrugged, the gesture easy to interpret.

You're asking the wrong person, mate.

'Maybe they thought he was still alive and it was quicker,' Kincade suggested.

'Too much TV, more like,' Angel said.

Again, it proved nothing either way. Lynch could have gone into the garage, locked the door and hanged himself. Or a killer could have taken him in, locked the door, hanged him and let himself out the front doors. The residue of fingerprint powder on the lock and all along the door edge confirmed that somebody had already considered that possibility.

Leaving the garage, they walked around the fountain and viewed the house from a distance.

'No CCTV,' she said.

'If I had a house like this, I wouldn't stick ugly bloody cameras on it.'

'Then you'd have to live with the fact that the person who murdered you might get away with it.'

'I'd be dead. What do I care? There might be CCTV cameras in the lane. Sometimes the council puts them up to stop fly-tipping.'

They stopped at the front door on the way into the house. Again, she took the lead in stating the obvious.

'No sign of forced entry.'

Angel crouched down, inspected the bottom of the door. There was no evidence of a potential killer Lynch didn't know using their foot to stop Lynch from closing the door in their face, no scuff marks or damage to the paintwork.

Inside the house, they went directly to the large kitchen where a SOCO looked up as they entered. Angel recognised him vaguely, nodded at him, then looked around the room. A rustic-style table sat in the middle, four wheelback chairs arranged around it. One chair had been pulled out and turned around, its back against the table. It had been tagged.

'What's this?' Angel said to the SOCO.

He saw a smile behind the man's face mask. *It's a chair, sir*. He clarified his question.

'Why have you tagged it?'

The SOCO leaned down and to the side, angled his head to look at the chair seat at a narrow, oblique angle.

'There's a faint stain. Could be urine.'

Angel did the same and saw it, now that it had been pointed out to him. It was consistent with Roy Lynch wetting himself. If it turned out that the stain was indeed Lynch's urine—and his doctor confirmed that he wasn't incontinent—it proved that he'd lost control of his bladder before death, not at it. Something, or some*one*, had made that happen.

'Where's the laptop with the suicide note?'

'Forensics have already taken it.' He pointed at a marker on the table. 'That's where it was.'

'What about the deceased's mobile phone?'

'They've got that, too.'

Although the work the SOCOs did was invaluable in determining the *what*, when it came to the *why*, mobile phones and computers often held the answers. People's lives have moved online, as have their crimes.

'Anything else of interest?' Kincade said.

'Only this.' He held up a water glass in an evidence bag. 'It looks as if it had been rinsed thoroughly and left to drain on the counter. But you never know.'

'If you've gone to the trouble to wash it, why not dry it and put it back in the cupboard?'

The SOCO shook his head, went back to dusting the sink taps, then thought of something. 'There's a drinks cabinet full of booze in the sitting room. Something to give him Dutch courage before he topped himself, perhaps?'

Or someone slipped him something to make him compliant, Angel thought.

They left the SOCO to it, took a quick look at the door from the kitchen into the garage. As expected, it showed signs of having been violently kicked a number of times until the door frame splintered. The door was a solid-looking affair, as Angel would've expected in an older house like Lynch's. The cleaner's husband was obviously a large man. As were his feet, as evidenced by a number of black footprints clearly visible against the white paintwork of the door that his wife worked her fingers to the bone to keep clean.

In addition to the door into the garage, there was a second door on the back wall leading into a mud room. A row of wooden shaker-style pegs ran the length of it, waxed-cotton jackets and heavier coats and scarves hanging on them. There were both men's and women's coats. Angel couldn't stop himself from wondering whether Lynch hadn't been able to bring himself to clear out his wife's clothes after she died, or he was just lazy.

The sudden lump in his throat told him something about himself.

As with the door into the garage, the one that led out onto a weathered brick terrace and the garden beyond had security bolts top and bottom. They were both slotted all the way home. The key was in the lock. Fingerprint powder covered everything. It was possible that a potential killer had found it all unlocked and had entered that way, then locked it behind him, but it seemed unlikely.

'Is that how the door was found?' Angel asked the SOCO as they came back into the kitchen.

'Exactly like that, yes.'

The relief in the man's voice was palpable. For now, at least, they would concentrate their efforts on the house and garage unless somebody further up the food chain who didn't have to get down and dirty their own knees decreed that the garden should also be searched.

'Not a lot for us here,' Kincade said drily. 'He might have topped himself, or someone might've done it for him. Wasn't that where we were when we arrived?'

He couldn't disagree.

On the way out, he stuck his head into the front sitting room. The whole house, including the basement and attic, would be thoroughly searched in the days ahead, but for now it was worth a quick look for those most revealing of household items—family photographs. They were often a mine of useful information, the sentimental attachments blinding the person displaying them to the things a stranger sees.

He crossed the room to where an antique display cabinet sat against the wall, Kincade following behind him. She looked around, took in the room with its massive fireplace, sunlight streaming through the leaded windows dappling its aged brickwork, chopped logs arranged neatly beside it awaiting the chillier nights ahead. She echoed his earlier remark.

'Whoever said crime doesn't pay doesn't know their arse from a hole in the ground.'

He picked up one of the framed photographs from the half dozen or so on the cabinet. Roy Lynch looked a damn sight better in it than in the others Angel had seen of him taken by the crime scene photographer. His wife was standing beside him, smiling, the two boys in their early teens in front of them not so much. Kincade took it from him, studied it.

'*Aw*, almost like a normal family. I wonder if one of those little tykes had anything to do with it?'

He didn't reply as she replaced the photograph. The investigation of Lynch's finances would reveal whether his sons had anything to gain from his early demise.

'What's your gut feel?' he said. 'Not about his kids doing it, but in general.'

She took up the *elbow resting on her other arm across her body* pose again, studying him. If she did it again, he was going to call it *position #1* for ease of reference.

'Is this you trying to determine whether you've been lumbered with somebody who likes to jump to early unsubstantiated conclusions?'

He held up his hands, showed her his palms.

'You're right. An unfair question.'

Despite the initial prickly response, she gave an answer of sorts.

'We've got the means of death at the scene and injuries that are consistent with being self-inflicted. But did he have a reason to kill himself? Too early to say. Did someone else have a motive? I should be asking you that. I've only been here a day.'

He browsed the bookshelves that lined the alcoves on either side of the chimney breast. There were a lot of books. Angel thought it incongruous in the home of a man who'd made his money selling drugs and ruining lives. Maybe his wife had been the book lover.

He didn't have the time or the inclination to read all of the spines or pull them out. But a quick scan didn't identify a biography of Sir Thomas Browne, the man whose quote had been used as a suicide note.

They left the house, started back down the drive towards the front gate. Despite her understandable reticence to stick her neck out after fifteen minutes at the scene, he asked another question, thinking aloud.

'Say it's murder. How many people?'

'That depends. If he was drugged, one person could do it. We'll have to wait for the tox report. And the results from the kitchen chair. See if they sat him on it while they prepared the garage for his final send-off. Otherwise, two people minimum. Again, we'll have to wait to see if there's evidence of being restrained or defensive injuries. If someone was going to hang me, I'd fight like hell even if they had a gun on me. Take one of the bastards with me.' She hooked her thumb over her shoulder at the house and garage behind them. 'I'd rather get blown away than die like that.'

He shrugged, kept his counsel.

Feeling the heat of the pitiless desert sun on his back, its endless dust and grit in his mouth. A dying man's dirty fingernails digging deeper into the flesh of his hand. A hand he prays will deliver him from his pain, intestines glistening wetly in the relentless glare, the bloody aftermath of the 7.62mm rounds that ripped through his flesh in the space of a heartbeat.

I can think of someone who'd disagree.

4

THEY HEARD THE COMMOTION AT THE FRONT GATE BEFORE THEY saw it. An angry shout in stark contrast to the air of quiet concentration at the house and garage behind them.

It's my father's bloody house. You can't stop me going in.

They quickened their pace down the drive, saw a man trying to dodge around the constable standing guard. Stepping from side to side like two people in the street who both go one way, then the other in a synchronised attempt to get past. The front end of an older dark-red Bentley was visible behind them. A woman with long, bleached blonde hair and sunglasses perched on top of her head was standing half-in, half-out of the open passenger door watching the argument, a cigarette held away from her body in her left hand.

She took a long final drag as if her life depended on it, dropped the butt and ground it out, then clip-clopped over to lend her man moral support. It only irritated him more, his voice condescending, dismissive.

'Get back in the car, Sam. Fix your make-up or post a picture of yourself on Instagram.'

'Do as he says, please, madam,' the constable echoed. 'And

you, too, please, sir.'

The voice of a man pissing into the wind.

Neither of them moved as he looked from one to the other. When Angel and Kincade were twenty yards away, the officer heard them approaching from behind him. He turned. Only momentarily, but it was enough. The driver of the Bentley shoved him to one side, ducked under the tape and set off running down the drive, veering off to the right between a couple of trees onto the lawn when he saw them coming towards him.

The uniformed officer recovered his footing, only to be pushed sideways again by the woman, standing at the tape and yelling like she was selling fish down on the docks.

'Go for it, Gav!'

Out on the grass, Gav sprinted forward, arms pumping, Kincade and Angel only yards behind him. He reversed direction abruptly like they were a bunch of kids playing tag in the park. Kincade lunged. Threw out an arm. Caught his shoulder and dug her fingers into his jacket half-pulling it off his back. The next thing they were both on the ground, an untidy mess of flailing arms and legs, the man squirming and yelling at her to *get the fuck off him* from under her as she tried to control him.

Eventually he stopped struggling, lay still on his back, chest rising and falling. She pushed herself onto her knees and up, dusted herself off as Angel offered the man his hand. He ignored it, clambered to his feet without assistance. Eyeing up the house as if he was contemplating a second attempt. The way he was heaving the air into his lungs suggested not. It hadn't been much of a chase, either.

'You must be Gavin,' Angel said, remembering the name of Lynch's son who'd followed in his father's drug-dealing footsteps from his earlier discussion with DCI Finch.

'Yeah, I'm Gavin. Alistair called me yesterday. I was away on business. I came as soon as I could.'

Angel and Kincade looked across the lawn to where Gavin's companion was still standing outside the tape, the constable keeping a wary eye on her. They didn't need to look at one another to share a thought.

That's what you call business, is it?

Angel had no doubt it would be hard work whatever you called it. He went back to Gavin Lynch.

'Your father's body isn't here, obviously. There's nothing you can do. And the house is a crime scene.'

'That's what I said,' Gavin yelled, jabbing his chest with his middle finger as if Angel had been arguing with him. 'Alistair started spouting some bollocks about suicide. No way. Some bastard did him in. Of course it's a bloody crime scene.'

It didn't occur to Gavin that he'd just confirmed the reason why he shouldn't be allowed anywhere near his father's house.

'Which is why we can't allow you in there,' Angel said, his voice neutral while all he wanted to do was take hold of Gavin's elbow, point him at his car and tell him to get lost and take his peroxide bimbo with him. They'd be in touch to interview him when it suited them—and count yourself lucky we don't charge you with assaulting a police officer.

He saw when it registered in Gavin's eyes that he could spend all day arguing the toss or running around his father's garden with them in hot pursuit, but he wasn't getting any nearer than he already was to the house. He changed tack, a sneer entering his voice. It suggested whatever answer Angel gave to his next question, it wouldn't be good enough.

'Who's in charge? You?' He looked at Kincade, the curl in his lip intensifying. 'Or this candidate for the England dyke's, sorry, I mean women's rugby team here?'

'I am.' Angel stuck out his hand in the full expectation of it being ignored again. 'Detective Inspector Max Angel. And this is DS Kincade.'

The woman who's an inch away from putting you on your cocky arse again.

Gavin proved him right, ignoring the hand and giving him a look that suggested he had more confidence in one of the sheep in the neighbouring fields getting to the bottom of how his father had died.

As is often the case, asking who's in charge fills a certain type of person with a false confidence. As if that officer now reports to them. Already, he appeared to have forgotten the farcical chase around his father's garden and the way Kincade had got the better of him. He leaned into Angel's personal space.

'I'm telling you now, it wasn't suicide. Somebody killed my old man. And if you lot don't find out who, I will.'

'We'll be in touch, sir,' Angel called after him as Gavin turned on his heel and headed back towards his car to work his anger out on his hapless girlfriend.

Kincade had something more pithy to contribute, muttered under her breath.

'*Prick*. I thought we had the monopoly on arseholes up in London.'

They watched as the uniformed officer held up the tape for Gavin to duck under with an exaggerated *after you* sweep of his hand to emphasise his contempt. He glanced at them watching him. Angel gave him a thumbs-up back.

'What's next?' Kincade said. 'A car chase around the country lanes?'

'Maybe later.' He glanced at his watch. 'Post-mortem's at four. Plenty of time to talk to the woman whose husband likes to kick down doors first.'

5

Mrs Dot Boyle, the deceased's cleaning lady, had been in no fit state to give a statement after following her husband through the door between the kitchen and the garage that he'd just kicked in and finding her now ex-employer swinging by the neck from the rafters.

Her husband, George, had already given a statement, although it was of limited use. He confirmed that he'd taken a call from his wife at approximately 9:15 a.m., a quarter hour after she arrived. She'd sounded very agitated and was convinced that her employer had come to harm, that conviction reinforced by her inability to get into the garage. George had walked to the house—a distance of approximately three-quarters of a mile—since they only owned one car and his wife had taken it.

In the fifteen minutes it took him to get to Roy Lynch's house, his wife had worked herself into a frenzy, persuading him to kick the door to the garage open. He'd seen it done on TV and was happy to give it a go. There were two security bolts on the house side of the door, top and bottom, but not on the garage side. The door frame had given way on the second attempt after Mr Boyle put all of his seventeen stone behind the kick. He hadn't said whose face he might have been imagining painted on the door as he did so.

He'd gone in first and immediately called to his wife to remain in the kitchen. True to form and consistent with their thirty years married, she'd ignored him, came into the garage and promptly fainted when she saw Lynch twisting on the end of a clothesline. After helping her back into the kitchen and putting the kettle on to boil, he'd dialled 999. The call had been logged at 9:39 a.m. He'd then waited with his wife until the police arrived ten minutes later.

In terms of providing background information, he had nothing to add. He'd never been to the house before, had never met Roy Lynch and wouldn't have recognised him in the street—despite it subsequently coming to light that they both used the same village pub, the White Horse, on a regular basis.

Angel guessed George Boyle hadn't needed to put his hand in his own pocket in the White Horse since finding Lynch, and would milk that situation for as long as he could find people to listen to his suitably and increasingly-embellished story.

They drove to the Boyles' house directly from Lynch's property, passing the pub in question as they drove through the village and out the other side. As is the case in most small English villages, a row of council and ex-council houses was located on the outskirts of the village. The Boyles lived in the very last house. There was a weed-infested vegetable patch at the side of it, a small, scruffy lawn behind and open fields beyond.

George Boyle answered the door to Kincade's knock. Early sixties, a full head of silver-grey hair cropped close to his skull, most of the seventeen stone he'd used to kick down Roy Lynch's garage door concentrated at the front hanging over his belt.

He didn't look pleased to see them, a situation Angel

accepted as simply one of the many crosses he had to bear as a police officer.

In this case, Angel got the impression from the way George glanced at his watch that it was less to do with protecting his wife from the stresses of being interviewed by the police and more to do with getting himself to the White Horse and making the most of his new-found celebrity status while it lasted.

He led them through to a small uPVC conservatory stuck on the back of the house that looked as if George had built it himself in a single afternoon after visiting the White Horse first. It was stiflingly hot inside, the sun beating down on a glass roof with no blinds. The double-glazed windows and door were all shut tight. A cynic might have said that the aim was to keep the interview as brief as possible by making the environment intolerable.

Angel thought it felt a lot like Iraq as the first trickle of sweat started its journey down his back.

Dot Boyle was around the same age as her husband, as thin as he was overweight. She had the air of having been beaten down and worn out, a lifetime of cleaning other people's houses taking its toll on her limbs and on her face. She was sitting on a floral-print sofa, a cup of tea and an ashtray on the side table, a copy of *Woman's Own* magazine beside her. The front cover featured two minor-league celebrities, who Angel couldn't have named to save his life, above a headline that demanded to know, *Is it all over?* He got the impression Dot was making as much of her husband's forced attentiveness as he was cadging free drinks in the White Horse.

'You run along now, George,' she said once he'd delivered the two officers into her presence. 'You don't want to miss last orders.'

George didn't need to be told twice. He took a step towards the sitting room and freedom with a speed that belied his bulk.

Angel and Kincade exchanged a look, then Kincade took it upon herself to assume the role of *the enemy*.

'It's best if you stay, Mr Boyle.'

He slumped visibly. Looked at his watch again doing a very poor job of keeping the annoyance off his face or out of his voice.

'I already gave a statement. I'm not surprised you lot are over-worked if you do everything twice. And I never knew the bloke, anyway.'

Kincade smiled politely, a patient look on her face that was easy to interpret.

Make as many excuses as you like, you're not going anywhere.

'In case your wife has another funny turn re-living the experience,' she said, then added something Angel wasn't sure anyone in the room believed. 'You'd never forgive yourself.'

Reluctantly, George Boyle sat on the low windowsill off to the side. That too was easy to read.

I'm still here, but don't expect me to participate.

Except his wife had other ideas.

'If you're staying, you might as well make yourself useful. Open the doors and then make the officers some tea.'

'Not for me,' Angel and Kincade echoed as George opened the doors onto the garden to let in some much-needed fresh air.

He went to sit back down. Again, his wife had other ideas. She finished the tea in her cup with a final slurp, held it out towards him.

'I'll have another one.'

He took the cup, disappeared into the kitchen scowling at his tormentor Kincade as he went. Angel crossed the room to stand by the open door.

'Talk us through exactly what happened.'

'I got there at just after nine like I always do—'

'How often do you go?'

'Three hours, twice a week. Mondays and Thursdays.'

'And when you arrived yesterday, the Jag was on the drive outside the garage?'

'That's right. I thought it was strange . . .'

Angel got the distinct impression that despite fainting at the scene, Dot Boyle was now about to morph into a cross between Miss Marple and DI Jane Tennison, solving the crime for them by the time George got back with her cup of tea.

'He always puts it away at night,' she said. 'It cost more than we paid for our house. I saw the invoice when I was tidying his study.'

'And the Tesla was parked in front of the house?'

'The what?'

'The Tesla. The white car.'

Mrs B. threw her eyes, her tone dismissive.

'Oh, *that*. George calls it a toy car. It's electric, you know. You can't hear them coming. I nearly got run over by one the other day . . .'

Angel felt a potentially endless list of anecdotes about electric cars and all the other evils of the modern world on its way. Seemed Kincade's antenna were twitching, too.

'Was it outside the house, Mrs Boyle?' she cut in.

Mrs B. looked a little put out at the interruption. If a story was going to be told at all, it should be told properly.

'Yes, it was. He'd never put it in the garage and leave the Jag out. Who'd want to steal an electric car?'

'Meaning you were expecting Mr Lynch to be at home? He doesn't go for an early-morning walk perhaps? Get out of the house so he's not under your feet while you get on with the cleaning?'

Briefly, Mrs B. looked as if she might take umbrage at the suggestion that her employer went out of his way to avoid her, however reasonably Kincade might have phrased the question.

'No, he's always in the house. Up and dressed. He goes to bed early and gets up early.'

Angel caught the look on Kincade's face as she made notes. Wondering how Mrs B. knew her employer's bedtime routine.

'I let myself in,' Mrs B. continued.

'Was there anything unusual about the front door?' Kincade asked. 'Was it open? On the latch?'

Dot shook her head firmly.

'No, nothing like that. Then I called out *hello* like I always do.'

She showed them exactly how.

Hell-oh-oh.

With an irritating rising inflection at the end.

'And there was no response,' Angel said, thinking if he heard that being called in his direction, he'd run a mile. Perhaps not hang himself in the garage.

'No. I went into the mud room but the door was still locked so I knew he wasn't in the garden. Then I tried the door to the garage.'

'Would you have expected him to be in the garage at that time in the morning?' Kincade said.

Dot gave her the look of a woman with the perfect answer to what she suspected was an uncalled-for sarcastic remark.

'That's where the freezer is. Sometimes Mr Lynch liked a sausage with his breakfast. He doesn't have one every day because the doctor said he should avoid fatty foods, so he freezes them.'

Probably not something that needs to be written up, Angel thought, the mention of the doctor prompting his next question.

'Do you know if he'd seen the doctor recently? Maybe he'd had some bad news?'

Dot's hand flew to her mouth at the implication, everybody's worst fear in her mind.

'You mean cancer?'

'It's possible. We need to find out why he might have wanted to take his own life.' Thinking the longer Mrs Dot Boyle believed it was a suicide, the better things—particularly the job ahead of them—would be. 'How did he seem the last time you saw him?'

'The same as always. A bit bad tempered first thing in the morning until he'd had a cup of tea.'

The mention of tea made her realise that she was without sustenance, herself. She turned her head towards the kitchen and yelled.

'What's happened to that tea, George? I hope you didn't forget to buy tea bags again.'

George appeared a moment later carrying a solitary cup of tea as if it was the crown at a coronation. A point was being made. He put it on the side table, took up his position on the windowsill with a surreptitious glance at his watch.

'To answer your question, I don't know if he'd been to the doctor recently,' Dot said.

Angel moved on, thinking that Lynch had obviously kept his doctor's letters in a better hiding place than his car invoices.

'So, the garage was locked,' he said.

The cup of tea stalled halfway to Dot's lips, her voice dropping to a melodramatic whisper.

'From the inside.' Making *inside* sound like one of the further planets in the solar system. 'The key was still in the lock. That's when I started to get worried. I told myself to calm down and called his mobile. Well, I almost jumped out of my skin when I heard it ringing in the sitting room. Mr Lynch never goes anywhere without it. He's as bad as the young people. George says they're going to get chips inserted into their heads soon and everybody will be walking around as if they're talking to themselves.'

She glanced at George who'd found something interesting to

look at on the sole of his shoe. It didn't stop him from mumbling under his breath when she looked away again.

'At least your sister will fit in then.'

Angel felt the interview getting away from them.

'That's when you called your husband,' he said

Dot nodded once.

'That's right. I told him to hurry—'

'I got there as quickly as I could, woman,' came from the windowsill.

Kincade turned to him.

'Just to confirm, your wife let you into the house, told you she was worried something had happened to Mr Lynch and that he might have locked himself in the garage. You kicked the door in, went inside and found him hanged from a rafter. Your wife followed you and fainted. You helped her back into the kitchen, sat her down and made her a cup of tea. Then you dialled 999.'

George nodded.

'That's right.'

'Did you do anything else while you were waiting?'

'Like what?'

Kincade shrugged.

'Take a look around the house?'

'Definitely not.'

'George likes that American TV programme, *CSI*,' Dot chipped in. 'He knows better than to touch anything.'

George nodded again. He looked vaguely embarrassed as if his wife had told them he liked watching *Shaun the Sheep*.

'The chair you sat your wife on after she fainted . . .' Angel said to him. 'Did you pull it away from the table or was it already pulled out?'

The Boyles looked at each other, then answered in unison.

'Already pulled out.'

Angel turned to Dot Boyle.

'We'll need to take the clothes you were wearing yesterday, Mrs Boyle.'

'What for?'

Angel knew that whatever he said, George Boyle was going to put it together, even if his wife didn't. Work out that they were looking at the possibility of an intruder in the house. An intruder who had murdered Roy Lynch. George Boyle wasn't going to be able to drink the free pints of beer fast enough in the White Horse.

George then confirmed it, answering for Angel.

'They need to check for fibres, Dot. Eliminate any that came from your clothing.'

He gave her a pointed look that everyone in the room understood.

I'll explain later.

'Do you need all of them?' Dot said, worry edging into her voice as she emphasised the word *all*.

Kincade handled that one even though it was addressed to Angel.

'I'm afraid so.'

'What about my underwear?'

'That too.'

Angel knew Kincade was praying as hard as he was that Dot didn't ask why. Neither of them would've relished telling her that they needed to determine whether she'd lost control of her bladder after she fainted and it was traces of her urine on the kitchen chair, not Roy Lynch's.

'I'll get them,' she said getting up out of the chair and heading towards the hall.

She was back a couple of minutes later carrying a plastic Tesco carrier bag filled with neatly-folded clothes. She handed it to Kincade looking as embarrassed as her husband had about the TV programme revelation.

Angel was aware that his final question for her would make it clearer still that they weren't convinced Lynch had committed suicide.

'Did you see anything out of the ordinary on any of your previous visits? A car parked nearby? Somebody you didn't recognise hanging around?'

Angel waited for her as she thought about it. She desperately wanted to remember something. In the end, she couldn't.

'No. Nothing. And George says I'm very observant.'

Angel could believe it. Although he'd have used a different word, the one he guessed George preferred. *Nosy*. It wasn't necessarily a bad thing. Nosy neighbours made their job a lot easier at times.

'I'm sure this is going to be all round the White Horse,' Angel said to George as he showed them out. 'Call us if you hear anything of interest.' The rest of it remained unspoken.

That you didn't start yourself.

6

'Something's confusing me,' Kincade said once they were back in the car. 'I got the impression Mrs Boyle wears the trousers in that house...'

'Me, too.'

'But the whole time it was George says this, George thinks that.'

She had a point, even if he didn't have an answer for her. But he could understand why George Boyle escaped to the pub at every opportunity.

'I feel more exhausted after that interview than I did chasing after Gavin Lynch,' she said.

'I was impressed that you caught hold of him, by the way. You don't actually play rugby, do you?'

It was a throwaway line, a joke. The answer took him by surprise.

'As it happens, I do. Or, I did, before I got sent down here. For the Met Police ladies' team.' She pointed a finger at him. 'And don't laugh.'

He worked a hurt expression onto his face, who moi?

'Why would I?'

'Most men do. Puerile schoolboy jokes about getting their head stuck between your legs in a scrum. *Where's the soap?* in the communal bath afterwards. Men never grow up. So, what's next? Talk to the regulars in the White Horse?'

He nodded, impressed at the way she'd segued from rugby to beer.

'Is that the lady rugby player talking? A few beers after working up a sweat chasing Gavin Lynch?'

'I wish. Even if it wasn't enough of a chase to warrant a mouthful.'

The pub was up ahead as they discussed it, fifty yards on the left. He kept on going, a handful of locals standing outside smoking watched them as they drove past.

'We need to get back for the post-mortem at four o'clock.'

She echoed his own comment to DCI Finch when she'd told him about it.

'You certainly know how to show a girl a good time down here.'

'You have a problem with them?'

She shook her head as if she didn't know what he was talking about. When it came to watching a cadaver being opened up like it was a suit carrier, the organs removed like so much dirty underwear stuffed inside, all in the cold, clinical environment of an autopsy room, there was no getting used to it. Not completely. Everybody just pretended they had.

They lapsed into as comfortable a silence as is possible with a person you've known for less than half a day. Except he felt that she was building up to something. The mention of her time in the Met, the phrase she'd used—*sent down here*—making it obvious what. It didn't take long before she proved him right.

'I'm surprised you haven't asked me how I ended up here as a DS.'

He shrugged like it had never crossed his mind.

'I'm happy to wait until you're ready.'

She took a deep breath, looking out of the side window. Her face when she turned back said it all.

I'll never be ready, but here goes.

'We might as well get it out of the way. Before you look it up on the internet or get the Chinese whispers version from the station gossip. I'm surprised you haven't already been told.'

'Superintendent Horwood and DCI Finch were both very keen that you should tell me in your own words.'

'Very considerate, I'm sure. They're probably hoping I'll open up to you and you can report back exactly how bitter and resentful I am.' Her mouth snapped shut aware of how badly it had come out. For a moment he thought she was about to put her hand on his arm as she apologised. 'Sorry, that's not fair. I know you wouldn't do that. Anyway, the misconduct hearing found me guilty of using excessive force whilst arresting a fifteen-year-old boy. A boy who'd pass for twenty any day of the week. I was demoted from inspector down to sergeant.'

'You were lucky you weren't kicked out altogether.'

She didn't immediately reply. He glanced briefly at her. The look on her face told him he'd touched on a part of the problem. She confirmed it soon enough.

'The other officer making the arrest with me was.'

'I'm guessing that caused some resentment.'

She coughed out a bitter laugh, the sound strangled and without humour.

'Just a bit.'

She looked away at the roadside trees whipping past the window, her hands in her lap. He glanced down, saw the flesh at the side of her thumbnail picked red raw. He wondered if she'd done it sitting in their shared office while she waited for him to arrive.

He hoped not.

'What happened?' he said.

'It was at a tree huggers demonstration in Hyde Park. The little prick spat on me. Called me a *fucking Nazi*.' She shook her head, anger and frustration in the gesture, tempered by a resigned acceptance of her own stupidity and lack of professionalism that followed the incident. 'I've got his spit dribbling down my face and then he laughs, says, that looks like spunk, except a fucking dyke like you wouldn't know what that is. What I should've done is taken him aside, said, if you didn't spend so much time wanking in front of the internet, sonny, you wouldn't know what it is, either. And then sent him on his way.'

'Except you didn't know he was only fifteen at the time.'

'True. Anyway, I lost it. It wasn't my finest hour. Things were going to shit at home, but I don't want to make excuses. Turns out the kid's mother is a big-shot tree-hugging civil rights lawyer. She kicked up a stink.'

Angel sucked the air in through his teeth, wondering how she'd got away with it.

'Sounds like you really were lucky not to be kicked out.'

'Yeah. Except it gets worse. I don't suppose you've heard of him, but my uncle is James Milne.'

He shook his head, the name meaning nothing to him.

'That's *Chief Superintendent* James Milne to you. He's a big cheese in SO15.'

Angel didn't need her to explain what SO15 was—the Metropolitan Police's Counter Terrorism Command, a specialist division working alongside MI5 and other intelligence and security agencies.

'People find out,' she went on, 'however quiet you try to keep it. Apparently, it makes me think I'm better than everyone else. Whatever happens, I've got Uncle James looking out for me. And of course, according to some people who've been stuck at detective constable for fifteen years, that's the exact same reason why I progressed as far as inspector in the first place.' She blew the air from her cheeks, the outburst draining her. The bitterness was gone from her voice when she spoke again. 'Bet you wish you'd never asked.' She paused, her timing perfect. 'Oh, I forgot. You didn't. Anyway, everyone agreed that it was best if I got a transfer to go with the demotion. The further, the better.'

'Including you?'

'At the time, yeah.' She glanced at her watch as if checking how long she'd been in her new role. 'Although I reserve the right to change my mind.'

'Of course you do.'

She shifted in her seat to face him at an angle. He couldn't say whether she was about to challenge him on the remark —*was that a sexist dig at women changing their minds at the drop of a hat?*—or whether she was looking for him to reciprocate with the soul baring and explain the reason for her predecessor, DS Stuart Beckford's absence.

'Any thoughts other than the confusion over who wears the trousers in the Boyle household?' he said to head off either of those possibilities.

'Quite a few.'

'Like?'

Her answer rolled out on the back of a self-deprecating laugh.

'Be thankful that my marriage only lasted eight years. I don't think I could do thirty or forty.'

'I meant about the case.'

She sat back in her seat properly again, facing front, the moment of danger over. Extended her arms and interlaced her fingers as the smile faded from her face. Pushed until the knuckles cracked.

'Not really. It could go either way.'

'What about Gavin Lynch? What did you make of him?'

The smile made a brief reappearance, although it was more of a sour scowl.

'Apart from being a jumped-up prick with a second-hand Bentley and a dippy blonde girlfriend, you mean?'

Angel agreed, apart from that, yes.

'I think he's already putting out feelers about who might have wanted to do away with dear old dad. I also think he's already got some names in his head. None of which he plans on sharing with us.'

'So we can expect retaliation?'

She looked at him, mock horror on her face.

'A gang war? I thought that sort of thing only happened up in the big city.'

'You thought it was all sheep rustling down here, did you?'

'Sheep *what*?'

It didn't deserve an answer. Nor did it get one. Besides, they'd arrived at University Hospital Southampton. There, in its bowels, a man's body awaited them, soon to be gutted like a fish in the name of the truth so that he might share the secret of how he had died.

7

THEY WERE FIVE MINUTES LATE. THE POST-MORTEM HAD ALREADY started, although they hadn't missed anything important. The forensic pathologist, Dr Isabel Durand, was talking quietly into her lapel microphone, giving a general description of the body. She looked up as they entered the room.

'It's a bit late for you, Padre.'

Angel smiled at the old joke between them, one that he enjoyed as much as she did.

'You say that every time, Isabel.'

Kincade looked at him, a question on her face, got a small headshake back.

Later.

Durand then pointed at Angel with the scalpel in her hand, her voice taking on a harder edge.

'And don't even think about it.'

He smiled again, said nothing. Once more, Kincade looked to him for clarification. She didn't get it. He kept his eyes front, concentrating on the proceedings.

Durand worked a gloved finger down between the clothesline and Roy Lynch's neck, lifted sufficiently to get the tip of a scalpel into the gap and cut the ligature—at the side of the neck, away from the knot at the back in order to preserve it. She handed the clothesline to a bored-looking exhibits officer waiting nearby.

She removed the paper bags that had been placed over the deceased's hands at the scene for evidence preservation, examined the hands and collected samples from under the fingernails, then moved onto the rest of the body.

The trousers claimed more of her attention than all of his other clothes put together.

She sniffed the stain on the crotch extending down the legs—not a particularly scientific procedure but effective nonetheless—and nodded to herself.

Angel would've expected as much. What he didn't expect was the length of time she spent on the lower legs, using adhesive tape to collect a number of fibres. In contrast to the upper trouser legs that were relatively uncreased, the material of the lower legs showed visible creasing—not a lot, but the opposite of what you'd expect. Typically, the upper legs crease around the crotch when a person sits down, the knees and seat become baggy over time, but the lower legs remain flat.

'Someone held him by the legs,' Kincade whispered to Angel without turning her head. 'While the material was still damp.'

He nodded, didn't say anything, the same thought having crossed his own mind.

Durand then cut away Roy Lynch's clothes, passing them to the exhibits officer. With the deceased's trousers she cut out a number of small, square pieces where the fabric was stained with what was likely to be dried urine, put them to the side for further examination.

She finished the first, non-invasive, phase of the autopsy with a visual examination of the ligature mark around Lynch's neck.

Angel was aware of Kincade becoming very still beside him once the body had been washed, weighed and measured awaiting the final indignity—the long Y-shaped incision from shoulder to shoulder meeting at the breast bone and extending all the way down to the pubic bone.

He dropped his own eyes to the floor as Durand peeled back the skin, muscle and soft tissue using a scalpel before pulling the chest flap up over the face to expose the ribcage and neck muscles. She made two cuts on each side of the ribcage, dissected the tissue behind it with a scalpel, and lifted the ribcage free from the skeleton to expose the internal organs.

She took a breather at that point, then turned towards the two detectives, addressing her remarks to Angel after a cursory glance at Kincade.

'Mindful that your colleague looks a little green around the gills, and given an initial presumption'—she paused, held up a finger until Angel nodded his agreement—'of death caused by asphyxia due to ligature strangulation, I'll start with a quick look at the hyoid bone.'

'I'm fine,' Kincade said sounding mildly indignant.

The pathologist ignored her, went back to the body.

'Don't worry about me,' Kincade whispered to Angel.

'I'm not. I don't have to hose the floor down.'

Durand came back to them a minute later.

'The hyoid bone is fractured, which I would expect to see in anything up to seventy-five per cent of deaths due to hanging or strangulation. However, from my brief initial inspection, I would say that the extent of the fracture suggests gradual strangulation consistent with short-drop or suspension hanging, rather than a more severe break caused by long-drop hanging. I'll leave it to you to decide what that might imply.'

Angel waited until Durand had gone back to what she referred to as her *client*, leaned in and whispered to Kincade.

'Exactly how okay are you?'

She took a deep breath, in exasperation rather than to dispel any queasiness.

'I'm fine. Really. I don't know what she was talking about.'

'Good. I've got a few things to do. Call me when you're finished here and I'll come and get you, give you a lift back to the station.'

Durand had just detached her client's larynx and oesophagus. Kincade's mouth flapped soundlessly as if hers had been taken out at the same time as she watched Angel's back disappearing through the door.

8

Angel picked Kincade up from outside the hospital two hours later. She noticed that the Tesco carrier bag containing Dot Boyle's clothes that had been on the back seat was no longer there. He'd obviously been back to the station. Two Sainsburys bags filled with groceries were in its place. It made sense. He'd been away for six weeks, after all. What didn't make sense was the cat basket sitting next to them, a white cat with tabby markings on its face inside.

'I left him in the cattery for an extra day,' he said. 'Give myself a chance to get straight after the trip.'

'What's his name?'

'Leonard.'

She groaned, sagging in her seat.

'Not after Leonard Cohen? I refuse to work with anyone who listens to Leonard Cohen.' She extended her left arm, made slashing motions across her wrist. 'Music to commit suicide to.'

'You don't have to worry.'

'Thank Christ for that. So why Leonard?'

'He'd already been named when I got him.'

'He was a rescue cat?'

'Something like that. He belonged to the victim on a murder case I worked. He was locked in a bedroom with her for thirty-six hours. You don't want to hear the details.'

She could imagine, wondering how difficult it had been to get the cat back into the habit of eating cat food.

'You don't occasionally wake up to find him sitting on the end of the bed looking at you in a funny way?'

'Licking his lips, you mean?' He smiled rather than say more, changed the subject. 'Did Dr Durand give anything away, or do we have to wait for her report?'

Kincade rocked her hand.

'She gave us a few teasers.'

He waited to hear what they were. Nothing was forthcoming, although a smug smile was developing at the corners of her mouth.

'Will there be a team briefing tomorrow morning?' she said.

'Uh-huh. Eight-thirty. You'll get a chance to meet everybody then.'

'Good. I can let everyone know what Dr Durand said then.'

'Including me?' His tone making it clear that as the SIO on the case he expected an early heads-up.

'Unless you want to answer some of my questions first, that is.'

He'd known this moment would arrive ever since she'd given him the questioning looks in the autopsy room. What he hadn't expected was to be blackmailed about it. He looked at her a long while, assessing her. She looked right back.

Enjoying every minute.

'What do you want to know?' he said eventually. 'About DS Beckford?'

She shook her head, the smile still on her lips.

'That can wait. When we walked in, the first thing Durand

said was, *it's a bit late for you, Padre*. I'm assuming that means you're the sort of goody two-shoes who's always early—'

'No.'

Her brow creased momentarily before she moved on.

'Why did she call you *Padre*?'

'Why do you think? Did you get the impression Dr Durand is the sort of woman who says things for no good reason?'

He watched the realisation filter into her eyes, saw them widen. Her voice was incredulous, a hint of suspicion that maybe he was winding her up behind it.

'You were a priest?'

'Yep.'

'What kind?'

'The religious kind.'

'You know what I mean.'

'Catholic.'

She nodded like she'd expected as much, her mouth becoming a perfect O.

'The real deal. My parents are Church of England. Summer fetes and jumble sales. Not so much incense or talking in Latin. Although I know for a fact they baptised my kids in the bath. I think it's all a load of bollocks, myself.'

'Maybe I do, too.' A pause. 'Now.'

'Do you?'

'I'm not sure.'

She leaned away from him, appraising him. And not getting far.

'I wouldn't have guessed in a million years. That's what she meant by being too late. Administering the last rites when he's already dead. So, why *Padre* and not *Father*?'

'I was an Army chaplain. Everybody gets called *Padre* whatever denomination they are.'

She was looking at him very differently now. As if she was six and her parents had taken her to the zoo for the first time to see the giraffe-hippopotamus cross the zoo keepers had accidentally bred when they left a gate open.

'Why the Army?' She shook her head, her voice incredulous. 'The only man in a war zone without a gun.'

'Long story. For another time.'

For her, maybe. For him, it was already too late. His brother, Cormac's, voice was in his mind, the anguish not diminished by the passage of time.

I don't know what to do, Max.

Kincade looked as if she was going to push him, momentarily. Until she saw his face. She made an obvious remark, instead.

'That's a hell of a career change.'

'It is.'

'Some really bad shit must have happened while you were in, where? Iraq? Afghanistan?'

'Both. And the answer to that one isn't covered in this round of questions, either. But I'll say this. It made me realise that believing in the essential goodness in people won't stop bad things from happening, but accepting the underlying evil in them allows me to bring them to task after they have.'

'Deep,' she said, sounding impressed. Then said something shallow. 'I joined because I thought I'd look good in the uniform.'

'I bet you do, too.'

She sucked air in through her teeth, surprise in her voice—although no offence taken—at his reckless words.

'You'd get demoted like I did if I reported that remark.'

'It'd be worth it.'

'Anyway, it wasn't about the uniform.'

'No?'

'No. And before you ask, that question's off-limits in round one, too. Anyway, my turn isn't over. After she called you *Padre*, she pointed at you and said, *don't even think about it*. Like she was worried you were the one who might be sick all over her nice clean floor.'

'You'll be sorry you asked.'

'I'll take that chance. I'm a big girl.'

He slipped his hand into his jacket pocket. She thought he was going to pull out his phone, show her something on it. A photograph, perhaps. Hopefully not of a puddle of sick. Instead, he brought out something she didn't immediately recognise, expecting to see a mobile phone. Then it clicked.

'A mouth organ?' Sounding as if he'd snaffled Roy Lynch's liver from the autopsy while Durand wasn't watching.

'*Harmonica*, please. Or Blues Harp.'

She took it out of his hand. Inspected it like they'd found a piece of meteorite in the street. She went to put it to her mouth, realised what she was doing and stopped. Gave it back looking like she wanted to wipe her fingers on her trousers.

'You didn't play that during an autopsy, did you?'

He held up his left hand, index finger extended. Guilty smile on his lips.

'One time.'

'I don't believe it! What did you play?'

'*The Last Post.*'

She stifled a snort.

'On a mouth organ? I mean harmonica.'

'Uh-huh. I can play it now if you like. It sounds better than you'd think.' The harmonica already halfway to his mouth as he said it.

'Don't you dare. What made you do it?'

He shook his head, a gentle smile on his lips at the memory of the smile on Isabel Durand's face that she'd tried so hard to suppress.

'It seemed appropriate at the time. The guy on the slab was ex-Army. He'd been living rough on the streets. I thought he deserved a send-off. With hindsight, the autopsy room wasn't the right place.'

'Was it someone you knew?'

'No. Anyway, Isabel never lets me forget it.'

She gave him the head-pulled-back appraising look again.

'That's another thing. I notice it's always *Isabel* with you, and not *Dr Durand*. Should I read anything into that?'

'Not what you're thinking, no. But we're good friends. We go back a long way.'

She was mulling it over, trying to decide whether she believed him, when the full horror of the harmonica situation struck her.

'Hang on. You don't carry that thing around the whole time, do you? Play it in the car when you're on a stake-out?'

'I do requests.'

She looked away, out the window. He knew it was to stop him from seeing the smile trying to break out on her face.

'*Jesus*,' she said,' I thought it was bad enough being stuck with someone who listens to Leonard Cohen.'

'Want me to play something now?'

'No, I do not. Why harmonica, anyway?'

'I learned to play when I was in the Army. It's a lot easier to carry around in the desert than a guitar or a drum kit.'

'I suppose. Or a church organ. C'mon, drive me back to the station.'

'The station? Or...'

'You're right. I need something to wash away the taste of that place.' Flicking her head towards the hospital and the autopsy room in its bowels. Immediately, she glanced at the back seat. 'What about Leonard?'

'He drinks lager shandy, if you're buying.'

'I meant, will he be okay?'

'We'll leave all the windows open. He'll be fine.'

'He won't pee in the basket?'

He leaned around, put his fingertips through the mesh door for the cat to nuzzle.

'If he does, we'll take a sample, bag it and log it. Slip it in with what was found at Roy Lynch's house. Give forensics something to think about.'

The look on her face was easy to read.

If I hadn't needed a beer before, I do now.

9

He drove west, crossing the River Test at Redbridge, then dropped down to Eling. There, he parked on the quayside overlooking Bartley Water next to The Anchor Inn. They could have gone somewhere closer, but neither of them had anything to get back home for.

He ordered a pint of Ringwood bitter for himself and a half of Stella Artois—popularly known as *wife beater* on account of its perceived historical association with binge drinking and domestic abuse—for her. They carried the drinks outside and found a vacant picnic table on the terrace facing the water.

'Eyes front or to the right,' he said. 'The view's better.'

She did as he suggested, couldn't disagree. Yachts lined the quayside directly ahead, and beyond that, across Bartley Water, the church of St Mary the Virgin nestled in the trees on the far side. To the right, more yachts, a forest of gently swaying masts, the Eling Sailing Club in the distance. She glanced to the left. Rusty red shipping containers were stacked four and five high in a storage yard, two massive electricity pylons in the distance beyond them.

Eyes right it was.

She was still trying to get her head around working with a cop who used to be a priest.

'I bet you get a lot of stick about it.'

'Yep. The team work their butts off, don't eat or sleep, do irreparable damage to their relationships and marriages, and when we finally make an arrest, I forgive the suspect and let them go.'

'It must have its advantages.' She pointed upwards. 'Divine inspiration. And I bet you're great at confessions.'

'Yeah. Shame I'm not allowed to hand out Old Testament-style punishments.'

'You seem very happy to joke about it. You must have believed in it at some point.'

He took a long, thoughtful swallow of beer, the conversation suddenly having taken a serious turn. It was all about tolerance as far as he was concerned. Something that was missing in other —generally sandier—parts of the world hell-bent on returning to medieval customs and attitudes. He didn't want to get into any of that now, lightened the mood again.

'Thank God we don't burn heretics at the stake any longer.'

He felt the weight of questions piling up behind her eyes, knew what was coming next. She didn't disappoint. He was surprised it had taken as long as it had.

'Catholic priests are celibate, aren't they?' Making *celibate* sound interchangeable with *castrated*.

'Uh-huh.'

'Were you?'

'Are you asking me if I broke my vows, DS Kincade?'

Face dead-pan as he said it, panic suffusing hers at the thought that she'd offended her boss on their first day working together.

'No, of course not—'

He held up his hand, stopped her from digging herself

further into a hole over a question he hadn't taken offence at to begin with.

'I was.'

'For how long?'

'Ten years.'

She shook her head like she'd heard some strange and dreadful things in interview rooms over the years, but this had them beat hands down.

'I don't know how you did it. I couldn't.'

He gave her the answer he always did to the question that was always asked.

'A lot of ugly people go without sex for a lot longer.'

There was a brief pause as the unexpected response sank in, then an explosion of laughter. It felt like an appropriate time to change the subject. Go out on a high, with a laugh, rather than risk getting caught up in something heavy. He waited for her laughter to water down to an amused smile.

'I think that's your twenty questions.'

'I've got a lot more.'

'I'm sure you do. Tell me what the pathologist said, first.'

She downed the last of her half pint of Stella, held up the glass.

'You want another one?'

'Not when I'm driving.'

'Especially with your new DS in the passenger seat?'

She shrugged, *suit yourself*, when he didn't answer, went inside. Five minutes later she was back with another half and two packets of cheese and onion crisps.

'Dinner?' he said.

'Yep. Alcohol, fat, salt, food additives. All the major food groups covered. High blood pressure's better than no blood pressure at all.'

'Roy Lynch would probably agree.'

He waited while she devoured the first of the two packets, declining her offer to share them with him.

'Did she give you a time of death?' he said.

She emptied the last of the contents of the crisp packet into her palm, tipped them down her throat, wiped her palms together.

'Somewhere between midnight and two a.m.'

He thought back to what Lynch's cleaner had said about her employer.

He's always in the house. Up and dressed. He goes to bed early and gets up early.

Lynch hadn't been dressed for bed when he died. He'd answered the door fully clothed. Different people have different ideas about what constitutes early, but assuming it was around ten p.m., they'd been doing something else before the visitor took him into his garage and hanged him. Talking? Drinking together? Arguing?

Already he'd slipped into the pattern of thinking in terms of murder, not suicide.

'She confirmed cause of death was asphyxia due to ligature strangulation,' Kincade went on, interrupting his thoughts. 'The condition of his liver suggests that he was a moderate drinker. We'll have to wait for the tox report to know whether he'd been drinking on the night before allegedly topping himself. And for evidence of anything else he might have taken.'

'Or had administered against his will.'

'True. There was no evidence of cirrhosis or anything sinister. It's unlikely he'd received a letter from his doctor telling him he only had weeks to live. And I asked her what she'd found under his fingernails.'

'Let me guess. She said trace evidence?'

'Yeah. Her way of telling me to shut up and wait for her

report. Maybe she'd have been more forthcoming if you'd stuck around.'

'What? And left Leonard in the cattery for another night?'

They sat in silence for a while longer. Looking out over the water, the occasional sound of a halyard slapping against a mast in the gentle breeze providing a backdrop.

'Talk me through the trousers,' he said, a choice of words that would have turned heads had anyone been within earshot.

'Yeah. Creased below the knee.' She clasped her forearms together in front of her. 'As if someone had been holding him around his legs while the material was still damp. It can't have been nice given that he'd pissed himself. But it fits with what she said about the damage to the hyoid bone. The killer stood him on the stepladder, took up the slack on the clothesline in a controlled manner. Tied it to the shelving. Then clamped his arms around Lynch's legs, pushed the stepladder away and let go of him.'

'I was thinking the same thing. Maybe even held him like that for a while to torment him.'

She saw that his drink was finished, threw the last of hers down her throat, the conversation at a natural end.

'I'm glad we did this,' she said as they made their way towards his car.

'Found out a few things you weren't expecting?'

'You're not kidding. Another couple of beers, and I might start thinking they've put us together as an experiment. Except I know it fits with DS Beckford being off. And no, that's not me bringing the conversation around to asking about him.'

'Good. I already feel like I've been on the wrong side of the table in the interview room.'

She gave him an incredulous look.

'Seriously? You'd know it if you'd been interviewed by me.'

After only twelve hours together, he could believe it.

She was thoughtful in the car as he drove away. He didn't think there would be any more probing questions about the lost ten years he'd spent as a Catholic priest. Not tonight, anyway. He waited to see what it was as he navigated his way through the thinning post-rush hour traffic. It wasn't what he was expecting when it arrived.

'I've been thinking about how you're going to explain about my situation. People are going to find out, but I don't want to stand up tomorrow morning and have to explain myself in detail.'

'Fair enough. Have you got something in mind?'

'As it happens, I have...'

Leonard was more excited about getting back to the empty house than Angel was. He prowled from room to room, a look of vacant curiosity on his face as if he'd never seen them before, rubbing his scent on table legs and the corners of anything protruding. Angel put the kettle on and made himself cheese on toast. A step up from Kincade's dinner of cheese and onion crisps, but not a very big one.

Going forward, he'd get into the habit of cooking properly for himself. Make sure he got his five-a-day.

Of course, he would.

He took his meal out into the garden, fighting his way through grass that hadn't been cut for six weeks, and sat in the small gazebo at the bottom of the garden looking back at the house.

Was it too big now?

When did it become the law that a man on his own had to live in something the size of a shoebox?

Bollocks.

Maybe he liked rattling around in the place. Had they thought of that?

He realised he was angry at *them*, whoever *they* were, that unidentified mass of humanity to whom everything said and thought is attributed.

Nobody had said anything to him. But he felt the weight of their expectations now that his life had changed.

Was it the discussion with Kincade that had unsettled him, steering his thoughts into the dark places in his mind that were best avoided? The knowledge that it had only been round one? There was something about her made him feel that when she asked him the difficult questions that lay ahead, he wouldn't be able to say *no* to her.

Back in the house, he wandered from room to room as Leonard had. Not leaving his own scent on the furniture, of course. But acutely aware of the one that clung to everything—in his mind, if nowhere else—that would gradually fade with time until there was nothing left.

It was the way of the world. That life should go on.

But nobody said it had to be easy.

10

'How are you getting on with your new DS?' Olivia Finch said to Angel's back as he stood staring out of her office window at seven-thirty the next morning.

He looked down at his feet before answering. She might have thought it an admission that things hadn't gone well, had she not known him.

'You make it sound as if she's a new pair of shoes you gave me for Christmas. It's the word *your*.'

'Okay, Mr Pedant. How are you getting along with *DS Kincade*?'

'Extremely well, ma'am. Even if I'm getting the feeling it might be some kind of social-engineering experiment devised upstairs.'

Finch looked up from the papers she'd been skimming, not paying particular attention so far.

'Really? What does she think?'

A mental image came to him of Kincade's incredulous face when he confirmed that, yes, he'd been a priest in a past life, one that felt now as if it had never existed.

'I think she might be thinking the same. After I answered a few of her questions.'

Finch was seriously interested now. Off came the glasses. She even went so far as to put her pen down, give him her full attention.

'What sort of questions? About you?'

'Uh-huh.'

'How much did you tell her?'

Kincade's incredulous face grew larger in his mind.

'More than she was expecting, that's for sure.'

'I'll bet. Your previous . . . is it a career?'

'*Calling*, ma'am. Or vocation. Yes, we talked about that. Including the obligatory prurient question about celibacy.'

'No doubt you gave your standard ugly-person answer?'

'I did. But without suggesting any examples around the station to prove my point beyond doubt.'

'Very thoughtful, I'm sure. I hope the mouth organ—'

'*Harmonica*.'

'—didn't make an appearance.'

'It was Isabel Durand's fault. And I didn't actually play it.'

'Thank the Lord for small mercies. Did Kincade tell you about her situation?'

'She did.'

'And what do you think?'

He'd thought about it a lot the previous evening after dropping Kincade off. He hadn't got far. Leonard hadn't been any help when he'd put the question to him, either. Too busy reacquainting himself with every nook and cranny in the house he'd been away from for six weeks. He told her the only conclusion he'd arrived at.

'Having never been a female police officer, I don't know how I'd react in a similar situation. I'd like to think my training and professionalism would allow me to rise above it. I can't honestly put my hand on my heart and advise anyone to bet on it.'

What he didn't mention was the vague doubts he'd felt rousing themselves at the back of his mind, in part as a result of Kincade's uncle's connection to SO15. What he'd call a pay-grade feeling—that the truth was above his.

Finch smiled gently. Picked up her pen again and held it up vertically inspecting the tip as if performing an eye test.

'Most people would just say, *I don't know*, Max.' She stopped him, pointing the pen at him, before he could respond. 'I realise you're not most people. Have you thought about how you're going to introduce her to the team?'

'She came up with a good idea herself...'

Finch laughed out loud when he told her.

'I like it.'

'I thought you would.'

That got him a sorry headshake, less of the amusement in her voice.

'Not that it would've made any difference even if I didn't.'

It wasn't necessary for him to answer that one.

'I hope you didn't tell her what you call me,' she said.

'Calling you *ma'am*, you mean?'

'Don't be an obtuse arse, Max. *In-between*.'

It was a private joke between them. She'd accused him one time of taking the concept of answering to a higher power too far. She'd been forced to remind him that there were other levels in-between—herself as his immediate superior, as well as everyone on the floor above. He'd referred to her as *in-between*, or *IB* for short, ever since.

'No ma'am,' he said.

'Good. How did you get on yesterday? Is Roy Lynch a suicide, or not?'

'I'm leaning towards not. As you identified yesterday, there's the question of him having wet himself...' He took her through the other findings. The kitchen chair that the deceased may or may not have left a matching urine stain on; the evidence of him having been held by the legs; the damage caused getting the car out of the garage. 'And there's something not right about the timing.'

'You mean he should've done the world a favour by doing it ten years ago? Or has Isabel Durand got the time of death wrong?'

'Neither of those things, no...' He then told her his concerns about Lynch being up so late in his daytime clothes. 'If it's suicide, he sat up for a long time thinking about it—'

'That's more likely to make someone decide *not* to go through with it. If you're going to do it, you need to get on and do it, not sit around thinking about it.'

'You sound as if you've coached people.' He ignored the despairing look she gave him, continued with his thinking. 'Say it's murder. Unless the killer turned up after midnight, which seems unlikely, he arrived earlier and they sat around doing something together.' He made quotes in the air as he said it. 'That suggests they knew each other.'

'Strange thing to do, too. Sit chatting to a man you know who you plan to kill.'

'Agreed. Talking of people he knew, his son Gavin isn't happy.'

'You interviewed him?'

'Not yet, no. He turned up, tried to get into the house. DS Kincade prevented him from doing so.'

She leaned back in her chair, folded her arms across her chest. Considering him. Then mimicked his words.

'*Prevented him from doing so.* Why do I get the impression that's a hugely edited version of what happened? I'm tempted to say, sanitised version.'

He shook his head, no idea, ma'am.

'I'm trusting you to tell me, Max, if you see any signs of the sort of problems that resulted in her joining us in the first place.'

He nodded. Understood.

'Anything else I need to know?' she said.

'We might have some additional help.'

'The unwanted kind? From Lynch Jnr?'

He nodded again.

'His exact words were, *if you lot don't find out who, I will.*' He held up his hand, his index finger and thumb an inch apart. 'His nose was this far from my own when he made the offer.'

'I'm surprised you didn't bite it off.'

He didn't share with her how close he'd been.

11

STANDING IN THE INCIDENT ROOM PREPARING TO BRIEF THE TEAM of detectives, uniformed officers, civilian and auxiliary staff assembled before him, Angel felt like he always did in these circumstances.

As if he was back in the pulpit, about to deliver a sermon.

The group in front of him were like every congregation he'd ever addressed. Some of them would soon be glazing over or picking at their fingernails wishing they were elsewhere. Others hanging on his every word convinced that the answers they sought—either the details of Roy Lynch's death or the route to eternal salvation—could be found in the pearls of wisdom that spilled from his mouth.

He'd faced a lot of rooms full of soon-to-be-disappointed people in his life.

Beside him, Catalina Kincade had her butt parked against a desk, texting on her phone. One or other of her daughters, he guessed. Reporting back on her first day. Telling them that *unusual* might be a better word to describe her new boss rather than *nice*. Those thumbs that flew across the keypad would be getting a good work-out in the days and weeks ahead as she winkled more information out of him, as he was sure she would try to do. Whether it would all be appropriate material for her six and eight-year-old daughters was another matter.

He waited for her to finish, caught her eye, then cleared his throat to get everyone's attention. A deep voice immediately resonated from the back of the room.

'Dearly beloved, we are gathered here today...'

The room erupted into laughter, a call of *good to have you back, Padre* coming from somewhere off to the left, a woman's voice.

Angel waited for it to die down, then looked directly at the man at the back grinning at him.

'Any time you want to take my place up here, DC Gulliver, just let me know.'

'Will do, sir. I do weddings and funerals, too.'

'Good to know, Craig.' He extended his hand towards Kincade. 'I'd like to introduce everybody to DS Catalina Kincade. She'll be taking Stuart Beckford's place for the time being.'

'When's he coming back, sir?' a trainee detective sitting at the front said, then immediately pulled his head down into his shoulders, tortoise-style, as somebody behind him threw a scrunched-up paper ball at the back of his head.

Kincade raised a hand in greeting, on the face of it not troubled by the implication hanging in the air that everybody couldn't wait for good ol' DS Beckford to get back.

'We've prepared a joint statement to explain what she's doing here,' Angel said with a glance at Kincade. He cleared his throat again. 'She was kicked out of the Met for good police work. Nobody in this room needs me to tell you that they don't put up with that kind of shit up there.'

Again, the room erupted, laughter and catcalls. And a muttered, *wankers* that Angel suspected was Craig Gulliver again. If it had been *twats*, it would've been Gulliver's partner, DC Lisa Jardine. It was good to know your team.

Despite the atmosphere of good-natured inter-force rivalry produced by the tongue-in-cheek statement, Angel saw a uniformed officer pull out his phone. It didn't take a rocket scientist to figure out what the search string put into Google would be.

Metropolitan Police misconduct hearing + Catalina Kincade

He was unlikely to be the first to do it.

'Roy Lynch,' Angel said, bringing the room to order. He turned to Kincade, gave her the floor.

The trainee detective who was missing DS Beckford was ready with a question as soon as she'd finished taking them through it, an attempt to claw back lost ground.

'We're definitely treating it as murder, are we?'

'We wouldn't be here now if we weren't looking at that possibility,' Kincade said, putting the emphasis on the last word.

'You need to keep an open mind,' Angel warned. 'Suicide is still a possibility. We'll be looking at why he might have wanted to—'

'Do the world a favour,' came from the back.

'Thank you, DC Gulliver. I was going to say, kill himself. We'll be talking to his doctor, friends, neighbours, family. On that note, I need to tell you that Lynch's son, Gavin'—a faint call of *wanker* came from Gulliver's direction—'has already offered his assistance.'

Everybody in the room knew what assistance meant, even the fresh-faced trainee detective. The case had taken on something of the characteristics of a race. Not against time, but against retaliatory bodies piling up.

Angel glanced at Kincade, got a *why not?* twitch of her shoulders back.

'DS Kincade had the pleasure of making Gavin's acquaintance on her first day,' he said. 'She dumped him on his arse on the ground.'

'Accidentally, of course,' Kincade said modestly.

'What are you drinking?' Lisa Jardine called, and got more replies from the whole room than she was expecting.

The trainee detective raised a finger. Angel nodded at him.

'Are we looking at the possibility of it being drug-related, sir?'

'We are. A warning to Gavin Lynch, rather than a grudge held for ten years. Talk to your sources on the street, everybody. Any turf infringement, some upstart Johnny-big-bollocks trying to make his mark... you know the drill.'

'Could it be murder but not related to the business he used to be in?' Craig Gulliver said.

Angel resisted the temptation to preface his reply with a remark that it was nice to have something intelligent coming out of Gulliver's mouth for a change, paused to let the question sink in.

'It could. So, barring a random nutter passing through on his way to a week's camping in The New Forest, we're back to looking at friends and family and other acquaintances.' He slapped the sheet of notes in his hand against his other palm. 'Okay, let's get to it.'

The deep voice resonated from the back of the room once more.

'Here endeth the lesson according to Saint Maximilian The Fallen.'

. . .

'I WANT TO INTRODUCE YOU TO OUR RESIDENT HECKLER AND HIS partner,' Angel said, waving Craig Gulliver and Lisa Jardine up to the front as everybody dispersed.

They made their way across the room, loose-limbed and straight-backed, youth on their side. Angel always thought they looked less like police officers and more like a pair of advertising execs, on their way to coffee and croissants in a converted warehouse with exposed brickwork and mis-matched chairs.

'Is that a Geordie accent I detect?' Kincade said, shaking hands with Jardine.

'It is, sarge. Sunderland.'

Angel saw something flash across Kincade's face at the word *sarge*. Was it the first time she'd been addressed as *sarge* and not *ma'am*? He wondered how long it would take her to get used to it. She soon recovered, pulling a face as if she'd made a faux pas.

'*Oops*, sorry. A Mackem.'

Jardine smiled broadly, made Angel see why she'd be called a *canny lass* back home.

'That's okay. I'll forgive you this once. At least you know the difference.'

'A northerner's a bloody northerner,' Gulliver said under his breath.

Kincade ignored the remark, not wanting to fuel what might be a long-running spat between them. She made a comment based on his height and powerful build, instead.

'You look as if you should play rugby second row, Craig.'

He smiled modestly, as if embarrassed by his stature.

'I used to.'

'I thought so. Who for?'

'Only at university.'

'Where was that?'

Gulliver hesitated, as if he couldn't remember.

'Portsmouth.'

Angel was well aware of the reasons behind Gulliver's reticence. He also hadn't missed that Kincade had said nothing about playing rugby for the Met police. He said nothing about it himself despite the small bond it would have created.

'Weren't you two about to start the door-to-door of Lynch's neighbours?' he said to the two DCs, instead.

'Door-to-door?' Gulliver echoed, sounding like he was having trouble reconciling the phrase with the task ahead. 'More like field-to-field out there. The houses must be fifty yards apart.'

'Then you better get going, hadn't you?'

'They seem okay,' Kincade said after Gulliver and Jardine had collected their gear and left.

'They are. You might change your mind when Jardine starts calling you *pet*.'

'Better than saying nothing at all. Getting information out of Gulliver felt a bit like getting blood out of a stone.'

'You noticed that?'

'Noticed? I thought I was interviewing an uncooperative witness.'

'There is a reason...'

Given his build, Craig Gulliver gave the lie to the idea that a person is blessed with either brains or brawn. He told people that he'd attended what used to be Portsmouth Polytechnic before all polytechnics promoted themselves to universities. In fact, he'd boarded at the renowned independent school, Winchester College, and from there went on to read Politics at Oxford University. Despite that, he'd chosen not to join the fast-track graduate scheme. It was a decision that endeared him to his peers, but did nothing to enhance his career prospects—the view from above being that when offered a leg-up, the sort of men and women they were looking for grabbed the opportunity with both hands.

'He was uncomfortable lying to me about it,' she said.

'Probably. Anyway, you seem to have made a good impression on them both. Anyone would think you were trying to impress me with your powers of observation.'

It's a pity I haven't worked you out as easily yet, she thought and kept to herself.

12

'What did you think of her?' Lisa Jardine said as Gulliver drove them out to start canvassing Roy Lynch's neighbours.

'DS Kincade, you mean? Too early to say. I was impressed that she knew the difference between you and a Geordie.' Making it sound like the difference between two similar-looking invertebrates that lived in the mud at the bottom of ponds.

'Not everyone's as geographically challenged as you are.' She studied him, a mischievous grin creeping across her face. 'You went bright pink when she said what a strapping big lad you are.'

'No way.'

'Deny it all you like. It's happening again now.'

He refused to lean sideways to inspect his face in the mirror, concentrated on driving.

Jardine moved on, having failed to get a rise out of him.

'You know that she was a DI in the Met? Got demoted for using excessive force arresting a little twat who spat on her and called her a dyke. She was lucky she didn't get thrown out.'

He looked sideways at her to see if she was joking. He knew

her well enough to know the look she got on her face when she was winding him up. For once, she wasn't.

'I didn't know that.'

'Of course you didn't. You walk around with your head up your arse all day long.'

'If that's the same as not spending all day gossiping instead of getting on with the job, I'm guilty as charged.'

'Head up your arse,' she muttered to end the conversation—if it qualified as such.

Fifteen minutes later, they pulled up outside Roy Lynch's immediate neighbour on the right-hand side. Gulliver had exaggerated about the distance between the houses, but not by much.

An old-fashioned cottage garden sat behind a white picket fence. Plants that neither of them could identify ran riot encroaching on both sides of the path leading to the front door, drooping under the weight of the recent rain. They were both wet through from the knee down by the time they'd fought their way to the door.

Gulliver gave the iron door knocker a particularly hard double knock in his irritation, as if they were bailiffs come to seize possession of the house. Despite the force of the knock, there was no answer. He was about to do it again when a voice called from the far side of the garden.

'They're away on a cruise for six weeks.'

They picked their way through the wet vegetation to where a woman in her thirties stood in the gap between a couple of mature shrubs smoking a cigarette.

Gulliver gave her a disapproving look.

'You probably shouldn't say that to everyone who knocks on their door.'

'I don't say it to *everyone*. I'm not stupid. You two might as well have *cop* tattooed on your foreheads. After all the police activity after Roy was murdered it doesn't take a brain surgeon to figure it out.'

Gulliver immediately worked a broomstick up his backside, his voice taking on a pompous note.

'We're currently working on the basis that Mr Lynch committed suicide, madam. Can I ask who said he'd been murdered?'

'Everyone. I think it was his son, Gavin, said it first. I wouldn't like to be the murderer if Gavin gets hold of him. He's a nasty piece of work, is Gavin.'

She took a long drag of her cigarette looking as if she was about to give them a couple of choice examples. Jardine cut her short.

'Did you see or hear anything, madam?'

The neighbour shook her head, blowing smoke straight up.

'I was away myself. Just for a few days to visit my sister. Not six weeks like them.' Flicking her cigarette at the house behind them and making it sound like a crime against humanity. 'Are you sure it was suicide? I heard he was a bit dodgy. Not the sort of bloke you'd want to get on the wrong side of.'

'Almost certainly suicide,' Jardine said, knowing that her next words contradicted the statement. 'How about before you went to your sister's? Did you notice anything unusual in the days leading up to when you went away?'

The neighbour shook her head again, although nodding would have been more appropriate to accompany the look in her eye.

I knew it.

They made their way out of the front garden and onto the road, looked left and right.

'Where did you learn to talk like such a pompous prick?' Jardine said, then mimicked what Gulliver had said. 'I suppose that's what they teach you at Oxford.'

He ignored her, regretting, as he often did, that he'd told her the truth—one of the few people he had. He looked past the house of the woman they'd just talked to, nothing but open fields beyond it, all the way to a line of trees in the distance.

'There's nothing that way.'

They about-faced, went past Lynch's drive nodding to the uniformed constable still standing guard, arriving at the immediate neighbour on the left thirty yards further down the lane.

'I wonder if another ex-criminal lives in this one?' Jardine said as they went through a wooden five-bar gate set into the middle of a privet hedge that looked as if it could be used to calibrate a spirit level. 'Probably find some rivals buried under the hedge which is why it grows so well.'

'I'll leave you to ask him that, shall I?'

The door was opened by a man in his late sixties wearing raspberry-coloured cords and a windowpane-check shirt with a frayed collar.

'You don't look like Jehovah's Witnesses, so that makes you police officers. You're here about . . . next door?'

Neither of them missed the pause before his choice of words. The lack of anything along the lines of *poor old Roy* was also very evident.

'We are,' Gulliver said. 'I'm DC Gulliver and this is—'

'DC Jardine, Mr . . . ?'

'Barclay. Robin Barclay.'

'Can we come in and ask you a few questions, Mr Barclay?' Gulliver said.

Barclay immediately surprised them. Not by saying, *no*, but by stepping outside himself leaving the door ajar.

'I want to show you something.'

He led them back across the gravel drive and out through the five-bar gate, stopped on the narrow roadside verge.

'The day before it happened, I was trimming the hedge.' He pointed at the ground. Small hedge cuttings were visible in the grass and on the road. 'I sweep it up, of course, but you can't get everything.'

Gulliver refused to look at Jardine. He'd laugh if he did. He knew exactly what she wanted to say.

That's okay, Mr Barclay. We're prepared to let it go on this occasion.

'You can see how narrow the verge is,' Barclay went on. 'Sometimes I'm standing in the road when I'm working. Some people steal traffic cones from roadworks and put them out, but I'm not prepared to do that.'

'You have to watch out for the traffic,' Gulliver said, rather than congratulate him on his honesty.

'Exactly. Most people are careful and considerate when they see me.'

A silver Range Rover went past at that point, as if Barclay had arranged it with one of his neighbours to illustrate his point. They all stood back. The car gave them a wide berth, anyway. Barclay recognised the car and its driver, raised a hand in greeting as it went past. Then it was time for the *but*.

'Of course, other people aren't so considerate,' he said. 'Young people on their mobile phones most of the time. A quick glance at the road every thirty seconds and then back to playing games on their phone or texting.'

'I'd be tempted to buy some cones,' Jardine said, 'if you don't want to steal them.'

Barclay glared at her, unsure whether she was being facetious or not. After a moment, he moved on, stepping out into the road in order to point directly at the entrance to Roy Lynch's drive.

'Like I said, I was out here trimming the hedge when a car

came out of there. A convertible Mercedes. The sort of car I'd expect his visitors to drive.'

He worked an impressive amount of loathing into the word *his*. One small word that conveyed so much.

What was the world coming to when one was forced to live next door to such people?

'And Mr Lynch's visitor almost hit you?' Gulliver suggested.

'Exactly. He came out of the drive and floored it.' Barclay dropped the arm pointing at Lynch's gates, went to inspect a portion of his own hedge. 'I had to throw myself into the hedge to avoid being hit. Luckily I don't think it's damaged too badly.'

'Or yourself,' Gulliver said as Barclay continued to inspect the hedge, teasing out a couple of broken branches.

Barclay waved it off.

'I'm more concerned about the hedge. Anyway, I got the bastard's registration number. He made it easy for me. A personalised plate. *PB 267*. Exactly the sort of pretentious thing his visitors would have.'

Gulliver duly made a note of it. Barclay waited until he'd done so before continuing.

'I know what you're thinking. We're investigating a man's death and this silly old fool wants to make a complaint about dangerous driving—'

'Not at all, sir.' This from Jardine.

'—but there is a point to it. Come with me.'

They exchanged a look, followed him as he marched back across the gravel drive and then into the house. They went down the hallway and into the kitchen where a similarly-aged woman was sitting at a weathered-pine table doing the crossword, a cup of tea in front of her. There was another cup at the other end of the table going cold, a Thompson & Morgan seed catalogue open beside it.

'This is my wife, Hilary,' Barclay said, not bothering to introduce them. 'Tell the officers what you heard, Hilary.'

Seemed the Barclays were well suited. Either that, or they'd grown alike over the years as people do. Like her husband, Hilary Barclay was not content with simply relaying the facts. Another demonstration was called for.

She got up from the table, went over to the back door and led them outside. They crossed a brick patio with an expensive-looking teak table and six chairs, then down across the lawn heading to the right in the direction of the boundary between their property and Lynch's.

Unlike the four-foot-high hedge that fronted the road, the hedge separating the two properties was a good seven foot tall. An old apple tree was growing up into it, the ground around it littered with windfalls.

'It's a never-ending job,' Hilary said, stooping to pick up a semi-rotten apple. 'Anyway, I was out here picking up apples when I heard an argument.' She pointed at the hedge, mouthed, *over there.*

Again, Gulliver refused to look at Jardine, knowing what was in her mind.

You don't have to whisper, Mrs Barclay. Mr Lynch can't hear you.

'What was the argument about?' he said instead.

Hilary's face compacted, disappointment and apology in her voice.

'I didn't catch it all, but the visitor was talking. Shouting really. It was something like, you were always a cheating . . . he used the C-word. Then he said, and you haven't changed. Lynch told him to F-off. That's exactly what the visitor did. He stormed off and then he nearly ran Robin over as he drove away because he was so angry.'

'Did he make any parting threats?' Jardine said.

Hilary had bent to pick up another apple. She straightened up at the question.

'He did, yes. But it was only something like, *you'll be sorry* as he stormed off.'

'Maybe now we'll get some decent neighbours,' Barclay said.

Hilary gave him a disapproving look. He glared right back at her.

'You think the same. You just don't want to say it in front of these two. They're not going to arrest you for thinking it, Hilary.'

'Did you have a lot of trouble with Mr Lynch?' Jardine said, addressing them both.

The Barclays looked at each other, then Mrs Barclay started the answer.

'Nothing was ever said—'

'But he wasn't our sort of person. He was a criminal.'

'*Robin!*' Hilary exclaimed. 'You don't know that.'

He gave her a pitying look, his tone weary. As if it was an argument they'd had many times, one that never changed.

'*Everybody* knows it. The officers here know it. You just refuse to admit it. As if you're worried people in the village will point at you. *That's the woman who lives next door to the criminal.*'

Gulliver jumped in to head off the looming domestic row.

'Were there any other incidents or arguments recently?'

'Not that I can think of,' Barclay said. 'It's not as if we spend our whole lives out here eavesdropping.'

Of course not, Gulliver heard Jardine thinking as they left the Barclays to their fallen apples and petty bickering.

There were no more houses on that side of Lynch's property. A continuous thicket of hawthorn lined the opposite side of the road, open fields behind. They made their way back to the car still parked outside the house of the neighbours who were away on a cruise.

'It's strange,' Jardine said, as they drove away.

'What is?'

'The Barclays. The way they've both got a first name that can either be a man or a woman. Like they're interchangeable.'

Gulliver shook his head at the often-random thought patterns his partner exhibited, attributing it as always to her upbringing in the frozen wastes of the North where he'd been told that people still ate their young.

'Let's hope a more useful insight than that comes from running the registration he gave us.'

13

Guy Yardley clicked on the first attachment to the email he'd just opened and felt sick to his stomach.

The body of the email itself had been short and not at all sweet.

We know what you did.

He'd been expecting the attachment to be a photograph. It was, but not of him in bed humping a woman half his age with greedy eyes and silicon-filled breasts.

That, he could've lived with.

Not this.

It was a copy of a form taken on somebody's mobile phone. Specifically, Companies House form NM01: Notice of change of name by resolution.

In the top box was the company number. He knew it by heart.

Below that, the original company name. Cameron Marine Engineering Ltd.

Then the proposed new name. Yardarm Marine Technology Ltd.

A name that still filled him with pride after all these years. A clever play on words, even if he did say so himself. Half of his own name incorporated into the traditional nautical saying about the sun being over the yardarm—time for a drink. And of course, Marine *Technology* was so much classier than Marine *Engineering*, which always made him think of grease and bilge pumps.

Below that, the signature of the person authorising the change. *His* signature. The same now as it had been back then.

There was no date. It had always struck him as strange that there was no requirement for it, no box for it. He'd always thought of undated documents as a bit suspect, not quite pukka. It was a government form so maybe that explained it. Like the company number, he knew the date that wasn't there by heart.

8th August 1993.

He got up from his desk suddenly feeling his age. Nobody would be catching him *in flagrante* in bed with a woman half his age the way he was feeling at the moment. He needed a stiff one, pardon the pun, before he opened the other attachments.

He went to the drinks trolley, grabbed the nearest bottle of Scotch. Poured himself a large one, forget about the jigger. Knocked it back and poured another. Took that one back to the desk now taking on the appearance of the dock in a courtroom.

The email was still there. It hadn't been a dream or the onset of dementia.

He opened the second attachment. Another Companies House form.

List of past and present members Schedule to form 363a, 363b.

There in the top box was a name he'd never forget. Lucas Cameron. His address below. A very nice house in Ampfield. He knew it well. In the next column, the number of shares currently held—zero. Nil. Zip. Nada. Beside that, shares transferred—one thousand. The whole of the company's share capital at that time. And the date, 6th August 1993.

The second line down showed the matching reverse entry.

His own name and address, shares held, one thousand. Transferred to him on the same date.

The day the company became his. The turning point of his life.

The third attachment was form AP01: Appointment of director. Himself. Guy Yardley. Company director and soon-to-be captain of industry. A proud day indeed. He raised his glass to himself, a mocking gesture with what now felt like a condemned man's last request in his unsteady hand.

And the last attachment. Form TM01: Termination of appointment of director. The details those of Lucas Cameron.

The pedantic wording devised by government pen-pushers had always amused him. Termination of *appointment* of director. Why not save yourself some ink and taxpayers' money, make it more accurate at the same time. Termination *of director*.

Somehow the joke wasn't so funny today.

He got a feeling it wouldn't ever be so again.

Now all he could do was to sit and wait for the blackmail demand to arrive. Questions about how much would be demanded and whether he could afford it paling into insignificance beside the only question that mattered.

What bastard was behind it?

Except that wasn't strictly true. There was another equally-important decision to make. *Should he tell Gavin?* It was the way to go if he wanted to guarantee a scorched-earth-style reaction. But it was one of those decisions you don't make lightly. There was no putting that genie back in the bottle once it was out.

No.

It wasn't a good idea. Not after Gavin's old man had just hanged himself. He'd wait to see what the blackmailers demanded, then decide.

. . .

GUY YARDLEY HAD NO IDEA JUST HOW GOOD A DECISION IT WAS. Gavin Lynch was in a foul mood. That tended to be bad for people around him. Which is why he was sitting alone in his car in a lay-by off the A27. He was angry at what had happened at the old man's house the previous day. The way the dyke bitch cop had dumped him on his arse. That silly cow Samantha laughing at him when he got back to the car hadn't improved his mood—until he spoiled hers right back. His fingers flexed involuntarily at the memory of it.

Worst of all, he was angry at himself. He regretted running his mouth. Threatening to do the pigs' jobs for them. That was plain stupid. They remembered things like that. Always at the most inconvenient times, too.

He closed his eyes, head back on the rest. Blew the air from his cheeks.

Was it possible that the old man had topped himself? It sure as hell wasn't because he was suffering from a broken heart as he lay alone in his bed each night. The old bastard didn't have a sentimental bone in his body. He'd ask the cleaner to give him a quick hand-job while she was hoovering if he felt a sudden urge. Gavin shuddered, tried not to think about it.

Besides, he'd spoken to him on the morning of the day he'd died. He wasn't thinking of topping himself. He was too busy ranting.

Can you believe it, his old man had yelled down the phone loud enough to make the instrument redundant, *that fucking Jewboy called me a cheat? I'll break his legs.*

Did Brent get to him first? Did he even have it in him? Back in the day, absolutely. But now? The two old farts would give each other a heart attack if they got into it.

Still, he'd have a quiet word.

He pulled out his phone, dialled Brent's number.

'Gavin. How are you bearing up?' Brent said, an oily

ingratiating note in his voice that made Gavin want to give him some of what he'd given Samantha.

Be patient.

'Not too bad, Phil, not too bad. Still in shock, I suppose. It's like there's suddenly a great big hole in my life.'

What a load of bollocks, he thought as the words rolled out. It wasn't like that at all. But people expected you to say shit like that. And it was important to play the game.

'I feel the same,' Brent said. 'He was a good man, your father.'

Lying insincere bastard, Gavin thought, then worked a conciliatory note into his voice.

'Look, Phil, I heard you had a disagreement with him the day before he died.'

A wary silence came down the line.

'It was nothing. Two stupid old men who ought to know better arguing about something neither of us could remember ten minutes later.'

Gavin chuckled with him.

You two-faced old git.

'I know that. The trouble is, do the cops? You know what they're like. They like a nice easy result. Keep the statistics looking good. You had an argument with him, next thing you know, he's dead.'

'Nobody overheard us. We were at the bottom of the garden—'

Gavin talked over him, a harder edge to his voice.

'I don't care. We need to get our story straight. Meet me at the old Star Line container yard in an hour's time.' His tone ensuring it was very much an instruction and not a suggestion open to negotiation.

'You really think it's necessary?' Brent said, an uneasy note entering his voice at the mention of the disused yard. Like everyone else, he'd heard the stories about the *conversations* Gavin Lynch and his associates conducted in the privacy of the rusty old shipping containers.

The dial tone in his ear suggested Gavin didn't merely think it necessary, he was already on his way.

14

THERE WAS SOMETHING WRONG WITH ANGEL'S PHONE. IT KEPT switching itself to silent. He'd missed a call from his father the previous evening. Only one, not six at two-minute intervals, so nothing to worry about. He hadn't spoken to him since getting back. Who knows what might have happened in the six weeks he'd been away? The fact that he hadn't taken a call from his sister was more confirmation that nothing had blown up, that the world hadn't come to a premature end.

He didn't have time to call him back now.

It was seven-thirty in the morning. He was in his office reviewing what they had, or didn't have, a meeting with DCI Finch scheduled for eight o'clock.

In front of him, the various reports they'd been waiting on— forensics, post-mortem, and so on—as well as Gulliver and Jardine's report from talking to Lynch's neighbours. Plus, a ton of other accumulating paperwork that viewed his desk as its natural home.

He was halfway through the forensic report when Kincade walked in. He looked up, couldn't stop himself from stating the obvious.

'You've got a face like a smacked arse.'

'Good morning to you, too, sir.'

She dumped her bag on her chair. Glanced at his desk and saw that he'd still got a full cup of coffee, went to the machine to get herself one.

He tried again when she got back, her phone in one hand, polystyrene cup in the other.

'Domestic problems?'

She blew on her coffee, took a sip. Shook her head.

'I don't want to talk about it.' A moment later, she contradicted herself. 'You know what I said about my husband? How we manage to behave like reasonable human beings? I lied. He called me this morning as I was leaving. I know he's got a CCTV camera mounted somewhere so he can monitor me, catch me at exactly the wrong time to dump shit on me. He's talking about wanting custody of the girls.'

Angel put the report he'd been reading to one side, picked up his now-cold coffee. Swivelled towards her on his chair, the irritating squeak not having fixed itself while he was away. Then waited. The best policy—and not only in the interview room. It didn't take long.

'He came out with all this shite about how I'm not settled, I don't even know how long I'll be down here. Then he made some snide remark about the possibility that my anger management issues—his words—might cause a problem here, and I'll get demoted again and shipped off to Manchester or some other northern hell-hole. And of course, it would be unfair if the girls had to follow me around the country in the wake of my professional cock-ups. Again, his words.'

He was scared to ask his next question.

'What did you say?'

'I was having trouble getting any words out. But I managed

to squeeze out something short and to the point that I'm not going to repeat in front of a senior officer.'

He gathered all the papers on his desk together. It didn't look as if he'd be reading through it before the meeting with Finch. He'd read it all once, anyway.

'What do the girls want to do?'

'Isla—'

'She's the eldest?'

'Yeah. She wants to be with me. Daisy can't make her mind up. She's a bit of a daddy's girl. But they both can't stand his new partner. Hannah. They're eight and six and even they can see that she's a bunny-boiler. She's only after his money, anyway.'

'Has he got a lot of it?'

She rocked her hand.

'He's a banker. That's with a *B*. This morning, he's very definitely one with a *W*, as well. He does okay. Not multi-million bonuses sort of okay, but he's never going to starve. Certainly, enough to keep a gold-digger like her in facelifts and boob jobs. Not that the frigid cow has ever had any kids to make them sag in the first place.'

He wasn't regretting asking—it was better out than in, after all—but he did feel as if he was standing in front of an automotive wind tunnel. Or caught in the middle of a sandstorm in the desert.

'I know what you need to cheer you up.' Touching his pocket where the harmonica lived as he said it.

She looked at him as if he'd said he thought her husband had a valid point.

'Make me take a leaf out of Roy Lynch's book, more like. You know, I've never actually seen or heard you play it. I think you use it as a threat, a means of control. You touch your pocket and everyone falls into line.'

'It seems to work with you.'

She shook her head—*shows how much you know*—as she sipped at her coffee.

'That's because I'm new. Once I'm settled in, it'll be different. I also think you use the mouth organ to change the subject. You thought I was going to ask you about kids.'

'If that's your way of asking now, I haven't got any. Not that I know of.'

She leaned back in her chair, assumed position #1. Eyes narrowed.

'That sort of suggests that before your period of—'

'Lunacy?'

'Celibacy, yes, you lived a lifestyle that might have resulted in there being children you're not aware of littering your past.'

It hadn't been true what she'd accused him of—threatening to get out the harmonica every time he wanted to change the subject. But there was no denying it was a good idea. He used it on her now seeing as she'd suggested it, touching his pocket.

She was right on it.

'Okay. More questions for another time. We're going to have to book a long session.'

You have no idea, he thought as he got up, waving the sheaf of papers at her.

'C'mon, DCI Finch is waiting for us.'

15

'I FEEL A BIT OUTNUMBERED, HERE,' ANGEL SAID AS THEY ENTERED Olivia Finch's office.

The pathologist, Isabel Durand, was already there, standing in Angel's usual spot looking out of the window. Almost as if she'd had an argument with Finch and they were studiously ignoring each other.

She turned around at the sound of his voice.

'Don't make it sound like a war, Padre. Men versus women.' She looked at Kincade before Angel could respond. 'Don't put up with any of his sexist remarks, Sergeant.'

'Is he known for them?'

'It's not his fault,' Durand said, not answering the question directly. 'All that time closeted with all those frustrated young men in the seminary. It's bound to leave a lasting mark.'

'Don't you have a cadaver to violate, Isabel?' Angel said, looking at his watch. 'You shouldn't keep the dead waiting. It's disrespectful.'

'And don't put up with any of his Papist nonsense, either,' Durand countered.

'Isabel believes we're like all the rest of the animals. We just happen to be top of the food chain.'

'And not all of us are right at the top.'

Finch was sitting back enjoying the show, or indulging the pathologist. Whatever it was, she brought it to an end.

'What have we got, Max? I know you've got Isabel's report there.'

Angel held it up to confirm it, a pointless gesture, then extended his hand towards the pathologist. She extended hers right back at him.

'A couple of things,' he said, 'in addition to what Isabel already told us. Multiple scratch marks—'

'Excoriation or gouging.' This from Durand.

'—on the victim's neck—'

'As opposed to abrasions from the clothesline.'

'—in addition to his own skin under his fingernails. What Isabel would no doubt call excoriated tissue.'

'Very good, Padre. There's hope for you yet.'

'It's consistent with trying to get his fingers under the clothesline to relieve the pressure. It doesn't mean anything in itself. Or to use a phrase that meets with Isabel's approval, *per se*.'

'The boy's learning.'

'Even if he committed suicide, he'd still panic once he'd kicked the stepladder away. That's why you want a sharp drop rather than a slow strangulation.'

'I'll bear that in mind,' Finch said drily, 'should I ever be considering it myself. What else?'

'The alcohol content in his bloodstream is consistent with what the publican at the White Horse told us. Lynch popped in at about six p.m. on the night he died and stayed for an hour and a half. He only drank two pints which dispels any ideas about him getting hammered before he killed himself.'

'Gulliver and Jardine spoke to the landlord,' Kincade cut in. 'Lynch was his usual self. He wasn't the most sociable of people, but he wasn't sitting alone in the corner drowning his sorrows. He also said, *see you tomorrow* as he was leaving.'

'More importantly,' Angel said, 'there were traces of the date rape drug GHB in his system.'

Off to the side, Isabel Durand cleared her throat.

'Gamma-Hydroxybutyric acid is not exclusively a date rape drug, Padre. I'd describe it as a party drug.' She made the word *party* sound as if it was a term she'd heard used, but she'd never actually been to one. Angel knew exactly how wide of the mark that was, akin to suggesting that Roy Lynch had died of a gunshot wound. 'It produces feelings of euphoria, relaxation and sociability, as well as increasing the sex-drive.' Making that sound as unexciting as a Women's Institute whist drive.

Angel nodded his thanks for the pedantic clarification, then continued.

'In this case it's fair to assume it was used as a date rape drug would be used to subdue the victim. Moving on to the forensic report, the stain on the kitchen chair is confirmed as being Lynch's urine, as is the stain on his trousers. Basically, he wet himself while still alive, then sat on the chair in his urine-soaked trousers. His bladder didn't empty at the time of death.'

Finch hadn't said anything beyond her tongue-in-cheek reference to her own possible suicide, listening to the conversation going back and forth between the other three. She stated the obvious now.

'Something, some*one* scared him sufficiently to make him wet himself. The threat of being strung up.'

'Exactly,' Angel said. 'The rope used was a steel-core clothes line available online or in any hardware shop. It was abraded where it passed over the rafter. Given the height of the stepladder and Lynch's height, the distance between the noose and the abrasion wasn't sufficient to give him any slack to get the noose over his head as it hung down from the rafter. It was put over his head first, then tightened before being tied to the shelving unit. He couldn't do that himself standing on the stepladder. No other rope was found in the house or garage suggesting that the length used to kill him was brought to the scene specifically for that purpose.'

'Whoever it was, they set out to hang him,' Finch said, 'rather than kill him another way. Is that relevant?'

Kincade fielded that one.

'Easier to make it look like suicide. Not everyone has access to a gun, an overdose doesn't always work...'

Finch acknowledged the point, then looked to Angel.

'Okay, Max. What does the divine inspiration tell us, freshly recharged after your visit to the cathedral in Santiago?'

It struck Kincade that she was the only one who didn't know all about Angel's six-week walking holiday. The reasons that made him need it. Reasons that she felt in her bones were connected to her predecessor, DS Stuart Beckford's leave-of-absence—still unexplained beyond the vague catch-all umbrella of stress. She pushed the thought and growing sense of paranoia that went with it aside, concentrated on what Angel was saying.

'The killer arrived at Lynch's house at some point after seven-thirty. There's a good chance Lynch knew him—'

'Or *her*,' Durand chipped in.

'Or her, and let them in. Or they had their own key, which suggests family. Maybe one of his sons. They then slipped GHB into his drink. There was a single, washed-up glass in the kitchen. To me that also suggests familiarity. *Get me a glass of water, will you?* The visitor then waited for the GHB to kick in. Lynch would've been aware of what was going on, but unable to control his limbs sufficiently to do anything about it. When he was suitably disabled, the killer took him into the kitchen and sat him on a chair while he went into the garage to get things ready. That's when Lynch lost control of his bladder. You see a man who's just drugged you carrying a rope into your garage, you know what's coming next.

'He moves the Jag, damaging the rear wing in the process, gets the rope and stepladder into position. Collects Lynch from the kitchen, loops the noose around his neck and takes up the slack. Lynch is forced to climb the three steps to the top as the noose tightens. Once he's on the top step, the killer ties the rope to the shelving unit. Then he waits. That's what I couldn't understand at first. The interval between when he arrived at the house at a time early enough for Lynch to still be up and dressed, and the time he died...'

'Sometime between midnight and two a.m.,' Durand said. 'He or she was waiting for the GHB to work its way out of Lynch's system. They just didn't wait long enough.'

'Not for Dr Isabel Durand, they didn't,' Angel said, his voice filled with admiration.

Durand smiled at him with a warmth Kincade thought held more than pleasure at the compliment. Coupled with the easy banter back and forth between them, it made her wonder if Angel had been less than honest with her about his relationship with the pathologist.

'Flattery will get you everywhere, Padre,' Durand said.

I'll bet, Kincade thought.

'What I'm thinking,' Angel said, 'is that after waiting until he believes the drug has washed through Lynch's system, he wraps his arms around Lynch's legs, takes his weight and knocks the stepladder away. Maybe he holds him like that for a while. Enjoying the moment—'

'Despite his nose being inches away from Lynch's urine-soaked groin,' Kincade said quietly.

'True. But this has got to be personal. Maybe he talks to him.

Taunts him. *Not so tough now in your piss-soaked trousers.* Or he pretends to drop him a couple of times before doing it for real. That's when the fibres got transferred to Lynch's legs. The GHB has pretty well worn off by now. He'll be struggling. Then, at one o'clock, say, the killer gets bored and lets go of him. Watches him die. Probably videos it to be enjoyed later.'

'Or shared,' Kincade said. 'Although probably not on YouTube.'

Everybody was silent for a couple of beats, waiting for Finch to say something. Durand cut in before she did.

'You left out the best bit, Padre.'

Finch gave him a sharp look as if it was always the same.

'Left to *last*, not *out*,' he said. 'As well as the fibres, Isabel recovered a human hair from Lynch's trousers. It came from a woman.'

Kincade was the one to shoot that down, stop everybody from getting overly-excited.

'It doesn't necessarily mean anything. It's possible the killer was a woman and the hair was transferred directly onto the victim's trousers. It's equally possible that it came from a woman the killer knows. It was transferred from her to him at some point, maybe even from being in a drawer with some of her clothes, and from him onto the victim's legs.'

Finch thought about it, looking at each of them in turn, then gave her verdict echoing the view of everybody in the room.

'It's looking like a poorly-concealed murder. What have we got in terms of identifying a suspect?' She immediately turned to Durand. 'Anything other than his own skin under his fingernails, Isabel?'

'I'm afraid not.'

'It makes sense,' Angel said. 'The only time he would've had a chance to hit the killer was when he was holding him by the legs. He'd already tried to get his fingers under the clothesline to relieve the pressure. If he stopped doing that to hit the man holding him, the pressure on his throat would increase. What's he going to achieve? Give his killer a slap to make himself feel better before he chokes to death?'

'What else?' Finch said.

Angel felt as if he'd done all the talking, a curiously unreal situation for a man in a room full of women. He looked at Kincade.

'What's this?' she said. 'If we're going to shoot the messenger, it might as well be the new girl?'

'Not a lot, then?' Finch said.

'There's nothing of any interest on his computer,' Kincade said. 'Classic car sites, some porn. No kinky auto-erotic sites telling you how to get the most out of your orgasm by taking GHB and then hanging yourself in your garage. Funeral directors after his wife died. There was also a parking management company website around the same time. Maybe he got a ticket at the funeral. No death threats on social media. To all intents and purposes, he's not on social media. He's not even on Facebook spying on what his kids and grandkids are doing.'

'What about his phone?'

'He didn't use it much. That's not particularly unusual for a man of his generation. And it's not what anybody would call state of the art. My kids would be ashamed to be seen in public with it. Mainly it's calls to and from his two sons. He made a long call on the morning of the day he died to his son, Gavin. The only thing of any real interest is a call he received at just after eight p.m. on the evening he died.'

'The killer calling to arrange to come around?' Finch said.

'Could be. The trouble is, it's from a burner. We obtained the cell-site data from the service provider hoping to track its movements, but it looks like it was switched off a lot of the time. Everyone's watched too many crime dramas on TV to make silly mistakes. It'll be somewhere at the bottom of the docks by now. There were also a couple of calls back and forth with a man called Phil Brent. He's a retired loan shark. The sort of person a retired drug dealer like Lynch might know. Or who his still-active son, Gavin, might still know.' She looked at Angel. He nodded for her to carry on. 'One of the neighbours interviewed by Gulliver and Jardine overheard an argument between Lynch and Brent. Brent threw out a generic threat as he was leaving. *You'll be sorry*. Brent then almost ran the neighbour over as he drove away. Luckily the neighbour got his registration.'

'I sense a *but*,' Finch said. 'A *not-so-luckily*.'

'His wife hasn't seen him or heard from him since yesterday.'

The implication wasn't lost on anybody in the room.

'Okay,' Finch said. 'Maybe we should talk to Gavin Lynch about that. I hear you've already made his acquaintance.'

It was said with a hint of knowing amusement in the voice that made Kincade feel comfortable smiling in response.

'I have, ma'am. And, yes, we'll be talking to him again. The whole thing has a sort of predictable feel to it. Lynch and Brent argue. Lynch tells his son Gavin about it during their phone call. Lynch dies in suspicious circumstances. Gavin kicks off at the crime scene. Brent disappears.'

'He probably regrets making a fuss at the scene.'

'He probably does, ma'am.'

'What about the satnav in the victim's car?'

'It's being checked out as we speak.'

'Be useful to take a look at the satnav in his son's car.'

She didn't need to spell out what everybody knew. They had nothing on Gavin Lynch to justify applying for a warrant to requisition it.

'Are the two sons the sole beneficiaries to the will?' Finch said.

Kincade looked at Angel.

'We haven't had sight of it yet,' he said. 'I'm guessing it will be a fifty-fifty split between them. We'll be looking into the state of both of their finances. See whether either of them has an urgent need for a quick cash injection.'

Finch gave him an incredulous look, one that suggested he'd led a very sheltered life.

'There's nothing quick about the way solicitors work. Probate will take months. That's not going to help if one of Gavin Lynch's suppliers wants his money by the end of the week.'

'Even if it's not that,' Kincade said, 'the woman with Gavin when he turned up at the scene looks as if she knows how to spend a man's money.'

Angel couldn't resist it. The words were out of his mouth before he could stop them.

'Is that a professional opinion, DS Kincade, or based on personal experience?'

16

Angel wasn't expecting what Kincade said to him once they were back in their office. The way she put on a gravelly man's voice—which he guessed was meant to mimic his own—should've alerted him before the words themselves.

'*We're good friends. We go back a long way.*' She left it a moment for him to make the connection, then asked, 'Care to revise your description of your relationship with Dr Durand? I mean, *Isabel.*'

'This is because of what I said about you and spending money, is it?'

'Don't avoid the question. But yes, that was unkind and hurtful.'

He peered at her, eyes narrowed.

'You don't look very hurt.'

'I'm good at putting on a brave face. And you still haven't answered the question.'

Nor did he do so now, what he did say sufficient to deflect her.

'You know, I almost feel sorry for Gavin Lynch.'

She gawked at him, concern creeping into her voice.

'Is this what Durand warned me about? What did she call it? Papist nonsense? You're determined to see the best in everyone. *Including* Gavin Lynch. You don't have a portable confessional you carry around, do you? Flat-pack from the Ikea God-squad range.' Then, when he didn't answer, 'Are you going to tell me why?'

Angel leaned back in his chair, swivelling from side to side, the squeak as irritating as ever.

'Gavin can't win. We're looking at him from both sides. Either he killed his old man himself, or he's done something to Phil Brent who he thinks might have something to do with it.'

She squinted at him as if she was missing something obvious.

'And there's something wrong with putting a prick like him in that impossible situation?'

'Not at all. That's why I said *almost* sorry for him.'

She relaxed, the worry that he was reverting to his past life receding with his words.

'Now seems like a good time to go see him. Put him in that situation face-to-face.'

'Not yet. I want to talk to his employer first. When Gavin turned up at the scene, he said he'd been away on business. He wouldn't have volunteered that if it hadn't been above board and easily verifiable. I'd like to ask his employer about it first.'

'You keep saying *employer*. This isn't a company he owns and uses as a front?'

He shook his head, tapping away on his keyboard to pull up the company details.

'According to this, he's only an employee.'

'Bloody well-paid one if he drives a Bentley. Even if it is second-hand. And the owner of the company is happy to have a known drug dealer use his established business as a front? A business he presumably spent years building up.'

'Maybe he owes him. As far as we know, he's clean.' He went back to his computer, shook his head. 'No, nothing.'

'Sounds a bit too good to be true, you ask me. What's his name?'

'Guy Yardley. The company's called Yardarm Marine Technology Ltd.'

KINCADE'S MOBILE RANG WHILE THEY WERE IN THE CAR. ANGEL laughed out loud when he heard the ringtone. It sounded like a flock of seagulls fighting over fish heads in her pocket.

'Aren't you going to answer that?'

'Nope. It's my mother.' Her mouth turned down, weariness mixing with irritation in her voice. 'And I know exactly what it'll be about.'

'The situation with your husband and the kids?'

She shook her head at the crushing inevitability of it, staring out the window.

'Yeah. If you want, I can tell you at least three things word for word she will absolutely definitely say.'

'Give me one and I'll let you know if I want any more.'

She cleared her throat.

'Okay, here we go. You don't even have to work at all, Catalina. Elliot earns more than enough to support you and the children. I wish your father had earned as much as he does.'

Angel bit his lip to stop himself from smiling.

'I've only known you a few days, but already I get the feeling that's about the worst thing anyone could say to you.'

'At least there's nothing wrong with your gut instincts.'

'Interesting ringtone you've assigned to her.'

'Yeah. I tried a few others first, but seagulls seemed to fit the best.'

The sound of his own mother's harsh Belfast accent was suddenly in his head, prompting his next remark.

'You don't have a problem with not knowing the difference when you answer and your mother starts talking?'

'I didn't know you'd met her.'

They passed the rest of the journey in silence. Kincade staring out of the window once more, her thoughts on her developing family situation exacerbated by her interfering mother, the arguments with both her and her husband that lay ahead. And worse, should they be unable to arrive at an amicable compromise.

For him, the exchange reminded him that he still hadn't called his father back.

Yardarm Marine Technology was housed in a modern brick and glass office block located close to Southampton Docks Gate 4. It looked as if it had been finished earlier that week, the sun reflecting off the spotless glass of the full-height glazed atrium at its centre.

'No sign of Gavin Lynch's Bentley,' Kincade said as he pulled into a narrow space reserved for visitors.

'No, but somebody else is doing okay,' indicating the much newer Bentley in a wider parking space nearest the front doors. 'I'm assuming that belongs to Guy Yardley.'

They were shown up to a dual-aspect corner office on the top floor that wasn't a lot smaller than the operations room back at the station. Yardley himself was a large man wearing a crisp white shirt and a striped tie that was meant to imply either past service in an elite regiment or current membership of an exclusive club. The effect was spoiled by the sweat rings under his armpits despite the arctic chill of the air conditioning.

'Nice offices you've got here,' Angel said as Yardley showed them over to a pair of cream leather sofas arranged in an Lshape that made the most of the view from the floor-to-ceiling windows. 'They look new.'

'Thank you, and yes, we moved in at the end of last year.'

'Business must be good. I noticed the Bentley parked outside.'

Yardley rubbed his hands together as if to dry the sweat both Angel and Kincade had felt when they shook hands.

'Very good, yes.'

'What do you do?'

'Project management, mechanical and electrical breakdown repair, structural collision damage. And we've got our own welding and fabrication shop—'

The door opened on the other side of the room just as Angel was regretting asking the question. They waited in silence as Yardley's secretary made the long trek towards them carrying a tray loaded with three cups, a glass cafetière of coffee and a plate of assorted biscuits.

'Can I ask what this is about?' Yardley said once she'd left the room.

'We've got a few questions about one of your employees,' Kincade said. 'Gavin Lynch.'

'Terrible business, his father killing himself like that.' Yardley's face fell as the obvious conclusion occurred to him. 'Does your presence here mean you don't believe he killed himself?'

'We're working on the basis that he did,' Kincade said. 'But we wouldn't be doing our jobs properly if we didn't investigate other possibilities.'

Her face said it was a nasty unpleasant job, intruding at such a difficult time, but someone had to do it.

'Did you know Roy Lynch?' Angel asked as Yardley leaned forward and depressed the plunger on the cafetière.

The question took Yardley by surprise. A few more beads of

sweat popped out on his top lip—and it wasn't from the heat coming off the cafetière.

'No. Why should I?'

You tell me, felt appropriate for reasons he couldn't identify. He softened it.

'No particular reason. So, about Gavin?'

He left it hanging. See what the nervous Yardley might volunteer. Nothing, as it happened.

'What about him?'

'What's his role?'

'He's the national business development director.'

'He's not an owner?'

Kincade kept the emotion off her face as Angel asked the question they both knew the negative answer to. Watching Yardley.

He looked horrified at the suggestion.

'Absolutely not. I own the company outright. We've got an employee share scheme, of course—'

'I wish we had one of those,' Angel said. 'Get a share of all those speeding fines.'

Yardley didn't know how to respond, understandably.

'Yes, quite.' He poured coffee into all three cups, added sugar and milk to his own. 'As I was saying, we have an employee share scheme, but I still have one hundred per cent control.'

It felt to Angel that there was something worth pursuing. Yardley was clearly proud of what he'd achieved, but there was something unsettling him.

'Has the company been in the family a long time? Or did you start it yourself?'

For a simple question, it took Yardley a while to get his words out.

Angel stated exactly that.

'It's a simple question, Mr Yardley.'

'It was neither, actually. I took over a small, failing company and built it into what it is today. I don't see what any of this has to do with Gavin's father committing suicide.'

'Nor do I. But until I ask, and the question's out there, that doesn't become apparent.' Yardley didn't look as if he followed or agreed with the logic. Angel didn't really care, moved on. 'You can appreciate how difficult this is. Gavin has recently lost his father and yet we are obliged to ask him what could be seen as insensitive questions. We talked to him briefly when he turned up at his father's house. He said he'd been away on business. We were thinking that if you were able to provide us with the details, we wouldn't need to ask him so many questions. Ask him for his alibi, basically. *Show us the hotel receipts*, sort of thing. *Let's see the new orders you got.*'

'Of course. I understand.'

They waited. Angel helped him along when nothing more was forthcoming.

'Can you confirm that he was away on business on the night of July twelfth? That was last Wednesday.'

Yardley became a little more vocal, but not a lot.

'Yes.'

'Can you give us the details? Where? For how long? Alone, or with other members of the sales team?'

Yardley took off his glasses which had been slipping down his nose as he sweated. He wiped the nose pads on his tie, put the glasses back on. They immediately slipped again.

'I'm afraid I don't have the details.'

If asked, Kincade would've said Angel overdid the look of disbelief on his face, although he got the voice just right.

'Really?'

Yardley found some composure from somewhere, assumed the smug attitude of a self-made man addressing a public-sector employee whose wages were paid out of his taxes.

'The secret to success in business is not to try to do everything yourself, Inspector. Not to micro-manage. It's the results that count. If Gavin can continue exceeding targets by spending his whole time on the golf course, that's fine by me. I'm sure that if you want to come back at the end of the month when he submits his expenses, we'll be able to let you have as many receipts as you like. Now, if that's all, I really am very busy. Gavin is a vital part of our operations, but I don't exactly sit here on my backside simply watching the money roll in.'

'YOU CERTAINLY SHOOK HIM UP,' KINCADE SAID WHEN THEY WERE back in the car.

Angel continued to stare through the windscreen at Yardley standing at the window in his big corner office, the master of all he surveyed.

'He was shaken up already. He's hiding something.'

'I agree. But I'm not sure it's anything to do with Roy Lynch's death. I think it's worth getting hold of a picture of Gavin's wife, comparing it to the woman in the Bentley with him when he turned up at the scene.' She flicked her finger at the top floor as Angel backed out of the parking space and straightened up. 'Just because Yardley's happy for Gavin to spend his life playing golf so long as he hits target, it doesn't mean he's going to admit to him screwing around on the company time, not even if he doubles his bloody target.'

'Making it sordid, but not suspicious. And Yardley doesn't want to be the one to drop Gavin in the shit. He might resign. Find someone else who's happy to turn a blind eye to him using their company as a cover for his drug-dealing and extra-marital activities so long as he hits target. But is it only about the money? Or does Gavin have some hold over him?'

She didn't have an answer for him, just another unknown.

'I don't think he was telling the truth when he said he didn't know Roy Lynch, either.'

'Maybe not. But if he was sweating like a pig at the prospect of a few questions from us, he hasn't got it in him to murder Lynch.'

GUY YARDLEY'S CRISP WHITE SHIRT WAS LIKE A USED DISH CLOTH now, sticking wetly to wherever it touched his skin, his collar tight and clammy. He was aware of his hand reaching inexorably for his mobile without any conscious input from him. His first knee-jerk reaction was to call Gavin. Demand to know what the hell was going on.

The police suspected Roy Lynch had been murdered, however much they tried to play it down.

Was it connected to the threatening email he'd received?

Equally worrying was Angel's interest in how the company had started. Was that simply coincidence after the email? Or had the blackmailer alerted them somehow? Sent an anonymous tip. *Ask Yardley how the company started.* To let him know they weren't messing around. Don't worry, it had worked. They had his full attention, one hundred and ten per cent.

Just tell me what you want.

He got his hand under control, his mind less so. There was no point calling Gavin. Another unwelcome thought had just crossed his mind, made something loosen in his bowels.

The cops suspected Roy Lynch had been murdered.

They were looking at the possibility that Gavin was responsible.

Did he do it? Kill his own father?

Was this a deck-clearing exercise until there was nobody left who knew what had happened back then? He'd be right at the top of that particular list himself.

The anticipation is said to be worse than the event. He couldn't argue with that, counting the minutes until the blackmailer made contact, put him out of his misery. He only hoped that wasn't too literal a phrase.

Trouble is, everybody knows you can wish in one hand and shit in the other, but see which one fills up the fastest.

17

'You did tell Dr Gupta that we're police officers, didn't you?' Lisa Jardine said. 'That we're not a pair of work-shy skivers looking for someone to sign a sick note.'

The receptionist at The Limes Medical Centre stopped typing long enough to give Jardine a long-suffering look, then immediately held up her index finger when the phone rang.

Jardine looked around the almost-empty waiting room wondering how so few patients could cause such a long wait. Craig Gulliver was sitting on a bench along one wall happily reading a two-year-old copy of *Top Gear* magazine. Jardine could see him salivating from across the room. She turned back to the receptionist who was explaining to the caller that yes, she understood that he had her on the line now, but that he'd still have to hang up and call back to make an appointment on the automated system. It was more than her job was worth to try to bypass it.

'Some people are so rude,' the woman said when the caller slammed the phone down in frustration. 'I don't make the rules.'

'Should I ring the automated system to make an appointment?' Jardine said.

The receptionist's lips pursed.

'There's no need—'

A call rang out from the other side of the room cutting her off.

Gulliver and Jardine.

Jardine joined Gulliver still carrying the magazine, heading towards where a middle-aged Indian doctor waited for them.

'I bet everybody thinks we're here for the family planning clinic,' she whispered.

'You wish.'

'Sorry to keep you waiting,' Dr Gupta said, holding out his hand to shake with first Gulliver and then Jardine, before leading them down a corridor to his consulting room at the back overlooking the staff car park.

Gulliver took the chair at the side of the doctor's desk after Gupta offered it to him. Jardine remained standing rather than sit on the examining couch and wrinkle the fresh paper sheet on it.

'What can I do for you?' Gupta said. 'You both look fit and healthy.'

They smiled with him at his joke hoping he was a better doctor than he was a comedian.

'We'd like to ask you a few questions about one of your patients,' Gulliver said.

Gupta nodded and turned towards his keyboard, started tapping away.

'Roy Lynch,' he said, proving that, as always, the doctor knows why you're there but still insists on asking.

Five minutes later, they knew everything they needed to know about Lynch. Like them, he'd been fit and healthy, and on virtually no medication, surprising but heart-warming in a man of his age.

'Good genes,' Gupta said.

Jardine asked if he could prescribe some for her.

'If only,' Gupta said, then confirmed, somewhat redundantly, that no, there had been no life-threatening condition hanging over his head promising a slow painful slide into an eventual merciful death. Gupta further confirmed that Lynch had not been suffering from depression as a result of his wife's early death in her mid-sixties a few months earlier.

'He'd had a long time to get used to the idea. And plenty of time coping with living on his own when she was in and out of hospital. It was no surprise when the end came. Not to anybody who knew her.'

'What do you mean by that?' Jardine said.

Gupta looked uncomfortable at the interest he'd aroused with an off-the-cuff remark he clearly didn't expect to be picked up on.

'Mrs Lynch was a lifelong smoker. She admitted to a pack a day, but like everyone talking to their doctor about their bad habits, she no doubt halved it. It's no surprise that lung cancer got her in the end. But in her younger days, she had something of a drug habit.'

If it wouldn't have been so obvious, Gulliver and Jardine would've shared a look.

Supplied by her own husband?

'She wasn't as robust as all those ageing rock stars who abuse their bodies their whole lives and still live into their eighties,' Gupta said.

'Not such good genes.' This from Jardine.

'Exactly.'

The interview felt as if it had come to a natural end. As with all visits to the doctor, a twenty-minute wait had been followed by less than five minutes with the man himself. Gulliver had one last question before they left.

'Was there a post-mortem?'

He was aware of Jardine staring at him, *where did that come from?* Gupta also seemed a little confused.

'No. Why?'

'Just wondering. After Shipman.'

Harold Shipman, nicknamed *Dr Death* and *The Angel of Death*, was a doctor and serial killer, considered to be one of the most prolific serial killers in modern history. With an estimated two hundred and fifty victims, he targeted vulnerable elderly people exploiting the trust they placed in him as their doctor, killing them by injecting them with a lethal dose of the painkiller diamorphine.

He was found guilty of murdering fifteen patients under his care. Sentenced to life imprisonment with a whole life order, he subsequently hanged himself in his cell at HMP Wakefield, aged fifty-seven.

His murders raised troubling questions about the powers and responsibilities of the medical profession. In particular, about the adequacy of procedures for certifying sudden death, after one of his patients, an eighty-one-year-old woman, was discovered dead in her home only hours after Shipman visited her. Until then, she had been in good health and her will had recently been changed to benefit Shipman, the estate valued at four hundred thousand pounds. Crucially, Shipman had insisted that no autopsy was necessary.

Gupta was clearly uncomfortable at the reminder of one of his profession's most shameful episodes.

'That man was a monster. Despite what he did, it's not necessary to conduct a post-mortem on every patient who dies in a hospital or hospice after suffering from a long-term life-threatening illness.'

'Did Mrs Lynch die in hospital?'

'Not hospital, no. St. Joseph's Hospice. It's only a quarter of a mile down the road from here. It's still run by the nuns. The

Daughters of the Cross. Although I believe they are talking about stepping down. They're all getting on a bit themselves.'

'I KNOW WHAT YOU'RE THINKING,' JARDINE SAID WHEN THEY WERE back outside, standing looking at each other over the roof of the car. 'I bet DI Angel knows all the nuns in the hospice. You think we should go and say *hello* from him?'

Gulliver turned his head, put his finger behind his ear.

'I think I can hear him now. *You were how close? And you didn't go there?*'

'We can't even say we were thinking about the taxpayers' money and saving petrol.'

Gulliver cocked his head again.

'*I've just walked four hundred and ninety-two miles. You two lazy bastards can walk a quarter of one.*'

'It'll be half a mile total if we have to walk back again.'

'Which we will. Unless you're thinking of checking in?'

Needless to say, they drove.

18

They were shown into Sister Veronica's office, a small private oasis of calm and simplicity within the greater oasis of serenity and peace that was St. Joseph's. Although it was difficult to tell with the habit she wore, she was most likely in her late fifties or early sixties, the only thing keeping the average age of the sisters from hitting the eighties.

She kicked off with a question that wasn't as easy to answer as it should've been.

'May I ask why you are interested in Mrs Lynch's death?'

Jardine looked at Gulliver. *Over to you, pet*. It was his question about a post-mortem that had resulted in them being here, after all.

Gulliver was acutely aware of the carved wooden crucifix on the wall behind Sister Veronica's head. He wasn't religious, but it still felt as if his answers would be judged by a higher power than the two women in the room with him. Or even DI Angel when they reported back. Although the absolute truth bore no resemblance to anything that could be justified in a court of law or the incident room, it was the only way to go.

'We're investigating the circumstances surrounding her

husband's recent suicide,' he said, getting no response from the nun at the news of the death. 'We talked to Dr Gupta and he mentioned that his wife died here. Seeing as it was so close . . . we thought, why not?'

Sister Veronica smiled. Gulliver thought it was a nice smile, especially for a nun, having always believed that being on the plain side was a basic entry requirement.

'Serendipity,' she said. 'The act of finding something not looked for.' She studied them both a long moment, the only sound the ticking of the clock on the wall. Then disappointed them.

'If you're wondering whether Mr Lynch smothered his wife with a pillow to put her out of her misery and has now killed himself out of guilt and shame, I would have to say that you watch too much television, your jobs notwithstanding. Mr Lynch wasn't even here when his wife died. He was distraught, but it's often the way things turn out. A relative or spouse sits with their loved one for hours on end and they slip away as soon as the visitor gets up to go to the toilet. That didn't happen in this case. Mr Lynch wasn't even in the building at the time.'

'Were there any unusual circumstances at all?' Gulliver said, feeling as if he was clutching at straws.

'Now that's a different question.' She took hold of the silver cross she wore around her neck running her thumb over the smooth metal. 'Mrs Lynch had two other visitors before she died.'

'Her sons?'

'No. Neither of them visited her whilst she was with us.'

It was a fact, plainly stated. Her voice was not judgemental. She had seen it all before, had long ago ceased to be surprised by people's behaviour, even at the end. It was what it was. To adopt any other attitude when voluntarily surrounding oneself with death was to invite madness. It helped if you believed that a higher power would take care of any retrospective judging that needed to be done.

'They were both women,' Sister Veronica said. 'The first one was an older lady who said she was Mrs Lynch's sister. They'd fallen out years ago and hadn't spoken to each other since. She didn't say why, and I don't like to pry. She'd heard that her sister was dying. As is so often the case, she wanted to make her peace with her before it was too late. I hope for her sake she wasn't placing too much hope on the idea that it would stop the feelings of guilt once her sister was gone.

'The second visitor was a much younger woman. Don't ask me who she was because I don't know. She slipped in and didn't stay very long. No doubt we should improve our security, but there are so few of us left it hardly feels worth it now. And it goes against the grain. You've probably got an officer who could come here and give us a lecture on what we should do. Tell us not to be so trusting, basically.'

'What did the woman do?' Jardine said.

'Nothing that you could arrest her for. One of the other patients, Mrs Dalton, overheard her say, *I hope you burn in hell.*'

Sister Veronica smiled again, a strange gesture on the face of it after what she'd just said. But it was more at them, at the obvious uptick in their interest. And at what she now said.

'I do have to add a caveat. Mrs Dalton died a week after Mrs Lynch, so you won't be able to talk to her yourselves. Even if she were still with us, I suspect it would be of limited value. She regularly claimed to see both Jesus and St. Peter standing at the bottom of her bed. She was also prone to bouts of confusion. She said to me on one occasion, *you should know this sister, you're a nun, but Jesus is the one with the long beard, isn't he?*'

'What did you say?' Jardine asked, unable to help herself.

'Luckily she fell asleep as I was trying to formulate an answer. Maybe she imagined what she claimed to have heard the young woman say to Mrs Lynch, or maybe it was a fleeting moment of lucidity. We'll never know.'

'I don't suppose you've got CCTV?' Gulliver said.

'No. We've never felt the need for it. And even now, if you find this young woman? What has she done? Are you going to charge her with saying spiteful things to a dying woman?'

Gulliver admitted that no, they wouldn't be doing that. He was about to come out with a trite bromide about how it can be the most insignificant-seeming piece of information that proves to be the vital missing link, when Sister Veronica demonstrated that it might be her who watched too much television.

'Or are you thinking that if this young woman carries such strong and vitriolic feelings around with her, then perhaps she is connected to Mr Lynch's death?'

Gulliver nodded, hoping his expression was that of a man confirming what had crossed his own mind some time before.

'It's certainly something we're looking into. Just to confirm, nobody saw this woman apart from the other patient, Mrs...'

'Dalton. I'm afraid not. And all she said was that it was a young woman. Unfortunately for you, when you're in your late eighties as she was, everybody under fifty qualifies as young. The only reason that we became aware of it at all is because Mrs Lynch was so distressed that night, which is understandable. That's when Mrs Dalton volunteered the information.'

'Did you ask Mrs Lynch about it?'

'We tried. Obviously, we didn't repeat what Mrs Dalton claimed she'd heard in case she'd imagined it, but we asked her what was wrong. She said, *I don't want to talk about it.*'

'Which implies there was something to talk about,' Jardine said, 'rather than saying, *it's nothing.*'

'I suppose so.'

'Did her husband visit her after this incident?'

'One last time, yes.' She became thoughtful, still fingering the cross around her neck. 'It did seem that their conversation was particularly intense that day. Obviously the nearer it gets to the end, the more difficult things become. But it could be that she told him what had happened.'

'Did you notice his mood afterwards?'

'I didn't see him, myself. I think it's fair to say that if anyone had noticed that he was angry, for example, they'd have mentioned it. Everybody knew about the mystery visitor, after all. But I can ask, if you like.'

'We'd appreciate it.'

'I noticed that we had to pay to park,' Gulliver said.

Sister Veronica's face took on more of the appearance that Gulliver expected in a nun.

'Yes.' Just one small word, but she managed to convey that she was not in favour of the situation. 'We were persuaded that it was necessary. As people lead more secular lives, donations fall. The building is getting older, as are we. It all costs money. It was also put to us that if hospitals charge to park, then why shouldn't we? I don't believe that's a valid argument to support anything. It simply accelerates the general decline in standards.'

'Are cars caught on camera as they enter?'

'I believe so. We use the latest technology. I know it's not LGBT...'

'ANPR?' Gulliver said as Jardine coughed into her hand.

'That's it. I can ask Sister Kathleen to dig out the details of the company who installed the system and manages it for us if that helps. I'll email it to you.'

Both Gulliver and Jardine's faces gave them away, their preconceived attitudes condemning them. A broad smile crept across Sister Veronica's face, her pleasure at their embarrassment surely a sin of some kind.

'Were you expecting rolled parchment with a wax seal? Hand delivered by a penitent wearing a hair shirt, perhaps?' She held up her hand, stuck out her little finger. 'I forgot to put on my signet ring this morning. Email it is.'

'WHAT ARE YOU THINKING?' JARDINE SAID AFTER SISTER VERONICA had delivered them from the all-embracing calm of the hospice into the jarring bustle and endless noise of the outside world, a car horn sounded in anger coming from somewhere close by welcoming them back.

'That it might be the best one-pound-fifty I've ever spent. I'm going to save the parking ticket.'

'What? To bore your grandkids with if you ever have any, God help us. *This is the clue that helped me solve the Roy Lynch murder.* I can hear their excited little voices already. *Tell us again, Granddad.*'

'Sour grapes, Lisa, sour grapes.'

'I bet you can't even remember the word she used.'

He gave her a tight smile. Shows how much you know.

'Serendipity.'

'I always thought that was a national park in Africa. Live and learn.'

'I wish you hadn't said that. Now I'm going to have *Serengeti* stuck in my mind and I'll forget.'

Jardine looked very pleased with herself. As if that had been the whole idea. Stop her partner from raising the bar unnecessarily as far as report writing went—it was already bad enough with him dropping all those Oxford Bloody University words in.

'So, who's the woman?' she said. 'And was it only Lynch's wife she hated?'

It wasn't necessary to remind one another that a woman's hairs had been found on Roy Lynch's trousers.

19

'Did you say Lynch visited the website of a parking management company around the time of his wife's death, or am I imagining it?' Angel said to Kincade.

She looked up, glad of the interruption. Stretched, tapped the screen of her phone sitting on her desk to bring it to life, see if anything had come in while she had it set to silent.

'You're not imagining it. Why?'

He held up the printout he'd been going through.

'I'm going through Lynch's satnav log. Most of it is what you'd expect. Golf club, Sainsbury's, garden centre, his sons' houses. Makes you not ever want to retire. But he also visited the premises of Southern Parking Management Limited. I say premises, but it looks like it's a Portakabin in a scrap yard.'

She rooted through the papers on her desk, found the printout of websites Lynch had visited.

'It's the same one. Maybe he was still arguing about a parking ticket.'

A quick look at the company's premises told Angel everything he needed to know. They were the sort of cowboys who clamped car wheels before it was made illegal for private individuals. They tended to be large aggressive men accustomed to heated arguments as they went about their business ruining people's days. They weren't in it to make new friends, or let people off fines.

'No. They're not the sort of people you argue with. Not unless you want to lose a couple of teeth as well as paying a hundred-pound fine.'

Kincade navigated to the company website. She found their postcode from the footer and copied it, then pasted it into Google maps. She was now looking at the location in satellite view.

'I see what you mean. I think I can see a rabid dog on a chain. Lynch must have gone there twice. He wouldn't have looked them up on the web back when his wife died and waited until now before he went there. The first visit was around the time his wife died, and then again . . . when?'

'Three days before he was killed. Roughly four months between the two visits. It might be worth talking to them at some point about what he wanted.'

She panned around in Google maps inspecting the site from above.

'You wouldn't want them living next door to you. Although I'm not sure anyone would hang you in your garage over an unpaid parking fine.'

'No, they'd feed you to the junkyard dog, instead.'

The speculation—both the serious and the not-so-serious—was cut short by the appearance of Gulliver and Jardine in the doorway elbowing each other out of the way to get in first.

Angel waved the satnav report at them.

'Don't bother coming in. You're on your way back out. You don't have a problem with vicious dogs, either of you, do you?'

'I think we've got something that's going to put that on the back burner, sir,' Jardine said. 'We've just come back from the hospice where Lynch's wife died. The nuns say *hi*, by the way ... they'll see you in heaven, if not before. Although I think they're going to be there a lot sooner than you are.'

Gulliver saw his chance to jump in and took it.

'Lynch's wife had a visitor before she died. A woman. Apparently, she said to her, *I hope you burn in hell*. The nuns don't know who she was but we're hoping to get a line on her through the company that manages the car park—'

'Southern Parking Management Limited,' Kincade said.

Gulliver and Jardine both stared at her, open-mouthed and deflated. Kincade hooked her thumb at Angel.

'He's not the only one with divine inspiration. It rubs off.'

'It explains why Lynch went there the first time,' Angel said. 'He wanted to find out who the visitor was. But why go back again months later?'

'Maybe they told him to get lost the first time, then something happened recently that made him try again,' Jardine said.

'There's only one way to find out.'

'I suppose you'll be wanting to go out there and talk to them yourself now, sir?'

He'd planned on talking to Gavin Lynch after they'd spoken to Guy Yardley. It wasn't a conversation he was looking forward to. He guessed Kincade felt the same. The new information regarding Roy Lynch's attempt to identify his wife's visitor offered another opportunity to catalogue Lynch's movements before confronting his son.

'You suppose right, constable. Bet you wish you hadn't made that crack about heaven, now.'

'How do you think the nuns ended up with a bunch of cowboys like this?' Kincade said as Angel navigated around the potholes in the unmade road leading to Southern Parking Management's site in Millbrook, immediately north of the railway line.

'They didn't visit first, obviously. The company's got a professional-looking website. That hides a multitude of sins. At the end of the day, it was probably down to cost.'

Kincade looked around as they drove through the gates set into the chain-link fence, the company offices, aka the Portakabin on the far side of a weed-infested concrete yard. At least there was no sign of a rabid dog on a chain.

'Bit different to Yardley's set-up,' she said. 'You get what you pay for, I suppose.'

'Let's hope this is the exception that proves the rule.'

They parked next to an older 5-series BMW, not a Bentley in sight. There was also a red Mini with a vaguely personalised number plate if you had a good imagination, as well as a Ford Transit van with the company name on the side. The left-hand rear door had been replaced at some point in the past but they hadn't bothered re-doing the livery. Anyone following the van would only see *Management Limited* on the right-hand door.

Their pre-conceived ideas continued to be reinforced when they entered the Portakabin. It smelled of coffee and a cloying woman's perfume, and would've benefitted from the door being left permanently open.

A stocky man running to fat and wearing a white polo shirt with *SPM* and the company logo on the chest was sitting at the desk nearest the door reading a copy of *Professional Security* magazine.

He looked up as they entered, identifying them immediately.

'Uh-oh. Looks like one of the lads gave the old bill a ticket.'

It was said for the benefit of the only other person in the room, a middle-aged woman with hair that was a shade of red not on God's original colour palette. She was also the source of the toxic perfume. Angel guessed she was the owner of the Mini. A desperate last-ditch attempt to hold onto her already-long-gone youth. It was obvious from the state of her desk compared to the man's, as well as the row of battered, grey metal filing cabinets behind her, who did all of the work at Southern Parking Management Limited.

The assessment was confirmed by the man who clearly had a lot of time on his hands to work on his one-liners.

'You didn't have to come here in person to pay it, officers.' He glanced at the woman. 'Steph, get the receipt book out.'

Angel got the impression that at times the day felt very long for Steph sharing a small office with the man he guessed was the owner, Conor Hoskins.

'Who would be the best person to speak to regarding someone coming here asking for information about a vehicle entering one of your client's premises?' he said, despite the overwhelming evidence pointing at Steph.

'That would be Steph,' Hoskins said, indicating her with a sweep of his hand as if they hadn't noticed her. 'I'm business development.'

'And I'm everything else,' Steph said.

Hoskins immediately reacted to the emphasis she put on the word *everything*.

'You don't do installations or maintenance.'

'I'm sure the day is coming.'

Angel had a feeling they could have kept at it all day. There was no radio playing in the background. He guessed a continuous low-level banter was better than silence.

'We're interested in a visitor on March fifteenth,' he said to Steph.

Hoskins put down the magazine he'd continued to idly flick through as they talked.

'I'll be off.'

'It's best if you stay, too, Mr Hoskins,' Kincade said.

'You know who I am, then?'

'It's on the company website.'

'It's good, isn't it?' Steph said. 'My daughter's husband did it.'

The comment might have been expected to elicit an equally-proud response from Hoskins. Instead, he scowled.

'You'd think Bill Bloody Gates himself did it, the amount he charged.'

Steph ignored him, looked to Angel and Kincade. Angel got the impression she already knew the answer to the question she now asked.

'Who was the visitor you're interested in?'

'Roy Lynch,' Kincade said.

Hoskins immediately cut in, the scowl on his face intensifying.

'I remember him. He kicked up a fuss. Wanted us to give him a list of the names and addresses of everybody who'd parked at . . . where was it, Steph?'

'St. Joseph's.'

'I had to tell him, it doesn't work like that, pal. If you think you can walk in here—'

'Why don't I tell it, Conor?' Steph said. 'I dealt with him, after all.'

Hoskins picked the magazine up off his desk, pretended to start reading it.

'Whatever.'

'He was very angry,' Steph said. 'Things didn't get off to a good start.' She avoided looking accusingly at Hoskins, but the point was made, nonetheless. 'I explained that it doesn't work like that. If people buy a ticket after being recorded by the ANPR, we don't keep the details. Who wants a long list of honest people who pay for their parking? It's not up to us anyway. We're members of the BPA . . .'

'British Parking Association?' Kincade guessed.

'That's right. They don't actually tell you how long, but you're not allowed to keep ANPR data for very long without a reason, especially if no offence was committed. Of course, it's a different story if they don't buy a ticket or they overstay what they paid for. That's when we apply to the DVLA for their details so that we can pursue them. You have to give the DVLA a valid reason why you want them.'

Despite pretending to read his magazine, Hoskins had been thinking about their presence, what it implied.

'You're only going to get lucky if you're looking for an idiot.'

'That's generally the case,' Kincade said.

'Anyone with any brains will buy a ticket. Only stupid people think, I won't buy one because it links me to the scene. Not buying one does that.' The look on his face suggested he believed he was the first person to see the logic.

'Did he say why he wanted the details?' Kincade said. 'As you implied earlier, you don't give out a list of number plates to everyone who walks in—'

'Of course not.'

'—so they presumably come up with some sob story.'

'They're all sob stories at that place,' Hoskins chipped in. 'It's a hospice.'

Angel stopped himself from interrupting. *And yet you still pursue them, these people visiting a dying relative.* It wasn't going to move things forward.

'I remember what he said because his story was unusual,' Steph said. 'Lots of people forget to pay at St. Joseph's. Normally they say they received an emergency call and they were so upset they forgot. He said the person he was looking for scared his wife, said to her, *I hope you burn in hell.* He said to me, call the hospice and ask the nuns. They'll tell you. They don't lie. He said he suspected it was his wife's sister. They'd had a falling out years ago. Over money, like it always is. He wanted to give her a piece of his mind, but he wanted to make sure it was her first. He knew her registration number. So I gave him a list of everybody who'd parked on the day he was asking about. It was only the day before he came here so we still had it. And I said to him, you give me a call if you find them. I'll help you teach them some respect.'

I bet you would, Angel thought and kept to himself. If they'd had a junkyard dog on a chain, he'd have taken his chances with it first.

'You gave him the whole list?' he said instead.

'That's right.'

Hoskins had been checking his phone for messages when she'd said it a moment ago. He was on her case immediately as Angel got confirmation from her.

'You didn't tell me that.'

She came right back at him, a guilty overreaction at being found out.

'Of course I didn't. Not after you nearly started a fight with him.'

'He had a bad attitude.'

'And you don't?'

'For Christ's sake, Steph, we could be shut down. All because you felt sorry for him.'

Again, Angel got the feeling they could keep it up all day long. He interrupted, addressing Steph directly.

'You didn't think to ask him for his wife's sister's registration first, and you'd look to see if it was on the list?'

The look she gave him was easy to interpret.

And the safety of our streets is entrusted to people like you?

'Obviously he didn't have it with him. Nobody is going to keep their sister-in-law's registration number in their head. Most people can't even remember their own.' She swept her hand across the mass of paperwork on her desk, irritation edging into her voice to accompany the dirty look she gave her boss. 'I'm rushed off my feet here. I didn't want him calling back with it, so I printed the list out, gave it to him.'

Angel and Kincade shared a look.

A list of car registration numbers would only be of use to Lynch if he had a contact with DVLA access. One who was prepared to put their job on the line for him. Unless he had been looking for a specific registration as he'd claimed—but not necessarily his sister-in-law's.

One of them needed to ask a pointless question. He let her do it.

'Have you still got a copy of the list? Or can you retrieve it from the system?'

Steph shook her head.

'Not after all this time. Like I told you, the BPA would be all over us. Data protection and all that rubbish.'

'What about people who didn't buy a ticket that day?'

'We'll have a record of that, if there are any. Proceedings could still be ongoing if they decided to take their chances in court.'

They waited as she tapped away at her keyboard. It was a very long shot. The number of visitors at St. Joseph's would be counted in the tens, not hundreds or thousands as in a busy shopping mall. Would the young woman have decided to save a pound or two because she was only popping in to whisper spiteful words in a dying woman's ear?

'Nothing,' Steph confirmed a minute later. 'Whoever you and Mr Lynch are looking for bought a ticket. She's an honest evil bitch. She's the one who deserves to burn in hell.'

Both Angel and Kincade knew what that implied. A search of Roy Lynch's house in the hope that he'd kept the list. That's if Angel's next question didn't throw any light on the situation.

'The satnav log on Mr Lynch's car shows that he came here a second time six days ago. What did he want that time?'

The question was directed at both of them. Steph had looked uncomfortable enough as what she'd done for Lynch came to light. Now, she looked as if she wanted a hole in the floor to open up and swallow her. Hoskins looked confused on its way to angry.

'I don't know anything about that,' he said.

'You weren't in that day. That was the day you went fishing.'

'I did not. I had back-to-back client meetings all day.'

Steph's face said she'd been interested to know how much business he was expecting to get from a shoal of bream or roach.

'What was the purpose of his visit?' Angel said, directly to Steph this time.

She took a moment to compose herself. Made sure her keyboard was straight, exactly parallel to the edge of her cluttered desk. A faint pink glow had climbed up her neck.

'I was in Sainsbury's last week and I bumped into him. It was in the beer and wine section. I asked him if he ever got to the bottom of what we've been talking about. He said no. But he did say it wasn't his sister-in-law. I felt a lot better about everything knowing I'd helped him avoid a nasty argument accusing her.' She glanced briefly at Hoskins to see if the happy outcome had done anything to wipe the scowl off his face. It hadn't. 'Then he told me that his wife had died, but it had been a blessing and he'd pretty much come to terms with it. And I said to him, you men are all the same. Hiding away your feelings because you think it makes you look weak. All he had was booze in his basket. It's not healthy sitting at home getting drunk and feeling sorry for yourself, I said. I told him if he ever wanted someone to talk to who wasn't family or friends who'd known her, he could give me a call. And he said, we could go to lunch if you like. So that's what we did. He came here and picked me up. We went to The White Swan and very nice it was, too.'

She glared at them all in turn, daring them to accuse her of any wrongdoing. Only Hoskins took up the challenge.

'This was the day I was out all day? Who was looking after the place?'

She gave him a withering look, her tone reflecting how long she'd worked there, what it was like.

'What? You're worried a big new client might have turned up unannounced while I was out for a couple of hours? Even if they had, they'd have still been here when I got back, stuck in one of the potholes you won't pay to have filled in. That's another thing. Roy said that if the road wasn't in such an appalling state, he'd have picked me up in his vintage Jag. So. That's what it was about. He picked me up and we went to lunch. It's not a crime. Or if it is, the world's gone down the toilet even faster than I thought.' The glare that accompanied the last couple of sentences was for Angel and Kincade alone.

'How did he seem?' Angel said.

'He didn't break down and cry on my shoulder, if that's what you mean.'

'Fat lot of good that would've done him,' Hoskins chipped in. 'You'd get more sympathy out of a . . .'

Steph turned on him as he struggled to find the word he wanted.

'Out of a what?'

'I don't know. I can't think of anything.'

'That's you all over. Open your mouth before you put your brain in gear.'

'Did he seem anxious?' Angel said to put an end to the bickering. 'Anything bothering him other than coming to terms with the loss of his wife?'

Steph stuck out her bottom lip, thought about it.

'I don't think so. Why?'

'I'm afraid he committed suicide a couple of days later.'

Angel and Kincade left them to it. Hoskins' voice came to them as the Portakabin door swung shut behind them.

Remind me never to ask you for any sympathy.

'You think we should charge her with wasting police time?' Kincade said as they bumped and bounced down the lane Hoskins wouldn't pay to maintain. 'Here we are thinking we might be onto something, and it's just a frustrated woman who wears too much perfume and who won't accept she's getting old wanting to get laid.'

'Wait and see how you feel when you get to her age. Besides, it doesn't change the fact that the young woman exists. If Lynch's wife told him about it and he took it seriously enough to try to track her down, there's got to be something worth looking into.'

'You think he found her, despite what he told Steph? He's not about to say, yeah, I found her and strangled her with her tights.'

'It's possible. There's definitely more to it. Nobody would go to the lengths he did, just to say, *how dare you talk to my wife like that?*'

'Maybe it was her who called him on the night he died? *I'm the woman who visited your wife.*'

'I'm getting a feeling we're going to find out soon enough.'

20

'She refuses to give her name, Mr Yardley.'

Guy Yardley's heart leapt into his throat at the irritation in his secretary Madeleine's voice.

This is it.

Except he hadn't expected a woman.

'Shall I put her through, or not?' Madeleine said, as frustrated with him as she was with the intransigent caller.

He kept his voice steady despite the sudden weakness in his limbs, the liquid feeling in his bowels. It was only money after all.

Relax.

Take deep breaths.

'Put her through.' Then, when Madeleine did so, 'Who are you?'

'Your past catching up with you.'

If he hadn't spent a sleepless night worrying about the email he'd received, its attachments condemning him, the rewards he'd reaped for the past thirty years laid bare, he might have wasted time bluffing. But the pounding in his head, the tight knot in his gut, wouldn't let him forget.

'What do you want?'

An incredulous silence followed, the stupidity of the question throwing the woman on the other end of the line momentarily.

'Isn't it obvious? Money. You cheated us.'

Again, had the email not existed, he'd have worked a pompous note into his voice.

I haven't cheated anybody.

Backed it up with some bullshit about how it was dog eat dog out there on the streets. If you can't stand the heat, get out of the kitchen, and all that bollocks.

Instead, he asked the only question that mattered.

'How much?'

'Half a million.'

'*What?*' It came out as a scream. Had his office not been the size it was, Madeleine would've poked her head around the door to see what was the matter. 'I can't afford that much.'

A harder edge entered the woman's voice.

'Don't make the mistake of treating me like an idiot. I've proved I know how to access company information. You want me to quote your turnover and profits for the last five years? The dividends you've paid yourself? I didn't pick half a million out of the air. It'll hurt, but it's doable.'

Yardley pushed himself to his feet. Went to stand at the window looking down on the car park like he'd stood watching the two cops after they left.

He felt sick, his legs barely able to support him.

The woman was right. Half a million was feasible. But he couldn't just roll over and agree.

'I can't raise that sort of money at the drop of a hat.'

'Nobody's asking you to. We'll accept an up-front payment now, come to an arrangement about the rest.'

'How much now?'

'Ten thousand.'

'Five. I can let you have it today.'

'We're not in some street market in Marrakesh haggling over the price of a rug. You don't need me to remind you that you're not in a position of strength. Ten thousand today or I call the detective in charge of looking into Roy Lynch's death—'

'That was you, wasn't it?'

'—and point him in the right direction.'

'How do I know I can trust you?'

'You don't. But you don't have any options. And if you mention a word of this to Gavin Lynch, I'm calling the cops. Then you won't have to worry about me coming after you. It'll be every shower time in prison. Will it be a shiv in the kidneys or a cock up the jacksy today? Your choice.' She laughed suddenly, an unhinged sound. 'About the money, not what happens in the showers.'

'Where do you want to meet?'

She snorted, suppressed anger behind the sound.

'Don't insult me, Yardley. I'm not an idiot. Give me your mobile number. I'll call back in two hours. If you don't have the money by then, the deal's off. You'll get more instructions when you've confirmed it.'

THE PHONE CONVERSATION KINCADE WAS HAVING WASN'T IN THE same league as the one Guy Yardley had just endured. That didn't mean she was enjoying it. It didn't help that her mother insisted on calling her Catalina, and not Cat. Coupled with the disapproving tone of voice, it made Kincade feel like a naughty six-year-old who'd walked mud all through the house.

She'd popped to the ladies' after getting back from Southern Parking Management when her mother had called again.

'I get the feeling you're avoiding me, Catalina.'

'I'm busy, Mum. It's difficult to talk at work.'

Although they were only twenty seconds into the conversation, there was a chance that the line about not needing to work at all could make an early appearance. She waited, but it didn't come. Not yet.

Her mother was still stuck on being avoided.

'It's because you know what I'm going to say.' She paused to give what she saw as her killer line more weight. 'And you know I'm right.'

Kincade resisted the temptation to say, *you think you're right about everything so you're going to have to help me out.*

'I assume Elliot called you,' she said instead, the phone wedged under her chin as she washed her hands.

Her mother's tone softened at the mention of Kincade's estranged husband's name.

'He did. He's very busy, too. But he still makes the time to call me. He's very concerned.'

He also needs to learn to fight his own battles.

'About what, specifically?'

If her mother was going to side with her husband, she wasn't about to make it easy for her. She could spell it out.

'The situation with the girls.'

'And what exactly is that? That they come to live with their mother and not with a—'

'I won't tolerate bad language, Catalina. I happen to think Hannah is a very nice lady.'

'She's a bunny-boiler.'

'I don't even know what that is. I'm sure it's something disgusting you've picked up at work.'

'And she's a gold-digger.'

She noticed how her mother didn't say she didn't know what one of those was.

'She said she's looking forward to coming to church with

your father and myself. I can't remember the last time you saw the inside of a church.'

Don't hold your breath.

'She's only trying to get on the right side of you.'

'I feel sorry for you, Catalina, I really do. You see the worst in everyone. We didn't bring you up to be like that. It must be—'

'My job?'

'I wasn't going to say that.'

'No? What were you going to say?'

'It doesn't matter. Besides, I know what you're doing. You're trying to distract me from what needs to be discussed. It's not fair that the girls should be uprooted every five minutes—'

'*Every five minutes?*'

A brief silence came down the line that brought to mind pursed lips, the air of a person expecting to soon be elevated to sainthood for their long-suffering patience with a difficult child.

'It's an expression, Catalina. You don't have to take everything so literally. You seem to be forgetting that I'm not a suspect you're interviewing picking them up on every wrong word.'

It was the perfect lead in to the *not-working* line. Kincade waited, but still it didn't come.

Instead, her mother continued to regurgitate what her husband had primed her with. Kincade was tempted to stick her hands under the dryer, drown her out. Except it would only be a temporary reprieve. She shook the excess water from them instead, waited for her mother to continue.

'Elliot is worried that the girls move down there with you and as soon as they get settled it happens again.'

'It?'

'You know perfectly well what I'm talking about, Catalina.'

Kincade took a deep breath, let it out slowly. Fat lot of good that did.

'Is this my anger management issues, by any chance?'

'Yes, that's exactly what Elliot called it. And you can take that sarcastic note out of your voice right now.' Kincade smiled to herself. At least her mother had held off from finishing the reprimand with *young lady*. 'I think he's got a point. Look how you're getting annoyed at me now.'

Kincade bit back the words that were so very close.

You want to see annoyed, I'll show you and Elliot annoyed.

'I'm only trying to help,' her mother said.

That required a hand over her mouth until the urge to scream, *you call this helping?* subsided.

Then another deep breath and a softening of her voice.

'I know you are, Mum. Unfortunately, it's only making it more difficult. I know you don't want to hear this, but I'm afraid Elliot is using you.'

'There you go again, seeing the worst in people. Whenever I get off the phone after talking to you I can't help thinking that everyone is in the wrong except for you. Why is that?'

Kincade didn't have an answer for her. Didn't have much of a will to live, either. She felt like she did at the end of a long *no-comment* interview. Like she wanted to shake her mother. Yell at her, *I might see the worst in everyone, but at least I don't see the good that isn't there.* She knew that one of these days she was going to take a call from her mother sobbing down the line, telling her how their bank account had been emptied out after a nice man from the bank called to say that there had been some suspicious activity on the account and he needed her to verify the log-in details...

'I've got to go now, Mum.'

'Does that mean you'll agree to Elliot and Hannah having the girls?'

A sudden thought struck Kincade, a spontaneous *aha* moment that made her smile despite everything. Forget about her leaving the job, they'd ship her mother in. Stick her in the interview room with the most close-mouthed suspect and she'd have them admitting to every unsolved crime committed in the last six months in five minutes flat just to get her out of the room.

'No, Mum, it doesn't mean that at all. I really do have to go now.'

She couldn't swear to it, but she thought she caught the start of, *you know you don't have to work at all, don't you?*

21

'WE'VE MANAGED TO GET HOLD OF PHIL BRENT,' CRAIG GULLIVER said coming into Angel and Kincade's office. 'He's the one Lynch's neighbour overheard him arguing with. Called him a cheating...' He glanced at Kincade who laughed.

'I'm touched by your chivalry, sparing a lady's blushes, DC Gulliver. And yes, we remember what he called him.'

'He's agreed to come in. Should be here any minute.'

'The last we heard, his wife hadn't seen him for twenty-four hours.'

'Apparently he was away on business.'

'Without telling his wife?' Angel said. It was turning into excuse of the month after Gavin Lynch also used it.

'You're asking the wrong person, sir. I'm not married.'

Kincade watched the colour rise inexplicably up Gulliver's face. She looked across at Angel. She might as well have been looking at a stone statue of one in a churchyard for all the expression on his face.

'Let us know when he gets here,' Angel said.

'Will do, sir.'

'I'm glad I wasn't standing in front of the door,' Kincade said after Gulliver bolted from the room. 'He'd have mowed me down in his panic to get out. What was that all about?'

Angel shook his head like it was as much a mystery to him. She looked at him a long moment knowing she was missing something. Something to do with the chair she was sitting in. DS Stuart Beckford's old chair. It had to be.

He became aware of her staring at him.

'What?'

'Nothing.'

He shrugged, went back to what he'd been doing.

And she wondered if there would ever be a good time to ask.

THE FIRST THING THEY NOTICED ABOUT PHIL BRENT WAS THE splint on the little finger on his left hand. Angel worked a concerned note into his voice.

'What happened there?'

Brent looked at it as if he'd only just noticed it himself. He smiled apologetically.

'I fell over in the garden and broke it.'

Angel nodded like it made sense, a different question running through his head.

Are you sure Gavin Lynch didn't break it because he heard you'd had an argument with his father immediately before he died in suspicious circumstances?

Trouble was, Brent was old-school. He'd accuse his own grandmother, dead or otherwise, before he pointed the finger at Gavin.

'I understand you've been away on business,' Angel said instead.

'That's right. A last-minute thing.'

'And you didn't have time to let your wife know? A quick call or text? *If you're wondering where I was at dinner time,* sort of thing?'

Brent produced the apologetic smile again, sharing it with Kincade beside Angel. It was the sort of thing made you want to wipe it off with an open palm.

'We had an argument. I stormed out. Childish, I know.' He shrugged. 'Especially at my age.'

Angel could have kept going, increased his discomfort. Asked him who he'd visited on business. Whether the supposed meeting had taken place in an empty shipping container in the docks with him tied to a chair. There was no point. They all knew it was a lie.

'You seem to be having a lot of arguments recently, Mr Brent,' Kincade said. 'We hear you had a particularly nasty one with Roy Lynch a day or two before he died.'

Brent tried hard to look horrified. He needed to work on it.

'I wouldn't call it that. A disagreement, that's all.'

Kincade produced the statement Brent's neighbour had given from the file in front of her. Ran her finger along it line by line as if searching for the section she was after.

Her eyebrows went up, something Angel guessed she practiced in the mirror.

'I wouldn't like to be in a nasty argument with you if you use the C-word in a disagreement. In fact, I'm interested to know. What word would you use, Mr Brent? If we were having a proper argument right now, not just a disagreement?'

It was obvious what word he wanted to use with her. The one that was written out in full on the neighbour's statement.

'Okay, maybe it got a little heated.'

She nodded to herself, good word.

Angel cut in, clarification needed.

'The sort of heated that immediately cools down? Ignoring for now that you nearly ran over Mr Lynch's neighbour as you were leaving. Or the sort of heated that gets worse? Festers away until you can't think of anything else and you want to kill him?'

Brent leaned back, held up his hands.

'Hang on. I came in voluntarily. If you're going to start throwing out accusations, I want my lawyer.'

Angel backed off, physically and verbally. Thinking, *you started it with two big fat lies.*

'Sorry, I shouldn't have said that. Let's back up. What was the argument about?'

Brent relaxed visibly, the tension easing out of his shoulders. Both Angel and Kincade knew then that in contrast to every word he'd uttered so far, what he was about to say would be the truth.

'We were in business together. Part-time. More like a hobby, really. We bought old cars at auction, restored them and then sold them. Very profitable it was, too.'

Angel was aware of Kincade deflating beside him, as was he. He ploughed on, nonetheless.

'Was Mr Lynch's Jaguar XK150 one of these vehicles?'

The anger that flared in Brent's eyes confirmed that it was. His words made an important distinction.

'It wasn't *his*. It was *ours*.'

'And what was the argument about?'

'Roy said he wanted to keep it, not sell it. We'd bought it together, paid for all the work that needed doing together. He offered me what I'd spent back plus a bit extra.'

'But not half of the increase in value resulting from the restoration.'

Brent looked as if he wanted to spit.

'Nothing like. It was an insult.'

'And that's why you called him a cheating . . .' Kincade said. 'I can't say the word. My mother would wash my mouth out with soap.'

Brent nodded, the resentment still smouldering in his eyes.

'And what did you mean when you said, *you'll be sorry* when you left?'

'Nothing. I was angry. What was I going to say? I hope you enjoy driving around in your new car, Roy. It doesn't mean anything. Another day I might have just said, *fuck you*.' He leaned forwards, tapped his middle finger on the table in front of Kincade, their obvious acceptance of his answers lending him confidence. 'I can tell you for free why I wouldn't have killed Roy. We didn't have a company or anything. We bought the cars and put them in one of our names. You can't register a car in two people's names. We took it in turns.'

'And the Jag was registered in Roy's name?' Angel said, trying hard not to smile at the way fate had conspired against poor hard-done-by Phil Brent.

'Yeah. And now he's dead, it'll be going to his sons or whoever he left all his money to. I won't even get the money I shelled out back, forget about the profit. There's no paperwork. It'll be more trouble than it's worth paying some shyster lawyer to try to sort it out. So, no, detectives, I did not have anything to do with Roy Lynch's death. I hope the bastard burns in hell.' He recoiled at the looks on their faces, mistaking it for horror. 'Jesus, don't tell me you're thinking of doing me for speaking ill of the dead.'

Angel looked at Kincade.

'I think we can let it go this time, don't you, Sergeant?'

'Just this once, sir, yes.'

Brent smiled with them thinking the interview was at an end. Except Angel wasn't going to let him go that easily.

'Talking of Mr Lynch's sons, have you spoken to either of them since their father died?'

All of the confidence of a moment ago went out of Brent. He

looked down at his little finger in the blue finger splint, then back at them.

'I spoke to Gavin.'

'What about?'

'To express my sympathies, what do you think?'

'It wasn't because you wanted to ask Gavin for what you're owed for the Jag?'

Brent did his best to look insulted at the suggestion, indignation in his voice that fooled nobody.

'Of course not. He's just lost his father.'

'Who called who?'

He saw Brent thinking back behind his eyes. He wasn't a young man, his grasp of technology not what it could be. *Can they tell whether the call was incoming or outgoing?* He decided it wasn't worth risking lying.

'He called me.'

'What for?'

'To tell me his old man had died, what else?'

'To tell you about it?' He flicked his own, unbroken little finger out. Looking at it as he asked his next question. 'Or to ask you if you knew anything about how it happened?'

He pushed back in his chair before Brent came out with another lie. He'd achieved what he wanted to. Made it clear everybody knew Brent was lying his face off.

'I'd be careful in that garden of yours, Mr Brent. Sounds like you got off lightly this time.'

'What do you think?' Angel said, once they were back in their office. 'What was the final score?'

Kincade started counting off on her fingers.

'Away on business. That was a lie. So was the argument with his wife and falling over in the garden. All the stuff about the car was true. The fact that you could actually see the pound signs spinning in his eyes means he definitely didn't kill him. But then he ended on a lie about not asking Gavin for his money back. I've lost count.'

'Four-two.'

'Except the big truths outweigh the little lies so it's a draw.'

'And we've wasted half an hour of our lives we'll never get back.'

Nobody needed to say it: *that's the way it goes.*

'Interesting that he used the same phrase about burning in hell,' he said. 'I wonder if he's got a daughter who visited Lynch's wife in the hospice?'

They talked it through, decided that if there had been any long-running animosity between the two families, Lynch and Brent would never have gone into business together.

'You're looking thoughtful,' he said. 'Still think it's worth looking into?'

She shook her head.

'Wrong word beginning with *T*.'

She made him work it out. It didn't take long.

'Thirsty.'

'Got it in one. I've got an irritating conversation with my interfering mother to wash away.'

'I can't do it tonight. I'm driving up to Salisbury to see the old man before my sister puts him in her car and drives him down here. Ask Gulliver and Jardine. They're usually on for a beer.'

'We'll see.'

He didn't push it. But he knew she wouldn't. It was his bones she was after picking.

22

Angel had just passed The Shoe Inn at Plaitford on the A36 when his sister, Grace, called him. Reluctantly, he turned the volume down on the CD player as Van Morrison's *And It Stoned Me* started up, took the call.

Grace didn't waste time saying *hello* or asking how his trip had been.

'I've just found out he didn't turn up for his appointment.'

She didn't need to spell out who *he* was. Their father, Carl Angel. The man he was on his way to see.

'I thought you were going with him.'

'Something cropped up at the last minute. You're not the only one with a demanding job, Max.'

She never missed an opportunity to remind him of it, either. Or the fact that it was his abrupt decision to about-face and change jobs so dramatically that had given fate the opportunity to indulge its twisted sense of humour, putting them on opposing sides of the justice system. Grace was a criminal defence lawyer. And while she'd never defended a case of the gravity he was currently investigating, it made for interesting conversations around the Christmas dinner table.

Like the year he'd worn a Hugo Boss suit, allowing Grace to damn him with faint praise as she'd complimented him on how well it suited him. She'd then reminded everyone at the table that it had been Hugo Boss who'd made the uniforms for the Nazis. It was therefore fitting that Boss' descendants should clothe her brother, a man employed to hound innocent citizens on the basis of race and creed, not criminal intent—her take on all police forces' default modus operandi.

The situation with their father wasn't as acrimonious, but that didn't mean they agreed on everything.

'Maybe he forgot,' he said.

'You know as well as I do that's not what happened. He's an awkward old . . . whatever, who insists on sticking his head in the sand.' She deepened her voice mimicking their father. 'In case you'd forgotten, I was a warrant officer class one. So, what's his problem with a blood test? Is he scared of needles?'

'Did you ask him about it?' Deciding *ask* was less provocative than the more accurate *grill*.

'Of course. And he said, it must be whatever you and Max think I've got made me forget. Then he said, it's lucky you didn't land on a different page on the internet or you'd be accusing me of having AIDS. *Accusing!* He's impossible . . .'

Angel turned the volume up slightly as Grace continued to let off steam. He couldn't help thinking that their father had a point. Grace was a hypochondriac. The internet was not her friend. She could convince herself she had pretty much anything if she put her mind to it.

But she might be right about their father.

Late Onset Huntington's Disease. Although the typical age at the onset of symptoms is in the forties, an increasing number of patients were being diagnosed at a much later age. A special punishment reserved by a spiteful god for proud ex-British

Army men who dared try to impose *Their* Majesty's rule on the God-fearing people of Northern Ireland.

If she was right, it was scary stuff for everyone concerned. There was a fifty-fifty chance of the faulty gene being passed on to each of his children. Watch out Grace and his good self. Their younger brother Cormac was already beyond the reach of any disease, however insidious.

Their grandfather, Frank, their father's father, had been described by people who knew him as *twitchy*. Back then, everybody expected things to start going wrong as you grew older without feeling the need to put a label on everything.

'I'm actually on my way to see him now,' he said, cutting her short. 'I'll see what I can do. Try to catch him after a couple of pints when he's more mellow.'

'*Mellow?* We're talking about Dad, Max. He doesn't do mellow.'

At the moment it didn't appear that his daughter did, either. He didn't point that out.

'I better go.'

'You're right. Don't want to get caught on the phone by one of your own traffic Nazis.'

'Bye, Sis.'

Although the suggestion that a couple of pints would mellow their father had been met with derision from his sister, it didn't change the fact that the conversation would start the same way as it always did.

Let's go to the pub.

His father would have three pints while he nursed one. At the end of each pint his father would ask if he wanted another one, to which he would reply that he had to drive home. His father would then remind him of friends of his back in the day who only had to flash their warrant card if they got pulled over.

Their *get out of jail free* card. It was at that point that Angel would go to the bar to buy his old man another beer.

He was struck, as he always was when he drove up to Mill Cottage in the picturesque village of Middle Woodford, four miles north of Salisbury, that it was by far the nicest place his dad had ever lived. Better than Belfast, better than Colchester. A damn sight better than HMP Whitemoor.

True to form, his father must have been waiting behind the door when Angel knocked, his coat already on.

'Let's go to the pub.'

Angel suspected that in the years ahead, should Grace's internet-inspired diagnosis prove to be correct, his father would insist that they meet at the pub itself. That way, his son wouldn't see the effect of the movement disorders associated with Huntington's disease, the impaired gait and balance, and he could blame it on being half-pissed on the way home.

'How was the Camino Way walk?' his father said as Angel put two pints of Hopback Brewery's *Citra* on the table they'd snagged in the window of The Duck Inn on the banks of the River Avon.

'Cathartic.'

It didn't matter what he said. He could've said *red* or *octopus*. His father wasn't listening. He was preparing the answer Angel could've seen coming for all of the Camino Way's four hundred and ninety-two miles.

'We'd have done it with a sixty-pound pack on our backs.'

If it hadn't been his father, WO1 (retired) 2nd Battalion, Parachute Regiment, he might have asked facetiously, *barefoot?*

Except any remark along those lines would be taken as a slur on the regimental honour, rather than a gentle nudge back into the realms of reality.

'Did it work?' his father said, as if Angel had just changed the fuse in a plug.

'I feel a lot better for it, yes.'

His father nodded approvingly. Positive, no unnecessary detail. Carl Angel had no time for whingers. And he certainly didn't want to get into the dangerous territory of emotions. He downed a third of his pint in one mouthful. Seventy-one or not, he could still put it away. That was something else that would change if a diagnosis of Huntington's was made. Difficulty with speech and swallowing were common symptoms.

'How's work?' Then, before Angel could take it in a safe direction, 'How's your mate Stuart Beckford doing?'

Short of lying, there was no way to avoid provoking a negative reaction.

'Still off with stress.'

His father didn't say anything. But Angel got the look he expected before his father raised his glass to his mouth again to cover it.

Stress? You don't know what stress is.

'I've got a new DS working with me in the interim,' he said to move the focus away from Stuart Beckford. It wasn't a topic he wanted to get into with someone like his father. Grace had told him that lack of flexibility was another symptom of Huntington's. Angel wasn't sure it was that. Thirty-five years in the military plus what came after tended to make a person set in their ways and attitudes. 'She's transferred down from London.'

'A woman, eh?'

'We do have them in the police, Dad. Just like they let them in the Army now.'

'Is she nice?'

Angel did the translation.

Is there a possible future romantic involvement?

'Very nice. She's got two girls. I can't remember their names.' Then, in an attempt to put an end to any further probing, 'Happily married—'

'Bollocks. Everybody knows coppers can't hold down a marriage.'

'Just like forces personnel can't, eh?'

His dad pretended he didn't hear. Made a point of holding his glass to his mouth long after the last drips had gone down his throat. Then banged it down on the table. Angel didn't miss his cue.

'Another one?'

'I thought you'd never ask.'

Angel went to the bar before his father asked him if he was also having a second pint. A quick glance at the two-thirds-full glass on the table in front of his son's seat should've told him the answer.

His father was sitting ramrod-straight in his chair, as if he was strapped into an electric variety in an American prison, when Angel carried his beer back. At the bar he'd decided not to let his father off so easily ignoring his remark about forces personal and their marriages.

'Spoken to Mum recently?'

'She hasn't called me, no.'

'You ought to get yourself one of those new two-way telephones. The ones that let you make calls out as well as receiving them.'

'Not that I receive many. Not ones I want.'

Angel wasn't sure whether it was a dig at him for not calling his father sooner, or a reference to Grace's earlier call to grill him about his missed appointment.

Whatever it was, they'd finally got to it.

'I suppose your sister sent you here to nag me.'

'Nobody *sent* me. And I don't do nagging.'

'I don't want a bloody test. Why can't she understand that?'

'You never served in Africa, did you?'

The glass that had been on its way to his father's mouth stalled halfway there.

'Huh? What are you talking about?'

'That's where ostriches live. Thought maybe you'd picked up some of their traits.'

The beer glass resumed its journey to his father's mouth, a quarrelsome question following a large mouthful.

'What's the point of bloody tests? If you've got it, you've got it.'

An obvious answer sprang to mind and remained in the land of the unspoken.

Maybe if it had been diagnosed and on your medical record you wouldn't have gone to prison for eleven years.

Except that wasn't the sort of thing you said to a WO1 (retired) 2 PARA, not unless you wanted the rest of the clientele falling silent to watch the argument taking place at the big table in the window.

Despite Angel's restraint, the alcohol was working on his father—and there wasn't a lot of mellow in it.

'Tell you what, why don't I get two phones?' He stuck out his thumb and little finger in the universal sign for a telephone on both hands, held them to his ears. 'I could have your mother on one line and your sister on the other, both nagging me at the same time.' He dropped his hands. Shook his head. 'You don't know how lucky you are.'

There was a moment's awkward silence when his father might have realised he'd said something insensitive. Except, just like he didn't do mellow, Carl Angel didn't do apologies.

Had Angel inherited more of his old man's belligerent genes, he might have come back at him.

Define lucky for me, Dad. I know, I'll start running through all the things I miss, apart from having someone who cares for me nagging me, that is, and you put up your hand if we get to the point where you think maybe lucky isn't the right word after all.

He didn't, of course, his father holding up his already-empty glass to move things along.

'You sure you don't want another one?'

Angel would've killed for one. He found conversations with his father draining in so many ways. But that didn't mean he was going to give in to temptation.

'You can sleep in the spare room,' the tempter said.

'Maybe another time. We've got a lot on at the moment.'

And I've got a feeling it's only the beginning.

23

GUY YARDLEY HATED HIS WIFE'S CAR. IT FELT SO CLAUSTROPHOBIC after the Bentley. So cheap and nasty. As if the indicator or windscreen-wiper stalks might snap if they were handled too roughly. And something somewhere squeaked incessantly, of course.

He was happy to put up with it when they went out to dinner or for drinks at a country pub, and she drove him home in it afterwards, but this was different.

Don't come in the Bentley, the woman had said.

As if he was the idiot, needed telling.

His wife hadn't been happy.

A business meeting? she'd said, her voice not so much incredulous as accusing. *At this time of night?*

He'd thought she was going to say more. Looking down her nose at him as she did so often these days.

Got your business condoms?

In the end, she'd made do with turning her back on him, *you must think I'm stupid* muttered under her breath as she shut the sitting room door in his face.

If only she knew. He'd have given his right arm to be having an affair like she thought and all he had to worry about was getting caught with his pants down.

But there was no way he could tell her the truth. As far as she was concerned, she'd married a success story. A self-made man who'd dragged himself up by his own bootstraps, left behind his humble beginnings.

Actually, it wasn't quite like that, dear...

He couldn't believe it after the woman on the phone had directed him back and forth from one side of the city to the other only to find himself back where he'd started—not that evening, but thirty years previously.

Solent View Industrial Estate on Pitt Road in Freemantle. The most inappropriately named site ever. Maybe it had been possible to see The Solent back when it was first built, but not for the last fifty years. Nowadays, anybody wanting to catch a glimpse of the sea would need to be hovering in a helicopter above the estate, and none of Solent View's tenants ran to one of those.

Not a towering glass atrium or award-winning-architect-designed, energy-efficient building in sight. Just pre-World War II brick-built units with corrugated asbestos sheeting roofs and windows so thick with the accumulated deposits and staining from acid rain and chemicals banned decades earlier that the light had given up trying to get through.

Whoever was behind it wanted to make sure his mind was focused. Don't worry, he'd got the message loud and clear.

This is where you started, where you'll wish you never left if you mess with us.

The last call he'd received had confirmed it.

Don't go to your old unit.

Then directions to another unit at the shitty end of the estate. Yes, it was possible to have degrees of shittiness even in a place like this. It had been the arse end of the estate thirty years ago and it still was. It hadn't seen a lick of paint in all that time. And because most of the units were empty most of the time, the owner hadn't bothered with CCTV down at this end.

It was asking to be vandalised by the local kids. It wasn't even necessary to drive in through the main entrance. It was possible to park on Lakelands Drive then cut across the unlit Freemantle Lake Park. There was a chain link fence but that wouldn't be a problem to a glue-sniffing toerag intent on mischief. It wasn't as if it was topped with razor wire.

He'd already been parked outside his old unit—now advertising cheap MOTs—when she'd told him not to. He left the car there and walked to where she directed him, the cash in an envelope in a Tesco carrier bag. A briefcase would've looked too conspicuous. Dressed in the old jeans and coat he wore for gardening, anyone seeing him would mistake him for a wino looking for a place to sleep, out of the rain that had been coming down for the past hour.

He picked his way around the puddles of dirty water and past piles of discarded car parts, peering at each unit until he found the one she directed him to. The roller shutter was raised six inches off the ground, the interior in darkness. He raised it sufficiently to duck under, not dipping low enough and scraping his back on the bottom of the shutter anyway, then stood staring into the gloom.

He felt he'd known the woman's voice that barked at him from the back of the unit all his life.

'Shut it.'

He did as she said, the shutter coming down as smoothly and quietly as a roller shutter can, as if it had been oiled in preparation. The moment it hit the ground and the outside world was cut off, a flashlight flicked on, a powerful one by the amount of light it emitted, dazzling him as she shone it directly in his face.

He raised his hand to shield his eyes, the woman invisible in the blackness behind the light. Off to his right unseen and unafraid rodents foraged in the accumulated filth.

The unit smelled of motor oil and stale urine, both rodent as well as human, and something else he couldn't identify.

He felt increasingly unnerved as she continued to say nothing. What did she expect him to say? *I'm sorry, whoever you are.* Spotlighted in the beam of her flashlight like a frightened rabbit, the words that had gone through his mind earlier—*it's dog eat dog out there*—didn't feel like they wanted to roll off his tongue so glibly.

He held up the Tesco bag like an offering.

'I've got the money.'

A stupid and obvious thing to say, but fear does that to a person.

'I didn't think it was a takeaway curry.'

'You want me to throw it on the floor?'

'Yeah, why not?'

He lobbed the bag towards her. The rats off to the side stopped scurrying momentarily as it hit the ground.

He wondered why he didn't rush her, overpower her. He got the impression based on nothing he could justify of a smallish woman.

Except he knew why.

She wasn't stupid. She'd already demonstrated that. She wasn't likely to be alone either, not threatening a man with everything to lose in a shitty industrial estate late at night.

He felt another presence in the unit. To his left in the blackness that the light in his eyes reduced everything to. Watching him.

The silence was eating away at him from the inside like a cancer.

Somebody had to say something. He didn't recognise his own voice when it was him.

'How does this work? The rest of the money, I mean.'

'You're the businessman. You suggest something.'

His mind went blank. Why hadn't she got everything worked out in advance? The fear in him knew the answer to that. They weren't interested in the money.

A sound off to his left made him startle. More like the scrape of a shoe than the scrabbling of tiny claws.

He couldn't stop himself from looking. Then wished he hadn't. The dark silhouette of a man was like a malignant patch of deeper darkness against the side wall.

He looked back at the woman into the full force of the flashlight's beam, better than the alternative. He hadn't answered her question about how things worked.

'I don't know. I've never done this before.'

'It's okay,' she said, the sharpness leaving her voice. 'I haven't, either. We can work something out. You can go now.'

He wasn't sure he'd heard her properly. He didn't need telling twice. He felt an almost irresistible urge to say, *thank you*. He bit the words back, his dignity maintained.

'Don't panic. I'm turning the flashlight off now. We don't want the nosy neighbours to see you leaving.'

A sudden all-encompassing blackness engulfed him, disorientating him. He swayed as he turned away from her, feeling blindly for the roller shutter somewhere in the gloom ahead of him.

He would've agreed, *good idea* if he'd been given the chance. By the time the *goo* of *good* was out of his mouth the man was behind him, the piano-wire garotte already looping over his head.

24

'If one more person says to me, *I've got a living to earn, mate* or *I've got bills to pay*, I'm going to—'

The uniformed PC standing in front of the crime scene tape stretched across the entrance to the Solent View Industrial Estate stopped mid-sentence as Angel and Kincade walked up. Craig Gulliver whose ear he'd been bending looked thankful for the interruption. He lifted up the tape.

'This way, sir.'

Angel let Kincade go first, then dipped under, Gulliver bringing up the rear. Once inside, they made their way to where a pair of crime scene technicians were going over a burgundy-coloured Ford Fiesta. It was parked outside unit B4, the business it housed offering cheap MOTs.

Underneath the blue and white *Vehicle Testing Station* sign screwed to the white-painted wall was a smaller sign. Black lettering on a yellow background made to resemble two number plates: *MOT PARKING*. The top plate, *MOT*, had a broken corner and hung down at a forty-five-degree angle.

Angel made a mental note not to bring his car here, however cheap, however egregious the failures they turned a blind eye to.

'It's Guy Yardley's wife's car,' Gulliver said.

Angel glanced around, the air of fighting a losing battle with life itself that hung over everything depressing him more than what awaited them.

'I can understand why he didn't bring the Bentley.'

'Me too. No idea why he parked here and not further down, though.' He pointed down the road. 'Unless he was worried about it going down one of those potholes and getting stuck.'

Nobody needed to point out that he'd ended up with a lot more to worry about than a potential flat tyre or damaged wheel rim on his wife's car.

'Who found him?' Angel said.

'Michail Doukas. He leases this unit. He turned up at seven o'clock this morning and found the car parked across his roller shutter preventing him from getting in ...'

'Let me guess. He's got a living to earn, bills to pay?'

'He has indeed, sir. His first reaction was to scout around, see if he could find some other early bird to help him push it out of the way. Then it crossed his mind that they'd have to leave it in front of somebody else's unit. The owner of the estate, Mr Singh, goes berserk if anyone parks on the access road itself. They get a lot of deliveries, big lorries. Mr Singh happened to turn up himself at that point. He said he'd see what he could do and went to his office to make some calls. Mr Doukas went walkabout to fill in his time.' He pointed down the road as before, this time at the larger police presence further down, not the potholes. 'That's when he saw that the roller shutter on one of the units down there was open a few inches. Unit C2. He claims he'd been thinking of moving to an older, cheaper unit and he wanted to take a look inside. See how they compare to the one he's currently in.'

'And after he saw what was inside, he decided to stay where he is?'

'I didn't actually ask him that, sir. He's still in Mr Singh's office if you wanted to ask him yourself.'

Kincade had already started making her way towards the unit where Guy Yardley's body had been found. She stopped halfway there. Not to let Angel catch up, but to point to the small dome CCTV cameras mounted on the wall.

'Cameras stop here.' She looked in the direction they were headed. 'I'd do the same if I was the owner. I wouldn't want to be caught on my own CCTV when I'm burning down the worst units on the estate prior to making an insurance claim.'

Angel shook his head in mock dismay.

'I can't think what can have happened to make you so cynical.'

'I'll introduce you to my mother. You'll get on like a house on fire.'

The glare of the arc lights spilling out of unit C2 intensified, the constant drone of the portable generator growing louder as they approached, interspersed with the regular hiss of camera flashes recharging and shouted instructions. The pathologist, Isabel Durand, was already inside. So too were the SOCOs and photographers, the uniformed PC who had been first to arrive at the scene, Lisa Jardine and now Gulliver, Angel and Kincade. They could expect DCI Olivia Finch to make an appearance in the next half-hour.

Michail Doukas might have welcomed as much activity at his own unit, but not for the same reason.

Guy Yardley was lying on his back in the middle of the unit, Isabel Durand crouched over him in her white protective suit.

'You look like you've just made a kill in the jungle and you're protecting it from scavengers, Isabel,' Angel said.

'Thank you for that observation, Padre. Rest assured, I won't be eating it.'

'Doesn't look as dapper as when we saw him yesterday,' Kincade said.

Durand looked up at her.

'I can see you two are made for each other.'

Funny, I was thinking the same about you, Kincade thought and kept to herself.

Angel squatted down next to Durand, his own protective suit rustling.

'What have we got?'

She pointed at the thin red weal circling Yardley's neck.

'I'd say manual strangulation with thin flexible wire. Piano or guitar most likely.'

'A DIY garotte?'

'Almost definitely. A length of loose wire makes the job ten times harder. Even wearing gloves, the wire would cut into the assailant's fingers as the victim struggled. Cause of death was asphyxia due to strangulation.'

Angel pointed at a dribble of blood that ran from the corner of Yardley's mouth, down and across his cheek, its journey ending where it settled against the ligature weal.

'And the blood? Bit through his tongue?' Already knowing he was wrong as the words came out of his mouth.

'Not bit, no.' She opened Yardley's mouth with a gloved finger and thumb as a dentist might to reveal what remained of Yardley's tongue. 'Cleanly severed with a sharp blade.'

'Post mortem?'

'Definitely. There'd be blood everywhere otherwise. And it would take six of them to hold him still if they'd done it while he was still alive. He'd be covered in bruises.'

'Any sign of the tongue?'

'Nobody's found it so far.'

They both stood up and shared a smile as their knees clicked in unison.

Kincade had been studying the floor between Yardley's body and the roller shutter. She pointed to the disturbance in the accumulated dirt and dust.

'I'd say he was leaving, facing the door, when the attacker stepped up behind him. Whipped the garotte up over his head'—she demonstrated as she said it—'then dragged him backwards away from the door to where he is now.'

Durand agreed.

'There's dirt and scuffs on the backs of his heels consistent with that scenario.'

'How many people?' Angel said.

Durand looked to one of the SOCOs who had his back to them.

'Andy?' Then, slightly louder when he didn't turn around, '*Andy!* How many people?'

The tech startled, lost in his own little world of fibres and footprints and all things microscopic.

'Two at least, plus the victim.' He walked to the back of the unit, pointed at the floor. 'Somebody stood here. Either a man with small feet or a woman. Probably size five shoes. There are two distinct sets of prints in the scuffle between the shutter and where the body is. That's consistent with one person dragging the victim backwards as he garrotted him.' He pointed to the side of the unit. 'There are footprints over there which are most likely the same as one of the sets in the scuffle. Same size, same tread pattern.'

'Sounds like two people to me,' Angel said.

'There's also this,' Andy said, pointing at a disturbance in the dirt and dust approximately halfway between Yardley's body and the back wall. 'That looks to me like something was thrown and landed on the floor.' He threw his hands outwards and up, made a puffing noise. 'The dust went flying in all directions. There's no sign of it, so the killer must have taken it.'

'What about his phone?' Kincade said.

'That, too. Unless he left it at home.'

'What? A captain of industry like him? He'll be one of those irritating jerks who stands at the urinal talking on his phone.' She was aware of Angel, the tech Andy as well as Isabel Durand all staring at her—how would you know? 'My husband complains about it all the time.'

She wasn't sure they looked as if they believed her.

Angel and Kincade left Durand and the SOCOs to it. They went outside in time to see DCI Finch striding down the access road in her protective suit.

'She looks good in it,' Kincade whispered, echoing Angel's own thoughts.

'I heard that, DS Kincade,' Finch said, then looked at Angel. 'What have we got, Max?'

'Guy Yardley, the man Gavin Lynch works for. We interviewed him yesterday. From the SOCOs' first impressions, it looks as if Yardley came here to deliver something last night. He entered the unit, threw a package to a woman or small man waiting at the back of the unit, then turned to go. A man who'd been standing off to the side then stepped behind him and garrotted him. One or the other of them then cut out his tongue, post mortem.'

Not surprisingly, the last sentence had the most impact. Finch had been looking past him to where Durand crouched over Yardley's body talking into a hand-held digital recorder. Her head snapped around.

'Cut out his tongue?'

'That's what Dr Durand said.'

'He didn't bite it?' Finch said in the hopeful but resigned voice of the person who would be tasked with fielding difficult questions at the inevitable press conference, supplying the voyeuristic grist to the media mill.

'Not according to Durand. The tongue is also missing. Unless a hungry rat had an unexpected stroke of good luck, it looks as if the killers took it with them.'

'The implication being that he was a grass, a snitch?'

'That's one possibility. It could also be that his killers objected to things he'd been saying, although not necessarily to us.'

'That's some objection.'

'We all have to watch what we say these days, ma'am.'

He'd meant it as a gentle dig at Kincade about her comment regarding Finch looking good in a protective suit. Too late, he realised it could equally well be a reference to the protester that Kincade used excessive force arresting at a demonstration after he insulted her.

As it happened, Kincade wasn't paying attention. She was looking at the chain-link fence twenty yards away. Beyond it was a path running through a small park. The back gardens of the surrounding houses ran down to it on either side. A small boy aged six or seven sat on his bike staring at them from the other side of the fence.

'I'm guessing they parked at the far end,' she said, 'made their way down the path on foot, then climbed over the fence. It looks as if it's sagging at the top. We'll need to get the SOCOs to take a look. Better stop that kid from putting chocolate fingerprints all over it.' She raised her hand to wave at a man in striped pyjamas leaning out of his back-bedroom window to get a better look at all the excitement. He waved back. 'Get somebody to talk to that nosy old git, too.'

'Do you want me to notify Yardley's wife?' Finch said, as she and Angel made their way back towards the entrance to the estate leaving Kincade behind to speak to the uniformed PC who'd been the first to arrive at the scene.

'Up to you. I don't mind doing it. Take DS Kincade along...'

'See if she's got a softer side, you mean?'
'Can't hurt.'
'Okay, you've got it.'
'There is one other thing . . .'

Something in his tone of voice gave him away. That, and the fact that she'd known him too long.

'Don't even think about saying it, DI Angel.'

He didn't need to now.

Kincade was right. You look good in that protective suit.

HIS PHONE RANG WHILE HE WAS SITTING IN THE CAR WAITING FOR Kincade. It was his sister.

'Can you talk?' she said.

'Yeah. Just taking a break. It's tiring work beating confessions out of prisoners in the cells.'

He pictured Grace's face on the other end of the line, the weary acceptance of his not-so-subtle dig at her *Guardian*-reading, tofu-eating leftie attitudes.

'That'd be funny if it wasn't so true. How was Dad?'

'Same as always.'

'You make it sound as if I'm imagining this.'

'I can only tell it as I find it.'

'Did he agree to go for a blood test?'

He closed his eyes, let a guilty silence answer for him. Got the reaction he deserved.

'*Jesus*, Max, you didn't even ask him, did you?'

He was reminded of what his father had said about being lucky, made a mental note to ask Kincade where she'd got the seagulls fighting ringtone. He'd assign it to Grace.

'It slipped my mind.'

'What did you talk about that was more important than our father's health? Rugby? Cricket?'

He ignored the sarcasm and her attempt to make him feel more guilty than he already did, happier thinking about what else they hadn't discussed—which had made a pleasant change.

'This and that. We didn't get onto what a disappointment I am to him, for once.'

'At least you went into the Army in the first place.'

'Yeah, but coming out again is an even bigger crime.'

He could have been more specific. Coming out again *voluntarily*. Except that would take them into dangerous territory. Their younger brother, Cormac, had come out in the most *in*voluntary fashion. Feet first. The event that had started their father's life circling the drain.

He glanced sideways out of the window, saw Kincade striding towards the car, only ten yards away.

'Gotta go, Sis. The suspect in the cells has stopped screaming. We can't have that, can we?'

'Funny, if it wasn't so true.'

He ended the call thinking he hoped she never met Kincade, learned the reason Kincade gave for her demotion.

'Everything okay?' she said, climbing in.

'Yeah. Just getting interrogated by my sister. Can you let me know where you got the seagulls squawking ringtone?'

25

'I THOUGHT HE WAS HAVING AN AFFAIR,' IRENE YARDLEY WAILED, dabbing at her eyes with a crumpled Kleenex, then blowing her nose vigorously.

Angel smiled, a soft sympathetic gesture that reflected the sadness inflicted by fate's little games.

The sounds of Kincade making tea came from the kitchen.

You used to be a priest, you tell her, she'd said when Angel suggested she might like to take the lead.

So much for seeing her softer side.

Irene Yardley pulled her fluffy pink dressing gown that looked as if it shouldn't be held too close to a naked flame tighter around her.

'He said he had a business meeting. That was a lie. At least he wasn't having an affair.'

Now wasn't the time to point out that he could have been doing both, just not on the same night.

'I didn't know he'd taken my car until after he'd gone,' Irene said. 'I thought to myself, the bastard's gone to a sleazy motel and he doesn't want to risk getting a scratch on his precious Bentley. Then when he didn't come home last night, I said to myself, *I knew it*. I went into the garage and got a screwdriver.' She held up her hand, her finger and thumb a hair's width apart. 'I was this close to running it all the way down the side, show him what a proper scratch looks like. And all the time he was already dead.'

Angel waited patiently while she sobbed, great chunks of air heaved deep into her lungs, sniffing snot and swallowing, a constant cycle. He didn't need to hear any of what she was saying, but it was best to let it come. He felt as if he was back in the confessional.

Finally, Kincade came in carrying a mug of tea, handed it to Irene. She took a sip, relaxed. The pink dressing gown gaped giving Angel an eyeful of something it was far too early in the morning for—even after coming directly from the crime scene.

'Did he give any details at all?' he said.

Irene shook her head.

'Just that it was a business meeting. I didn't ask who it was with.' She dropped her eyes, sniffed loudly. Looked back at Angel. 'I thought he was going to meet a woman. I didn't want to challenge him, have a big argument. Head in the sand, that's me.'

He was reminded of how he'd accused his father of the same thing not much more than twelve hours previously.

'Did he take anything with him?'

'Not that I saw. But he was acting suspiciously when he got home from work. He had something in a Tesco bag he didn't want me to see. He said it was work papers. I said to him, why don't you put them in your briefcase? And he said he'd spilled coffee all over it. I thought it was a present for the woman he was going to see.'

Angel had no doubt that it was neither. The obvious suspicion would be confirmed soon enough.

'How did he seem in the last few days?'

'He was in a filthy mood when he got home the day before yesterday. When I asked him what was wrong, he snapped at me. Said it was just work. Except I always know when he's lying.'

'Have you got any idea what it was about?'

'Not really. I know he was upset about Roy Lynch . . . killing himself.'

Nobody could miss the hesitation before she'd said, *killing himself*. Kincade jumped on it.

'The way you said that suggests you think there's some doubt about that, Mrs Yardley.'

Irene pulled her dressing gown tightly around herself again, much to Angel's relief. Took a sip of tea. Time wasting, basically.

Kincade softened her voice.

'You can tell us, Mrs Yardley.'

She didn't look convinced, came out with it anyway.

'Guy said he thought it wasn't suicide. He said he got the idea from you when you went to his office the other day and interrogated him.' She caught the look they exchanged, her voice suddenly defensive. 'That was the word he used. Anyway, he said you thought Roy's son Gavin was involved.'

Kincade shook her head, *easy mistake to make*.

'I don't know where he got that idea from, Mrs Yardley. We haven't even spoken to Gavin Lynch yet.'

'So you don't think Gavin's involved?'

'Can we concentrate on your husband's relationship with Roy Lynch,' Angel cut in. 'They must have been close if he was that upset about his death.'

A lot of the grieving widow went out of Irene's face at that point, replaced by something harder, more cynical.

'I don't want to speak ill of the dead, Inspector, but you didn't know my husband. Guy was only ever concerned about what happened to other people in relation to how it would affect him. His pocket, generally.'

Angel leaned forward on the sofa, elbows resting on his knees as something worth pursuing appeared on the horizon.

'In what way would Roy Lynch's death impact your husband?'

The sudden and obvious uptick in interest unsettled Irene, made her backtrack.

'I don't know. If it was anything, it would be to do with the company.'

The comment, vague as it was, was sufficient to bring to mind how uncomfortable Yardley had become when Angel tried to quiz him on the company's early years. He asked his wife the same question.

'How did your husband's company get started?'

She waved the question away, her voice reflecting boredom with all things business-related.

'I've got no idea. That was all long before my time. The only thing I know is that Roy Lynch was involved. That's how Gavin ended up working for my husband. Guy felt he owed Roy, so he gave his son a job. A very well paid one, considering how little he does to earn it.'

Mrs Irene Yardley wasn't anybody's fool. She was well aware of the true nature of Gavin Lynch's employment. Her mouth turned down, but it wasn't anything to do with her husband allowing Gavin to use his company as a front.

'There must be something in the water at that place. Even if my husband wasn't having an affair, Gavin Lynch certainly is. You know what his nickname at work is?'

Both Angel and Kincade shook their heads, surprised at the unexpected turn the conversation had taken and the even-more-unexpected question.

'No idea,' Angel said.

'Keyhole.' The way she looked at them suggested she expected a reaction of some sort. Laughter at what should be an obvious joke. She threw her eyes when it didn't happen, her voice taking on the long-suffering tone of a person having to explain a very simple concept to an even simpler person. 'Because he'd fuck one, pardon my French, if there wasn't already a key in it.'

'She seems to be getting over her grief nicely,' Angel said after they'd seen themselves out, leaving a Family Liaison Officer with the new widow.

'You're not kidding. She'll have worked her way through all five stages of it by the end of the day. I bet she sells the company and buggers off to the south of France by the end of the week.'

Angel wasn't so sure about that. There was something not quite right about Yardarm Marine Technology. He had a feeling that any potential buyer doing their due diligence might find something they weren't expecting.

'We better get over there fast before she does.'

Guy Yardley's secretary, Madeleine, had already heard the news by the time Angel and Kincade arrived at the Yardarm Marine Technology premises barely forty-eight hours since their last visit. She'd called Yardley's mobile phone when he hadn't shown up for a ten o'clock meeting, then tried the house and had spoken to his wife.

She was as upset as Mrs Yardley, although Angel got the impression it wouldn't wear off so fast. Then again, she wasn't in line to get the Bentley, the business and the house. They waited while she repeated, *I can't believe it* half a dozen times, then Angel got them started.

'How long have you worked for Mr Yardley?'

'Fifteen years, give or take.'

'Are you the longest-serving employee?'

She chewed a nail, thinking about it.

'I think so. I'm trying to remember if Gavin Lynch was here when I joined.'

'Meaning you knew Mr Yardley and the company better than anyone.'

'I suppose so.'

'Did he confide in you? I don't mean personal matters. Did he bounce ideas off you?'

Madeleine smiled at the thought of it.

'No. Sometimes he asked my opinion about someone he was thinking of employing. I got the impression he only ever took any notice when my opinion confirmed what he'd already decided.'

He smiled back at her. *That's bosses for you.*

'Would he have told you if the company was in trouble?'

'That's more difficult to say seeing as it isn't.'

He acknowledged the point with a dip of his head.

'Did you have anything to do with Roy Lynch at all?'

The question took her by surprise, a crease appearing in her brow.

'No. Why would I?'

'I got the impression he was involved in the company in some way.'

'Are you sure you don't mean Gavin Lynch?'

Angel was very sure, but he wasn't getting anywhere.

'Maybe it was back in the beginning.'

Madeleine shook her head, not disagreement, more a subconscious manifestation of not understanding where any of this was going.

Nowhere, was the answer. Angel had been fishing. He now brought them bang up to date.

'How would you describe Mr Yardley's state of mind and his behaviour over the past week or so?'

'I thought you'd never ask,' Madeleine said.

Angel was aware of Kincade smiling to herself. He ignored her, concentrated on Madeleine.

'Why's that?'

'Because it's what the police always ask. And I've been thinking about it. Something happened the day before yesterday. It must have been an email he received because I didn't put a call through to him. And I would've heard him talking on his mobile.'

Angel doubted it, the size of Yardley's office still fresh in his mind from their last visit.

Whatever the means of communication, Madeleine's comment gelled with what Yardley's wife had said.

'Mrs Yardley told me he was upset when he arrived home that day,' he said, down-grading *filthy mood* to *upset*.

'I wouldn't call it that. He was scared. I brought him in a cup of coffee and he almost jumped out of his skin. He looked guilty as sin. As if I'd caught him looking at porn on his computer. But it was his email.'

'We'll take a look in a minute, if that's okay.'

'Of course. Then yesterday, he got a call from a woman who refused to give her name.'

Angel resisted the urge to say, *size five feet? Hopes people burn in hell?*

'Young or old, would you say?'

'Young definitely. Very pushy. Aggressive. I'm used to people calling who expect you to jump to it, but this woman was worse.'

'And Mr Yardley agreed to take the call?'

'He seemed to be in two minds, but then he did.'

'How was he when he'd finished?'

'Like a ghost. I've never seen anybody so pale. He went out immediately without any explanation. It wasn't like him at all.'

Angel didn't suppose it was. You don't take a call from the person who's going to kill you within the next few hours every day of the week. He also had a good idea what was in the package he'd handed over to them.

'I'd like to take a quick look at his computer now. Someone will come to take it away, but we might as well have a quick look while we're here.'

Madeleine led them into Yardley's office and they made the long trek from the door to his desk. Angel saw her assessing the distance.

'Maybe I wouldn't have heard him talking on his mobile, after all.'

Angel got himself settled into Yardley's real-leather executive chair, Kincade standing at his shoulder as if they were preparing for a portrait for the company brochure. Madeleine leaned across him and logged in using Yardley's credentials, a strangely intimate moment, the smell of her perfume in his nose.

'Does he have access to the company bank accounts on here?' he said.

Madeleine looked at him a long moment. She knew what he was thinking. She chose not to say anything about it beyond confirming that, yes, Yardley could access the company bank accounts online.

She pulled out the top left-hand drawer without being asked, fished out a tattered slip of paper.

'All the log-in details for the online banking and everything else are on there. Mr Security Conscious, he wasn't.'

They waited until Madeleine took the hint and left them to it. He started with the online banking. Kincade pointed over his shoulder at the screen a minute later.

'There it is. Ten thousand withdrawn yesterday afternoon.'

He scrolled back, then adjusted the search settings to the last three months. There were no other suspicious withdrawals.

'Strange,' he said. 'Extort him for ten thousand, then kill him.'

'Unless they weren't interested in the money. It was a ploy to get him to agree to meet them.'

'Or *her*, as he thought at the time.'

They had less success with Yardley's email. Angel started three days previously and worked all the way up to the present time. Then checked the deleted folder.

'Whatever it was, he's permanently deleted it,' he said. 'Forensics might be able to get it back or it could be on the company mail server.'

He closed the email client, studied the computer desktop for anything that stood out. She leaned over his shoulder.

'I can't see anything called *blackmail demand*.'

They were interrupted by a knock at the door, then Madeleine poked her head in.

'If you wanted to talk to Gavin Lynch, he's just arrived.'

They shared a look.

They wanted to very much indeed.

26

Outside Yardley's office, Angel called Madeleine back as she set off to take them to Gavin Lynch.

'Does Gavin know about Mr Yardley's death?'

'I certainly haven't told him. The only reason I know is because I called the house.' She dropped her voice to a conspiratorial whisper. 'Mrs Yardley isn't a big fan of Gavin's. She wouldn't have called him.'

The remark confirmed the impression they'd already formed from talking to the widow Yardley. It was worth pursuing, nonetheless.

'Why not?'

'Nothing specific that I know of. But it annoys her that Mr Yardley was pressured into employing him. If there's any pressuring of Mr Yardley going on, Mrs Yardley wants to be the one doing it.'

It made him wonder if Yardley had been conducting an affair as his wife suspected—with his secretary. What she'd just told them wasn't exactly run-of-the-mill office gossip.

'And no-one else knows?'

'Not from me. I expect Gavin will have to tell everyone. I would have told him as soon as he arrived if you hadn't been here. I thought it would be best coming from you.'

Best for us, Angel thought, *maybe not for him.*

'Is he aware of the things bothering Mr Yardley? The young woman who called?'

'I don't think so. Mr Yardley went out immediately after talking to her, as I told you. I got the impression that whatever had shaken him up, he wanted to keep it completely private.'

Between him and his maker, Angel thought with the benefit of hindsight.

GAVIN LYNCH'S OFFICE WAS A LOT SMALLER THAN YARDLEY'S AND without the double-aspect views. It was still a damn sight bigger and plusher than anything either Angel or Kincade had ever worked in—or were likely to.

It also lacked the two sofas for entertaining visitors that Yardley's contained. For a brief moment, it looked as if Gavin was going to remain seated behind his desk while they stood in front of it. As if he'd summoned them for a dressing down. He got up and came around the desk when the dynamics of the situation crossed his own mind, parked himself on the edge of his desk instead. It now felt like a more relaxed dressing down.

He was clearly surprised to see them, and immediately jumped to the wrong conclusion.

'You didn't have to come here. I would have come into the station.'

It would soon become clear that they hadn't made a special trip to talk to him, but for now they were happy to leave him believing it. It helped with stage one of the interview. What Angel thought of as baiting the interviewee.

As far as he was concerned, grieving son or not, Gavin Lynch had set the scene for all future exchanges between them the previous day. He'd insulted Kincade and left them with a parting threat.

If you lot don't find out who, I will.

Angel started with that.

'The last time we met, you implied that you would be making your own enquiries into your father's death. How's that going?'

'I was upset and angry. Not thinking straight.' He lifted his hand, opened and closed his fingers and thumb like a bird's beak squawking. 'I was giving it some of that.'

'And once you calmed down, you decided against it?'

'Yeah.' He tried an obsequious smile on them, one that years of working in sales had perfected. 'Leave it to the professionals.'

'So you haven't been asking around?'

'We heard you'd spoken to Phil Brent,' Kincade cut in before Gavin could answer. 'Met with him, in fact.'

It was a stretch, but they suspected him of breaking Brent's finger and that was hard to do down a phone line.

Gavin shifted his butt on the edge of the desk. Tried to make light of it. *Of course I spoke to good ol' Phil.*

'He's a friend of my dad's. I thought you meant, you know, asking around.'

Angel and Kincade both cocked their head at him, as in, keep going...

'We did,' Angel said.

'Well, I haven't.'

'Who haven't you spoken to?'

Kincade liked Angel's style. There was no easy way to answer a question like that, as Gavin was demonstrating.

'I haven't spoken to anybody.'

'Apart from Phil Brent.'

'Apart from him, yeah.'

Everybody looked relieved to have got that settled.

'What happened to his finger?' Kincade said before Gavin could relax.

Momentarily, Gavin looked as if he was going to play the stupid card.

Finger? What finger?

Instead, he proved that, if nothing else, Brent had been consistent with his lies.

'I think he fell over in the garden.'

Angel and Kincade enjoyed the brief silence that followed, even if Gavin didn't. They were all reminded of the last occasion on which they'd met, in Gavin's father's garden. And how Kincade and Gavin had ended up rolling on the ground together after he'd tried to get past them.

Angel let Kincade capitalise on Gavin's discomfort.

'It's just that we know your father argued with Mr Brent a couple of days before he died. Then you had a long phone conversation with your father on the morning of the day he died.' She extended her arm as if holding a phone away from her ear. 'I bet he was really ranting?' She paused, gave him the chance to agree. Continued when he didn't. 'Then your father died in suspicious circumstances. You made a threat in our presence that you were going to get to the bottom of the matter. The implication was that you would be more successful because you won't be constrained by the need to stick within the law—'

'I told you, I was angry, running my mouth.'

'Let me finish, please. Then Mr Brent disappeared on an alleged business trip that his wife knew nothing about. And when he reappears, he's got a broken finger.'

She left it at that.

Your turn to talk now.

Gavin folded his arms over his chest as if he needed to keep his hands under control to stop himself from taking a swipe at her.

'Since you obviously know all about it, you'll know that the argument was over a car. Nobody kills anybody over a car.'

Kincade shook her head.

'What it was about ultimately was money. And the two factors behind the majority of murders are money and sex. I'm assuming your father and Mr Brent weren't in a sexual relationship? That this wasn't a lover's tiff that got out of control?' Gavin had the sense not to rise to the bait. Kincade carried on whilst he was attempting to formulate an appropriate response. 'Of course, I might be completely off base—'

'You can say that again.'

'—and you talking to Mr Brent had nothing to do with you thinking he might have been involved in your father's death. Maybe it was a warning to keep his mouth shut about something.'

'Like what?'

'You tell us. We've only got Mr Brent's word that the argument was about the Jag. That could be a lie.'

'You be sure to let me know what it is if you find out.'

'Count on it, Mr Lynch. Before we move on to another matter, I need to ask you where you were on the night of your father's death. When we saw you at your father's house, you mentioned something about being away on business, but then things got a little out of hand. We asked Mr Yardley about it but he didn't seem to know much about it at all.'

She looked at Angel. He nodded in agreement.

'Very vague.'

'Sketchy.'

He nodded again. Approval this time.

'Good word. Make sure you use it when you write it up.'

They looked at Gavin. Help us out here.

'I stayed overnight at the Royal Hotel in Winchester.'

Kincade's brow creased.

'I've only just transferred down here, but that isn't very far away, is it?'

'Ten miles,' Angel said, ever helpful.

Kincade looked surprised to hear that it was even closer than she'd thought.

'If I had a Bentley, I think I'd drive home.'

Gavin gave her a self-satisfied smile. One that suggested that since she wasn't ever going to own one, her opinion was of no relevance.

'You know what business meetings are like. Or maybe you don't. I'd had a few drinks with the clients. That's why they call it *wining* and dining. And I never drink and drive.'

'Glad to hear it, Mr Lynch. Were any of your . . . colleagues on the trip with you?'

Angel liked the pause before *colleagues*. Gavin didn't. He didn't like answering the question, either.

'Samantha,' he said eventually.

Kincade's face lit up as if she'd just made a connection she was proud of.

'And that would be the lady in the car with you when you turned up at your father's house?'

'Yeah. Sorry to spoil your little game—'

'None of this is a game, Mr Lynch.'

'—but no, when you check with the hotel, you won't find two rooms booked for that night. We shared a room.'

Both Angel and Kincade nodded. As if they approved of Gavin's cost-conscious attitude when spending the company's money, although they stopped short of putting it into words.

It wasn't necessary to ask who slept on the couch.

'We will of course need to confirm that with the hotel and

with Samantha,' Angel said, 'but I'm sure everything will be fine. Can you give us Samantha's surname?'

Kincade liked the ambiguous nature of the phrase, *can you give?* Without phrasing the question as, *do you know?* he still made it sound as if Gavin might not. Or even that she might not have one at all, having abandoned it years ago, being the sort of woman men didn't know long enough to ask.

'Lee,' Gavin said. 'Samantha Lee.'

Briefly, Angel considered immediately asking Gavin to confirm his whereabouts the previous night when Guy Yardley was murdered. But Gavin was on the back foot already. To lead into the news of Yardley's death by asking for his alibi felt unnecessarily callous. For all they knew, the two men might have been good friends despite what Yardley's wife had said about her husband being pressured into employing him.

All of the antagonistic tone that had characterised their conversation so far was absent when he next spoke.

'I'm afraid I've got some bad news, Mr Lynch. Your employer, Mr Yardley, was found dead in an industrial unit in Freemantle earlier this morning. He'd been murdered.'

When they talked about it later, both Angel and Kincade would agree that in their opinion it wouldn't be possible to fake the impact the news had on Gavin Lynch. He sagged visibly, jaw slack, a bark of stuttering laughter dying on his lips.

'Guy? Murdered?'

'I'm afraid so.' Sounding as if it had been his own best friend.

'How?'

'We can't divulge that at the moment.'

'Not hanged?'

'No, not hanged.'

'And it was definitely murder?'

'At this early stage there are lots of things that need to be established, but that isn't one of them.'

Gavin pushed himself upright. Staggered around his desk, sank into the chair behind it. He didn't look so much of a cocksure drug dealer at the moment.

Angel had planned on maintaining the pressure. Taking a similar line to the one taken by Kincade. Say how Yardley made it abundantly clear that Gavin spent the night his father was killed in a hotel with a woman who wasn't his wife. Leave the suggestion hanging in the air that maybe Gavin had killed him for having a big mouth. Given Gavin's reaction, that approach was inappropriate.

The man needed a drink, not a grilling.

'Where did you say it happened?' Gavin said.

'The Solent View Industrial Estate in Freemantle.'

'What the hell was he doing there?'

To Angel's ear, the question wasn't a simple expression of bewilderment. It felt as if Gavin was questioning Yardley's judgement in going to a location he knew would be the last place Yardley would go.

'Does that location mean anything to you, Mr Lynch?'

The question took Gavin by surprise, pulled him back from wherever he'd been, lost in his thoughts.

'What? No. I know where it is, but it doesn't mean anything to me.'

And Angel thought, *liar*. Despite being in shock at the news of Yardley's death, Gavin Lynch still had the wherewithal to lie. That was something to be borne in mind.

He took things in a different direction. Circling towards the question that was starting to obsess him.

'We've spoken to Mrs Yardley and his secretary, Madeleine. Everything's up in the air. Nobody knows what's going to happen with the company now that Mrs Yardley owns it.'

Gavin looked at Angel sharply. As if he'd just realised that the woman who thought he was a waste of space was now in charge. That he might be on borrowed time already.

'Maybe she'll run it herself with you in charge,' Angel said. 'Or maybe she'll sell it.' He paused, the relieved look on his face of a man who was happy he wasn't the one with such uncertainty hanging over his head. A man to whom an innocent but related question had just occurred. His tone conversational, as if he was no longer a cop talking to a man whose employer had been brutally murdered. 'Do you know how Mr Yardley got started in the first place?'

Gavin shook his head.

'You should've asked my dad that. Obviously, you can't, now.'

Angel was aware of the small smile on Kincade's face—*bet you wish you still had your direct line to the man upstairs.*

'Didn't he ever tell you?'

'It was thirty years ago. I was still at school.'

And that isn't an answer.

Gavin was recovering rapidly after his initial shock. As if he was processing the implications, and maybe Guy Yardley's death wasn't such an inconvenience after all. That he could see ways in which the situation could be used to his advantage. And part of that meant not telling them the truth.

The realisation knocked the conversational tone right out of Angel's voice.

'We were told your father was behind Mr Yardley employing you.'

Gavin stared back at him. *So?*

'You'd be a pretty shit dad if you didn't look out for your kids. Have you got children?'

'No.'

Gavin looked at Kincade.

'You?'

'No.'

The answer didn't surprise Angel. It wasn't simply a question of keeping all personal details out of the conversation. They were talking about parents doing the best for their children. She didn't want to give him an easy shot.

Do them a favour, tell them not to follow in Mum's footsteps.

'I can understand why your father would want to help you out,' Angel said. 'What I can't understand is why Mr Yardley would agree.'

Gavin had recovered all of his composure by now. Chin up, leaning back in his chair, arms crossed over his chest. The vaguely mocking tone was also back.

'Maybe he thought any son of his good friend Roy can't be all bad.'

And that isn't an answer, either.

'That must be it.'

'What's any of this got to do with who killed my dad? Or Guy?'

Angel shook his head, beats me.

'Just pulling at loose threads. Did your father or Mr Yardley have any enemies you know of? Any recent disputes or arguments?'

'Nothing and nobody off the top of my head.'

'Talking of enemies, did your father tell you about the young woman who visited your mother in the hospice?'

'My mother?' Gavin's face compacted in confusion momentarily. 'You mean my step-mother? Marianne.'

'Sorry, I should've been more specific.' Hoping it sounded a lot more like a slip of the tongue to Gavin than it did in his own head and to Kincade.

'Yeah, he told me. Some sicko who whispered, *I hope you burn in hell*. We reckoned she must have escaped from the local asylum. A nutter.'

'You didn't try to find her?'

Gavin laughed. It sounded as false as Angel's remark about a slip of the tongue.

'What for? Tell her not to be so horrible to a dying woman? Or tell her doctor to double her meds?'

Angel and Kincade shared a look. Was it possible Roy Lynch hadn't told his son he'd visited Southern Parking Management? Didn't want him to laugh it off as he was trying to do now.

'Your father obviously thought differently,' Angel said. 'He went to the company that manages the parking to try to get a list of everyone who'd parked there that day.'

'If he did, he never mentioned it to me.'

'Maybe he didn't think you'd care. Is your own mother still alive?'

'She is. I can't see what that's got to do with anything.'

'Probably nothing. Do you see her at all?'

'Not as much as I should.' He did a mock double-take. 'You're not thinking she's the woman who cursed Marianne because she stole her husband all those years ago?'

'Anything's possible when families are involved. We'll need her contact details in case we need to talk to her.'

'Why would you need to talk to her? She hasn't spoken to my dad for thirty years and she never even knew Guy Yardley.'

'At the moment, I have no idea. But that might change. And we don't want to have to bother you unnecessarily, given how busy you're likely to be in the aftermath of Mr Yardley's death.'

Gavin grudgingly pulled out his phone and recited his mother's name, address and phone number.

'Just go easy on her, okay?' He tapped his temple with his middle finger. 'She's not all there.'

Kincade brought things to a close, finally asking Gavin his whereabouts on the previous evening. He had no problem coming straight back at her, the speed and confidence in his answer that he'd been at home watching TV with his wife making the need to follow up and confirm it almost redundant.

Angel had some parting words for him as they left—words that would ultimately prove to be wasted.

'Good luck with working for Mrs Yardley. You're going to need it.'

27

'It doesn't look real,' she said, then immediately corrected herself. 'I don't mean not real like it's made of plastic. It doesn't look like a person's tongue is what I mean.'

He could've asked her whether she'd had an idea in her mind about what a severed human tongue would look like, how the real thing measured up. Whether it was a disappointment. It wasn't a conversation he was about to rush into.

'More like an ox tongue,' he said instead.

Big mistake.

She immediately got out her phone, searched Google for *ox tongue*.

'*Yuck!* That's disgusting.' She showed him the phone screen. He couldn't disagree. 'It looks more like a severed penis in a really thick condom.'

He couldn't disagree with that either.

She shuddered as she continued to look at the image, a strange reaction from a person who'd had no qualms watching him cut Yardley's tongue out of his mouth. She swiped across to the next image. It showed a cooked ox tongue on a white plate, a mixed-leaf salad on the side. She closed the browser in disgust.

'I can't believe people actually eat it.' She poked Guy Yardley's tongue in its Ziploc bag with her fingernail. 'It's a lot smaller than an ox tongue.'

'Yes, well, a person is a lot smaller than a cow.'

'I suppose. I wouldn't like to see an elephant's tongue.'

He agreed, nor would he.

'Are you sure we can't send it to him?'

She looked at him as if it was three days until Christmas and they were standing outside a pet shop, looking through the window watching the puppies play.

'It'll spook him. Make it ten times harder.'

She let out a heavy sigh, her voice resigned.

'I know. I'm going to make him eat it when we get him.'

That was another thought he didn't want to dwell on. Not for the first time since she'd knocked on his door out of the blue all those months ago, he wondered what he'd allowed himself to get caught up in. He couldn't think how many times she'd watched the video of Roy Lynch jerking on the end of a clothesline like an epileptic marionette manipulated by a madman. She refused to give the phone back now. The longing in her voice—*I wish I could've been there*—kept him awake at night.

As did the questions concerning what it said about him.

He changed the subject. Something more practical and less gruesome.

'Have you had any more trouble with the nosy cow in the downstairs flat?'

She'd told him how she'd heard the woman and another old crone gossiping, whispering as she walked past them the day after he'd first gone to her flat.

Old enough to be her father.
Disgusting.
Whore.

She should've ignored them. But she came right back at them. Showed them that if there was anything disgusting, it was her language. They'd remember her now. Stupid, but he could understand why it had happened.

She wasn't the most stable young woman, after all. His own flesh and blood, too.

'What are we going to do with it?' she said again, a hint of petulance in her voice.

'I already told you.'

He told her again, all the same. It was the only way to stop her from suggesting whatever poisonous ideas might be floating around in the dark recesses of her brain. Her response was as unsurprising as it was disturbing.

'I want to be the one to do it.'

28

Kincade was looking distinctly nervous.

They were back in the car, still parked in the Yardarm Marine Technology car park. Gavin Lynch was standing at the window of his office staring down at them, much as Guy Yardley had from his. As if it was his first job as the new chief exec—to glare at departing coppers.

'We should tell him not to watch us for too long,' Kincade said leaning forward to look up at him through the windscreen. 'Look what happened to his predecessor.'

That was when she noticed the harmonica in Angel's hand.

'What are you doing?'

'Thinking of what to play.'

'You are joking?'

'It helps me think.'

She nodded like it made sense. Put her hand on the door handle.

'Clear the car, you mean? Give you some time alone.'

'I've just added a minute to the play time.'

'Right, I get you. It's like being in court and every time the toerag in the dock gives the judge some lip, he gets another month on his sentence.'

'And another one.'

'Are you sure you've got enough puff?'

'And another.'

'We keep on like this and I'll be getting overtime listening to it. So, are we going to grab some lunch?'

'I thought you were getting out of the car?'

'You haven't started playing yet. If you're going to, can you do it before we eat? I don't want to get indigestion.'

'This is shaping up to be one of the longest songs I've ever played.'

'It'd be wasted on me.'

'It's wasted on everybody.'

Much to her relief, he slipped it into his pocket, backed the car out. Perhaps he only ever threatened to play, although she wasn't banking on it. He was like all men. Had to be fiddling with something. Men with beards and moustaches played with them incessantly, he turned his mouth organ over and over in his fingers.

Something to do with their mothers, most likely.

'What are you thinking?' he said as he pulled away.

'Pizza.'

He glanced at her, saw the small curl at the corner of her mouth.

'I meant about this morning's revelations.'

'Oh, right. It's got to be the same woman in all three situations. At the hospice, the hairs on Roy Lynch's trousers, and now the woman who called and wouldn't give her name.'

'I agree. Does the fact that Gavin lied at least twice imply he knows who she is?'

She assumed position #1. Left arm across her body, right

elbow resting on it, knuckle of her index finger resting against her lips.

'Two lies?'

'Uh-huh. He must have known his father went looking for her.'

'Unless the old man didn't want junior to know who she was. He had an idea, and didn't want Gavin to know about her.'

They'd stopped at a red traffic light. Angel took the opportunity to look at her properly. See if she was being serious or just kicking it around.

'A long-lost illegitimate daughter, something like that?' he said when he saw that she was serious.

'Could be. Like you said to Gavin, anything's possible with families. What was the other lie?'

He pulled away as the lights went green. On the other side of the junction two lanes merged into one. The car beside them, a twenty-year-old VW Golf with tinted windows and an illegal exhaust, floored it in a puff of blue smoke to get ahead of them.

'Wanker,' Kincade said, as Angel let the Golf cut in ahead of him.

'Him or me?'

'Him, of course, sir.'

'I've only known you a few days, but I get the impression you wouldn't have let him cut in.'

She shrugged like she'd never really thought about it.

'Depends on how I'm feeling on the day.'

'And today? After our meeting with Gavin Lynch?'

She pretended to think about it. Except she wasn't.

'We'll never know. Not until you stop insisting on driving the whole time.'

She got the strangest feeling then. That she'd inadvertently touched a raw nerve. The problem behind the DS Stuart

Beckford mystery. Had he hit and killed a pedestrian while Angel was in the passenger seat? A child? That'd make a person go off with stress. A vivid mental image went through her mind, made her shudder. One of her daughters flipped high into the air by a speeding unmarked police vehicle. Turning head over heels in mid-air twisting gracefully like an acrobat in slow motion. Then *Splat!* as real time resumes, the sickening sound of soft flesh and brittle bone meeting unforgiving concrete and stone.

She shook herself out of it, an involuntary tremor rippling through her, the image still clinging on.

'Someone walked over my grave,' she said in response to his curious look. 'What was the other lie Gavin Lynch told?'

'That the Solent View Industrial Estate meant nothing to him. The way he said, *what the hell was he doing there?*'

She nodded to herself as she thought back.

'As if Gavin knew a very good reason why it would be the last place Yardley would ever go. Something to do with his past.'

'It's to do with that bloody company, I know it is.'

He pulled to the kerb in front of Enzo's Pizzeria in the West Quay Retail Park, switched off the engine. It was only five hundred yards as the crow flies from the station, but he had a feeling she was looking for an opportunity to talk.

'You want to share?' she said.

'If you like. You choose.'

'You like spicy?'

'Fine by me. But no anchovies.'

'Count on it,' she said, taking the twenty-pound note he offered and getting out.

He spent the ten minutes she was away with his eyes closed, head against the rest. Allowing a picture of the young woman who linked the two murders to form in his mind. Had she been the one to cut out Yardley's tongue? What horrors lay behind her ability to do it, if she had? Did she derive any satisfaction from it? Find relief from whatever demons haunted her?

He didn't get far.

Life and people will always find new ways to wrong-foot you, however many times you've been around the block.

'Spicy Italian sausage and jalapeño,' Kincade said when she got back in the car, pizza box in one hand, two bottles of sparkling water in the other.

'With extra chili oil?'

'*Damn.* I forgot that.' She then proved his earlier premonition right. 'What do you think about the idea of no talking shop while we're eating?'

'Depends on what the alternative is?'

She offered him the open box, then dug in her pocket for the paper napkins.

'PNG.'

'I'm guessing that isn't *persona non grata*?'

'Uh-uh. Personal nitty-gritty.'

He couldn't stop himself from laughing at the brazenness of it.

'To give me indigestion in case the spicy pizza doesn't do the trick?'

'You get used to it.'

'Which?'

She'd just put too much pizza in her mouth preventing her from answering. By the time she'd chewed and swallowed it, the question was forgotten, another one taking its place.

'What's the worst thing anyone ever told you in the confessional?'

The question took him by surprise. Hijacked his subconscious at the same time. That didn't stop it from kicking back, the taste of desert dust and grit in his mouth, his head suddenly awash with memories. Of distraught young men trained in the theory of killing until they were consumed by an insatiable thirst for the opportunity to try it for real, only to find themselves sickened and horrified at the too-late, Road-to-Damascus realisation that hidden away under the statistics for enemy dead and ordnance destroyed, there's only one casualty that matters in any war—and that's a man's own humanity. Because there's no such thing as a prosthetic conscience for when the one you were born with that you've ignored for so long gets blown to hell.

He didn't put it to her quite like that, of course, mildly-disapproving humour leading the way.

'You asked the other day if I'd kept my vows of celibacy. Now you'd like me to violate the confidentiality of the confessional?'

'I was forgetting about that. I suppose it's necessary or people wouldn't tell you the good stuff.'

'*The good stuff?* You mean the stuff that goes on the wall next to the board with the hymn numbers? Sin of the week.'

'Do you have one of those?'

'No, but you could put it in the suggestion box.'

'It might make more people come back to the church.'

'And how about a list of the worst sinners? Like the list of past captains in a golf or cricket club.'

'Now I know you're not being serious. What made you become a priest in the first place?'

He looked back at her as she waited expectantly, considering her, now that the conversation had taken a serious turn.

'Is this you starting chronologically? Or starting easy working towards what you think will be the difficult questions?'

'It's probably the same thing, so, yes. And I don't want you to get indigestion. Not today.'

He finished the last mouthful of the slice of pizza he'd taken, held up his hand at the offer of another.

'It's not very exciting. There were no visions or blinding white lights.'

'Not even any stigmata?'

He showed her his hands, unblemished palms upwards, his voice apologetic.

'Sorry.'

'Let's hear the boring, then.'

He rested his head against the rest, closed his eyes again. The indistinct image of the young woman was still there, captured in negative as if he'd been staring too long at a lightbulb. He pushed it aside, concentrated on his own past.

'At university I was what people like you would call *normal*. Partying, drinking, girls . . .'

She pulled a face of mock horror, as if seeing him in a different light.

'No drugs I hope.'

'Heaven forbid, officer.'

'But you knew people who did.'

'Doesn't everybody? Anyway, one day I woke up with a particularly evil hangover. I was in a strange bed with a girl whose name I couldn't remember snoring beside me. Clothes strewn around the room, the smell of sex coming off the sheets like I could taste it. And I thought, *what's it all about?*' He ignored the sly smile that suggested it sounded good to her, carried on. 'My mother's family are from Belfast. Strict Catholics. That's how I was brought up. I left it behind—'

'When you discovered girls with forgettable names?'

'Exactly. My mother's—'

'What's her name?'

'Siobhan. Her brother Malachy is a priest. He was visiting from Ireland. It was just after they'd signed the Good Friday Agreement. Malachy was a staunch nationalist. A united Ireland and the withdrawal of British troops from the North. It put him somewhat at odds with my father, but that's another story. His personal standpoint aside, he was active behind the scenes during the peace process facilitating meetings between republicans and loyalists. The thing is, Malachy could talk for Ireland. I'm sitting there listening to him talk about it with a stinking hangover, thinking, *will you ever shut up?* Except, by the time he did finally shut up, I knew what I wanted to do with my life.'

'You became a priest because of a hangover?'

He ignored her attempt to trivialise it, carried on as if she hadn't spoken.

'If Uncle Malachy had been a cop, I'd probably have gone straight into the police, skipped the previous ten years. So? How does that compare to stigmata or visions appearing in a blinding white light?'

She scrunched her face, head rocking from side to side as if it was a close call.

'Maybe I'll embellish it a bit when I tell the girls.'

'That's your children, the girls, or the girls'—making air quotes as he said it—'you go out partying with?'

'Both. But embellished in different ways. So—'

He stopped her with a raised hand as he felt her about to move onto more difficult questions.

Why did you go into the Army?

And what made you leave?

Except, once again, it was already too late. The anguish in Cormac's voice subtly distorted, turning to bitter accusation somewhere on its journey from a hell-hole halfway across the globe to his own guilt-ridden mind.

I don't know what to do, Max.

He showed her both of his empty palms.

'I'm not eating anymore, so that's me done.'

'You only had one slice.' Thrusting the box at him as she said it.

He patted the flat expanse that was his stomach, got a roll of her eyes back.

'Whereas you're still eating,' he pointed out.

'What do you want to know?'

He followed suit, started gently.

'Why did you join the police?'

'That's easy. My uncle, same as you. He just happened to be a rising star in the Met.'

'Or you might have become a priest yourself?'

'Who knows? Anyway, that was so easy, you can have another one.'

He was tempted to call it a day there. She'd already told him about the incident that resulted in her demotion. Although he wasn't sure he believed it completely, suspecting that a lot of careful thought had gone into the final version, now wasn't the time to attempt to unravel it. That only really left her family situation.

She was well aware of it, too.

'Go on,' she said, the challenge coming through a mouthful of pizza, 'ask.'

'What went wrong in your marriage?'

She swallowed, took a swig of water. Contemplated another slice, decided against it.

'The usual.'

'Putting the job before your family?'

'Yep. It's even more boring than your story. He wasn't cheating on me or abusing me. Or the girls. It gives him an irritating smugness. I put my career above a good marriage, not even a crappy one. All because some deep-seated personality defect one of his expert friends could charge me thousands of pounds to diagnose meant I was determined to go one better than Chief Superintendent Uncle James.' She raised a finger in a way that suggested the same had been done to her on more than one occasion. 'Who, by the way, managed to stay happily married.'

'I feel like we're moving away from boring now.'

She flipped the lid shut on the remaining slices of pizza, belched politely behind her hand.

'Yep. And now I'm finished eating, too.'

29

'Who's been murdered?' Eric Vale said as soon as he'd answered the door to Gulliver and Jardine's knock.

They were both pleased to see that Vale had changed out of his striped pyjamas that DS Kincade had seen him wearing as he leaned out of his back-bedroom window to see what was going on at Unit C2 in the Solent View Industrial Estate.

'Nobody said anything about a murder, sir,' Jardine said.

Vale gave her a withering look.

'When did you start putting live bodies in a body bag? I saw them carrying it out.'

'That's true, sir, but it's too early to say how he died.'

He waved it off with a dismissive flick of his hand.

'You don't get half of the Hampshire Constabulary out at the crack of sparrow fart for some wino who died in his sleep, or a junkie who did the world a favour and overdosed. Good luck with collecting trace evidence in that shithole.'

Gulliver and Jardine exchanged a knowing look. Should they ever get past the front step and be shown into the living room, they could expect to see the largest television on the market permanently tuned to cop dramas.

Mrs Vale appeared behind her husband at that point.

'Stop talking and invite them in, Eric. Let them do their job.'

'If I stop talking, there's not much point in them coming in, is there? You were fast asleep in bed snoring the house down. Fat lot of use you'd be in court. *I was asleep, your honour.*'

Mrs Vale was approximately one and a half times her husband's size and weight. She extended her meaty arm, pushed him aside as if moving a curtain out of the way.

'Come in, officers.'

She led them through to a sitting room at the back of the house overlooking the rear garden. A low fence separated it from the path crossing the park they were assuming Guy Yardley's killers had used to approach the unit where they killed him.

Mrs Vale offered them the floral sofa occupying pride of place in the room. Sitting side-by-side with Gulliver on it made Jardine feel as if they were about to announce their engagement to his parents.

'If you could talk us through what you saw, Mr Vale,' she said, as a small scruffy dog trotted into the room and immediately started sniffing her shoes.

Vale, who had remained standing, fished in his pocket and came out with a folded piece of paper. Jardine wouldn't have been surprised if he'd pulled out a surplus police-issue notebook that he'd bought on eBay.

He unfolded it, adjusted his glasses on his nose.

'I don't know why you bothered writing it down, Eric,' his wife said. 'You go out for a fag at exactly the same time every night.'

Vale ignored her, cleared his throat.

'It was ten-oh-five p.m. As my wife said when she interrupted—'

'You can't interrupt someone who hasn't started talking yet,'

Mrs Vale said. 'Someone who thinks he's being cross-examined in court in the biggest murder trial of the century.'

Vale gave her a look. *Finished now?*

'I'll make us some tea,' she said, disappearing into the kitchen.

Jardine hoped the dog would go with her. It didn't, still engrossed in sniffing her shoes. It was only a matter of time before it started humping her leg.

'I'd gone outside to have a cigarette,' Vale said. 'I don't like to smoke in the house.'

'I won't let him,' came from the kitchen.

He gave an apologetic smile.

'It's my one vice.' He waited momentarily to see if his wife corrected him—*What do you call pornography on the internet if it isn't a vice?*—then continued when she didn't. 'Sometimes I stand at the bottom of the garden. Chat to neighbours walking their dogs, that sort of thing. But it had been raining. The grass was soaking wet and I was wearing my slippers. So, I stayed by the house—'

'Where I could still smell the smoke coming through the bedroom window.' Mrs Vale from the kitchen again.

'That's when I saw them,' her husband said. 'A man and a young woman.'

'How do you know it was a young woman?' Gulliver cut in. 'Did you see her face?'

'No, they were both wearing hoodies with the hoods up. Like everyone going into that place who's up to no good. Somebody should burn the units this end to the ground. I'd do it for fifty quid if Gandhi paid me.'

'Gandhi?' Gulliver said.

'That's what he calls the owner, Mr Singh,' Mrs Vale said, as she came in carrying four mugs of tea in her large hands. 'He's being racist.' She placed all four mugs on the low coffee table in the middle of the room. Then dug in her pocket, came out with half a dozen sugar packets appropriated from a local cafe.

The scruffy dog watched her doing it. Seeing nothing of interest, it went back to Jardine's legs. As she'd expected, it jumped up, put its front paws on her knees.

'*Scout!* Get down,' Mrs Vale barked.

Scout ignored her.

'How did you know it was a young woman if you didn't see her face?' Gulliver said as Jardine tried to push Scout away.

'I'll explain in a minute,' Vale said. 'But I need to tell you, the man with her had a limp.' He said it as if only one person in the world, or at least in the greater Southampton metropolitan area, had a limp, and as such he'd just solved the crime.

Gulliver didn't need to ask how he knew about the limp, told him to carry on before Vale decided a demonstration was called for.

'It was obvious they were up to no good,' Vale said. 'You get a feel for these things.'

'And the path doesn't go anywhere,' Jardine pointed out still trying to get Scout off her legs.

'No,' Vale conceded. 'Anyway, they climbed over the fence at the end. It's not difficult. It sags in the middle from where so many kids have climbed over. Even so, the man slipped and almost fell. I suppose because he had a bad leg. He swore and she asked him if he was okay, which is how I knew it was a woman.'

'And she had no trouble getting over herself, which is why you think she was young?' Gulliver said.

'No, it wasn't that. Anyway, that's when I decided to take a closer look. It was obvious they weren't winos and they didn't look like junkies, so I thought, they're up to serious mischief.'

What was obvious to both Gulliver and Jardine was that Vale's story was benefitting from a large injection of hindsight.

The reality was that he was a nosy neighbour, and if it moved, he was going to take a closer look at it.

'I didn't go indoors to get some waterproof shoes. My slippers are ruined.'

'Ruined,' Mrs Vale echoed, the first thing she'd said in agreement with her husband.

'There wasn't time,' Vale went on sounding as if the future of the planet had hung in the balance. 'Let's go outside and I'll show you.'

Jardine came out of the chair like Scout had crawled under it and bitten her butt through the cushion. She shook him from her knee, set off for the kitchen where the back door was. The other three trailed after her. She stepped aside to let Vale unlock the door, then they all trooped down the garden.

It was immediately apparent where they were being led. A patch of the lawn looked as if a dozen people had been milling around on it. No doubt Mrs Vale and any of the neighbours who were interested had already been given the tour.

As expected, Vale stopped in the middle of the trampled patch. He looked down at it.

'This is where you were standing, is it?' Gulliver said before Vale had a chance to complain that the lawn was ruined as well.

'That's right.' He pointed to his left, across the neighbouring gardens and towards the industrial estate. Everyone looked. 'You can see the unit where it happened from here. It's lucky Jim from two doors down trimmed his hedge last week or you wouldn't be able to.'

'What's the lighting like at night?' Gulliver asked.

Vale shook his head, disapproval in the gesture.

'There isn't any this end, but there's still enough light to see from the lights further down. This is where things started to get strange. They went to the unit and he lifted the roller shutter halfway up. Then she backed away and took a picture of him bending down to get under it. That's what made me think it was a young woman. Who else but a stupid young person is going to take a photograph of them breaking into a unit where they plan to murder someone?'

Gulliver cut in and wasted his breath.

'We haven't confirmed it was murder.'

'I know they take pictures of everything,' Vale went on, slipping into a well-worn rut. 'Everything they eat. Probably coming out the other end when they go to the toilet. But the murder scene? You should look on Instagram.'

'She definitely took a picture?' Jardine said.

'Definitely. I saw the flash. At least they weren't totally stupid. He had his back to her. He wasn't smiling at the camera. A bit pointless, if you ask me.'

'What happened next?'

'They both went inside and closed the shutter almost all the way to the ground. There wasn't any light leaking out of the gap at the bottom. A little while later, I heard a car drive in from the far end. It stopped halfway down. A man carrying a Tesco carrier bag walked the rest of the way. He looked a bit like a bum. Old coat and trousers. He opened the shutter and went inside, then closed it all the way to the ground.'

'He knew what unit to go to?' Jardine said.

'It looked like it. He was peering at the numbers as if he was looking for a particular unit. At that point, I thought it must be a drug deal.'

'Could you hear anything?'

Vale shook his head looking very disappointed with himself.

'I heard them at the fence, but the unit is too far away. Especially with the shutter down. About five minutes later, the man and woman came out again. She was holding the carrier bag. They started coming back the same way they'd got in. They would've seen me if I stayed where I was, so I hid in the bushes.'

He indicated a large, dense shrub that neither Gulliver nor Jardine could have named. 'They walked past and I heard a car drive away a few minutes later. I crept back down the garden and waited to see if the man who'd come to meet them came out. I assumed he was getting high when he didn't, so I went to bed. You don't want to interrupt some crazy junkie when he's shooting up, risk getting stabbed with a dirty needle. When I saw all the activity this morning, I knew it was a lot worse than I'd thought.'

Bringing it into line with what you'd prayed for, Jardine thought and didn't say.

'I THOUGHT HE WAS GOING TO ASK IF WE NEEDED HIS CIGARETTE butt as evidence,' Jardine said after Eric Vale had reluctantly closed the front door on them, his role as prime witness at an end, at least for now.

'Interesting, though, what he said about the girl taking a photo of her accomplice in front of the unit. What's that all about? I can understand why they'd take one of what they did to Yardley—'

'Can you? I can't.'

'You know what I mean. A reminder. A memento.'

'If you're a certifiable lunatic, yeah. You think that's what we're dealing with here? Or you think they're going to send it to us? Taunting us.'

He shrugged, told her what he really thought.

'You watch too much TV.'

30

'What's the story with those two?' Kincade said, then added quickly, 'Don't look now.'

Gulliver and Jardine both turned immediately, caught Angel looking directly back at them, the pathologist, Isabel Durand, sitting beside him.

They were all in The Wellington Arms, the nearest pub to Southampton Central police station, an unspoken need for a night out together in the wake of the discovery of a second body and the resultant gearing up of the case that went with it. Angel, Kincade, DCI Finch, Gulliver, Jardine, plus the civilians—Durand, a couple of mortuary attendants, the stills photographer and various other hangers-on.

Angel raised his beer towards the three of them staring at him. Amusement on his face like a man who'd come home from work and caught his children playing doctors and nurses in the bathroom. Gulliver and Jardine turned back sheepishly, the look on Kincade's face easy to read.

What part of don't look now don't you understand?

'Nothing as far as I know,' Craig Gulliver said.

Jardine rolled her eyes heavenwards, mimicked her partner.

'*Nothing as far as I know.*' She leaned partially across him to put her body between him and Kincade. 'That's because his head's too far up the boss' arse to see anything.'

Kincade risked a fast glance across at Angel and Durand.

'You're saying there *is* something going on?'

Jardine leaned back, folded her arms across her chest.

'I don't think it's necessary to say anything. All you need is eyes in your head.' Then, hooking her thumb dismissively at Gulliver. 'Without a desire to deliberately close them.'

Kincade stood up. The sudden look of panic on Jardine's face suggested she thought Kincade was about to go across and ask them straight out. She relaxed when Kincade pointed at their empty glasses, then moved away to see who else needed a refill.

'I can't believe you did that,' Gulliver said to Jardine as soon as Kincade was out of earshot.

'What?'

'Tried to start a rumour about the boss and Durand.'

'It has to start somewhere.'

'You don't think that's a little inappropriate given . . . what happened?'

Anger at her own unthinking stupidity washed over her face.

'*Shit.* I forgot all about it. I'll tell Kincade I was only joking.'

'Don't bother. You'll only make it worse.' He pointed surreptitiously at one of the mortuary attendants, an unhealthy-looking young man with lank hair wearing a Motörhead T-shirt. 'I'm going to start one about you and *Keep Moving* to pay you back.'

The nickname was a reference to the young man's complexion—so deathly pale and sickly that his colleagues would have him in the freezer cabinet or on the dissecting table by mistake if he stood still for too long.

Jardine grinned back at him, already recovered from her faux pas.

'Who says it's only a rumour?'

A couple of tables away, Isabel Durand leaned in closer to Angel, dropped her voice.

'They're talking about us over there.'

'I know. Shall I put my hand on your knee or do you want to put yours on mine? Actually, no, I don't think I want your hand on my knee.'

'You don't know where it's been.'

'That's the problem. I know exactly where it's been.'

He could picture it now. Burying itself in Guy Yardley's innards with an unbridled enthusiasm for the visceral onslaught that was an autopsy. The post-mortem had been rushed through late that afternoon. Most of the people who'd attended it were now gathered in The Wellington Arms.

Durand had confirmed her initial unofficial statement regarding the cause of death—asphyxia due to strangulation with thin, flexible wire, most likely guitar or piano—as well as supplying a time of death at between ten and eleven-thirty p.m. the previous night

She'd suggested a long, slim, single-edged blade had been used to cut out Yardley's tongue.

'Something like a fish-filleting knife. Very sharp and used by someone skilled with it. Even somebody proficient couldn't help causing cuts to the lips with a double-edged blade. And they're accustomed to holding slippery things.' She'd taken hold of her tongue and pulled at it, her fingers slipping off to demonstrate the point.

'Someone who works in a fish-processing plant?' Gulliver had suggested.

'That's for you to determine,' she'd said as she fixed one of the attending mortuary assistants with a disapproving glare for sniggering at the words, *accustomed to holding slippery things*.

'Perhaps somebody who performs or assists at autopsies?'

Angel had suggested. 'Pretty well everything you touch is slippery.'

She hadn't bothered to reply to that.

Kincade arrived at their table, putting an end to the question about whose hand should go on whose knee. Durand downed the last of her wine, then got up to go to the bar with Kincade rather than simply hand over her empty glass. Olivia Finch immediately took her place looking very pleased to get away from the stills photographer.

'I'd rather look at autopsy photographs than his holiday snaps,' she said, then flicked her finger at Kincade already deep in conversation with Durand at the bar. 'How are you getting on with Kincade?'

Angel pretended to think about it as he finished his pint.

'She likes her pizza a bit on the hot side for me. But I like her sense of humour. That line about—'

'Me looking good in a protective suit?'

He nodded, that's the one.

'Anything on her skills as a police officer?' she said when he didn't volunteer more.

'She seems very competent from what I've seen.'

Finch shook her head as if wondering why she bothered.

'I'm going to ask to see your holiday snaps in a minute. I won't come away knowing any less about DS Kincade. Anything to give cause for concern?'

'Are you worried Uncle James is watching?' Then, when she didn't immediately pick up on the reference. 'Chief Superintendent James Milne. A big noise in SO15.'

She made a lazy, swatting motion at something unseen by anybody else in the room, her tone equally dismissive.

'I'm not worried about him.'

'You're right. Worried is the wrong word. But it can't hurt to be the senior officer responsible for getting his favourite niece back on track.'

She pulled a face, leaning away from him.

'I hope you're not implying I'm shamelessly pursuing my own career interests.'

'Aren't you?'

She allowed a guilty smile to creep across her face.

'Maybe a little bit. It can't hurt.'

Ask DS Kincade about that, he thought and kept to himself, their conversation about her marital rift in his mind.

THERE WAS A MESSAGE FROM HIS MOTHER WAITING FOR HIM ON HIS landline answering machine when he got home. She never called him on his mobile. She claimed she didn't want to call it and risk it going off at an inappropriate time. It suggested she wasn't a hundred per cent sure about exactly what he did, perhaps thinking he was a spy rather than a policeman.

The start of the message made him smile as it always did.

It's your mother, Max...

As if he got a lot of calls from women with almost incomprehensible Belfast accents.

He guessed she'd want to talk about his recent trip, whether he felt better for it. In his mother's case he could've understood it. Her faith in the glory and the power of the Catholic church would allow her to believe that a visit to a cathedral built on the grave of an apostle—the reputed burial place of Saint James—might result in a miracle for her son.

He put the kettle on before calling her back, got a couple of slices of bread from out of the freezer and stuck them in the toaster. Leonard came through the cat flap at that point carrying a mouse—as if he thought they'd have their late-night snack together. He dropped it on the floor, watched it as it made a dash for the safety of the junk in the corner under the kitchen table, then went after it.

Angel thought about trying to rescue it, as he often did, decided he didn't feel up to grubbing around on his hands and knees under the table. He called his mother back, instead. Her opening words surprised the hell out of him.

'Your father called me. He sounded like he'd had a good drink.'

Angel could believe it. His old man had drunk three pints in the pub, but Angel suspected he'd hit the whiskey—Jameson, most likely—when he got back home. He felt a twinge of guilt at not having stayed the night. He'd have been forced to join him rather than sit and watch him drink alone, staying up late into the night listening to anecdotes he'd heard a thousand times, but at least he could've moderated his old man's alcohol intake.

'Not too much, I hope.'

'He was well on his way. That's the only reason he called. He said you and Grace have been nagging him about going for a blood test. Something about Grace searching the internet for some horrible disease to accuse him of having.'

Ignoring her use of the words *nagging* and *accuse*—verbatim from his father—it made him think. The old man hadn't dismissed it out of hand, despite his protestations. The idea had lodged in his mind sufficiently to make him call his estranged wife about it—admittedly when under the influence of alcohol.

'What did he want you to do?'

He was expecting her to say, tell your children—always hers when something went wrong—to get off my back. He was wrong.

'Nothing. He just wanted to talk. It wasn't like him at all. I think he's scared.'

She was happy saying it to him, but she'd never have said it directly to her husband. He confirmed it, anyway, in case a minor miracle had occurred that he'd missed.

'I'm assuming neither he nor you actually used that word.'

A bark of incredulous laughter hit him in the ear, the only sound harsher than his mother's voice.

'Don't be stupid, Max. It's himself we're talking about. Do you think I should come over?'

Her use of the word *himself* when talking about her husband reinforced just how long she'd been back in Belfast. Coming up for fifteen years. She hadn't visited the mainland in all that time, not after the rift with her husband following their youngest son's death—for which she blamed him.

A visit now would have unwanted consequences for Angel. She wouldn't stay with his father. Too much, too soon. Grace had no room. She'd be looking for an invite to stay with him. He wasn't sure he was up for that, to have her fussing around after him.

It suddenly struck him that was the real reason behind the offer to come over. He avoided the issue.

'Did you run it past Grace?'

'She said to talk to you.'

He tried again.

'What do you think?'

Any minute now and one of them was going to ask Leonard. Probably get the most sense out of him.

'I'm not sure,' she said. Then her voice brightened as if something fortuitous had occurred to her. 'You could probably do with some company around the house.'

He smiled to himself at the confirmation, now out in the open.

'I've got Leonard.'

'Does he do a lot of cooking these days? That's another thing. I don't suppose you're eating properly.'

The toaster went *ping,* ejecting the toast as she said it. He expected to hear a triumphant, *ha! I knew it.*

'I thought you called because you're concerned about Dad, not me.'

'Don't change the subject, Max.'

'Talking of eating, Leonard's just decapitated a mouse he brought in.'

The sharp intake of breath that came down the line told him it had done the trick. His mother hated cats for that very reason —the complete or partially-eaten remains of rodents they left lying around the house. He made doubly sure.

'I hope I don't find what's left of it in the spare bed like last time. I got the blood out of the sheets, but it soaked into the mattress.'

'I don't believe you, Max. And I don't know what the world's coming to when a failed priest lies to his own mother.'

But she didn't say any more about coming to stay.

31

'It's got to be the same woman,' DCI Finch said after Angel finished relaying what Yardley's secretary had told them about the phone call from the woman who refused to identify herself. 'Do we know anything about her?'

'Yardley's secretary got the impression of a young woman,' Angel said. 'That tallies with what the witness who saw them enter and leave the scene said.' He rocked his hand. 'At the end of the day, all it amounts to is one impression based on tone of voice, and one prejudiced opinion based on a disapproval of young people's obsession with their mobile phones.'

'You can put me in that category,' Kincade said, a sour edge to her voice.

Whilst not adding anything to the discussion, Angel and Finch took something away from it—the complaint against Kincade for using excessive force during an arrest was likely to have been backed up by phone camera video footage supplied by the plaintiff's friends.

'Anything on the man?' Finch said, addressing the room in general.

'He's got a limp,' Jardine offered. 'Could be grounds for

bearing a grudge. Except it's a hell of a grudge to garrotte a man and cut out his tongue over a gammy leg caused by playing football when they were kids.'

Everybody in the room knew worse had been done for a lot less. And would be done for less still in a race to the bottom of mindless violence.

'Isabel?' Finch said.

Durand smiled, her words riding out on the back of it.

'I'm assuming you're not asking whether I'd do that to somebody who broke my leg?' She waited until the laughter had subsided, then continued. 'A long, slim, single-edged blade . . .'

Angel tuned out what he already knew, thinking about his conversation with his mother the previous evening. About what he hadn't told her—or his sister.

That his father had stumbled on the way home. He'd laughed it off. *Pissed again.* Pointed at a bump in the pavement that only he could see. Angel had laughed with him, joined in. *Not like in the good old days, eh?*

He'd spent a while on the NHS website when he got home, reading up on Huntington's disease. Balance problems were listed under the later symptoms section, not early symptoms. But everyone was different.

He'd said nothing. Avoided setting his sister on his old man like a hungry wolf going at a sheep, or have his mother crossing the Irish Sea. At least until they'd managed to get him to submit to a blood test—and one that came back positive.

Then another thought hijacked him. If his father had it, there was a fifty per cent chance he did, too. And Grace. They could have a blood test themselves. It would only prove it one way—the worst-case way—but it was something to consider. He'd keep that to himself for now, too.

Was that him wanting to stick his own head in the sand?

He was dragged back into the conversation by Finch asking him a direct question.

'Anything else, Max?'

'I think the ten thousand Yardley drew in cash and took with him was a ploy to lure him there. It can't have been a first instalment because they killed him.'

'Unless he told them, *that's all you're getting, now piss off*,' Kincade suggested.

'Did he strike you as that sort of a man when we interviewed him?'

She took a moment to think back to the meeting, her response unequivocal.

'Definitely not.'

'Then there's the change in M.O. Roy Lynch was made to look like a suicide. There was no attempt to disguise Yardley's murder whatsoever. They actually made a statement by cutting out his tongue. That implies they were worried that if Yardley thought Roy Lynch had been murdered, they wouldn't have been able to lure him to that industrial unit so easily. I also think the choice of that particular industrial estate is significant. Admittedly, it seems to be purpose-made for what they planned to do. Unused, unlit, no CCTV. But I think there's more.'

'Go on,' Finch said, elbows resting on her desk now.

'The car's satnav log doesn't show the journey from his house to the industrial estate.'

'Suggesting he already knew it. Could be that's where he started out before he became successful.'

'Exactly. We'll be talking to the owner of the estate, Mr Singh. See how far back his records go. Gavin Lynch also made a remark that sounded off when we told him where Yardley had been killed.'

'*Why on earth would he go there?*' Kincade quoted. 'As if he knew of a very good reason why he shouldn't.'

Finch took it upon herself to state the obvious once again.

'Be nice to know what that reason is.'

They were interrupted by a knock on Finch's open door. Moira Burrell, the Family Liaison Officer who had been left with Yardley's widow came into the room, then stood off to the side waiting to be invited to speak.

'It would,' Angel agreed. 'The trouble is, Yardley himself was determined to make it difficult. His secretary told us he received an email that spooked him shortly before he took the call from the woman. We checked his computer while we were there. It had been deleted. We thought there would be a copy on the company mail server which forensics would find...'

Finch's brow creased at his tone.

'And there wasn't?'

'No. They called the company IT department—'

'It's only one guy,' Kincade said.

'—and he confirmed that Yardley had full access to the server and must have deleted it himself. He'd been responsible for all the company IT before it got too big and he had to employ a dedicated IT professional. But he still had access and knew enough to go in and delete an email. Whatever it contained, he really, *really* wanted to keep it quiet.'

'The fact that his tongue was cut out suggests he didn't keep quiet enough about something,' Jardine said drily.

The comment was off-the-cuff and flippant, but it made everybody think, nonetheless. Moira Burrell tried to take advantage of the temporary lull, addressing Finch.

'If I could have a quick word, ma'am.'

Finch held up a finger. *In a minute.* Went back to Angel.

'I'm hoping I'm getting a best-to-last feeling here, Max.'

'Gavin Lynch,' he said.

'That's what I want to talk about,' Burrell said.

Finch showed her the *wait a minute* finger a second time, looking at Angel as she did so.

'What about him?'

'Roy Lynch's wife, Marianne, was his step-mother. His own mother is still alive, so there's potential for trouble there. He also lied to us when we spoke to him. Twice. He said he didn't know that his father tried to trace the young woman who visited his wife in the hospice. And he claimed the industrial estate meant nothing to him. He clearly knew its significance to Yardley.'

'And? I get the feeling there's more.'

'Mrs Yardley can't stand him. He might be out on his ear very soon.'

'I doubt it.'

The comment took everyone by surprise. It came from Moira Burrell, looking very uncomfortable as all eyes swivelled towards her.

'That's what I've been trying to say. Mrs Yardley got very upset last night. Not because she's missing her husband. I don't think she misses him at all. It was all, woe is me, what am I going to do? I said to her, what are you talking about? You can sell the company, go anywhere you like with millions in the bank. That's when she said—'

'I don't own the company.' This from Angel.

'Exactly, sir. She gets the house and Bentley and everything, but her husband left the company to Gavin Lynch.'

32

'Congratulations!' Angel said, his smile as insincere as the sentiment. 'I understand you're now the proud owner of Yardarm Marine Technology.'

Gavin Lynch stared back at him without responding, the scowl on his face eloquent enough.

They were in interview room number one, the room outside which Kincade had facetiously remarked should be changed to *confessional number one* when Angel was using it. Although they were a long way from charging him with anything, they'd decided their home turf would concentrate his mind.

'What I don't understand,' Angel went on, 'is why you didn't say anything when we spoke yesterday. I distinctly remember saying, *nobody knows what's going to happen with the company now that Mrs Yardley owns it*. And yet you said nothing.'

Kincade raised her hand to interrupt.

'You also said, *maybe she'll run it herself with you in charge, or maybe she'll sell it*.'

Angel nodded his thanks.

'Two chances to put me straight. Don't take this the wrong way, Mr Lynch, but I get the impression that you're the sort of man who'd jump at the opportunity to put a nosy copper like me straight. Put me in my place.'

Kincade tapped her chest as she joined in.

'I get the impression you're the sort of man who wouldn't ever pass on the opportunity to blow his own trumpet, either. *Look at me, Johnny Big Bollocks.*'

'Or were you unaware that Mr Yardley had left the company to you at that point?' Angel said. Then, when Gavin didn't respond, 'That's an actual question, Mr Lynch. It's not rhetorical.'

Gavin shifted on his chair, crossed his arms.

'I knew. And if you're seriously wondering why I didn't say anything, you're more stupid than I thought.' He swept his arm in a wide arc, took in the interview room as well as them sitting in front of him. 'I knew it would get your juices going and we'd end up in this discussion. I was hoping you might have made some progress before we did.'

'Fair enough,' Angel said. 'How long have you known?'

'Since I first went to work there. So, if you're thinking I killed Guy to get my hands on the company, I waited a bloody long time to do it.'

'Maybe the opportunity never presented itself before.'

'Or maybe you recognised that Mr Yardley was a better businessman than you,' Kincade said. 'And you decided to let him grow it until it was really successful before you got rid of him.'

'And maybe you two are talking out your arses,' Gavin said.

'Maybe we are,' Angel agreed, 'but we need to explore all the possibilities. Why did he leave it to you?'

Gavin's mouth twitched as if he'd been about to say, *you'd have to ask him.* He decided against it, kept it simple.

'No idea.'

Angel and Kincade shared an incredulous look. Then Angel

started them on what looked like being a long road to understanding and maybe the truth.

'You're telling us that on your first day when most new employees are being shown where the toilets and the coffee machine are, the big boss showed you around and said, *one day all of this will be yours*, and you just said, *okay, thanks*. You didn't ask why? That's also an actual question.'

'No, I didn't think that because it didn't happen like that.'

Angel smiled like now it was all falling into place.

'Everybody just knew that's the way it was. Is that it?'

'By osmosis?' Kincade suggested.

They both knew exactly why, but they were going to make him say it. It was all part of the same deal between Yardley and Gavin's father, Roy, which had resulted in him being employed in the first place. It also explained Irene Yardley's animosity towards Gavin. It had nothing to do with thinking he didn't do anything to earn his big salary. It was resentment that he would one day own the company and she wouldn't. It raised the question of why she hadn't mentioned it when they spoke to her, but that was for another time.

Gavin was very reluctant to answer. He wasn't stupid. He knew that whatever he said, it would only result in more awkward questions as he dug himself ever deeper into a hole.

'I don't know why. The deal was arranged by my old man.'

'Sounds as if he had a hell of a hold over Mr Yardley,' Angel said. 'Not only did he force Yardley to employ you, he made him sign the business over to you. I bet Guy Yardley had a few sleepless nights over the years.'

'Probably crapped himself every time he heard a cat outside in the bushes late at night,' Kincade added. 'But that's by the by. We're back to you, Mr Lynch, the man who never asks any questions. Because I'm assuming you're about to tell us that you never asked your father about why the deal was put in place.

You just thought, *thanks, Dad*. I'd do the same for my kids if I could, but I'd expect them to ask a ton of questions.'

They both saw what went through Gavin's mind. At their last meeting he'd asked them both if they had children, and they'd both said, *no*. He had the sense not to mention it now, to score petty points when he was so far on the back foot.

'I asked him,' Gavin said eventually. 'He said it was complicated.'

Angel gave him a head-cocked look.

'And your own father thought you weren't up to understanding it? Even though he was happy to strike a deal with Yardley that would ultimately put you in charge of a multi-million-pound company.'

Kincade had an answer for that even if Gavin didn't.

'Maybe he thought Mr Lynch here would've matured by the time the company came to him, sir.'

Except it put a crease in Angel's brow rather than clarifying matters. He turned to Kincade as if Gavin wasn't there.

'But surely when that happened and Mr Lynch had reached his full potential, they'd have had that discussion?'

They both looked at him.

Did you?

Gavin was looking as if he couldn't decide which one of them to launch himself over the table at first, the muscles along his jaw tensing.

'He said I didn't need to know.'

Angel nodded like now he really did get it.

'And your father was something of a Victorian-era patriarch. What he said was gospel, and no arguing. In his mind you'd be twelve years old until the day he died. My own father's a bit like that, but I think that was his Army service. Your father wasn't in the Army, was he?' He held up his hand. 'You don't have to answer that one if you don't want to.'

Kincade leaned across the table, confusion on her face and in her voice.

'Weren't you even curious?'

'You don't look a gift horse in the mouth.'

She leaned back again, her tone now resigned.

'A cliché to the rescue.'

'Are we done here?' Gavin said, pushing his chair back an inch.

Angel pulled his in an inch closer.

'Not quite. We need to ask you about your movements on the night Mr Yardley was murdered.'

'I already told you. I was at home watching TV with my wife.'

'Do you remember what you watched?'

Gavin laughed without any humour in it.

'I hope not. When I say we watched TV together, what I mean is we sit in front of it together. To spend some time together. We watch whatever she wants to watch. Complete crap most of the time. I tune it out. Let it wash over me as I think about other things.'

Angel got a sudden premonition that Kincade was about to go on the attack. Ask whether those other things included his supposed work colleague, Samantha, that he'd spent the night with on the night his father was killed. He headed her off.

'And what about specifically between ten and eleven p.m.? Were you still together in front of the TV at that point? Your wife didn't go to bed early?'

Gavin's lips arranged themselves into what might pass for a smile.

'Actually, I was the one who went to bed early that night. I was shattered. I've had a stressful few days.' His tone making it very clear he laid a lot of the blame for that at their door.

Angel cleared his throat, kept his voice emotionless as he asked his next question.

'Do you sleep in the same bed as your wife? You don't have separate bedrooms?'

Kincade was too quick for him this time, interrupting before Gavin answered.

'Given that you're having an affair with one of your work colleagues?'

Gavin had definitely made up his mind now. If he launched himself across the table, it would be Kincade's neck his outstretched hands were aiming for. Despite that, he did a good job of keeping the emotion out of his own voice.

'Yes, we share a bed. I'm sure that when you ask her, my wife will confirm that I was already fast asleep by the time she came to bed. I'm afraid I have no idea what time that was.' He'd addressed them both, but now he concentrated on Kincade. 'And I'd appreciate it if you don't repeat any of your snide remarks in front of her.'

Kincade gave him a cheery smile.

'I'll do my best, sir. Especially now that you're worth so much more than you were a couple of days ago. I'd hate to think what the divorce settlement would be.'

'WHAT'S THE VERDICT?' OLIVIA FINCH SAID ONCE ANGEL AND Kincade were back in her office.

Angel was helping himself to coffee from Finch's private machine. He extended his other hand towards Kincade.

'One big fat lie, and one brush with the truth. I believe his alibi even before we talk to his wife. It's got the ring of truth about it. But he's not stupid. If he's behind it, he wouldn't have done it himself.'

'And the definite lie?'

'Pretending he doesn't know what the deal was between Yardley and his old man. No way would he have put up with his old man saying, *I'm not telling you* all his life.'

Finch looked at Angel.

'Max?'

'I agree. We don't know if he's behind it, but looking into the company background is the way to go. And if he is behind it, we need to find a link between him and the couple who actually killed Yardley.'

Finch put into words what they all knew.

'It's not going to be as easy as waiting to see if he transfers a chunk of his newly-acquired shares to a pair of strangers, or makes a Yardley-style cash withdrawal.'

Everybody smiled, *wouldn't that be nice.*

'Something we seem to be forgetting,' Angel said. 'If he's behind Yardley's murder, it's too much of a coincidence to think that he isn't also responsible for his father's death.'

His words had a sobering effect on them all.

They'd be dealing with a very different kind of monster if that were the case.

33

The very different kind of monster was not having a good day. It was bad enough being summoned to the police station to attend a grilling over the ownership of the company.

Things only got worse once he got back.

He'd run the gauntlet of Yardley's secretary's disapproval and was lounging on one of the leather sofas in what was now *his* office, when his phone pinged as a text came in.

He thought about ignoring it. He had a list as long as his arm of people he didn't want to have to deal with in the aftermath of his interview.

The condescending female detective's parting taunt had really hit home.

I'd hate to think what the divorce settlement would be.

Worse, she'd known it, had enjoyed the effect it had on him.

A shudder rippled through him at the thought of some man-hating bitch of a lawyer encouraging his grasping cow of a wife to go after half of everything, the company included. And some arrogant old fart of a judge—also a man-hating bitch, but older—actually giving it to her on a plate. Like Janis had ever done anything other than sit on her fat arse in over-priced spa hotels getting pissed on prosecco with her friends, all of them in a competition to see who could blow through their husbands' money the fastest.

Janis won that one hands down every time.

A difficult conversation with Samantha also lay ahead. Yes, he remembered how he'd promised that they would take things to the next step very soon. But after the recent development, what they should actually be doing right now is backing off. Just thinking about her reaction gave him a shrivelling feeling below the belt line.

The text that had just arrived might well be from her.

Despite all of his concerns, he couldn't ignore it.

Which is when he discovered that it doesn't matter how bad you think things already are, they can always get worse. In fact, substitute *will* for *can*.

The text was short and to the point.

I know who killed Yardley.

There was an image attached. He wasn't sure he wanted to look, made himself do so all the same.

It wasn't as bad as he'd expected.

It showed a man in a dark hoodie, his face turned away from the camera, ducking under the roller shutter of the unit where Guy Yardley had been killed.

Gavin was sitting staring at the image, his mind a temporary blank, when his phone pinged again. This time he couldn't open it fast enough.

I've got another shot of him coming out afterwards. I'll be in touch to let you know what I want for it.

He pocketed the phone, slipped further down into the sofa as his mind tried to make sense of it all. A minute later, he pulled it out again, tried calling the number that had texted him. The phone was switched off. His fingers tightened around his own phone, wanting to throw it at the floor-to-ceiling windows in his shiny new office.

He forced himself to relax. Closed his eyes and concentrated on letting the tension in his neck and shoulders melt away. There was no point in getting angry, winding himself up to fever pitch while he waited. That was how mistakes were made. Like when he told the cops he'd find out who'd killed his father even if they couldn't.

Stupid.

Like breaking Phil Brent's finger. That was stupid, too. He wasn't going to do it a third time.

He pushed himself up out of the too-soft sofa, went to sit behind his expansive new desk. He couldn't blame the cops for thinking he might have killed Yardley to get control of it all. At times he wondered why he hadn't.

Then he thought things through.

How was the person sending the photograph supposed to have got hold of it? A nosy neighbour who happened to be looking out of their window at that exact moment? And with their camera in their hand to catch the guy in the three seconds it took him to duck under the roller shutter? Even if they did, how did they know it was Yardley who'd been killed? Or that he, Gavin, would be interested in his killer's identity?

Everything pointed to the killer having taken it himself, or with the help of an accomplice. And the purpose? To lure him somewhere as they'd lured that idiot Yardley.

Because he knew now what linked the two murders. And why they were hoping to make it three.

His fingers itched, he felt like texting back so badly.

Hello, Matt. How are you, you sorry sad loser?

Except that would be the most stupid thing of all.

No, he'd play along. Let them believe he was as stupid as they clearly were. That they'd got him well and truly hooked.

Only it would have a very different outcome to the one they had in mind.

He pulled out his phone, not to call them back in his irrational knee-jerk panic of a minute ago, but to call a man he knew. A man who would bring his own brand of psychotic sunshine into what little remained of their sorry lives.

And by the time he'd finished the call to Milan Broz five minutes later, he was feeling very differently about his afternoon. Looking forward to them making contact.

In the meantime, there was one more thing he wanted to do to make absolutely sure.

Half an hour later, he let himself into his father's house. It was the first time he'd been inside since the old man died. He went directly to the kitchen and through into the garage, making a mental note to get somebody in to repair the broken door frame.

The rope his father had supposedly used to hang himself was gone, obviously. To be analysed by the cops' forensic nerds. Identify what brand it was and then start trying to contact every Amazon customer in southern England who'd bought a clothesline recently. Good luck with that. He almost felt sorry for them. All they had to do was ask him and he could give them a name—although to be fair, he might have changed it.

Except even if they did ask, *could* give wasn't the same as *would* give.

He stood in the middle of the garage, fists bunching and un-bunching at his sides as he thought of the little shit. How he wouldn't have had a hope of getting the better of Roy Lynch back in the day when his old man was someone to be reckoned with. As Gavin liked to think of himself now—and as the little shit would soon find out the very hard way.

He stood for a minute longer enjoying the thought, then left the garage, went upstairs and into the attic. The old man had cleared out a lot of the junk that had been there the last time Gavin looked, but not the boxes and boxes of old classic car magazines. His father had always planned to have them bound, then proudly display them in what he liked to call his study, and which in a smaller house would be called a home office.

He shifted thirty years' worth of dusty boxes, found the year 1993 right at the back. Then spent ten minutes leafing through the magazines inside feeling strangely nostalgic. It wasn't an emotion he often suffered from. Nor did it last long now. A seething anger came next, quickly followed by excited anticipation at what was to come—a thrill in the gut that rivalled the feelings he'd experienced as a boy flicking through these same magazines, imagining himself behind the wheel of the cars featured.

He found what he was after tucked inside the July 1993 issue of *Classic Car Magazine*. He knew how his father's mind worked. He'd been unable to throw away the clipping from the newspaper, carefully concealing it between the pages of the magazine, instead. Gavin had discovered it there years ago. He'd never forgotten. It had been something of an *aha* moment concerning his dear old dad. Not the sort of thing easily forgotten.

A stupid man might have taken a photograph of the yellowing cutting on his phone, but Gavin was done with being stupid. He only wanted to check the dates, make sure his memory wasn't playing tricks on him.

It wasn't.

The headline was as he'd remembered it.

Local businessman Lucas Cameron commits suicide.

And so was the date. Thirty years to the day before his father had been strung up from a rafter in his garage two floors below where Gavin now stood, a faded newspaper clipping in his tightly-clenched hands.

In that same garage, as the newspaper article pointed out. A sad story of a man at the end of his tether. A man who felt as if there was no hope ahead in the face of the impact of the 1992 economic downturn on his once-profitable business, Cameron Marine Engineering Ltd. A despairing man who believed he would no longer be able to provide for the family he now left behind—a grieving widow and two teenage children, a boy and a girl.

It almost brought a tear to Gavin's eye.

Almost.

He put everything back where he'd found it, except for the dust, of course, and the newspaper clipping that he planned to burn later. He couldn't help wondering as he put the boxes back —*who was the message for?* The same location, the thirty-year anniversary of the date. Was it for him? Except that didn't make sense in advance of the pathetic attempt to lure him to a similar fate.

He'd be sure to ask the little shit when they met.

He pulled out his phone, checked for a signal and the battery level. He didn't want to miss the call or text when it came.

34

GIVEN GAVIN LYNCH'S PROMOTION TO NOT ONLY OWNER OF Yardarm Marine Technology but also to person of increased interest, a discussion with his natural mother, Dawn Howard, had moved up the list. Gulliver and Jardine had been duly despatched to Fareham, a little under twenty miles away, whilst Angel and Kincade were re-interviewing Gavin himself.

Dawn Howard lived in an uninspiring terraced house with uPVC double-glazed windows and front door, as different from the elegant country house her ex-husband had lived in as night and day.

The door was opened by a slim man in his late twenties, his long blond hair tied in a ponytail. Gulliver and Jardine couldn't help looking down at his feet. Clean-shaven and looking as if he didn't yet need to, it would be possible for him to be mistaken for a young woman by a confused old lady dying of cancer in a hospice. Like the second person in the industrial unit where Guy Yardley was murdered, the shoes sticking out of his faded jeans were Dr Martens—although a lot bigger than a size five.

'We're looking for Dawn Howard,' Jardine said, holding out

her warrant card. 'I'm DC Jardine and this is DC Gulliver. And who might you be?'

'Her son, Nick. I live here with her.'

Making you Gavin Lynch's half-brother, Gulliver thought knowing the same was going through Jardine's mind.

'What do you want with her?' Nick said, leaning against the door frame, his arms crossed.

Jardine gave him a smile that Gulliver knew well.

Just go and get her, sonny.

'To discuss a number of matters with her.'

If Nick Howard hadn't already crossed his arms, he'd have done so now.

'Unless you've got a warrant, which I doubt, you're not coming in until you tell me what it's about.'

Gulliver and Jardine exchanged their *too many TV cop dramas* look, then Jardine took the lead.

'Her ex-husband, Roy Lynch, is dead.'

'Yeah? Good riddance.'

If they hadn't already checked out his shoes, they'd have done so now.

'Why do you say that?' Jardine said.

'Because he was a piece of shit.'

They couldn't argue with that, although it didn't move them forward.

'Anything specific?' she said.

'Because of how he treated my mum.' He glanced behind him briefly at the empty hallway. 'She tried to kill herself when he left and took the kids. He did her a favour by taking them, if you ask me.'

Although no-one had, she did so now.

'Why's that?'

The question earned her a pitying look, the contempt also in his voice.

'You're saying you don't know?'

'Know what, sir?'

He took a deep breath, let it out through his nose. As if this really was becoming tiresome, telling them what they should already know, what the taxpayer paid them to know.

'Gavin Lynch is a drug dealer.'

'How do you know that? Do you buy drugs from him?'

'No. Because he's my half-brother, God help me. He's also my mum's son and I don't want anything he does coming back to bite her. I make it my business to know what he's up to.'

The sentiment was admirable, and in other circumstances they would have applauded it. But the reference to business, even though in a different context, prompted a question from Gulliver.

'What do you do for a living, sir?'

Both holding their breath. Just like they'd both be watching him walk if they ever got past the front door, see if he had a limp.

'Self-employed delivery driver.' He looked past them, pointed to a white Ford Transit that had seen better days. 'That's my van. Today's my day off.'

It looked as if they weren't moving off the front step for the moment. Might as well throw out a few questions, Jardine thought.

'When was the last time you saw Gavin, sir?'

Nick didn't even bother making a pretence of trying to remember.

'No idea. I make sure I'm out when he visits mum.'

'He can't be all bad if he still visits his mum.'

The look on Nick's face said it all. *And you're the people charged with preventing crime in this country?*

'Don't kid yourself. It's only when she calls him. And that's only when she wants something. If she's short of cash.' He left an exaggerated pause. 'Or anything else.'

If he was hoping to see a reaction at the implication that Gavin supplied his own mother with a few ounces of marijuana, he was disappointed.

'Did you ever meet Roy Lynch?' Jardine said.

Nick's nose wrinkled as if he'd been the one to find him dead after a week in the hot sun.

'Why would I?'

'How about to tell him personally that he's a piece of shit?'

'What? And have him set Gavin and his mates on me? He knows some seriously scary people. But I might go and piss on his grave if they allow him to be buried in a graveyard.'

It was evident that apart from watching how he walked, they weren't going to get anything useful out of Nick Howard.

'Do you mind if we have a word with your mother now?' Gulliver said.

Nick wanted to say *yes, he did mind* but couldn't think how to do it. He glanced at his watch, then led them into a sitting room on the left.

'Wait there. I'll get her.' He went to the bottom of the stairs and yelled. '*Mum!* Someone to see you.'

Gulliver and Jardine were both aware of what Gavin Lynch had told Angel about his mother—that she wasn't quite with it. It presumably explained Nick's easy, two-stage approach to letting his mother know the police wanted to talk to her. *Someone* would change to *the police* once she'd descended from the safety of her room.

But if they were expecting a wizened seventy-year-old woman to come shuffling down in her carpet slippers and hair curlers, they were mistaken.

Dawn Howard looked ten years younger than she was likely to be. On the wrong side of seventy, her heyday would have been in the mid-to-late sixties. It was clear she didn't ever want to leave them behind. She wore her long grey hair tied back in a ponytail similar to her son's in everything but colour, jangling as she came down the stairs under the weight of the silver and turquoise jewellery she wore. Jardine had never been, but she guessed the Glastonbury festival was full of similar-looking women, their numbers decreasing year on year since the first one held at Worthy Farm in 1970.

Dawn gave her son a disapproving look as she came into the room carrying a hand-rolled cigarette that was cloyingly sweet in the small room.

'If you'd said *cops* and not *someone,* I'd have put this out first.' She took one last drag, pinched the end and put the butt in her pocket. 'What can I do for you, detectives?'

'The arsehole's dead,' Nick said before either Gulliver or Jardine could put it more delicately.

It made no difference. She continued to look at them with as much emotion as if she'd been told the neighbour's cat had just killed her pet hamster.

'How?'

'Something painful, I hope.' This from Nick.

'Suicide,' Gulliver said.

Dawn shook her head.

'No way. Not Roy.' She narrowed her eyes at them. 'You know that anyway.'

Whether it was the promise of an interesting conversation to come, or a sudden awareness of the awkwardness of the four of them still standing up, she flicked her head at the kitchen.

'Make us all a cup of tea, will you, Nick?'

Her son didn't look happy to be excluded, but left the room all the same—without any sign of a limp, both Gulliver and Jardine noted.

'Ordinary tea for me,' Jardine called after him.

'What's Roy's death got to do with me?' Dawn said. 'I know

you aren't here to notify me. You don't think I had anything to do with it, do you? Or Nick?'

'Not at all,' Gulliver said in his best two-faced tone. 'We're trying to gather some background information.'

Dawn smiled, her teeth surprisingly good considering the substance abuse she'd most likely subjected her body to, a fact that she would shortly confirm.

'Gavin not being very talkative?' She didn't wait for them to confirm it. 'Too much of his father in him.'

'He was still a child at the time we're interested in,' Gulliver said, neatly avoiding the question.

Dawn raised a henna eyebrow at that.

'You're going back a long way.'

'To around the time you split up with your husband, yes.'

'My *first* husband,' Dawn corrected, managing to make it sound like *first mistake*. She glanced at a framed photograph of her standing with a man who clearly wasn't Roy Lynch. Gulliver and Jardine looked with her. 'My second husband, Alex, died two years ago. Heart attack.'

'Could you talk us through the circumstances of the break-up?' Jardine said, drawing Dawn's eyes back from the photograph.

'That's easy,' she said. 'I was a mess. An addict. That's how Roy got custody of the boys. Didn't matter that the reason I was an addict was because I was married to the man who supplied the drugs. That's harder to prove, of course.' There was an edge of bitterness to the words. And accusation, too, levelled at them.

You people like it easy.

Nick came back into the room—again, no sign of a limp—carrying a tray loaded with two cups of what Jardine had called *normal* tea, plus a mug that smelled of blackcurrant with the bag still in it, as well as one that smelled of apple and cinnamon. Secretly, Gulliver wished it was for him.

'Anyway,' Dawn said, 'Roy left me and took the boys, moved in with her.' Making *her* sound like the antichrist.

Something about the way she phrased it made Jardine question it further.

'Are you saying the house belonged to the woman he moved in with?'

'Yeah. Great big house. I've never seen it, obviously, but Gavin's mentioned it. Before he learned that I didn't want to hear anything about it.'

'Do you know anything else about . . .' Jardine hesitated, decided she couldn't continue talking about *the woman* even if Dawn couldn't bring herself to use her name. 'About Marianne.'

Dawn shook her head, took a sip of blackcurrant tea.

'No. When Roy left me, I didn't know what day it was. I was probably more upset that I'd lost my supply than my kids. After I got clean, I didn't want to know. I was advised that I'd be wasting my time and money if I tried to get the boys back. I was a recovering addict. I suffered from depression. And I tried to kill myself. Forget it.' She glanced at the photograph on the display cabinet again. 'Then I met Alex and started a new family. Never looked back. I'm afraid I can't see anything in any of that that's going to help you identify who killed him.'

'How well did you know Guy Yardley?' Jardine said.

'Not at all. I only ever met him once. We went out on his yacht.'

'I didn't know he had one.'

Dawn waved the remark away with a jangling flick of her hand.

'It wasn't anything fancy. No more than two people could sleep on it. The only reason I remember is because that's where I spent the whole trip. I was sick as a dog the whole time.' She smiled, a soft, self-deprecating gesture. 'And it wasn't anything to do with the sea being rough.' She put an imaginary joint to her mouth, pulled it away again. 'I was never invited again. I think Guy nearly got thrown out of the yacht club. They were all a bunch of stuck-up twats. Rear Admiral Pugwash and Roger the cabin boy. It was right at the end of me and Roy, anyway. Why do you ask about him?'

'You're aware that Gavin works for him?'

Nick couldn't resist interrupting.

'When he's not busy with his other job.' Making quotes in the air as he said the word *job*.

Dawn ignored him, concentrated on Jardine.

'Yes, I know he works for him.'

'Actually, he works for himself now. Mr Yardley was murdered recently and he left the company to Gavin.'

'Bastard,' Nick hissed. 'I bet he killed him.'

Again, Dawn ignored him, looking from Jardine to Gulliver and back again.

'Is that what you think? Is that what you've been leading up to by asking questions about the past?'

Jardine shook her head solemnly.

'Absolutely not. I can't deny that we have to consider the possibility of Gavin being involved, but our focus here today was most definitely on the past. To be honest, there are a lot of other people we would talk to first about recent events. Our investigations so far suggest that there was some kind of agreement between Mr Yardley and your first husband that resulted in Mr Yardley leaving the company to Gavin.'

'Well if there was, I never knew anything about it. I was a junkie. And one who was about to be shown the door. I didn't get invited into the boardroom. I'm afraid you've had a wasted trip if that's what you were after.'

'Do you know if your husband did anything for Mr Yardley that might have made Yardley feel he owed your husband?'

Dawn laughed out loud at that, then took another sip of blackcurrant tea.

'Apart from supplying him with weed, you mean? No, I can't think of anything. But as I said, I didn't know what day of the week it was back then. They could've murdered someone together in our bed and I wouldn't have noticed the bloodstains.'

Both Gulliver and Jardine smiled politely at the colourful example. It was time to call it a day. Before they did, Gulliver had one last question.

'Did Gavin mention that your ex-husband's second wife died a few months ago?'

Everybody expected Nick to interject with another comment about how he hoped it had been slow and painful. For once he surprised them by keeping silent.

'He didn't mention it, no,' Dawn said, sounding as if her life was in no way diminished by the lack of that information.

'Lung cancer,' Gulliver said aware of Jardine watching Dawn as closely as he was as he explained further. 'She died in St. Joseph's Hospice.'

'Really? What a coincidence. A friend of mine's sister works there. She's not a nun, of course.'

'It's a nice place, ignoring why people are in there, that is. Have you ever been?'

Dawn shook her head, regret at never having found the time.

'No, never.' She patted her pocket where the butt of her joint was waiting for her. 'Maybe I will one day if I don't give these up. Wouldn't that be a coincidence. Both of Roy's wives dying in the same place.'

As everyone would soon find out, there were a lot bigger coincidences hiding around the corner.

35

'THERE'S SOMEBODY HERE TO SEE YOU, SIR,' LISA JARDINE SAID, leaning around the door frame to Angel and Kincade's office. 'Somebody who's too important to speak to anyone below the rank of inspector. Roy Lynch's neighbour. The one who was away on a six-week cruise. I get the impression he was the one actually giving the orders on the bridge. He's just not wearing his captain's hat today.'

Angel pushed back in his chair, thankful for the interruption. It was unlikely to be of any use, since the neighbour had been on the other side of the world when Lynch was killed and during the weeks leading up to it. But you never knew.

Like everyone else connected to the case, Nigel Ambrose was in his mid-sixties. He was very well-preserved, wearing a short-sleeved linen shirt and pale-blue fitted shorts to show off his recently and expensively-acquired tan, scuffed boat shoes without socks on his feet.

Angel shook hands and introduced himself, couldn't help but notice that his hand was as tanned as Ambrose's from his own six-week holiday.

'Are you the SIO?' Ambrose said, proving that, patron of expensive six-week cruises or not, he liked a cop drama on the TV as much as the next man.

'I am. What can I do for you, Mr Ambrose?'

'I'm Roy Lynch's neighbour. I thought you'd want to talk to me.'

Angel extended his hand to lead the way to the nearest available interview room rather than let him down in front of everyone in reception.

'We would have, if you hadn't been on the other side of the world at the time of Mr Lynch's death. And for the preceding five weeks. Unless there's anything you can tell us about the period before that, of course.'

Ambrose made a show of thinking about it, his suntanned brow furrowing. It was obvious he was only going through the motions.

'Not really.'

'Did you have much to do with Mr Lynch? Did you socialise together? Either before or after his wife died?'

'No. My wife never liked him. I won't tell you what she said when she heard he was dead. Don't want you thinking she had anything to do with it.'

Angel smiled with him, thinking he'd give it another minute before it got to the point where he could gently show Ambrose the door.

'You didn't go for a quick pint at the local pub, just the two of you?'

'Once or twice years ago.'

'Meaning you wouldn't be aware of what was going on in Mr Lynch's life? It's not as if you went for a pint every day and he'd confide in you about things that were worrying him?'

Angel paused, let Ambrose come to the realisation in his

own time that he had nothing to offer, the disappointment reflected in his voice.

'I thought you'd want to speak to me, that's all,' Ambrose said. 'Tick all the boxes, that sort of thing.'

'You're right. The smallest things. Sadly, not in this case.'

Ambrose allowed himself to be led back towards reception looking as dejected as a failed job applicant being shown out by the interviewer who'd turned him down. Despite that, he made a game attempt at conversation, aka nosiness.

'Who gets the house?'

'Everything's split equally between his two sons seeing as his wife predeceased him.'

Angel wasn't surprised to see Ambrose's mouth turn down at the mention of Lynch's sons. Nobody he'd come across so far had a good word to say about Gavin Lynch. Ambrose followed suit.

'I hope Gavin doesn't move in. He's too bloody flash for my liking. Roy was okay. You wouldn't have known he was living there most of the time. Gavin will have noisy parties every weekend with all his druggie friends. And he's not the sort of person you ask to turn the music down.'

'I wouldn't worry. They'll probably sell it. If Gavin wanted to move in, he'd have to buy his brother out.'

Ambrose snorted, not looking convinced.

'I hope you're right. But they're going to have a hell of a job selling it now.'

Something in Ambrose's tone made Angel stop walking. Ambrose stopped with him in the middle of the corridor. They stepped backwards to let a couple of uniformed PCs get past, then Angel picked up the conversation.

'Why do you say that?'

Ambrose looked at him as if it was the stupidest question he'd heard in a long time.

'Who'd want to buy it? One suicide you could ignore, but two?' He shuddered theatrically as if a steward had shown him into a cabin without a window on the cruise ship. 'I wouldn't want to live there.'

Needless to say, they were back in the interview room less than a minute later, Ambrose now looking confused after being given the bum's rush only a moment ago.

'You didn't know? The previous owner killed himself as well. Hanged himself in the garage after his business went down the toilet.'

'What was his name?'

Ambrose took a minute thinking about it, then edged his way towards a name.

'It was the same surname as one of the Tory Prime Ministers . . .' He rubbed the back of his neck as if massaging the memory out, then came out with it in a triumphant exclamation. '*Cameron!* Lucas Cameron. I never met him. It was before my time. But the first time I went to the pub, one of the locals laughed and said to me, you're the bloke who moved in next door to the jinxed house or something like that. I think he called it *Noose Cottage* and everybody joined in laughing. I didn't bother asking his name at the time, but when I told my wife, she made me ask the next time I went to the pub. She likes a bit of local gossip.'

'Do you know when this was?'

'We've been there for twenty-five years, so it was before that.'

'Were any of the other neighbours there before you moved in who would've known Cameron?'

Ambrose was already shaking his head before the question was out.

'We've been there the longest apart from the Lynches. Looks like we'll be staying there now. Buying the house next door to the jinxed house is almost as bad as living in it.'

If Ambrose hadn't sounded so dejected at the prospect, Angel would've asked him what name the ever-imaginative pub gossips had come up with in the light of recent developments, whether they'd made the obvious connection between *noose* and *Lynch*.

THINGS FELT AS IF THEY WERE GAINING TRACTION—IN A VERY convoluted way—when Gulliver and Jardine got back from interviewing Dawn Howard and everybody was gathered in the incident room. Angel had the floor.

'Roy Lynch and his wife Marianne had both been married before. Roy was married to Dawn Howard, who told us that the house Roy was killed in was actually owned by his wife, Marianne. Lynch's neighbour told us that a man called Lucas Cameron hanged himself in that same house more than twenty-five years ago because his business went belly-up. Her previous husband, obviously. A search of the coroner's inquest records will give us the exact date and details, but the fact is Marianne's first husband committed suicide in the garage of the same house where her second husband Roy was murdered.'

'I'm glad I didn't marry her,' Gulliver said under his breath. He got an eye-roll from Jardine, the only person close enough to hear.

'Was the house in joint names, or owned solely by her?' DCI Finch asked more constructively.

'Just her. Given that her first husband had his own business, it's likely that they bought it together, but put it in her name only. That way, it would be protected if his company got into financial difficulties and he ended up bankrupt or owing money under a personal guarantee. At least they wouldn't lose the family home.'

Kincade laughed, regret at a missed opportunity mingling with bitterness in the sound.

'That's very trusting of him. I wish my husband had done the same. He'd be living in a tent right now.'

The remark got a polite chuckle from everyone in the room more than a belly laugh. The bitter edge was a little too raw for that. Angel moved swiftly on.

'The thing is, the company did get into trouble, to the extent that Lucas Cameron committed suicide. At the moment, this is hearsay based on what was said to the next-door neighbour when he moved in. We don't know anything about the company yet. The Companies House online records are a little inconsistent going back that far.'

'Could there be a link to Guy Yardley's company?' Lisa Jardine said.

'Potentially, yes. If we assume that Lucas Cameron's suicide was genuine—'

'And are we?' Olivia Finch cut in.

Angel smiled and promptly didn't answer the question as asked.

'For the purpose of what I'm about to say, yes. If his company got into so much trouble that he killed himself, somebody, Guy Yardley for instance, could have bought it cheaply and then turned it around. If that happened, then we have a connection from Lucas Cameron to Yardley to Gavin and Roy Lynch. That's on top of the personal connection between Cameron and Roy Lynch through Marianne, the woman they both married.'

'How exactly does Yardley fit into all this?' Finch said.

'We don't know yet. But if Marianne was left a worthless company when her husband died, Yardley might have been nothing more than the man who happened to buy it. It's likely that he was killed at the Solent View Industrial Estate because it was significant to him. He might have been in business there on a smaller scale, then bought Lucas Cameron's failing company and never looked back.'

'But why leave it to Roy Lynch's son, Gavin?'

Angel opened his hands wide, your guess is as good as mine.

'Roy might already have known Yardley. He persuaded Marianne to give Yardley first refusal on the company at a fire-sale price.'

'On the condition that he does right by his son,' Kincade suggested.

'Could be. Unfortunately, four out of the five people involved, Roy and Marianne Lynch, Cameron and Yardley, are dead. The fifth, Dawn Howard, readily admits that her brains were fried back then. She couldn't tell you who knew who when. But if Roy Lynch wanted a front for his illegal activities, he'd want it to be owned by somebody under our radar, somebody squeaky clean. Like Yardley.'

'Did Lucas and Marianne Cameron have any kids of their own?' Finch said

'That's something we're looking into.'

'If so, we could be dealing with the resentful children from Marianne's first marriage going after the men they believe stole their inheritance.'

That obvious conclusion had already crossed Angel's mind —with a major flaw.

'By all accounts there was no inheritance to steal. The company was worthless. It probably had a ton of debt. They were kids. What would they do with a company about to go under? Turn it around as a school project? They should be grateful to Yardley for taking what might have been a liability off their hands.'

It was left to Lisa Jardine to sum up how everybody felt when the briefing broke up.

'I feel like I've just finished a mergers and acquisitions

module on an MBA course at the university. I hope there isn't going to be an exam now.'

Angel smiled with the rest of them, the most difficult question in such an exam in his own mind.

How did any of it explain why the killers had cut out Guy Yardley's tongue?

UNSURPRISINGLY, ANGEL FELT A FIRM HAND ON HIS ELBOW preventing him from heading back towards his office.

'You want to answer my question about Lucas Cameron's suicide now?' Finch said. 'Was it genuine? Or is history repeating itself?'

'Too early to say. But given that Roy Lynch shacked up with Cameron's widow immediately after he died, and Roy's friend Guy Yardley might have taken over what remained of Cameron's company, we'll be taking a close look at it.'

She mulled it over, nodding to herself.

'Two suicides by hanging in the same garage can't be a coincidence. However, I agree with you about the company not being worth killing one man over, let alone two, thirty years after the event. We're missing something. We need to find out if there were any kids.' She noticed him smiling to himself. 'I'm thinking out loud, Max. I realise you're already thinking along the same lines.'

He dipped his head in acknowledgement as her mind continued to search for connections.

'Didn't the nun at the hospice say that Marianne's sister had visited her? As well as a young woman?'

The memory of the disappointing conversation was still fresh in Angel's mind.

'A woman claiming to be her sister visited. The name in the

visitors' book was simply Evelyn. We're working on it. Sister Veronica said she would also make enquiries.'

Finch's eyes crinkled as she pointed towards the ceiling.

'Maybe they've still got the direct line to the man upstairs that you seem to have lost.'

36

Gavin Lynch made his way through the tall stacks of dull-red and rusting shipping containers at Eling wharf, the container yard located next to The Anchor Inn, the pub Angel had taken Kincade to at the end of their first day working together.

Gavin was very glad he didn't live in America. He'd be feeling some lunatic's cross-hairs on his back right about now if he did. He'd never understood a country where any sicko or psycho could walk into the local branch of Walmart and buy a hunting rifle and a telescopic scope at the same time as they bought a new broom or doormat.

His mood was less up-beat than it had been earlier—and it wasn't only the limitless opportunities the container yard offered to a hidden gunman. It was all very well thinking that he was one step ahead of them, having worked out that they were using the promise of information to lure him to his own death, but were they one step ahead of him again? He pushed the thought from his mind. You could go on forever and still not know for sure.

The presence of his own pet sicko-cum-psycho, Milan Broz, made him feel a lot better about the whole situation.

The follow-up text had arrived as he was leaving his old man's house. It had been short and to the point.

10 p.m. Eling wharf container yard. £10,000.

A close-up aerial view from Google maps had been attached, the exact location circled in red.

He guessed they thought of it as the first instalment. What he knew would be the first, last and only instalment, immediately taken back as it slipped out of their hands while the blood flowed out of their veins. The last line had made him laugh out loud.

Come alone. We'll be watching you.

Is that a fact? he thought to himself as he immediately called Broz to give him the location. *Well, we'll be watching you first, shit for brains.*

He hadn't seen any sign of Broz as he'd made his way through the maze of containers, his footsteps echoing down the narrow aisles—and he was actively looking for him. He guessed they would be, too, if they had any sense.

So far, it didn't look as if they did.

Nobody was waiting for him at the designated rendezvous when he got there. It didn't surprise him. He was expecting another text or a call giving him further directions like in any cheesy spy movie.

Being careful.

Just not careful enough.

'IT'S TEN O'CLOCK,' SHE SAID. 'CALL HER.'

Her impatience worried him. Not as much as her increasing bloodlust, but, still, he could do without it. He was nervous enough himself. A positive outcome from the game of bluff and double-bluff was not a done deal by any means.

He'd found the number for Gavin Lynch's wife, Janis, in Roy Lynch's phone. They'd had the photographs for some time now—the ones of Gavin and his girlfriend, Samantha, leaving a motel together when he was supposedly on a business trip. He'd been surprised how much it had cost to hire a private investigator to follow them. The PI had given him a strange look when he said that Samantha was his wife. It had been easy enough to interpret.

I'm not surprised she's having an affair if she's married to you.

Let him think what he liked. They had what they needed.

And very soon, Mrs Janis Lynch would have it, too.

'Make the call,' she said again. 'He's not going to stay there all night when we don't turn up.'

He swallowed his irritation, the desire to snap at her. *I know that, I'm not stupid.*

He made the call.

Janis Lynch sounded suspicious. It wasn't surprising. A call from an unknown number late at night. Like a scam to get her bank details from an industrious scammer in Nigeria working overtime.

'Hello?'

'Is that Janis Lynch? Gavin Lynch's wife?'

'Yes. Who are you?'

'My name's Richard. I'm Samantha Lee's husband.'

He left the name hanging. Trying to determine if it meant anything to her. Whether she had her own suspicions.

Her voice when she spoke suggested not. A growing confidence was replacing the late-night wariness. Except he had a feeling it was more a false bravado in advance of what she feared was coming.

'I have no idea who that is. Or who you are. It's late and I want to go to bed . . .'

'Please don't hang up, Mrs Lynch. Your husband is having an affair with my wife, Samantha. I hired a private investigator to follow them. I've got photographs. I can send them to you.'

He waited as the process of denial set seed, the confidence already gone from her voice. Just another betrayed wife on the other end of the line now. Fighting hard to stop her voice from breaking as she spoke to the stranger who'd brought her world crashing down around her ears.

'Why would I want to see them? And how did you get my number?'

'The private investigator gave it to me. I can't give you any answers about why you might want to see the photos. I'm just offering them to you. I wasn't able to bury my head in the sand, but maybe you can.'

He let an uncomfortable silence stretch out between them as her own mind went to work on her, the niggling doubts and suspicions that must have plagued her coming to the fore. Connections being made. Unexplained behaviour now made all too clear.

'I can hardly say no now, can I?' she said sourly.

'I'll send a couple to you. Then I'll call you back. I'm afraid there's worse to come than your husband cheating on you.'

He ended the call before she could ask what exactly. Then sent two of the most incriminating photos. Ones that highlighted Samantha's—admittedly trashy—attractiveness. Janis Lynch wasn't going to be happy about the size of Samantha's chest, that was for sure. Or the pouty cock-tease lips.

He turned the phone off as soon as he'd hit *send*. He didn't want Janis immediately calling him back. He felt sorry for her, increasing her distress the way he was. It was her own fault. She shouldn't have married a cheating bastard like Gavin Lynch in the first place.

Beside him, his unstable accomplice was fit to burst. Rocking back and forth on her chair, her hands clamped under her thighs.

'Get us a couple of beers from the fridge,' he said to give her something to do.

A minute later, she was back, a large dent already made in the contents of her bottle as she handed the other one to him. She perched on the arm of his chair, bouncing her knee up and down as if she had an irritating involuntary tic. One part of her body always moving or twitching. Feet tapping, fingers flexing. Chewing her nails one second, drumming her fingers the next. He wondered if she had a drug problem, prescribed or otherwise. Whether she was on too many of them, or not enough. She took another swallow, glanced at her watch, then at the phone in his hand.

'That's long enough. Call her back. The bastard isn't going to wait all night.'

He took a swallow of his own beer to stop himself from yelling at her.

I know that. You already said it.

Then he switched on the phone, called Janis Lynch back to bring even more pain into her life.

'*Bastard!*' she hissed down the line at him. 'Gavin, not you. Although you're not exactly my favourite person at the moment, either. What's the worse thing you mentioned?'

He nodded at his partner as she looked expectantly at him.

She's taking the bait.

'Did he tell you about Guy Yardley being murdered?'

He felt the change come over her from the other end of the line. Horror at the realisation that he wasn't about to say, *this is the second or third or tenth affair he's had.* That it was indeed a whole lot more serious than a cheating husband who couldn't keep it in his pants.

The wariness was back in her voice. The vain hope that she wouldn't be forced further into this disturbing conversation.

'He mentioned it. He didn't go into any details. He said the police wouldn't tell him anything. Do you know what happened?'

He felt the contoured handle of the knife in his hand as he answered. The clever ergonomic design that ensured a good grip was maintained when things got messy, got slippery, the warm wetness of Yardley's blood flowing over his gloved hand, his bare wrist.

'No. And I don't want to know. It's not relevant, anyway. Did your husband tell you who Yardley left the company to?'

The sharp hiss in his ear told him she'd figured it out, her voice incredulous when she answered him.

'Not Gavin?'

'Yeah. Something to do with a deal Yardley made with Gavin's father.'

'That was before my time. How do you know all—'

The words died in her mouth as her mind processed the implications a second or two behind. There was horror in her tone when she voiced them, but not much disbelief.

'Are you saying Gavin killed him in order to get control of the company?'

Her horror was matched by the relief that swept over him as she cut short one question to ask another. Because he didn't know for sure whether the idea he was planting in her mind was true or not. He didn't have an answer for how he was supposed to know the details of Yardley's will. He'd have been forced to invent something. Now they were past the *how*. All that mattered was that the seed had been set. Let her own mind do the rest.

'I'm not saying anything. I'm stating facts. Yardley was

murdered. Gavin gets the company which must be worth millions. You make your own mind up. You know Gavin better than I do.'

He smiled to himself at the line. It was because she knew him so well that she found it so easy to believe. He extended his beer bottle towards his partner, toasting carefully and quietly.

So far, so good.

'There is something I do want to say,' he said. 'You won't want to hear it. But it's something you need to think very carefully about.'

He took a sip of beer to create a lull, force her into asking. Participation is key.

'What?'

'I don't know the exact numbers, but Gavin is now approximately ten million pounds richer than he was a few days ago. He's got a lot more to lose if you say you want a divorce because he's having an affair with my wife. If you divorce him now, it'll cost him five million. If you have an accident'—he coughed, *ahem*, into his hand after he said it—'before the divorce, he keeps all ten million for himself. Take another look at the photographs I sent you. Then ask yourself, how much does he love me?'

This time he let the silence stretch out for as long as she needed to process the information, arrive at an assessment of her husband's character.

It didn't take long.

'Do you think I should go to the police?'

He flinched involuntarily at the word *police*. That was the last thing they needed.

'I don't know what you would say to them.'

'What you've just told me.'

'They'd laugh in your face. They'd be rushed off their feet if they had to respond to every rich man's wife who finds out her husband is having an affair with his secretary.'

He closed his eyes. Hardened his heart to the anguish that now came down the line at him, his own wife's face intruding on his mind.

'What am I going to do? Wait until he tries something to make the police believe me?'

He did his best to work an equal note of helpless desperation into his voice. Gripping his beer bottle until his knuckles turned white, the tension flowing into his voice.

'I don't know. I'm still trying to get my head around it all myself. But I had to tell you. I know it's the last thing you want to hear, but I wouldn't be able to look at myself in the mirror if I hadn't warned you and then I read in the paper that you'd had a fatal accident. Is your husband at home at the moment?'

Bitterness and hatred filled her voice as she immediately jumped to the wrong conclusion.

'No. He said he had to go out. He wouldn't say where. I bet he's with the bitch. *Oops*, sorry. I mean your wife. Is she out?'

He wouldn't have been able to match the venom in her voice at the best of times. Now, it was all but impossible, exhilaration coursing through his veins as everything came together.

'Yeah. She said she was going out with a girlfriend. Except I called the girlfriend's husband. He told me she'd been at home with him all night. The only advice I can give you is to lock all the doors before he gets home. It'll buy you some time while you try to think what to do.'

There was a satisfying edge of malice in her voice as she replied.

'I'll do that right now. Make the bastard sleep in his car.'

Or hopefully his father's house, he thought as he ended the call.

. . .

CATALINA KINCADE WAS THINKING ALONG SIMILAR LINES. Not that she'd find herself sleeping at her parents' house—it being in London—but in her car.

She was on the rooftop terrace of her apartment block, staring down at the yachts in the harbour at Ocean Village, an up-market marina development situated at the mouth of the River Itchen, a little over a mile from police HQ as the seagull flies.

The luxury two-bedroom flat wasn't exactly hers, nor was she renting it. It was owned by one of her husband's banker friends currently on secondment for six months in New York. She'd done a quick search on the internet for similar properties when she first moved in, and was both horrified and rather pleased to see that it would cost six hundred and fifty thousand pounds to buy. Understandably, Elliot's friend hadn't wanted to let it to somebody he didn't know, but was happy to allow her to stay there.

So far, nobody at work had asked her where she was living. She wasn't sure whether she'd tell the truth or lie when somebody finally got around to it. Already guilty of the crime of coming from what people mockingly pronounced *Lahnden*, living in one of Southampton's prime locations would merely confirm what most people believed—that all Londoners thought and acted as if the sun shone out of their backsides.

After her conversation with Elliot earlier, it might not be a problem for much longer.

She didn't know if he'd actually do it—put pressure on his friend to threaten to throw her out if she didn't roll over and agree to him and his latest squeeze keeping custody of the girls, but it concentrated the mind.

It would be an ironic twist if it did happen after the remark she'd made and immediately regretted in the meeting earlier about Elliot living in a tent if he'd been stupid enough to put the house in her name only.

She hadn't helped matters when she'd sent her eldest daughter, Isla, photographs of the view from the roof terrace—the yachts and sleek motor cruisers in the marina below her—as well as pictures of what would be the girls' bedroom, should they come to live with her. If it were possible for her to feel any sympathy for Elliot—akin to feeling sorry for a cockroach accidentally trodden on—the thought of the girls' incessant whining about wanting a sea view from their bedroom would do it.

Elliot's opening remark had confirmed that the process had already begun.

What the fuck do you think you're doing, sending those photos to Isla?

Her disingenuous response as she sipped a cold beer—*she wanted to see where I'm living*—whilst true, did nothing to help.

Nor had, *fight your own battles and stop sucking up to my mother in order to get her on your side.*

Things had gone downhill from there, the phrase *sucking up* always guaranteed to help turn a minor disagreement into a full-blown argument, spiteful personal remarks optional.

If she hadn't already drunk two cold, gassy beers, she'd have worked the anger out of her system by going for a late-night run after Elliot hung up on her. Since she had, that only left a third one.

GAVIN LYNCH COULD'VE DONE WITH A COLD BEER HIMSELF TO HELP ease his own irritation.

He'd waited until eleven o'clock—an hour of his life he'd never get back—and still he or they hadn't turned up.

That idiot Broz must have given them away. Smoking those

filthy Eastern European cigarettes or playing beeping games on his phone as he hid waiting. And now they were spooked, they'd stay spooked.

Except anyone who'd already killed his father and Guy Yardley wasn't about to give up now. They'd find another way.

Just not tonight.

Look on the bright side. It gave him a bit of breathing space. A chance to try to find them before they tried again.

He pulled out his phone to compose a text to Broz as he stalked through the containers heading back to his car, not trusting himself to call him, speak to him in person. He wouldn't be able to stop himself from saying something. And Milan Broz did not take criticism well. Not even from the man paying him, the man allowing him to indulge his sadistic streak.

They're not coming. Call it a day. Speak tomorrow.

Back at his car, he sat for a while in the darkness, his anger growing. Not only a wasted evening, chilled through from not having worn a coat—he'd planned for some strenuous physical exercise of the bone-breaking variety to keep him warm, after all—but now he had to face Janis's seething anger and suspicion when he got home, her biting sarcasm. It had been obvious when he left that she thought he was meeting Samantha. He could hardly tell her the truth.

I'm off to kill a man who thinks he's going to kill me. Don't wait up.

Let her think it.

Besides, he was expecting a showdown any day. He couldn't swear to it, but he had a feeling she'd employed a private investigator to follow him a couple of weeks back.

She was biding her time. Waiting for the right moment. And now that wait would cost him five million. A paranoid man might think she'd arranged to have Yardley killed.

Bitch.

Fifteen minutes later, his suspicions were confirmed when he turned the key in the front door and it wouldn't open. She'd bolted it from the inside. He didn't need to check the back door in case she'd left it unlocked. He did so anyway, climbing over the also-locked side gate to get around to the back. She hadn't, of course.

He went back to the car on the front drive, sent her a text. As with Broz, he didn't trust himself to speak to her. A man can't afford a wrong word, the wrong tone of voice, when he's hoping that his bitch of a wife relents and lets him in to sleep in the spare bed.

I can't get in. Have you bolted the front door?

It was a waste of time and he knew it. The reply a minute later confirmed it.

I thought you were spending the night with Samantha.

Seeing Samantha's name was like a slap across the face. It proved that he'd been right. The bitch had hired a private investigator. She'd have photographs as well as Sam's name. There was no point in replying. She wasn't going to let him in whatever he said.

On any other night, he'd have broken in, risked her calling the cops. Tonight was different. He congratulated himself that he'd gone to the old man's house to find the newspaper cutting that afternoon. The key was still in his pocket. His reward for being thorough, making sure that he was right before he acted.

He was tempted to send Janis a final text.

No problem. I'll sleep at Dad's.

In the end, he couldn't be bothered.

He felt relieved as he drove there. Now that everything was out in the open, the shit well and truly having hit the fan, he felt as if a burden had been lifted. What was the worst that could happen? He'd have to give Janis five million. He'd still have five left for himself. The biggest hit would be to his pride. Besides, he'd be able to beat her down. He knew what she was like. Mrs Instant Gratification. Offer her less for a quick, uncontested settlement and the grasping cow would bite his hand off.

He'd dump Sam, too. She was getting to be too demanding, too whiney. And they weren't even married, God forbid.

No, he was about to enter a new phase of his life. A fresh start. And with a ton of cash in the bank. All legal, too. And all because of the old man and the deal he'd struck with Guy Yardley all those years ago. He felt a hot stinging at the backs of his eyes as he slipped the key into the oak front door and it actually opened when he pushed it.

It was the last positive emotion he would ever feel.

As he stepped into the house and stood for a moment in the dim hallway, a young woman he'd never seen before came out of the sitting room. For reasons he couldn't explain, he was overcome by a sudden intense feeling of wistful nostalgia. A disconcerting regret for things that might have been but never were—and now never would be—due to nothing more than fate's relentless malevolence.

She said something to him that made no sense. Lips moving, the words lost somewhere in the endless void of time and space between them, intensifying his sudden unnerving sense of loss.

Before his mind could make sense of the myriad thoughts crashing through it or his limbs react, a man materialised out of nowhere from the shadows behind him. He went to raise his arm but it was already too late, the heavy iron poker from the sitting room fireplace crashing down onto the back of his head. Off in the background somewhere the shrill whooping of the woman provided a deranged backdrop as his legs buckled and he crumpled to the polished parquet floor, the all-too-temporary relief of sweet blackness claiming him for its own.

37

DCI Olivia Finch's facetious remark to Angel about the nuns at St. Joseph's Hospice having a direct line to the man upstairs was more true than she knew—even if the reality was a little more prosaic.

Lisa Jardine took the call from Sister Veronica who told her that as a result of asking everyone a second time, the bursar, Sister Philippa, had remembered something. The woman who visited Marianne Lynch claiming to be her sister had given a donation to the hospice. A generous one, at that. Being financially on the ball, Sister Philippa had persuaded Marianne's sister to complete a Gift Aid form, enabling the hospice to claim back an amount equal to basic rate income tax on the donation. That necessarily involved giving her full name and current address.

A mini-miracle was how Jardine described it when she told Angel about it.

Serendipity, Angel had agreed using Sister Veronica's own word, immediately despatching Gulliver and Jardine to interview Mrs Evelyn Walker in Chandler's Ford, seven miles away.

They had their usual argument about which radio station to listen to as Gulliver drove.

Anything heavy metal—defined by her as aimed at and played by spotty adolescent teenage boys too immature to get a girlfriend—was out. He was equally against what he called *girly shit designed to cry yourself to sleep to*. In a rare meeting of minds, they were agreed that anything with phone-ins was an absolute no-no. Who needs to listen to uninformed opinionated pricks spouting off on topics nobody cares about when they had each other?

As usual, they settled on something blandly ubiquitous that got a lot of air time in care homes.

The conversation about music segued naturally—in their minds, at least—into one about Angel.

'I don't want to tempt fate,' Jardine said, 'but he hasn't got his mouth organ—'

'Harmonica.'

'—out since he's been back from his holiday.'

'It wasn't a holiday—'

'Anything that means you're not at work is a holiday.'

'—and if you'd been paying attention—'

'Also known as sucking up.'

'—you'd have noticed that he hadn't been playing it for a while before that. Not since . . .'

She nodded her understanding without him having to put it into words.

'I heard he was playing it at the time. Something like that would stop me from feeling like playing a happy tune on my mouth organ.'

'Did you realise that if you called it a harmonica—'

'Like teacher's pet does.'

'—it would avoid any unfortunate misunderstanding that

might arise when a woman uses the words *mouth* and *organ* in the same sentence?'

'In the mind of a certain type of man, yes. One who hasn't grown up yet, and probably never will. One who isn't happy listening to any music that doesn't make his ears and nose bleed.'

As usual, their conversation didn't achieve much, the world's many problems not a lot different from when they started. It passed the time, nonetheless.

Having dealt with Angel, they then moved onto Kincade. Rumours had naturally been doing the rounds of the station in the aftermath of the tongue-in-cheek explanation that she'd been thrown out of the Met for good police work, something that was not tolerated in the Big Smoke.

'What do you think about that story about why she was demoted?' Jardine said. 'Using excessive force making an arrest.'

Gulliver had actually made discreet enquiries himself. To the untrained eye, it looked a lot like going for a beer and a curry with a mate who'd moved up to London to join the Met when he was back home visiting his parents for the weekend. Gulliver hadn't said anything to anyone about the contents of that discussion. Unlike his partner in the passenger seat, he had no time for gossip and tittle-tattle.

Admittedly, what his friend had told him had also been based on rumour, but it was rumour a lot closer to the horse's mouth. He was well aware that if he said anything to her now, somebody at the station would be telling a suitably embellished version of it back to him by the end of the day. He kept it vague as a result.

'It sounds plausible.'

Jardine gave him the exasperated look of a person frustrated with someone who refuses to enter into the character-assassination spirit of things.

'Of course, it's plausible. But is it true?'

'Why don't you ask her?'

'*Ha, ha*, I don't think.' She was quiet a moment—one that Gulliver enjoyed—then her brow compacted. 'Do you think she's told the boss the truth?'

'Like in the confessional, you mean?'

'I hadn't thought of that. More likely in the car.'

He shook his head firmly.

'Based on my personal experience'—glancing pointedly at her as he said it—'the truth doesn't get much of a look-in during a conversation between two police officers in a car.'

She tried to look offended. Leaning away from him as if he'd suddenly become contagious, her head pulled back.

'Are you saying that things other than the complete truth come out of my mouth?'

'What I'm saying is, I'll let you know if I ever hear it. I might ask you to repeat it so that I can record it, if I do.'

As with the discussion about Angel, there wasn't much in terms of actual information being exchanged by the time they'd arrived at Evelyn Walker's house.

MRS WALKER WAS SURPRISED TO SEE THEM, BUT NOT AS SURPRISED as she was to hear that Roy Lynch was dead. Her response was immediate and enthusiastic.

'Good riddance.'

Gulliver and Jardine both experienced a feeling of déjà vu. It was the exact same reaction they'd got from Lynch's first wife's son, Nick, phrased in the same words. Unlike Evelyn, the only thing that was likely to surprise them was if they interviewed anybody who was saddened by the news.

Evelyn then appeared to contradict herself.

'Thank God I saw him at Marianne's funeral.'

Her eyes misted over at the mention of her sister's send-off. She made no attempt to explain her remark, forcing Gulliver to ask.

'You just gave the impression that you didn't like your brother-in-law.'

She looked as if she was about to form the shape of a cross with her index fingers, hold it towards them to ward off Gulliver's description of Roy Lynch.

'Don't ever call him that. It wasn't that I disliked him. I absolutely fucking hated him.' She saw the shock on their faces, as if they were down at the docks interviewing a whore in between turning tricks, didn't bother to apologise. 'I told him what I thought of him. I held my tongue for all the years Marianne was alive, but once she was gone, I wasn't going to hold back. I think he was rather shocked. And if you're wondering if I took it a stage further and actually killed the bastard, all I can say is that I wish I had. Unfortunately, I was at a very tiresome dinner party. Five incredibly dull people will be able to confirm that I was bored senseless at the dinner table all night long and drank far too much white wine as a result.' She laughed as if she'd said something amusing. 'My husband drove, for once. I made a note of it on the kitchen calendar, it's so out of character.'

'We weren't actually asking for an alibi, Mrs Walker,' Gulliver said. 'But we'd be interested to know why you felt so strongly about . . .' He paused, then selected the most accurate, least-contentious description. 'Mr Lynch.'

Evelyn shook her head, where to start.

'Because he ruined my sister's life. He drove a wedge between us and forced me to act in a way of which I am ashamed, now that she's gone.'

'Could we start with the first one?' Gulliver suggested tentatively. 'In what way did he ruin her life?'

Evelyn looked at him as if she was aware that police officers were getting younger by the day, but she hadn't realised they were also getting stupider.

'Because he turned her into the wife of a criminal, a drug dealer, that's why. Because he exploited a weakness in her that allowed her to be turned. Loathe as I am to say anything positive about him, I can't deny that Roy Lynch was a handsome man in his younger days. He also had plenty of money which he was happy to throw around seeing as the tax man hadn't taken his share. And he had a charm that appeals to a certain kind of woman.' Her nose wrinkled as she said it, her lips pursing. 'I certainly didn't appreciate it when he pinched my bottom, but my younger sister couldn't see past the paper-thin facade to the lecherous degenerate that lived below. It was as if she was sixteen all over again and had never been kissed.'

Jardine wondered if there was an element of sour grapes underlying the vitriolic diatribe. Had Roy Lynch pinched Evelyn's bottom and found it too bony for his liking? Too saggy? Then moved on to her riper little sister? She caught Evelyn staring at her as if she'd read her mind, gave her a polite smile back.

'I'd never argued with Marianne,' Evelyn went on, 'not until she met Roy Bloody Lynch. We did nothing but, afterwards. As a result, I cut her off. I didn't see or speak to her for the best part of thirty years. And that is what I'm so ashamed of. If I hadn't been back in Southampton having lunch with an old friend, and then bumped into another old acquaintance, I wouldn't even have known that Marianne was dying.' She dropped her eyes to her hands clasped in her lap, as if forgiveness for her sins might be found there. 'No doubt you found me because of the form I filled out at the hospice after giving them a donation. I got a bit carried away with the emotion of it all. It almost gave my husband a heart attack when he saw how much I gave them. I suppose it was my way of trying to deal with my guilt for abandoning my sister to that dreadful man for all those years.'

After hearing the anguish in her voice, neither of them needed to ask how well it had worked for her.

There was an awkward silence as Evelyn continued to contemplate her hands, turning her wedding ring around and around on her finger. The ticking of a grandfather clock in the hallway was magnified in the quiet atmosphere as if it was doing its best to compensate for the lack of conversation.

Jardine cleared her throat to bring them all back to the present, before asking about the past.

'We actually wanted to ask you about the period before Marianne met Mr Lynch. When she was married to her first husband, Lucas.'

It was as if the clouds parted, the sun now shining down through the sitting-room windows. Evelyn's face didn't exactly light up, but the permanent scowl that had sat on it as she talked about Roy Lynch and the effect he'd had on her sister fell away.

'He was a lovely man. Things must have been very bad for him to do what he did.'

Gulliver and Jardine shared a look at the phrase, *things must have been*. It implied that Evelyn didn't know for sure. She now confirmed it.

'Lucas Cameron didn't believe in washing his dirty linen in public. Whatever went on in his company—'

'What was it called?' Jardine interrupted.

Evelyn's brow creased as she took herself back thirty years, staring at the carpet as if she'd made a note of it there years ago but too much hoovering had worn it away.

'Cameron Marine Engineering, I think,' she said eventually. 'Something like that. The point I was making was that whatever went on in the boardroom, he didn't bring it home with him. I suppose he was old-fashioned that way. I don't know if he even told Marianne all of it. That's why it came as such a terrible shock when he took his own life. We all thought, surely things weren't that bad. Apparently, they were. After all these years I'm still surprised that he took the coward's way out.'

Neither of them pointed out that suicide is more often a mental health issue than a lack of moral fibre as Evelyn fell silent.

Jardine cleared her throat a second time when it felt as if Evelyn would never speak again.

'I understand no talking shop at the dinner table, but was there anyone he would have confided in? Nobody can keep everything bottled up inside.'

Evelyn snorted, shows how much you know.

'No? You haven't met my husband.' She pointed at the stone fireplace. 'You've got more chance getting information out of that than you have him. Lucas was the same. I suppose these days young people would be posting it all over social media. *Look at me, my company's going down the toilet.*'

'Who was the most likely?' Jardine persevered.

'His brother, Aiden, of course.'

Gulliver saw the words *of course* and the implication in them that the person asking the question was an idiot register on Jardine's face. Despite that, she remained professionally polite.

'Is he still alive?'

'As far as I know. We haven't been in touch for years. He couldn't stand Roy Lynch either. It gave us something in common. But people drift apart. You can't maintain a lifelong friendship on the basis of a shared hatred for one man.'

Jardine could've argued with that, but asked a more useful question instead.

'Can you let us have the most recent contact details you have for him?'

Evelyn pushed herself to her feet, went out into the hallway and over to a small table where the landline sat. A minute later she was back, an address book in her hand—if you can call a collection of loose pages between two hard covers all held together by an elastic band an address book.

'It won't be very recent,' she said as if they'd both been struck blind and couldn't see what was in her hands. They wouldn't have been surprised if it had disintegrated at her touch.

Despite that, she found an address and a phone number for Aiden Cameron easily enough.

Jardine went for broke after making a note of them.

'Have you got an email address?'

Evelyn shook her head, holding up the address book apologetically.

'Sorry. The fact that he's in here means he pre-dates my mobile phone and computer-literate days. I transferred anyone I thought I'd be in contact with going forward.'

'What about children?' Gulliver said.

Evelyn gave him the same *policemen getting stupider* look, then demonstrated that she was the one losing the plot.

'He'd hardly confide in them, would he? They were only fourteen and twelve at the time.'

Jardine jumped in, seeing her opportunity to get back at Evelyn for the unnecessary *of course*.

'I think what DC Gulliver means is, did Marianne and Lucas Cameron have any children together?'

There was no question of, *oh, sorry*. Evelyn answered as if she hadn't misunderstood at all.

'Two. Jessica was the eldest, Matthew two years younger.'

Gulliver knew that Jardine was doing the maths, as was he. According to the inquest report into Lucas Cameron's death, he'd committed suicide in July 1993. A girl of fourteen in 1993 would now be forty-four, her younger brother forty-two. It was possible that Matthew was the man they were looking for, but unlikely that his accomplice was Jessica—not unless the old woman in the hospice had been wrong about the age of the woman who hissed *I hope you burn in hell* at the dying Marianne Lynch.

'I don't suppose you've kept in touch with either of them?' Jardine said.

The question caused Evelyn to bow her head again, the guilt back in her voice.

'No. It wasn't deliberate. It was an unavoidable result of cutting Marianne off.'

'Were they at the funeral?'

'No.' She was thoughtful a moment, then hesitated. It became clear why a moment later when what she said compounded her shame. 'The only thing I can tell you is that Jessica and Matthew had a rough time when Roy Lynch moved in and brought his little monsters with him. Except they weren't so little. They were a year or two older. At that age, a year can make all the difference between being a child and a young adult.' She smiled softly, her words mocking herself. 'I think my husband would divorce me if I'd left a donation big enough to compensate for all the guilt I feel.'

Jardine phrased her next question carefully, so as not to lead Evelyn.

'Do you know if your sister had any other visitors?'

'Her husband, obviously.' Making it sound as if she'd allowed a cockroach to crawl over the bed covers. 'I don't suppose her stepsons bothered. And if either Matthew or Jessica visited her, she certainly didn't say anything to me about it. But it might be that she was too unsettled by me turning up after all those years.'

Not as much as by her other visitor, Jardine thought as they got up to leave. On the way out, Evelyn placed the remains of her address book back on the phone table. As well as the landline, there was a framed photograph sitting beside it. Jardine bent to get a better look. It showed two girls, one a few years older than the other.

'That's my daughter,' Evelyn said proudly, pointing at the younger girl. 'She's a doctor now.'

Jardine would've expected to be told the daughter's name. And maybe who her friend was. The two girls looked vaguely similar. Instead, Evelyn was looking as if she regretted saying as much as she had.

Jardine indicated the older girl.

'Who's—'

Behind them, the doorbell rang. Evelyn glanced at her watch.

'That's her now. She's early. She's taking me to lunch.' She inspected herself briefly in a tall, narrow mirror on the wall behind the phone table, tut-tutting at what she saw as she went to the front door. 'I haven't even put my face on yet. We're going to be late now, even though she's early.'

The remark was clearly aimed at them for having taken up her time when she should have been getting ready.

Evelyn's daughter had taken a call on her mobile phone by the time her mother opened the door. Pushing forty, she was medium height and slim with shoulder-length natural blonde hair—unlike her mother's which was the same style but out of a bottle. Apart from that, they could have been sisters—at least from a distance—an assessment that would please one of them no end and dismay the other.

She was halfway back to the front gate, pacing as she talked. Evelyn looked a little put out that she hadn't been able to introduce her in the flesh to the two detectives. She soon recovered when she realised that it gave her time to get ready. She held up her hand towards her daughter with her fingers splayed—*five minutes.*

It's going to take a lot longer than that, Jardine thought as she and Gulliver went past the daughter on the path. The woman nodded at them as they squeezed past, the same perfunctory greeting she'd have given the postman or a delivery driver. Then it was as if they didn't exist, back to a conversation that sounded very one-sided, a lot of nodding but not much more than the occasional *uh-huh* or *sounds good* coming from the daughter's end.

Jardine paused at the car, not getting in, even though Gulliver was already in the driver's seat and inpatient to go. Watching Evelyn Walker's daughter as she finished her call, then went into the house without a backwards glance.

'What are you doing?' Gulliver said when Jardine finally got in.

'I'm not sure. I got the impression there wasn't anyone on the other end of the line. The daughter was pretending so that she didn't have to be introduced to us.'

'How would she have known we were there?'

'No idea. It's just a feeling. Probably nothing.'

38

AIDEN CAMERON PROVED TO BE EASIER TO LOCATE THAN ANGEL anticipated. His details—including a current address that was not the same as the one supplied by Evelyn Walker—were on the Police National Computer. Four years previously, he'd been stopped for speeding doing forty-five in a thirty limit. He'd subsequently failed the roadside breathalyser test when the officer pulling him over smelled alcohol on his breath. He lost his licence for six months as a result.

Although Gulliver and Jardine were keen to follow up on the lead they'd identified, Angel decided to conduct Aiden Cameron's interview himself, taking Kincade along with him.

'Don't you trust me to drive?' she said as he led the way to his car, a metallic-grey Audi S6 Avant, the car of choice for any man who subscribes to Roosevelt's advice to speak softly and carry a big stick. She was tempted to point out that she'd completed the Met Police's eleven-week Armed Response Vehicle Officer course, and was prepared to put money on the fact that he hadn't. In the end, she decided against it.

She was even more convinced that whatever had happened with her predecessor, the much-loved and sadly-missed DS

Stuart Beckford, it had something to do with driving. The de facto short answer was that, no, he didn't trust anyone to drive. It wasn't only her, or even a typical chauvinistic bias against women drivers in general.

'I like driving,' he said simply, making her want to punch him in the side of the head.

She decided to say something foolish.

'At least you can't drive and play the mouth organ at the same time.'

He raised an eyebrow at her before backing out of his space.

'Is that a challenge, Sergeant?'

Seemed she'd eaten a double portion of foolish pills for breakfast that day, followed them with a big reckless one.

'Yeah, why not?'

'What do you want me to play?'

'God save the Queen. Or should that be King, now?'

He smiled to himself as if she'd chosen his favourite piece. Despite that, he kept both hands mercifully on the wheel as he pulled into the traffic on Southern Road.

'Maybe later.'

She almost felt disappointed. She knew what he was doing. He was going to make her beg for it.

'I don't think you ever play it.'

'Not for a while, no,' he admitted, a sudden sadness washing through his face.

And that was the end of that.

'Feels like we're getting somewhere,' she said when it became clear he wasn't going to say any more as he concentrated on driving.

'You mean about Lucas Cameron's company?'

'Yeah.'

After Evelyn Walker gave Gulliver and Jardine the company name, it hadn't taken long to establish that Cameron Marine

Engineering had changed its name to Yardarm Marine Technology—the company run until his untimely death by Guy Yardley, and left to Gavin Lynch in the wake of it. Lucas Cameron had resigned, posthumously, and had been replaced by Yardley, who had never looked back.

That news only served to intensify Angel's belief that something irregular had happened around the time of Cameron's suicide—if that's what it was.

Cameron's widow had been left with a failing company and nobody to run it. Had her new man, helpful Roy Lynch, come to the rescue? *I know a man who might be interested...*

Angel thought not.

'Hopefully Aiden Cameron will be able to shed a little more light.'

The door to Cameron's house in North Baddesley was opened by a tall blonde woman wearing faded jeans and an un-ironed man's white shirt worn outside them.

Kincade stated the obvious after they'd introduced themselves, warrant cards held forward, and she invited them in.

'You're from the States?'

'Uh-huh. Boston. You probably wouldn't have noticed if I hadn't just got back this morning from a trip home. I haven't even had a chance to unpack yet.'

'I'm surprised you didn't go straight to bed. I always do.'

'Who is it, Barb?' rang out from the interior of the house.

Barbara Cameron inclined her head towards the source of the call.

'Patient to look after.'

The reason behind the statement became clear when she led them through to the sitting room.

Aiden Cameron was sitting sideways on a cream sofa with

his leg up, a hospital-issue crutch leaning against the wall at the end of it.

'Hip replacement a couple of weeks ago,' he said, patting his left leg.

'And an operation on your hand at the same time?' Angel said indicating the dressing taped to the outside edge of Cameron's left palm. 'I hope you got a discount.'

Cameron smiled with him.

'It's only a scratch. I broke a glass and cut myself.'

His wife caught the look Angel and Kincade exchanged at the implication. That she'd deserted him in his hour of need to go to America, left him to hobble around the house hurting himself.

'My trip was last-minute. My mom's not well. She's ninety-one. My sister thought it might be the end. After seeing her, I figure she'll outlive me.' She hooked her thumb at her husband. 'Especially if his majesty here keeps giving me his orders.' She did a little curtsey. 'Another cup of tea, darling, for you and your special guests?'

'Thought you'd never bloody ask.'

Angel couldn't stop the thoughts that buzzed around in his head like a swarm of fat black flies. How well can a man recovering from a hip operation walk after two weeks? Does he need the crutch at all times? Can he climb over a chain-link fence? How about reversing a vintage Jag out of an unfamiliar garage? In short, was he milking the situation now that his wife had returned, but had been able to look after himself and get around perfectly well previously?

'My nephew was staying,' Cameron said, interrupting his thoughts. 'He looked after me.'

Even so, Angel thought, feeling the change come over Kincade at the same time it did him, an increased alertness, a sudden quickening of the pulse.

'Is that your brother Lucas's son, Matthew?'

'Matt, yes. We hadn't seen him for a while. It was pure coincidence that he called when he did. Took over nursemaid duties from Barb.'

'Careful what you say,' came from the kitchen. 'I can hear every word.'

Cameron smiled in the direction of the kitchen, then gave them his attention.

'What can I do for you?'

Angel started with what he'd been led to believe would be good news for his host.

'Were you aware that Roy Lynch died recently?'

The words took a moment to sink in, then Cameron sat bolt upright.

'Really?' He turned towards the kitchen again. 'Hear that, Barb? That bastard Lynch is dead.'

'Good riddance,' floated back.

Angel made a mental note to suggest to Gavin Lynch that it be inscribed on his father's headstone. Somebody was bound to spray paint it on afterwards if he didn't.

Cameron relaxed back into the sofa, his brow creasing as the further implications sank in.

'Your presence here suggests it wasn't a natural death.'

'No,' Angel said. 'He was found hanged in his garage—'

'Like my brother.'

'Exactly like that, yes. I'd like to ask you a few questions about what was going on back then. With particular reference to your brother, his wife, Marianne, and Roy Lynch.'

The spiteful satisfaction that had colonised Cameron's face at the news of Roy Lynch's death was suddenly gone as he took them back to a time when Lynch was the one having the last laugh.

'Depending on how unkind you want to be, Marianne was a

good-time girl, although gold digger would be equally appropriate. Everything was hunky-dory while Lucas was doing well. Then things started to slide. Suddenly it was a week's camping in The New Forest instead of a fortnight in a villa with a private pool outside St. Tropez. That was when Marianne started the affair with that bastard Lynch. You know that Lucas's company was going through a rough patch at the time?'

Angel nodded, accepted a cup of tea Barbara Cameron had just carried in.

'Don't worry,' she said, showing him her perfect teeth, 'I've had twenty years over here being trained on how to make it properly. I know how fussy you Brits are.'

Angel sipped, nodded his approval, then went back to her husband.

'We'll get back to that in a minute if we can.'

'I was working in the States at the time,' Cameron said. 'That's where I met Barb. But I talked to Lucas on the phone most days.'

The weight of vindictive coincidence contained in Cameron's innocent words blindsided Angel momentarily. A long-dead brother on the other side of the world calling for help—moral or business-related, it made no difference which—that in the end would prove to be too little, too late.

Except it was the one difference amongst the similarities that allowed Aiden Cameron to sleep at night whilst it accused him.

I talked to Lucas on the phone most days.

A stark contrast to the regret that plagued him.

I should have talked to Cormac every day.

Not the one solitary conversation that would haunt him into his dotage.

I don't know what to do, Max.

Kincade cleared her throat pointedly to bring him back into the conversation as Cameron continued to talk.

'Marianne's affair with Lynch certainly didn't help with Lucas's ability to concentrate while he was trying to keep the company afloat.'

'We were told you never liked Roy Lynch,' Kincade cut in.

Cameron snorted looking like he wanted to spit.

'Whoever told you that likes an understatement. I detested him.'

Angel leaned back in his chair and sipped at his tea, allowed Kincade to continue.

'Was that because you blamed him for your brother committing suicide? He'd got business troubles and then his wife has an affair with Lynch instead of supporting him.'

'That's right—'

'That's not what you told me,' Barbara Cameron said. 'You said you blamed ... I can't remember his name. It'll come to me.'

Angel and Kincade looked from her to her husband and back again.

'Bishop,' she exclaimed triumphantly. 'Somebody Bishop.'

Everybody looked at Aiden Cameron for confirmation. He nodded.

'Stephen Bishop. They were all to blame. Lynch, Marianne and Bishop.'

'Who is Stephen Bishop?' Angel said. 'And how was he to blame?'

Cameron extended a hand towards his wife. *You're so keen to interrupt, you tell it*. She shook her head.

'He's the owner of SBM Logistics,' Cameron said. 'A minute ago, I used the phrase *a rough patch* when talking about Lucas's company. That's what it was. Nobody expects it all to be plain sailing when you're running a business. It certainly wasn't the end of the world. He was waiting for confirmation of a big order from SBM Logistics that would've turned things around, at least for a while longer. Then Bishop cancelled the order. Said his own company was having cash flow problems. It was the last straw. The bank knew that Lucas was waiting on the order. As soon as it was cancelled, they were on him like a pack of wolves. *Whoosh*, out comes the rug from under his feet. Bastards. A lot of the blame is on them, too.'

It appeared Cameron blamed everyone apart from himself. He'd grown increasingly red in the face as he laid bare their joint culpability. Angel saw his wife make a move as if to put a calming hand on his arm, then think better of it. Making tea wasn't the only thing she'd learned married to Aiden Cameron for twenty-plus years.

'Did you ever wonder if it wasn't actually suicide?' Angel said.

The question took Cameron by surprise. He adjusted his leg again, a spasm of pain rippling across his face.

'I don't think so. It was a hell of a shock. I came back for the funeral, but only stayed one night. Things were going crazy at work in the States. I didn't really have much time to think about anything at all.'

'Do you know a man called Guy Yardley?'

'I know the name. I never met him. Marianne sold what was left of Lucas's company to him. If you're thinking Lucas was killed so that Yardley could get his hands on the company, you're way off base. Without that contract, there really was no company. Just a bottomless money pit.'

'And yet Yardley bought it.'

The look on Cameron's face suggested he was getting bored with questions about a man he'd admitted he didn't know and whose relevance hadn't been explained.

'Some people would buy a dog turd if it was cheap enough.' Then, more practically, 'Presumably he didn't take over the debts. At least the blood-sucking bankers had to swallow those.'

Everybody nodded as if it sounded like there was at least some justice left in the world.

'Did you know Roy Lynch's son Gavin ended up working for the company?' Angel said.

Cameron's reaction suggested clearly not. He swivelled around, both feet on the floor now as if he was getting ready to stand.

'Really?' He narrowed his eyes at Angel as the implication hit him. 'Are you implying Roy Lynch was somehow behind the company's problems? Then, when it was sold to his friend Yardley for a pittance, Yardley reciprocated by employing his son?'

'I'm not implying anything. But you've just outlined a very plausible scenario.'

'How on earth could Roy Lynch be behind it?'

Angel opened his hands wide like the Pope at Easter, caught Kincade smirking at him out of the corner of his eye.

'No idea.'

Thinking Cameron had been the one to suggest it, not him.

'Speaking of children, what about Lucas's?'

The belligerence that had underscored the talk of Roy Lynch potentially being involved in the demise of his brother's company melted away, regret taking its place. Cameron leaned forwards, forearms on his thighs, a posture Angel consciously stopped himself from mimicking.

'I wanted to help with them, I really did. It wasn't healthy that someone like Roy Lynch was the only man in their lives. But it was impossible from the other side of the Atlantic.'

'What happened to them?'

Cameron responded by looking at his wife, the regret on his face now changing to apprehension as he addressed her directly.

'I've never told you any of this . . .' He tried a smile which only made him look as if another spasm of pain had gone through his hip. 'You might not have agreed to marry me if I had.'

She told him not to be so silly, clearly interested in what was coming. As were Angel and Kincade.

'As you know, Lynch moved in after Lucas's death and brought his boys with him. I believe his wife was a drug addict which is why he had custody.'

He then repeated what Evelyn Walker had told Gulliver and Jardine. That it hadn't worked out well for Lucas's children, being a year or two younger than the incomers.

He looked at his wife again, clearly uncomfortable that what he was about to say was only coming out now under direct questioning from the police.

'I've wanted to tell you this so many times...'

Seemed Barbara was getting as fed up with the prevarication as Angel and Kincade were.

'Just spit it out, Aiden.'

And when he did, everyone in the room wished from the bottom of their hearts that he hadn't.

39

'About a year after Lucas's death, Jessica got pregnant. She refused to say who the father was. She was fifteen at the time and didn't have a boyfriend. The suspicion was that Gavin Lynch was responsible. Consensual or rape, who knows? Roy Lynch put pressure on Marianne to put pressure on Jessica to have an abortion. She refused.' He paused, swallowed thickly. Cleared his throat. Managed not to look directly at any of the other three people in the room, spitting the words out as if they were contaminated. 'She died in childbirth. And so did the baby.'

His voice changed, became the flat monotone of a man deliberately distancing himself from his words. As if afraid that a stray emotion was all it would take to undo all of the healing work time had done.

'Jessica collapsed at week thirty-seven of the pregnancy . . .'

She'd been rushed to Princess Anne Hospital, the resulting emergency C-section classified as late preterm. She died on the day. The cause of death was ruled at the subsequent inquest as a combination of undiagnosed mitral valve prolapse—a common form of mitral valve disease affecting two per cent of the population that is harmless for most people, a lot of whom have no symptoms and are unaware that they have it—and ventricular fibrillation.

Her baby, whose name Cameron had never been told, was described as being in a poorly condition at birth and passed away two days later. Cause of death was severe hypoxic-ischemic encephalopathy—too little oxygen to the brain—compounded by the emergency delivery following sudden maternal cardiovascular collapse.

Angel was aware of Kincade's eyes on him the whole time Cameron spoke in his lifeless monotone.

Talk to me now about a loving God.

Nobody said anything for a very long time after Cameron's voice faded to nothing. Everyone far too fascinated by the pattern in the carpet.

Kincade broke the silence, made her own opinion clear in the process.

'The rape was never reported?'

Cameron cleared his throat again, his voice still hoarse when he answered.

'Obviously not. Jessica never accused Gavin. She was scared of him and his father. I hate to say it about my ex-sister-in-law, but Marianne was a waste of space. If Roy Lynch had said to her, get a coat hanger, I'll hold her legs open, she'd have done it.' He glanced at his wife after saying it, shrugged. It is what it is.

Barbara clapped her hands together. Jumped up and started collecting empty tea cups.

'Right. I'll just clear these away.'

Everybody busied themselves finishing off the dregs and holding their cup out, thankful of some activity in the room. Angel thought it was an excuse on Barbara's part to get out of the room, that he wouldn't see her again. He was wrong. She came back a minute later, a glass of water in her hand. She sat down, didn't bother asking if anyone else wanted one.

'Did you come back for Jessica's funeral?' Angel said to Cameron.

A look passed across Cameron's face as if Angel had asked whether they left her lying in a ditch.

'No. I wasn't well myself at the time.' He looked at his wife. 'You remember when . . .' He trailed off when she shook her head, *not really*, before he'd even said what was wrong with him.

'Who told you what happened?'

'Marianne, of course. It was hardly going to be Roy Lynch, was it?'

'Did you ask to see a copy of the inquest report?'

'No. Why would I?'

It seemed to Angel that there was a little too much aggression in the response. Guilt, he supposed.

'Your niece had just died in tragic circumstances. Sometimes people need to see it in black and white—'

'What? To make it real? It was real enough, I can assure you. I didn't need to read some dry legal document turning a family tragedy into a fucking statistic.'

'You've got a good grasp of the technical details, that's all. *Hypoxic-ischemic encephalopathy* and so on. That's a bit of a mouthful for a grieving mother to tell you in a trans-Atlantic phone call.'

'As it happens, Matt told me years later. Maybe he saw the inquest report. I never asked him.'

The mention of Jessica's brother presented a perfect opportunity to move on from what was deteriorating into an antagonistic line of questioning, one to which Cameron was responding in an increasingly aggressive manner. Angel jumped at it.

'Tell me about Matt?'

Cameron blew the air from his cheeks, looking like a man for whom the worst is behind him.

'He had a rough time, obviously. He was bullied by the older boys, two against one. I'm sure they were very cruel about his father's death, as children can be. He ended up running away from home when he was sixteen. I thought I'd never hear from him again. Then, one day after we'd moved back from the States, he made contact. We've kept in touch ever since. As I said when you first arrived, we hadn't heard from him for a while, then he called out of the blue just before I went in for my operation. He's been staying here for a few weeks.'

'What does he do for a living?'

'Self-employed website designer. Work's a bit slow at the moment which is why he took the opportunity to come down and stay. He lives in London. And he can always work remotely if he picks something up while he's here.'

Angel would rather not have asked his next question, casting doubt as it did on Matt Cameron, the devoted nephew who was happy to look after his recuperating uncle.

'I'm sorry to have to ask you this, but are you able to confirm his whereabouts on the nights of the twelfth and fourteenth of July?'

Cameron's first reaction was a mix of alarm and horror.

'You're not suggesting he had something to do with Roy Lynch's death, are you?' Confusion quickly took its place as the words rolled out of his mouth. 'Hang on . . . why two dates?'

'Guy Yardley has also been killed.'

Cameron shook his head vehemently, looking at his wife for support.

'You can't seriously think Matt had anything to do with either of those deaths.'

It was a statement, not a question. One that Angel was forced to contradict.

'We can't ignore any possibilities. Are you able to confirm his whereabouts on those two dates?'

Angel got the impression that if it hadn't been for his leg, Cameron would've leapt to his feet as he responded.

'Absolutely. He was here with me.'

'You seem very sure without checking.'

'I don't need to check. Last Tuesday we went to the Harbour Lights Picturehouse to see the new *Indiana Jones*. The Friday before that there was a quiz night at The Hunters Inn. Apart from that, we've stayed in every night.' He pointed at a well-stocked drinks cabinet against the wall. 'Had a drink here. Matt likes his whisky. But he's not what you'd call a party animal. He gets a bit morose if he has too much.' He tapped his left leg a couple of times. 'I'm not exactly up for it myself at the moment.'

'Aiden's not a party animal at the best of times,' Barbara added, which everybody ignored.

'And he didn't pop out at any time for an hour?' Angel persevered. 'Get some fresh air? Walk the dog?'

'We don't have a dog. But to answer your question, no. And before you ask, I'm not on any medication for my hip that knocks me out at night.'

The situation needed defusing. Cameron had continued to grow redder in the face as Angel fired question after question.

'You think I could have a glass of water, please, Mrs Cameron?'

'Sure. Help yourself.'

It wasn't what he was expecting, but it did the trick all the same.

'Anyone else?'

Kincade and Cameron shook their heads. Barbara drained her glass and handed it to him.

'Please.'

Whatever.

The tension had eased marginally when he got back. He gave an almost imperceptible dip of his head towards Kincade —*you take it from here.*

'Has Matt got a girlfriend?' she said, looking at both Cameron and his wife.

'He doesn't talk about anyone,' Cameron said.

Barbara gave him a look.

'You said you thought he was gay, but he hadn't come out yet. Except you said *queer*.' She looked at Angel and Kincade, smiled at them. 'I'll deny it if you try to arrest him for a hate crime.'

Kincade smiled back, moved on. Addressing Cameron this time.

'Has he always worked in IT?'

'As far as I know.'

Barbara jumped in again, the accusatory note still in her voice.

'You told me he could have been a professional footballer. He could've been earning millions.'

Cameron wasn't happy at the interruption. Whether he was simply getting tired of his wife's interruptions, or whether the reference to football annoyed him specifically was impossible to say. He sounded as if he was talking to the dog they didn't have —a puppy—when he replied.

'As a junior, yes. He wasn't good enough to make it in the Premier League.'

Was that because he'd sustained an injury? Angel wondered. *One that left him with a limp, perhaps?*

'Is he still staying with you?' Kincade asked.

Cameron reacted in the last way either Angel or Kincade would have expected. He chuckled, a good-natured sound after the hostile atmosphere of a minute ago.

'It's ironic what I said earlier about Marianne not wanting to go camping in The New Forest. It was something I pulled out of the air as an example of their reduced circumstances. But that's exactly what Matt's doing. A few days camping in The New Forest. He left the day before yesterday. He didn't say exactly where he was going.'

Kincade worked an amused look onto her face at the funny old ways of the world.

'That's okay, sir. If you give us his mobile number, we'll call him and ask him. If you could also let us have his address in London, while you're at it. I don't suppose you've got a recent photograph, have you? Patient and nurse, sort of thing.'

Cameron dug around for his phone which had slipped down the gap behind the sofa cushions as he slouched on it.

'I can give you an address and a phone number. But the last photo I've got of him is probably from before I went to the States. I think he was three at the time. Barb can go up in the loft and dig something out if you want.'

Much to Barbara Cameron's relief, Kincade shook her head as she took down the mobile number and address Cameron read out to her.

'Don't worry about it. How's he getting around down here?'

'He's got a car. A silver Ford Focus. It belongs to a friend. He doesn't have a car in London. And no, I don't know the registration number.'

Kincade shrugged. You win some, you lose some.

'We can't have you doing our whole job for us, sir. But ask him to call us if you speak to him before we do.'

They both knew as they got up to leave that he'd have done so before they were back at the car.

40

'Open the Companies House website on your phone,' Angel said to Kincade as they drove away from the little enclave of family tragedy that was the Camerons' house. 'I want to look up Stephen Bishop's company. All the details should be there if it's still active.'

By unspoken mutual consent, a discussion of what had happened to Jessica Cameron would wait until they'd distanced themselves sufficiently from it with a cleansing dose of everyday police work.

She'd already tried calling Matt Cameron's number and had left a message asking him to call her back when it went to voicemail. Neither of them was holding their breath. Now, she was expecting the usual interview post-mortem, scoring Aiden Cameron on how many truths, how many lies, the number of grey areas, and identifying matters to be followed up.

Instead, it appeared he'd made up his mind already.

She opened the browser on her phone, did as he'd said. Scanned the options available and suggested the most likely.

'Get information about a company?'

'That's the one.'

She entered *SBM Logistics* into the search box, hit *return*. Clicked on the top result.

Angel glanced across at the screen.

'You want the *people* tab. What's it say?'

'Five officers, four resignations. Stephen Bishop's there. Born 1940, making him eighty-three, if he's still alive. Appointed April 1970, resigned in June 2008. Either he's enjoying a well-earned retirement after almost forty years running the company, or he's six feet under after knackering himself.'

'Who else?'

'Oliver Bishop.'

'Must be his son.'

'Born December 1968, making him fifty-five. Appointed January 1998. No resignation. He's still there.'

She didn't need to be told to enter *SBM Logistics* into Google to find the company website.

'I wonder if Matt Cameron designed it for them?' she said, thinking aloud as she opened the site.

They exchanged a look. She flicked her way to the bottom of the page with her middle finger where a credit to the designer could often be found.

'Doesn't say. We can ask Bishop when we talk to him.' She navigated to the contact page, but held off from calling the number listed. 'What are you thinking?'

'I want to know why Stephen Bishop cancelled the order that ended up being the final nail in Lucas Cameron's company's coffin.'

'Maybe he found a better price elsewhere.'

'Only one way to find out.' He indicated and pulled to the kerb, left the engine running. 'What's the correspondence address for Stephen Bishop?'

'You're thinking we should go there now?'

'Actually, no. Call the company. Talk to junior to find out if dad's still alive first.'

She made the call, identified herself to the switchboard operator and was put through to Oliver Bishop's personal gatekeeper.

'He's not in the office today.'

She said it so quickly, Kincade suspected it was a default response whether he was there or not. So that Bishop could decide who he did and didn't talk to.

The woman sounded middle-aged to her. The bored tone of a person who's been in the same job for far too long. If so, there was a chance she'd worked for Stephen Bishop as well as his son.

'Maybe you can help me.'

'I'll try.' Making it sound as if it wouldn't be very hard.

'Do you know if Stephen Bishop is still alive?'

The gatekeeper's voice softened, the tone alerting Kincade to the bad news that was coming.

'No. I mean, yes I know, and no, he's not still alive. Thirty-eight years he ran the company, and he was dead within a year of handing over the reins to his son. I think he died of boredom, to tell you the truth. He should never have retired.'

Kincade gave Angel a thumbs-down as the gatekeeper talked.

'Do you have a mobile number for Oliver Bishop?' she said, then, before the woman could roll out the usual bullshit, 'I realise that you don't normally give out numbers, but this is a matter of some urgency. I'm not at liberty to say what, exactly, but we can't wait for Mr Bishop to call us back. I can give you a number to call if you want to check that I am who I say I am.'

The softness went out of the gatekeeper's voice, a prim, clipped tone that reinforced Kincade's impression of an older woman replacing it.

'That won't be necessary, Sergeant.'

She then recited the number by heart, asked if there was anything else in a tone that suggested there better not be, and they ended the call.

Angel was grinning at her when she'd finished.

'Full marks for pompous officialese. *I'm not at liberty . . .*'

'What would you say?'

'How about, I can't say?'

She shook her head, shows how much you know.

'She's an old biddy. The *not at liberty* line works better. Anyway, you want me to call junior? Interrupt him on the golf course. I mean, in a business meeting.'

He studied her a long moment as she waited for an answer, then said something she wasn't expecting.

'Is that an insight into the corporate world based on personal experience of being married to your husband?'

'Yep. They get paid the big bucks because they supposedly work so hard, but a lot of the time they're on a jolly.'

'Do I detect a hint of sour grapes?'

She shook her head, big side-to-side strokes, then showed him her eye teeth, a malicious pleasure in her eyes.

'Nope. He's got an ulcer from all those business lunches.'

He flicked his finger at the phone still in her hand.

'Make the call.'

Needless to say, it went to voicemail. She left a message, asked Bishop to call her back as a matter of urgency.

'You think his secretary called him while we've been talking, warned him?' she said as she pocketed the phone.

'Definitely. Whether that's why he didn't answer is a different matter.'

The time had come to leave behind the safety of dry talk about companies and cancelled contracts, move onto the emotionally-charged parts of the story Aiden Cameron had told.

Angel started by kicking it into Kincade's court, as was his right.

'What did you think of Cameron's story about Jessica?'

The anger she'd shown earlier at the mention of rape was gone, sadness in its place at the tragic consequences.

'I don't want to think about it at all. It's too depressing. But it needs confirming. We need to get hold of the inquest report.'

Although she hadn't said it in so many words, the implication was clear.

'What part don't you believe?' he said.

'I didn't like the caveat that it was all told to him across the Atlantic. He didn't come back for the funeral so he didn't talk to anyone in person, didn't ask to see the inquest report. It's as if he was preparing for being caught in a lie at a future date and wanted to be able to claim ignorance.'

'I agree. But that's not answering my question.'

They were still parked at the kerb where he'd stopped in case they needed to drive directly to Stephen Bishop's house. Now that it wasn't going to happen, he pulled back into the traffic heading for the station as she thought about his question.

'Okay. You want me to stick my neck out?'

'I thought it was quite clear I'm not going to stop until you do.'

She couldn't argue with that.

'What if Jessica's child didn't die? And she's the mystery young woman.'

He glanced at her, then back at the road ahead as the traffic came to a sudden unexplained halt. He leaned sideways to look around the car in front, then went back to her.

'And how would that work? No piss-taking about miracles and resurrections.'

She gave him a pained look. *Who moi?* Then counted the points off on her fingers.

'The inquest will be black and white. Either only Jessica died, or they both died. End of. If she didn't, there are only two possibilities. Aiden Cameron knows it and he just told us a very detailed lie...'

'Hypoxic-ischemic encephalopathy, you mean?'

'Exactly. I'm really impressed you keep remembering that.'

He smiled at the compliment, thinking, *one day soon I'm going to have to tell you why*, then made a joke of it.

'That's why I get paid the big bucks.'

Her mouth turned down at the outlandish remark.

'You're forgetting that I used to be the same rank as you, sir. Anyway, the other possibility is that Marianne lied to Cameron and he never bothered to check. You can sort of understand why she would. Her daughter's been raped by her new husband's son—'

'You seem very sure on that point.'

'That's because I am.'

'Based on what?'

'Having met Gavin Lynch is sufficient for me. So, her daughter's been raped and dies giving birth. What's she going to do with the baby if it survives? Bring it home? So that it can grow up asking, *where's Mummy, Granny? Who's my daddy?* Not forgetting the constant reminder of what Roy Lynch's son did to his wife's daughter. I don't think so. They give it away and decide to tell Great-Uncle Aiden that it died rather than risk him trying to intervene. Maybe they thought he was never coming back from the States and wouldn't ever find out.'

'And Matt Cameron goes along with the deception?'

She gave him a look. It suggested that although she'd never asked, she was now taking it as read that he didn't have children. Nor had he ever met one.

'They tell him the same thing. He's a thirteen-year-old boy, for Christ's sake. You think he was even listening when his mother told him what happened to his big sister's baby?' She put her hands together as if holding a games console, thumbs tapping up and down. 'He's too busy killing aliens and trying to get to the next level.'

He took it from there, even though he wasn't fully behind the idea.

'Then what? He runs away, wakes up one day and decides to find out the truth? Somehow locates his dead sister's child and together they go on a killing spree?' He left the words hanging a couple of beats, then knocked them down. 'The only trouble is, they seem to have killed everyone apart from the person the most responsible. Gavin Lynch. Why kill Roy?'

'Unless he raped her, not Gavin.'

'And Yardley?'

'Maybe he joined in.'

'I'm not sure it's completely healthy the way answers like that come so naturally to you without appearing to have to think about it. I hope for your daughters' sakes that you have a different thought process at home.'

'Apart from when we're talking about their father, yes.'

Despite the light-hearted remark about how her mind worked, something she'd said made him think. The way she voiced the sort of questions Jessica's child might have asked had she survived.

Where's Mummy, Granny? Who's my daddy?

'Awkward,' he said.

For a moment she thought he was continuing with the conversation about her girls and estranged husband.

'How do you mean?'

'Where was Jessica during her pregnancy? At home with her mother and Roy Lynch and his sons? That's as bad as bringing the child home if it had survived. All watching her belly getting bigger and bigger. Listening to her throwing up in the morning and complaining about not being able to get into the bathroom.'

'Maybe they had two? It's a big house.'

'You know what I mean. We should have asked Aiden Cameron. Call him and ask him now.'

She did as he said. As with everyone else she'd tried calling, it went to voicemail. She left a message to call her back, pocketed the phone. Checked her watch.

'I feel like I need something to wash away the taste of Cameron's story.'

'Listerine?'

'Only if all the pubs are shut.'

'Prior engagement, I'm afraid.'

She lifted her arm, sniffed her armpit. Shrugged.

'It can't be that. I'm starting to feel like a pariah. Last time you were rushing off to see your father. Who is it this time?'

He ran his fingernail from his throat down to his belt instead of answering. Refusing to look at her while she thought about it. An amused chuckle signalled when it clicked.

'Everybody's favourite pathologist, Dr Isabel Durand? I knew there was something going on there.'

'There isn't *something going on*. And there better not be *something going around* the station about what isn't going on when I get in tomorrow. She's cooking me dinner, that's all. I told you, we're old friends.'

A wide grin broke out on her face. If he was expecting further ribbing about romantic attachments, he was wrong.

'Rather you than me. Just promise me you'll leave immediately if she says she's cooked liver, kidneys, heart or brains. And I'd take your own red wine if I were you.'

41

Catalina Kincade was feeling as if she deserved a medal—loyalty in the face of overwhelming nosiness—when Lisa Jardine stuck her head around the door at just after seven o'clock.

'Boss not here?'

Very briefly, Kincade considered mimicking Angel's gesture, running her finger from her throat to her navel, and in doing so feeding Jardine's hunger for gossip.

'Something he had to do,' she said instead. 'What did you want him for?'

Jardine shook her head, already turning away.

'Doesn't matter. It'll wait.'

Kincade suddenly felt very much the outsider, the new kid on the block. She was tempted to ask, *don't you trust me?* It was obvious that Jardine had something on her mind, something she'd wanted to run past Angel. And she thought, *bollocks, I'll provoke a reaction.*

'Would it be any different if it was Stuart Beckford sitting here and not me?'

The question wasn't anything Jardine was expecting. Her

face made that very clear. Her reply was a lesson in not answering when she found her voice.

'That's impossible to say seeing as it isn't.'

'I suppose that's better than you saying, *absolutely*.' She gave a dismissive flick of her hand. 'I'll tell him you were looking for him.'

Jardine stayed standing in the doorway.

Kincade felt like carrying on in the same vein.

Yes or no? If you're going to say it, say it. Otherwise I've got things to do.

'Something about the interview with Marianne Lynch's sister, Evelyn?' she said instead, extending her hand towards Angel's chair.

Jardine grinned as she came into the room, lowered herself into it as if it was the gateway to hell.

'I hope I don't come over all religious if I sit here too long.'

'Could be worse. You might start playing the mouth organ. So, what's on your mind?'

Jardine rocked her head from side to side, face compacted.

'Evelyn Walker's daughter.'

'What about her?'

'I got a funny feeling she was trying to avoid us. And that was after her mother did her best to not tell us her name. I was looking at a photograph of two teenage girls and she said, *that's my daughter*. But she didn't say what her name was. All she said was that she's a doctor. She didn't say what sort, either. Whether she's a GP or a surgeon or something in the middle. But I couldn't help thinking, doctors are good with knives.' She stuck out her tongue, ran her thumb sideways across it, as if severing it. Then shook her head at herself and jumped up. 'Just saying it out loud makes it sound stupid.'

'What does Craig Gulliver think?'

'That I'm imagining things. And that he wishes his doctor looked like her.'

Jardine paused at the door, looking as if she had more to say. Which she did, and nothing Kincade was expecting.

'It wouldn't have made any difference if it had been DS Beckford sitting there.'

Despite having asked the question earlier, Kincade didn't know what to say. Then her phone rang, a diversion that both women welcomed. Jardine slipped away as Kincade pulled it out to check the display.

She wasn't expecting it to be Matt Cameron, and nor was it. It was his Uncle Aiden.

'I was wondering where Jessica was living while she was pregnant,' Kincade said.

'At home with her mother, as far as I'm aware.'

'You don't know?'

She'd only met him the once, but she had no problem picturing him shaking his head on the other end of the line.

'As I keep telling you, I was in the States.'

Excuse #1, she thought with a mental yawn as the now-familiar words rolled out.

'Didn't you wonder about how awkward that might be?'

'Probably. But it was thirty years ago. As I told you, Jessica never actually accused Gavin Lynch of rape. Besides, where would she have gone? A Salvation Army hostel for unmarried mothers?'

No, but you've just answered the question for me, she thought as they ended the call, the memory of Lisa Jardine sitting in Angel's chair and their recent conversation in her mind.

I was looking at a photograph of two teenage girls...

She sat for a while thinking it through, then went back to the internet search she'd done for *Campsites in The New Forest*. Wondering where to start on the disheartening sixty-seven campsites within a fifteen-mile radius when her phone rang again.

Oliver Bishop this time, the man currently running SBM Logistics—the company that pushed Lucas Cameron over the edge when they cancelled the contract that might have saved his business.

'I wanted to talk to you about something that happened in 1993,' she said.

The tide of relief that came down the line almost washed her away.

'That was before my time.' It was an automatic, subconscious response triggered by a time frame that pre-dated the year of his own appointment by five years. Then it registered in his conscious mind. 'Hang on . . . did you say 1993?'

'That's right.'

'I think I know what you want to talk about. The cancelled contract.'

She didn't miss the use of the definite article, *the* cancelled contract, the implication that it had been the only one. But clearly memorable.

'You know about it even though you weren't there?'

'Oh, yes. Dad never really got over it . . .'

A minute later they had an appointment booked for the following morning.

See what your gatekeeper thinks about that, she thought as they ended the call.

She stayed a while longer, put in a request for the inquest report into the death of Jessica Cameron from the Southampton coroner's office, made a couple of calls to ex-colleagues in London regarding Matt Cameron at the address in Islington they'd been given, and then called it a day. Wondering if Isabel Durand had indeed cooked liver, kidneys, heart or brains for

Angel. At the moment, she felt hungry enough to eat any of them.

Just not tongue.

'I'm complimented, Max,' Isabel Durand said. 'It's only linguine with samphire and prawns.'

He'd pulled out his phone as she put the bowl down in front of him and taken a couple of pictures.

'Don't tell me you've opened an Instagram account and you're going to post them to it,' she said. 'I didn't think you did social media.'

He pocketed the phone, picked up his fork and wound it into the pasta.

'I don't. It's evidence.'

'Really? Of what?'

'For when Kincade grills me tomorrow about what you've cooked us. She thought it would be either liver, kidneys, heart or brains.'

Durand smiled as if she was wishing she'd thought of it herself before defrosting the prawns.

'In a blood sauce?'

'No, that was to drink.'

'Cerebrospinal fluid, perhaps?'

He was starting to wish the phone had stayed in his pocket. Except he knew from long experience that it wasn't possible to spend an evening with Durand and not be made acutely aware of what she did for a living at some point. Trouble was, she was getting into her stride now.

'I'm a little disappointed at her imagination,' she said, 'if that's the limit of the organs she thinks I might have misappropriated from the autopsy room.'

'That's a conversation the two of you should have together.'
Thinking, *without me*.

'Maybe I should have invited her tonight, as well. Then she could've tried to guess what I served her.'

She was joking, he knew that. A third person, one whom neither of them knew well, would stifle the conversation she had in mind. A discussion that would leave him feeling as if he was back in the autopsy room, not outside the French doors of her house in the picturesque village of Beaulieu. Laid out on the dissecting table, rather than sitting at a rickety flea-market bistro table on the weathered brick patio enjoying an alfresco meal in the warm evening, the scent of jasmine on the night air, the light spilling out from the kitchen and a pair of paraffin storm lanterns providing the only illumination. He might show Kincade a picture of the food, but not the setting. He'd never hear the end of it.

'Anyway, this is excellent,' he said in an attempt to move the conversation on.

She smiled, not at the compliment, but at the way he was struggling with the linguine.

'You can have a spoon if you really want. Eat it like a true Englishman.'

He shook his head, absolutely not. A long time ago, she'd told him how Italians only ever use a fork to eat pasta. Only the English cheat by twirling it in a spoon, a habit that amuses the Italians no end. Now, it was a joke between them—to spoon or not to spoon. And he was determined not to give in.

'So, what's she like?' Durand said. 'Kincade, I mean.'

He broke off a piece of crusty sourdough roll, dipped it in his sauce as he thought about how to answer. He knew Durand wasn't interested in his assessment of how competent a police officer Kincade was. Or even if she was likely to throw up in the autopsy room as Durand had accused her.

'I'm not sure about the story she tells about being demoted. I did a search of the misconduct hearings, couldn't find anything about it.'

She took a sip of the Pinot Noir he'd brought, considering him over the rim of the glass.

'What do you think it might be? Presumably if it was something particularly egregious, she'd have been kicked out.'

'Except she's got Uncle James looking out for her.'

'The implication being that the problem was with the offence committed, not the person committing it. The hearing wasn't reported because the powers that be don't want whatever she was doing at the time coming to light?'

'Could be.'

She nodded as if he'd given her the definitive answer she'd been hoping for.

'I'll try to remember to use that phrase in my reports going forward. *Could be* a gunshot wound. *Could be* an overdose of heroin. *Could be* human skin under the fingernails or nasal mucus.'

He held up a hand, enough now.

'You'd like me to speculate based on no evidence whatsoever, instead?'

'No. Just a gut feel based on having worked with her.'

He concentrated on coaxing linguine onto his fork, aware of her not eating herself as she watched him in the flickering light. He felt like a junior pathologist making a hash of his first post-mortem while the learned professor looked on.

'There's definitely more to it, and to her, but I honestly don't know what it might be.'

Momentarily, he thought she was about to throw her bread roll at him. She took a bite of it, instead, talking as she chewed.

'Have it your way. I just hope you don't have a problem

working with someone with secrets.' Then mouthing to herself, *pot, kettle, black.*

He guessed it was better than her putting her fork and wine glass down, elbows on the table and an earnest look in her eye as she asked him, *how are you, Padre?*

It was also a neat way of putting the ball in his court. He could choose to say, *of course not*, and leave it at that. Or he could say more.

He took a deep breath, the smell of jasmine stronger now as a light breeze picked up. It caught his paper napkin, blew it onto the ground. He could've bent to retrieve it, the perfect opportunity to then sit back up and talk about something different.

He left it where it was.

'I keep hearing Cormac's voice. *I don't know what to do, Max.* Someone will say something, and *bang!* I'm right back there. And the nightmares are back.'

Now she did put down her fork. Stretched across the table to put her hand on his arm.

'It's understandable.'

'Maybe to you it is, but not to me. Why am I thinking and dreaming about that now? It's fifteen years. If there's anything that should be keeping me awake at night, I'd have thought it would be . . .' He faltered, the words that he spoke so often in his job catching in his throat. 'How can Cormac hijack that, for Christ's sake?'

'Who knows? We know so little about how the mind works.'

'Even though you cut brains up all day long.'

She withdrew her hand, leaned back, her head in the shadows now. Smiling at him, the length of time they'd known each other reflected in the softness of it.

'That's something we *do* understand. Changing the subject to avoid talking about what's really on your mind. I believe it's known as *male reaction number one.*'

He dropped his eyes to his lap briefly, a lascivious grin on his lips.

'I thought that was when a man sees a pretty woman?'

'There you go, doing it again.' She wagged a finger at him. 'I'd have thought that as an ex-priest you'd understand the value of unburdening yourself.'

'I think the clue's in the *ex*.'

'It's okay, I don't mind if you don't want to talk about it. I suppose a man who decides to go for a walk for four hundred and ninety-two miles has his own way of dealing with things. But I will say one thing . . .' She waited for him to stop mopping sauce with the last of his bread and look at her. 'You have to tell Kincade about it soon. It's not fair on her to be wondering what the hell the big deal is with her boss and her predecessor that nobody wants to talk about.'

42

Roy Lynch's former cleaner, Dot Boyle, had to admit that her husband had a point, although if you say anything enough times it soon comes to look like the truth.

All that booze going to waste.

Dot had been married to George long enough to know that pointing out that alcohol was not perishable was not what he wanted to hear.

'All those years,' he said, 'working your fingers to the bone. And for what? A pittance. If you'd left and the tight bastard had to employ somebody else, he'd have had to pay them double what he paid you.'

Little by little he was wearing her down. A bit like life itself.

'How much did you say he paid for that old Jag?' George went on. 'He could've afforded to pay you an extra pound an hour.'

Dot knew she'd give in eventually. But it felt wrong. Stealing from the dead. She said this to George. George had an answer, of course, a smug smile on his lips knowing that he was about to get his way any minute.

'No, you'd be stealing from his sons. They own everything now. It's not stealing, anyway. It's accumulated back pay.'

Dot tried one last tactic, knowing that it wasn't going to work as she trudged into the kitchen to fetch the key to Roy Lynch's house. She thrust it at her husband.

'There's the key. You get it. You'll be able to carry more bottles than I can.'

He gave her the look she'd been expecting. The same one he gave her when she asked if he'd help with the washing up instead of sitting on his fat arse in front of the TV.

'What if somebody catches me in the house? What am I going to say? You've got an excuse if they catch you. You tell them you wanted to come in and clean, keep the place nice for his sons. Because you've got a good heart.'

She knew when she was beat. There was no point asking him who he thought might catch him or her. She could've wasted her breath, said he could claim he'd come to cut the grass. A quick look at their own garden would soon put paid to that. As for trying to say that she was scared to go in because of the bad experience she'd had the last time . . . he'd come out with some old bollocks about having to confront your fears head-on. Not that he'd ever confronted his fear of a day's hard work.

Which is how she found herself on Lynch's front step, inserting her key into the lock as she had so many times before, a heavy-duty canvas tote bag in her hand.

She stood a while in the hallway listening to the quiet. Glancing at the stairs, she noticed mud on the bottom two or three steps. Careless coppers not wiping their feet, no doubt. Weren't they supposed to wear those blue booties?

Then it came to her.

The perfect solution to her mini crisis of conscience. She'd clean the house for real. Then take payment in booze. Now that she looked around, there was fingerprint powder everywhere. There'd be enough to do to justify a few bottles.

Before that, she was determined to do what she'd imagined George saying to her—confront her fears. She'd go into the garage. Prove to herself that it was only a garage. And apart from the sudden loss of her earnings, a garage with not much in the way of bad memories attached to it. She wouldn't miss Roy Lynch one jot.

She went through to the kitchen.

The door to the garage hadn't been mended after George kicked it in. If she'd thought about it when she was arguing with him, she'd have suggested he fix it in exchange for the booze he wanted. As it was, it had been closed, but couldn't be locked because of the splintered door frame.

She stood in front of it for a long while. Hand on the handle, the door cracked open an inch. Blackness beyond it. Heart going like a triphammer in her chest. Listening. For what, she had no idea. Putting it off, that's all.

She told herself not to be so stupid, wishing she'd asked George to come with her. Took a deep breath and pushed the door all the way open. Flicked on the light.

Nothing.

The room was empty. No body swinging gently on the end of a clothesline. Not even the Jag. It was still parked outside on the drive.

She felt stupid as she walked into the room. And relieved. She went to stand under the rafter from which Roy Lynch had been hanging the last time she was here. It was just a rafter.

Even so, she didn't close her eyes. Tempt fate to put an image of his grotesque face in her mind.

She felt a lot better when she came out again. A sense of achievement. She'd overcome her fear. And without a patronising lecture from George beforehand.

She collected the vacuum cleaner from the cupboard under the stairs, stepped carefully around the mud on the bottom steps and made her way upstairs. She'd start there, work her way down.

She stood a minute outside the door to the small, fourth bedroom as she often had in the past. She hadn't worked for the Lynches back then, but she'd heard the stories, the rumours about what had gone on. In this small bedroom, by all accounts. Except how any of George's drunken cronies in the White Horse would've known which bedroom, she couldn't begin to imagine.

Still, it had an air of sadness about it.

Suddenly she didn't feel so bad about stealing Roy Lynch's sons' booze. One of them had stolen a lot more from a young girl in this very room, robbed Jessica Cameron and all those who loved her of everything she was.

If she'd been Marianne Lynch, she wouldn't have settled for having the room hoovered and dusted once a week. She'd have taken a bucket of industrial-strength bleach to it. A flamethrower if she could've got her hands on one.

But all that was in the past now.

It was just a room. Like the garage was just a garage.

Except it wasn't when Dot pushed open the door and stepped inside, her knees buckling as the scream bounced off the walls.

It was an execution chamber.

43

Kincade wasn't quick enough with her prepared joke when Angel walked into their office the next morning looking very pleased with himself.

She'd thought about asking him to undo a couple of shirt buttons so that she could inspect his chest for a Y-shaped incision following his dinner with Isabel Durand the night before. She'd rejected the idea, decided she didn't know him well enough yet.

She was going to keep it to a simple question.

Was it Roy Lynch or Guy Yardley?

Hopefully not have to prompt him—*that you had for dinner last night*. It spoiled the effect if you were forced to explain.

Then Craig Gulliver walked in with a question of his own. One that took over.

'What's the worst thing you want to start your day with, sir?'

Kincade felt her blood run cold as she watched the same realisation come over Angel's face.

'Another body,' he said, sounding like a dead one himself.

'Yeah. Want to try to make it even worse?'

That was easy.

'Gavin Lynch.'

'Got it in one. Go for broke?'

'At his father's house?'

Gulliver had looked up at the ceiling at that point.

'You're getting help from someone up there, sir.'

After that, Kincade hadn't felt in the mood for joking about his dinner date with a woman who cut dead bodies open for a living. That didn't mean she didn't ask anything at all. But she kept it simple.

'Enjoyable dinner last night?'

'Very.'

He gave her a strange look that made her feel uncomfortable. As if he was assessing her. Trying to determine if she was being nosy, probing for salacious details following on from her remarks the previous evening about a possible romantic liaison between him and Durand. Except it didn't feel like that. She got a premonition that if the circumstances were otherwise, there was something he wanted to say.

Now, it would have to wait.

But it had something to do with the fact that this morning he'd told her that she could drive for a change.

All in all, agreeing that his evening had been *very enjoyable* didn't tell the half of it.

Ten minutes later, she could've asked Durand the same question. Except she was busy with Gavin Lynch's corpse in the small bedroom of his father's house.

'The same cleaning lady found him,' Gulliver told them.

'What was she doing here?' Angel said.

Gulliver smiled briefly.

'Supposedly to clear out all the perishables.'

'Really? I like a perishable and tonic myself. Or a malt perishable over ice. So, what happened?'

'It looks as if somebody was waiting for him in the house. At the moment, we don't know why he came back here. They hit him over the head as he walked in, then dragged him upstairs.'

Angel nodded to himself, remembered seeing the mud on the bottom stairs that they'd had to step around.

Gulliver smiled knowingly again.

'Mrs Boyle said she decided to give the house a quick clean in exchange for the perishables she was about to take. That's why she was up here.'

'Has anybody asked her about this particular room?'

'I don't know, sir. But she keeps calling it Jessica's room.'

Nobody needed to ask why.

Despite what Aiden Cameron had said about Jessica Cameron not accusing Gavin Lynch of raping her, somebody clearly believed that he had. And they were of the opinion this was the room where it happened.

They squeezed into the small room, already filled with men and women virtually indistinguishable in their protective white suits. Durand was leaning over Gavin Lynch's body laid out on the single bed. Spread-eagled on his back, his wrists and ankles tied to the bedpost at each corner.

Durand looked up when they entered—with a quick smile for Angel, Kincade couldn't help noticing.

'When was he killed?' Angel asked.

'I'd say thirty to thirty-six hours ago.'

'So, sometime late, the night before last.'

The interview with Aiden Cameron was immediately in his mind. Specifically, Cameron telling him how his nephew, Matt, had taken off for a few days' camping in The New Forest. A well-earned rest after killing Gavin Lynch the night before, perhaps?

'Cause of death?'

'Asphyxiation, most likely.' She stood aside so that Angel and Kincade could get a better look at the body. A strip of silver duct tape was wrapped all the way around Gavin's head, stretched tightly across his nose, flattening it.

'No tape over his mouth?' Angel said, a growing sense of dread building strength inside him at what he knew was coming.

'No. Asphyxiation was due to a foreign body lodged in his throat whilst his nose was taped shut.'

Angel didn't really hear the second half of the sentence. His mind was fixed on the words *foreign body*.

'I'm taking it we've found Guy Yardley's tongue?'

Durand opened Gavin's lips for them to see for themselves instead of answering. In contrast to the last time she'd done something similar to show them that Yardley had no tongue, Gavin Lynch now appeared to have two.

She then confirmed what Gulliver had told them, adding a few additional details.

'He was hit across the back of the head with an iron poker. The skin wasn't broken due to its smooth round profile, but I'll be surprised if I don't find a depressed skull fracture and some kind of intracranial hematoma when I take a closer look. They dragged him up the stairs...'

'Hence the mud on them.'

'Exactly. It came from his heels. They laid him on the bed. He would've still been groggy, which allowed them to tie him to the bed frame.' She indicated the ligatures binding his wrists and ankles. 'They were aware that a man choking to death will thrash around violently. As you can see from the bed covers.'

'Same clothesline used to hang his father?' Kincade said, stating the blindingly obvious.

'Very probably. They then taped his nose shut, forced what will no doubt prove to be Guy Yardley's tongue into his mouth, and clamped his mouth shut manually.' She placed one, gloved hand gently over Gavin's mouth as she said it, then the other one on top of it. Leaned forwards over the body as if performing CPR. 'They would have needed to put their full weight behind it. The human jaw muscles are extremely strong. There's also a good chance that you'd get bitten. Despite that, with a determined person's weight forcing a foreign body into the throat, death is inevitable if protracted.'

Nice and personal, Angel thought. Feel him struggling underneath you. Better than slapping a strip of duct tape on and standing back to watch as if it's on the TV.

Except that wasn't the thought he took away with him.

He'd interviewed a man recently with an injured hand.

44

'What does it mean?' Kincade said, as much to herself as Angel as she drove them away from the Lynch house, a property that was changing hands faster than they could keep up with. 'They cut Yardley's tongue out, the implication being he should've kept his mouth shut about something. What does using it to choke Gavin Lynch to death mean? I can't think of a connection that makes sense.'

Angel dragged himself away from the thought that had crossed his mind, an additional unsavoury implication of Gavin Lynch being the latest victim, considered the question.

'It doesn't necessarily have to mean anything. The fact that he was killed in Jessica's bed is making enough of a statement—'

'You're not kidding.'

'—but not everything has to have a hidden—'

'Or not-so-hidden.'

'—meaning. They cut Yardley's tongue out. They had to do something with it.'

Kincade laughed, a sudden explosive release of tension.

'You're right. They ran out of piano wire and clothesline, and they're thinking, shit, what are we going to choke him with?

Then one of them says, hang on, have you still got that tongue we cut out last week?'

'Waste not, want not, eh?'

'Exactly.'

The mood-lightening effect of the facetious exchange didn't last long, his thoughts of a minute ago soon back in his mind.

'What you were saying yesterday . . . about Jessica's child not dying and being the woman we're looking for? You know what the implication is now?'

'Now that they've killed Gavin Lynch, you mean? It implies she killed or helped kill her own father. Assuming he raped Jessica, that is.'

'And if your definition of a father is a biological one limited to the man who got your mother pregnant, and not the man who raised you.'

She sucked air in through her teeth as if she'd narrowly missed a pedestrian crossing the road.

'That's a bit deep for me, this early in the morning.'

They were on their way to a hastily re-convened meeting with Oliver Bishop. Angel had spoken to DCI Finch and she'd agreed to apply for a warrant to search Matt Cameron's London property. They'd put in a number of calls to the number Aiden Cameron had supplied for his nephew, but hadn't received a call back. Nor were they expecting to.

In the meantime, Angel was still keen to talk to Bishop. Despite what had recently come to light regarding the tragedy of Lucas and Marianne Cameron's children, the whole sorry chain of events had been set in motion following Lucas's suicide.

Bishop had asked if they could meet in a coffee shop halfway between Roy Lynch's house and another meeting he was hoping to attend after he'd finished with them, and for which he would now be late.

Kincade was disappointed not to meet the gatekeeper, but she soon got over it as a random thought crossed her mind.

'I'm not sure you should be allowed a social life, sir.'

Unsurprisingly, he wasn't sure what to say. He invited her to explain.

'Somebody ends up dead every time you have a night off. You went to see your father, Yardley was killed. You have dinner with Durand, Gavin Lynch gets his.'

'On the contrary. I should be encouraged to go out more.'

He was sure she muttered, *you've turned me down twice*, but she was looking away at the wing mirror in preparation for overtaking a pair of cyclists who were riding side by side, sitting upright as they chatted and held up the traffic.

'What do you think Gavin was doing at his father's house?' she said when she'd finally got past.

Angel had been giving it some thought.

'Obviously he was lured there.'

'Well, yes, I realise that. Hell of a coincidence if they happened to be waiting in the house with a poker, otherwise. But how?'

'The witness who saw them when Yardley was killed said he thought the woman took a photograph of the man entering the unit. I think they sent that or another one they took inside the unit to Gavin.'

She took her eyes off the road to give him a dubious look.

'And he agreed to meet them at his father's house in the middle of the night? On his own. After his father and Yardley had recently been killed. His father in that same house. I know he's a cocky bastard, but still. I'm sure he knows some nasty people to take along as back-up.'

He didn't have an answer for her. One thing was for sure. Gavin had paid the price if it had been a simple case of arrogant over-confidence on his part.

. . .

OLIVER BISHOP WAS ALREADY AT THE COFFEE SHOP WHEN THEY GOT there. On his phone, sitting at a table at the back. He killed the call as soon as they joined him, glancing surreptitiously at his watch.

'Why the sudden interest in something that happened thirty years ago?' he said by way of starters.

Angel gave him the usual bullshit back.

'We can't say at the moment. If you could tell us what actually happened. We're not so much interested in the details of the order that was cancelled, but the reasons why.'

'The fact that you remembered it from the year alone suggests it wasn't simply because your father found a better price elsewhere,' Kincade added.

The waitress turned up to take their order and everyone fell silent. They'd expected Bishop to hold off from talking in front of the girl, but he continued to say nothing once she'd gone.

'Mr Bishop?' Angel prompted.

'I was trying to think of how to phrase it, but what's the point? My father was threatened. He was attacked as he was leaving the office one night. Two men wearing ski masks so don't ask me who they were. They broke his little finger.'

Angel and Kincade kept their faces blank at the mention of the same modus operandi Gavin Lynch had used to get information out of Phil Brent, the man his father had argued with shortly before his death.

'It was the first thing they did,' Bishop said sounding as if he was re-living it himself. 'It wasn't as if they asked him something and then broke his finger when he refused to answer. They grabbed his hand and *snap!*'

'Demonstrating that they meant business,' Angel said, unable to fault the ruthless efficiency of their approach.

'I suppose. They told Dad to back out of the contract he was about to sign with Lucas Cameron. God knows how they knew about it. They said that for every day that went by without the contract being cancelled, they'd break another finger.'

'Did your father think about going to the police?' Kincade said.

Bishop took a deep breath, shook his head.

'No. One of them took a photograph out of his pocket, rolled it into a tube and stuffed it into Dad's mouth. It was all very corny like it was out of an old gangster film, but it scared the shit out of Dad. That's when they told him not to go to the police. The one who'd stuffed the photograph in Dad's mouth pushed it in harder, choking him. *This will be the consequence if you do*, sort of thing.' He fell silent, swallowed thickly. Looking like a man reliving a narrow escape he'd had thirty minutes ago, not thirty years. 'It was a picture of me. Dad pulled the contract the very next day.'

On the face of it, the incident Bishop had described explained why Yardley's tongue had been stuffed in Gavin Lynch's mouth. Another message. Another link to the past. But the killer would have needed to know the story behind the cancelled contract.

'Did your father ever tell anyone outside the family about it?' Angel said.

Bishop gave him a look. Is he serious?

'It's not the sort of thing you bring up at the monthly Rotarians meeting.'

'Have—'

'I told anyone? Is that what you were going to say? No. You're the first.'

His face said the rest of it.

And hopefully the last.

'Did you ever hear from the men again?' Angel said.

Bishop shook his head, eyes on the table as he shared his father's shame.

'Dad never forgave himself. He heard how Lucas Cameron's company went down the tubes afterwards.'

They both waited. Didn't prompt him about what else his father might have known. Bishop confirmed it soon enough.

'And he knew that Cameron committed suicide as a result.'

The waitress turned up with Angel and Kincade's coffees at exactly the wrong time and caught the word *suicide*. She put the cups down hastily, slopping the contents, and hurried away.

'How did your father learn about the suicide?' Angel said, mopping spilled coffee with a paper napkin.

'Cameron's brother told him.'

Both Angel and Kincade came alert. Angel stopped mopping coffee.

'Who? Aiden?'

'I think that was his name, yes.'

'What happened?'

'You should ask my secretary. She was there at the time.'

'The general gist of it will do for now,' Kincade said.

'He came into the office and made a scene. Dad was feeling guilty enough as it was. He never forgave himself. And suddenly there's this maniac in the office screaming at him. *You're responsible for my brother's death*. He kept on and on at him, *why did you do it?* In the end, Dad told him the truth to shut him up. Showed him his broken finger. Told him how his family had been threatened.'

Angel was immediately back in Aiden Cameron's house. Cameron's words in his mind as he told them about the contract being cancelled, the reason Stephen Bishop had allegedly given —that his own company was experiencing cash flow problems.

No mention of being told by Stephen Bishop that he'd been attacked and his son threatened.

Aiden Cameron had pieced it together. Marianne Cameron told Roy Lynch about the contract her husband was hoping would be his company's salvation—either maliciously or she let it slip. Roy Lynch and one of his enforcers then attacked Stephen Bishop to make sure it didn't happen.

And Cameron had failed to mention that fact to them, making something generic up instead.

The conclusion was obvious. He hadn't wanted them to know that he blamed Roy Lynch for his brother's death.

And the reason why not was more obvious still.

He'd told his brother's son, Matt, all about it.

45

ANGEL FOUND AN UNEXPECTED VISITOR WAITING FOR HIM IN reception when they got back from interviewing Oliver Bishop.

It was Sister Philippa, the bursar at St. Joseph's Hospice who'd supplied a name and address for Marianne Lynch's sister, Evelyn.

'I asked to speak to Constable Jardine,' she said, sounding a little put out. 'The desk sergeant told me she isn't here and that I should wait for you instead.'

Angel looked over at Sergeant Jack Bevan, an escapee from a South Wales mining town Angel couldn't ever pronounce correctly, got a wink back that luckily Sister Philippa didn't see.

The way Bevan leaned on the counter watching them suggested he was expecting them to do a Catholic-clergy version of the Mason's handshake, one left-footer to another. Maybe he expected Sister Philippa to hitch up her habit—ignoring for now that she wasn't wearing it. She was dressed in street clothes—a thick plaid calf-length skirt and blue sweater that looked hand-knitted, sensible brown brogues and a silver cross around her neck, even that not a definitive indicator of her calling in life.

Angel didn't miss the fact that Kincade was also enjoying the moment. He steered Sister Philippa by the elbow into the nearest interview room, aware of Kincade's voice in the background.

Glass of holy water, Sister?

He closed the door, sat down opposite the nun.

'I think I might have made a mistake,' she said. 'About the young woman who came in and hissed, *I hope you burn in hell* at Marianne Lynch.'

'In what way?'

'I didn't take much notice when Sister Veronica asked everyone if we'd seen a strange woman wandering around the hospice.' She took off her wire-rimmed glasses then produced a handkerchief from her sleeve and started to clean them. 'I need a new prescription. And I don't know how they get so greasy. It's not as if I ever touch the lenses with my fingers.' Satisfied that they were clean enough, she put them back on her nose. He wasn't sure whether she saw a hint of impatience on his face, but she felt the need to explain herself, nonetheless. 'I'm not wittering on for the sake of it. I'm trying to explain that my eyesight isn't what it used to be.'

'Which is why you think you might have made a mistake.'

'Exactly. Sister Veronica was asking us to try to remember whether we'd seen an unfamiliar woman wandering around. And I thought to myself, no, I've seen Mrs Walker on two separate occasions. I was doing some tidying up the other day and I came across the correspondence with Mrs Walker about the donation she made. I had to dig it out to give your colleague her details. And it reminded me of something I'd forgotten all about.

'On the second occasion that I saw her, or at least I believed it was her, I waved as she was leaving. And she completely ignored me. I thought it was very odd. And rude. Her donation was extremely generous, and she'd been so pleasant when I collared her to ask her to fill in the Gift Aid form.' She smiled guiltily, dropped her voice to a conspiratorial whisper as she made a personal admission. '*Collared* is the right word, Inspector. Sometimes I get a little overly enthusiastic. Sister Veronica says I pounce on people when they're at their most vulnerable. Maybe I do. But the bills don't pay themselves. It didn't matter in this case. Mrs Walker couldn't have been more pleasant, more amenable.'

That's guilt for you, Angel thought and kept to himself.

'And yet, the next time you saw her, she blanked you.'

'Exactly. So now I'm wondering if it really was the same person.' She took off her glasses a second time but didn't do anything with them. 'As I said, I need a new prescription. In my defence, if it was two different people, they look very similar. Mother and daughter, perhaps? The second woman's hair was a more natural shade of blonde. Mrs Walker's was out of a bottle.' She touched her own steel-grey hair. 'The sin of vanity, I'm afraid.'

Angel showed her out, remembering what Kincade had told him earlier about Lisa Jardine looking for him the previous evening. How she'd wanted to discuss her misgivings about Evelyn Walker's daughter, name currently unknown.

He smiled to himself as he made his way back to his office after saying goodbye to Sister Philippa.

Let them take the piss about divine inspiration and confession and holy water, he was having the last laugh.

Kincade looked up at him as he entered the room.

'She's confessed,' he said. 'It was her and the rest of the gang of killer nuns. They call themselves *the nuns from hell*.'

'What did she really say?'

'That she'll be making a formal complaint about the holy

water crack. See if you can find Jardine around anywhere, will you?'

She got up from her chair, unsure of what to make of it all.

You started it, he thought as she went to find Jardine.

They came back together five minutes later, the apprehensive look on Jardine's face making it clear Kincade had primed her, told her the boss was in a strange mood.

'How easy would it be to confuse Evelyn Walker with her daughter?' he said to her, then rocked his hand. 'If your eyesight isn't great.'

Jardine didn't need to think about it.

'Very easy. Even easier if Evelyn Walker paid to get her hair coloured instead of doing it herself.'

'And would the daughter pass as a young woman to an old woman in the next bed to Marianne Lynch?'

That one took a little longer, but not much.

'I think so. She's slim and that always helps.'

'Then I think it's time we brought her in. If I could leave that with you, constable?'

'What's going on?' Kincade said as soon as Jardine had left, her feet as good as skipping over the floor.

'I had a slurp of holy water from Sister Philippa's hip flask, myself. Together we figured it out.'

46

Evelyn Walker confirmed to Gulliver and Jardine that her daughter, Dr Tessa Walker, worked as an obstetrician at Princess Anne Hospital, the same hospital where her niece, Jessica, had died. She also gave them Tessa's home address and mobile number.

That was as far as they got. Dr Walker wasn't at work, where she was expected to be by her colleagues, nor was she at home or answering her phone.

'Maybe she's camping in The New Forest with Matt Cameron,' Angel said somewhat facetiously when Gulliver called him. He then asked if they were comfortable with notifying Gavin Lynch's wife, Janis, about her husband's death.

They were, deciding between themselves that Lisa Jardine would take the lead.

'It's sure as hell not because of your soft, feminine side,' Gulliver said as they stood on Janis Lynch's front step waiting for her to open the door onto the start of the worst day of her life.

Except it wasn't.

If they'd been forced to pick one emotion, Janis Lynch was resigned. As if it was nothing more than the latest and now the last in a long line of disappointments that had accumulated over the long years of being married to her husband, a serial philanderer. Despite that, she still found time for a spot of self-recrimination.

'I should never have locked him out.'

'Why did you?' Jardine said. 'Actually, let's back up. Where did your husband go before you locked him out?'

'I don't know. He said he had something he had to do. I thought he meant some*one*. His girlfriend. Except he's not normally so obvious about it. I know what he gets up to when he says he has to go away on business. But he doesn't usually pop out halfway through the evening to screw the bitch.'

'Do you know her name?'

Janis looked as if something had turned sour in her mouth as she spat it out.

'Samantha. I can't remember her last name. I'm sure she's in his phone.'

I'm sure she is, Jardine thought. The only problem was that Gavin's killers had taken his phone, as they had Guy Yardley's.

'I think she works at his company,' Janis said. 'She won't be hard to find. Look for the one with the biggest tits. He was like a fourteen-year-old schoolboy that way.'

Like all men, Jardine thought and kept to herself, despite the warm welcome the comment would get from Mrs Janis Lynch, herself somewhat on the flat-chested side.

It was possible that Gavin had indeed spent the evening with his girlfriend and had found himself locked out by the wife he'd pushed too far when he came home. Except it didn't feel right to Jardine. Janis appeared to take her husband's infidelity in her stride. As if she'd decided a long time ago to put up with it for the sake of whatever benefits she derived from the relationship that she didn't want to give up.

'Was something different about last night?' Jardine said.

'Apart from the fact that you thought he was being more blatant than in the past.'

'The phone call.'

Jardine and Gulliver came alert, both sitting forward on the sofa they were sharing. Janis carried on before either of them could ask the obvious question.

'Actually, no, that wasn't all. He'd been speaking to that animal, Broz...'

Neither of them needed to ask her to explain. Milan Broz was well known to them. Janis made her feelings clear, anyway.

'He's an Eastern European psychopath Gavin knows. You ask me, he was kicked out of the KGB for excessive cruelty. Anyway, Gavin called him. Next thing, he's walking around with this smug look on his face like a dog with two tails. And it wasn't the sort of look a man gets on his face when he's thinking about bending his secretary over his desk.'

Neither Jardine nor Gulliver asked her to elaborate. They didn't suppose she'd be able to put it into words. And nobody wanted a picture. It was sufficient that she, knowing her husband as she did, had identified that something was different —and different is rarely a good thing.

'You're saying he went to meet Broz?' Jardine said.

'Probably. But I don't know what for. All I do know is that if Broz is involved, somebody's going to end up in hospital.'

The assessment matched their own opinion of Broz. They'd be talking to him in the near future, for all the good it was likely to do them. For now, Jardine moved on.

'Tell us about the phone call you mentioned.'

'It was while Gavin was out. He said he was Samantha's husband. He sent me pictures of the two of them.'

'Can we see them?'

Janis got up as if it was all she could do to push herself to her feet, went into the kitchen. She was back a minute later, a mobile phone in a bright pink protective cover in her hand. She found the text message she was looking for, handed the phone to Jardine.

'He said he's got more, if I want them. I don't know why he thought I would. He hired a private investigator to follow them.'

There were two photographs, both of Gavin Lynch and his girlfriend, Samantha, coming out of a motel room. The front of Gavin's Bentley was visible in one of them. Jardine was familiar with most of the local no-tell motels but didn't recognise it.

'Seeing this is what pushed you over the edge, is it?' she said. 'Having your nose rubbed in it. That's why you locked him out?'

'No.'

'No?'

'It was what he said about Gavin owning the company after Guy Yardley was killed. Gavin didn't tell me about it. Then this man on the phone starts saying how Gavin's suddenly worth ten million and if I divorce him, it'll cost him five million. Then he says, I'd lock all the doors if I was you. I thought, I'm already doing it, mate. When Gavin came home, I told him to piss off back to his girlfriend. Except he went to his dad's house instead . . .'

The enormity of what she'd set in motion hit her like a freight train. She'd remained standing after she brought the phone in from the kitchen, looking at the photographs over Jardine's shoulder. Now, she sagged, slumped into the armchair opposite them.

It was obvious to Gulliver and Jardine what had happened. Gulliver nodded at Jardine—*you explain.*

'The man who called you wasn't Samantha's husband. It was the man who killed Gavin.'

Janis's hand flew to her mouth as her further—albeit unknowing—complicity became clear.

'He set you up,' Jardine went on. 'Made sure that you were sufficiently angry and upset—'

'And scared.'

'And scared, to lock your husband out. He took a gamble that your husband would go back to his father's house. Unfortunately for your husband, it paid off.'

'And it's all my fault.'

She knew it was pointless, but Jardine said the words that needed to be said.

'It's not your fault. You were tricked by a very clever man who's put a lot of thought and preparation into this.'

She didn't say the other things going through her mind.

It's actually your husband's own fault for making it easy for them by playing away from home so often.

As is often the case when presented with sudden and unexpected tragedy, Janis's mind focused on factors that weren't directly relevant to the present discussion.

'Why didn't he tell me about Guy Yardley leaving him the company? Do you think he killed Guy to get the company for himself and then he was going to dump me? Or worse? Is that why he called that animal, Broz?'

If Gavin Lynch hadn't been lying on a slab in the mortuary as they spoke, it would've been a very good question. Get himself out of the house and into his girlfriend's bed while his psychopathic sidekick put an end to the problem of his wife taking him to the cleaners before it even crossed her mind to do so.

'I'm sure he was just waiting for the right time to tell you the good news,' Jardine said.

Janis gave her a look that was easy to interpret.

I've lived with a lying cheating bastard for more years than I care to remember—you need to work on your lies, girl.

47

They didn't have Gavin Lynch's phone, but they did have something else. Forensics had found it inside Gavin's wallet. It was currently in an evidence bag sitting on Angel's desk.

'*The Daily Echo*,' he said. 'July thirteenth, nineteen ninety-three. *Local businessman Lucas Cameron commits suicide.*' He skimmed the article. 'Thirty years to the day before somebody strung Roy Lynch up in the same garage.'

'We knew it was a message,' Kincade said, 'but it's good to have it confirmed. Gavin must have gone back to the house to get it, meaning to destroy it before circumstances overtook him.'

'But why did Roy cut it out in the first place? A memorable event in all their lives...?'

'Or a memento of personally bringing that event about?'

'There's an easy way to find out.'

She'd only been paying attention with one ear as she worked. Now she looked up, her interest piqued.

'Really?'

'Uh-huh. If he's still alive. There's a quote from a DI called de la Haye in the article. Never heard of him, myself. It's not the sort of name you'd forget, either.' He pushed back in his chair, got to his feet. 'Jack Bevan on the front desk will know.'

But not before Bevan had his fun, as Angel soon discovered.

'Anything useful come out of interviewing Mother Teresa?' he said, referring to Angel's earlier discussion with Sister Philippa.

Angel leaned on the counter, dropped his voice as if he had a secret to share.

'She admitted that if she hadn't been a nun, she'd have made a pass at you. Seeing as you're about the same age. Which is why I want to pick your brains.'

'I can't say you're going about it the right way.'

'Do you remember a DI called de la Haye?'

As Angel had said to Kincade, it wasn't the sort of name you forgot. And Bevan hadn't.

'There was a Detective *Chief* Inspector de la Haye. He must have retired fifteen years ago. You want me to make a few calls, see if I can get a number for him? He left as soon as his thirty years were up. He's probably only in his sixties. Should still be alive.'

Make a nice change in this case, Angel thought as he headed back to his office.

HALF AN HOUR LATER, BEVAN CALLED BACK.

'You're in luck. Paul de la Haye. Retired in two thousand and nine, still very much alive. He's got a yacht down at the Shamrock Quay marina that he's refurbishing. He's living on it while he's doing it up. He says any time you want to drop by and help sanding down and varnishing, he'll be glad to see you. No need to take your own sandpaper and varnish.'

'What are you like with a paintbrush?' Angel said to Kincade when he got off the phone.

She took a moment to bridge the disconnect between what she'd been doing and his unusual question before replying.

'The best. I had to be. Elliot wouldn't know one end of one from a . . . I can't think of anything useless enough.'

'What about sandpaper?'

She shook her head, regret on her face.

'Sorry. That's men's work. Mindless, tedious, strenuous. The sort of thing you're good at.'

Which is why she didn't get invited to accompany him for the short drive across town to the historic Shamrock Quay to talk to de la Haye.

Located on the west bank of the River Itchen, the marina took its name from the famous J-class yacht, *Shamrock V*, built by Camper and Nicholson on the site in 1931. She was the first British yacht to be built to the new J-class rule, commissioned by Sir Thomas Lipton for his fifth America's Cup challenge, a lifelong ambition he never fulfilled.

Angel handed over a six-pack of Kronenbourg 1664—an appropriate gift given the French origins of his host's name, which de la Haye explained by pointing out over the sea in the vague direction of France and the Channel Islands.

'I'm originally from Jersey.' Sounding as if they should be able to see it from where they stood, had it not been so cloudy. 'Maybe if I'd made it to Chief Super I could've afforded to move back there. Except I was never any good at brown-nosing.'

Let's hope you were too busy getting on with the job, Angel thought as de la Haye led him down the jetty to where his yacht was moored. Angel was no expert, but it looked fully refurbished to his eye, the paint and woodwork immaculate, stainless-steel fittings gleaming, no hint of mildew on the tightly-furled sails.

Two directors chairs waited for them on the jetty, a cool box between them. Yacht refurbishment didn't look such hard work, after all. Angel almost felt guilty for not bringing Kincade. Almost.

The name on the back of the boat made him smile. Not a cheesy nautical play on words or a pseudo legal-investigative name like *habeas corpus,* but simply one that captured the spirit of how life should be lived.

Carpe diem.

Seize the day. Something most people only come to appreciate once it's too late. Angel hoped he didn't fall into the same trap. The job he was in pretty much guaranteed it—one reason de la Haye had got out on the dot of thirty years, perhaps.

They got settled in the directors chairs, admiring the fruits of de la Haye's labours. Well-earned, and colder bottles of Heineken from the cool box than the ones Angel had brought, in hand.

'I wanted to talk to you about Lucas Cameron's suicide.'

De la Haye cocked his head, put his finger behind his ear.

'Lucas Cameron's what?'

He didn't need to say any more. Angel was talking to the right man.

'Slip of the tongue. The *death* of Lucas Cameron.'

De la Haye nodded his approval.

'I know what we're talking about now. Why are you asking?'

Angel smiled in the knowledge that he was about to make a man who looked very happy with life—apart from not being able to afford a house on Jersey—even happier.

'Somebody hanged Roy Lynch from a rafter in his garage recently.'

'By the neck, I hope.'

'Definitely.'

'Good. It's what he deserved.' He raised his bottle and they toasted. 'Someone did to him what he did to Lucas Cameron.'

'Did you speak to Roy Lynch about it at the time?'

De la Haye leaned back, stretched out his long legs, ankles crossed.

'At length. On more than one occasion.'

'And?'

'And he had an alibi.'

For reasons he couldn't explain, Angel was suddenly back in what had been Jessica Cameron's bedroom, Isabel Durand pulling open Gavin Lynch's mouth to reveal Guy Yardley's tongue stuffed inside.

'Guy Yardley?'

De la Haye re-crossed his legs, nodded.

'Yep.' He flicked his finger at his immaculate yacht ten feet away. 'He was on Yardley's boat at the time. Moored off Buckler's Hard on the Beaulieu River. Or so the two lying bastards claimed.'

'Any other witnesses?'

A large great black-backed gull landed on the jetty twenty yards away, started picking at a discarded plastic bag with its vicious yellow bill, eyeing them warily at the same time. De la Haye laughed without humour.

'A few seagulls, probably. Yardley's dog might have been on board.'

'I think I'm getting a feel for the situation. What did Marianne Cameron, soon-to-be Lynch, say?'

De la Haye pretended to think about it for a couple of beats as he watched the gull. It had given up on the plastic bag and had landed on his boat. Looking as if it was about to crap on the scrubbed teak decking.

'*Where's my drink?* Something like that. She was a lush. And yes, I heard what subsequently happened to her and Lucas Cameron's daughter. It was some months later so I don't know the details.'

'Did you go to the inquest?'

'No.' His tone adding, *why would I?*

'Did you ever see the inquest report?'

De la Haye shook his head rather than say *no* again. Then he leaned forward in his seat, the chair flexing under his weight.

'Should I have?'

'Maybe. It's looking as if the person who strung up Roy Lynch also killed his son Gavin, as well as—'

'Guy Yardley?'

'Yep. The thing is, there's some confusion over whether Jessica Cameron's baby survived her death.'

'And you think, if it did, that child could be behind the killings?'

'That's why I want to see the inquest report.'

De la Haye said that made two of them.

They sat for a while in a companionable silence as Angel allowed de la Haye a minute to enjoy the thought of Old Testament-style justice prevailing before moving on.

'Do you know where Jessica Cameron was living while she was pregnant?'

'No idea. Why?'

Angel was well aware that, retired detective or not, de la Haye was not entitled to be privy to every aspect of the investigation. That said, he liked the man. And he knew nothing he said would ever go further than the jetty they were sitting on. There'd be more chance of the gull that was still sitting on de la Haye's yacht spreading it around.

'There's an inconsistency. Marianne Lynch's niece, Tessa. She's involved somehow. I was wondering if Jessica stayed with her aunt and got friendly with her cousin Tessa.'

'Who is actually the one putting things straight?'

'Maybe.'

De la Haye took the opportunity to demonstrate that he might be retired, but that didn't mean he'd let his mind atrophy.

'On her own? She'd need help.'

Again, Angel found himself in a difficult position. It was de la Haye himself who got him out of it, answering his own question.

'Jessica's brother, Matt.' He studied Angel as he sat not answering. 'I can see it in your face.'

'Does he have a limp?'

De la Haye took himself back thirty years as he sipped thoughtfully at his beer.

'It's possible. There was a rumour at the time his sister was raped that he tried to stop Gavin Lynch as he was going into Jessica's bedroom. Gavin pushed him down the stairs, broke his ankle. Roy Lynch didn't want him going to hospital with all the attention and questions that would have entailed. *It's just sprained and don't be such a big baby.* By the time it got to the point where his mother couldn't ignore it any longer, it was too late.'

'Did you come across Lucas's brother, Aiden, at all?'

De la Haye shifted in his seat, a strained expression on his face as if he had indigestion.

'How are my haemorrhoids, did you say? A pain in the arse. Like Aiden Cameron.'

Angel smiled with him, wishing he'd spoken to de la Haye before talking to Aiden Cameron.

'Did you interview him?'

'Nope.' He jabbed his chest with a thick middle finger. 'He interviewed me. At length.'

It gelled with what Oliver Bishop had said. Aiden Cameron had been busy in the aftermath of his brother's death, trying to get to the bottom of it, despite what he'd said about going directly back to America.

'I hope you were able to provide him with satisfactory answers.'

'Give him Roy Lynch's head on a plate, you mean? No. Why, is he taking an interest in this?'

'He's provided Matt Cameron with an alibi for all three killings.'

De la Haye's eyebrows went up into his forehead at that, the cynicism in his reply a result of a career spent being lied to.

'That's some family loyalty. Have you spoken to Matt, yet?'

'Not yet. Aiden told us he's camping somewhere in The New Forest. And he's driving a silver Ford Focus.'

De la Haye smiled the smile of a man who'd been there himself many times.

'He didn't feel like being any more vague?'

'I'm sure he's saving that up for when we ask him why he claimed he never suspected anything was questionable about his brother's suicide.'

They talked it through for a while longer, then moved onto other things as the sun finally broke through the clouds and bathed the righteous in its warm glow as they enjoyed a second cold beer each. De la Haye jumped up at one point and shooed the big gull away, but not before it crapped on his paintwork.

'Is that twat Marcus Horwood still there?' he said as Angel was getting ready to leave.

'*Detective Superintendent* Horwood is still there, yes.'

De la Haye nodded as if he'd been expecting as much.

'He was always good at brown-nosing.' He slapped Angel on the shoulder as he walked him up the jetty. 'That's what you need to do if you want to get on.'

It had been a bumper visit. Not only had Angel gained some valuable information from de la Haye that he would put to good use in the following days, he'd got a cynical lesson in life itself thrown in for free.

48

Angel and Kincade were in their office the next morning, as was Olivia Finch who'd brought a cup of coffee with her that anyone with a nose on their face knew didn't come from the machine next to the lifts.

They'd been discussing Janis Lynch, the woman who was now ten million pounds richer as a result of everybody else dying. Despite the other avenues being followed, nothing changed the simple fact that most murders are committed for reasons of sex, money or revenge by persons known to the victim—the closer, the more likely.

Janis Lynch ticked most of those boxes.

After leaving her the previous day, Gulliver and Jardine had visited what was now her business, Yardarm Marine Technology. There, they quickly identified her husband's girlfriend, Samantha Lee, although not using the method Janis had suggested—lining all the women up and selecting the one with the largest breasts. Samantha would have been chosen had they done so.

Samantha had been a lot more distraught than Gavin's wife had, immediately breaking down and sobbing her mercenary heart out. They managed to identify a number of key points in amongst the incomprehensible sniffles and heaved-in shuddering breaths as her mascara streamed down her Botox-enhanced cheeks.

She was indeed involved in an extra-marital relationship with Gavin Lynch.

He had promised to leave his wife for her—although to be fair, he'd been promising to do that since their second date, the occasion on which he first got into her knickers.

They had been together in a hotel on the night that his father had been killed.

But she had not been with him at any point on the night on which he was killed himself. She wanted to see him, but he told her that he had things to do. Things that he didn't share with her. Before the news of his death, she'd experienced a rare moment of self-awareness, suspecting that maybe she was approaching her own sell-by date.

All of which meant Janis Lynch ticked the money and revenge boxes for murdering her husband. Against that, it implied a degree of forward planning in killing the other two victims in order to make Gavin financially worth killing that she hadn't demonstrated when Gulliver and Jardine interviewed her. And she would have needed an accomplice, someone with both the physical capability and lack of conscience required to carry out the actual killings.

Cue Gavin Lynch's own enforcer, Milan Broz, now currently sitting in an interview room becoming increasingly irritated as Angel and Kincade kept him waiting while they kicked it around with Finch.

. . .

'Where are we as far as locating Matt Cameron goes?' Finch said to Angel as she walked with him and Kincade towards the interview room.

'Working our way through all of the campsites in The New Forest. Of course, we've only got Aiden Cameron's word for it that that's where he is. And we all know Uncle Aiden's lied to us before. For all we know, he could be on the way to France on Guy Yardley's yacht.'

'Has he still got it? His widow, I mean.'

'No idea. We'll check.'

'And Dr Tessa Walker?'

He shook his head.

'Nobody's heard from her.'

'You think she's with Cameron? Voluntarily, or hog-tied in a bin bag in the boot of his car?'

'Both are possible. What's happening with the search warrant for his London property?'

He got the feeling that wasn't quite so possible, the way she stopped dead having peeled off towards the stairs, turning back towards them.

'It's not going to happen.' Then, before he could remonstrate, 'What have you got on him?'

'A bloody good motive.'

She re-phrased it more accurately.

'A *thirty-year-old* motive. You think Gavin Lynch hasn't pissed off enough people since then to fill a football stadium?'

'A limp?'

'Check with Dr Durand, but I bet there are at least a million people in this country with a limp.' She held up a finger. 'And I hope you weren't about to try to clinch it by saying he's not returning your calls.'

As she'd said, it wasn't going to happen.

. . .

MILAN BROZ WAS EVERYBODY'S IDEA OF AN EASTERN EUROPEAN thug. Square and squat, he looked as if you could hit him with a stick until the stick broke. And unlike most men with closely-cropped hair who trim it themselves, his mouth full of uneven teeth suggested he'd also turned his hand to dentistry.

Angel figured he'd killed more people than malaria before he left the Motherland behind for the sunnier, softer climes of the UK, where offenders are not routinely abused and tortured. Or, if they are, it's not so well publicised.

Angel always felt the dismissive scorn of men like Broz when he sat across a table in an interview room from them. The open contempt for the rules and constraints that hampered the men charged with holding them accountable for their crimes.

You call this an interrogation? Back home, this is where they put us when they've finished.

Broz had come in voluntarily. He'd submitted to a non-intimate DNA sample being taken on arrival and was now working hard at looking bored as he sat without any outward signs of anxiety.

It was a sham, to a degree. They'd seen on the CCTV from the room next door how he'd bounced his right leg incessantly as he waited, only stopping once they entered and the game began.

Angel started by putting an unwelcome idea into Broz's stunted mind.

'We're currently looking into the possibility of Mrs Janis Lynch being behind the killings of her husband, her father-in-law and the man her husband worked for, Guy Yardley. She has a very good motive for wanting them all dead.'

'Ten million of them, in fact,' Kincade said.

Angel nodded his thanks for the clarification.

'That's a lot of money, Mr Broz. More than enough to pay for some help with the actual messy business of killing them.

Because she would have needed help. All three of the murdered men were a lot bigger and stronger than she is.'

'Not as big and strong as you, of course, Milan,' Kincade said in mock admiration at his pumped-up biceps straining the seams on the arms of his black T-shirt.

Broz stared at her making it clear he'd like to show her exactly how big and strong—in more ways than one.

'Gavin Lynch was hit over the head with a poker,' Angel said. He opened the manila folder in front of him, selected the top sheet of paper. Pushed it towards Broz. 'Recognise that?'

Broz glanced at it, then back at Angel. Shrugged dismissively without responding.

'It's a copy of the arrest report for when you were accused of attacking a drug dealer called Charlie Knight with an iron bar a couple of years ago. Do you remember that incident?'

Broz shrugged again. *Maybe.* Didn't say anything.

'It's not the same weapon that was used to attack Gavin Lynch, of course. That was a poker. Do you know what a poker is?'

He watched Broz carefully as he mimicked stoking an open fire. If he was hoping to see anger or unsettle Broz by questioning his command of the English language, he was disappointed.

He moved on, the scene set sufficiently to talk about another drug dealer who'd had the back of his head caved in.

'Tell us what the telephone conversation you had with Gavin Lynch on the night he was killed was about.'

Broz had the sense not to play the stupid card.

Telephone conversation? What telephone conversation?

'Can't remember. Nothing important. Maybe football?'

Angel nodded like it seemed reasonable.

'That must be it. I don't follow football, myself. More of a rugby man. But I know how passionate people get about it. I'm assuming you and Gavin support different teams? That's why he was so angry when he finished talking to you on the phone. That's what his wife told us. What was it exactly that she said, DS Kincade?'

Kincade opened the folder she'd brought in with her, consulted the sheet of paper with the message she'd typed out earlier as Angel dictated it. She cleared her throat.

'Stupid fucking Eastern European wanker.'

Angel nodded along, yes, I remember now.

'Why did he call you that, Milan?'

'No idea. I wasn't there.'

'What did you talk about to annoy him so much? Did you call his football team a bunch of useless wankers, perhaps? And that's why he called you a stupid fucking Eastern European wanker back?' He turned to Kincade. 'Did Gavin say anything else when he got off the phone to Mr Broz?'

She shook her head.

Angel tried prompting.

'He didn't say, all he's good for is hitting people over the head with an iron bar or a poker?'

'Afraid not.'

Angel tried not to let his disappointment show.

'That would've been ironic, wouldn't it? What we call poetic justice, here in England.' His tone took a patronising turn. 'You know, he says, all you're good for is hitting people with an iron bar, and then a few hours later, you go and show him exactly how right he is. *Whack!*' He slammed his palm on the desk to accompany the exclamation, startled Kincade more than Broz. Then worked a self-satisfied smirk onto his face. 'I bet you stood over him after you'd hit him and said, *who's the fucking wanker now, shit for brains?* Except they were more like mush for brains by then, of course. Is that how it happened, Mr Broz? And then you dragged him upstairs and killed him?'

Broz looked at him a long time without saying anything. Eyeball chicken. Angel was good at it. So was Broz. They were doing it a long time before Kincade got bored and interrupted.

'Answer the question, Mr Broz.'

Broz dragged his eyes away from Angel's. Slowly. To make it clear Angel hadn't won.

'No. That isn't what happened. There was no argument. His wife is lying.' He waved his hand dismissively in Angel's direction without looking at him. 'All this talk is bollocks.' He smiled thinly at her as he demonstrated his command of the vernacular.

'Did you meet Gavin Lynch on the night he was killed?' she said, as Angel continued to stare at a scar on the side of Broz's head.

Broz nodded.

'What was the purpose of that meeting? And don't say to talk about football. Or women. Or any other bullshit.'

Broz dropped his eyes to the table momentarily as if he'd made a note of the word he was looking for on it earlier.

'Security.'

'What do you mean, security?'

'You mean protection?' Angel said.

Broz nodded again.

'Gavin was meeting somebody.'

'Who?'

'No idea.'

It wasn't worth pushing him. In all likelihood, Gavin hadn't told Broz who he was meeting, or why. Broz hadn't been brought along for his intellectual input. His instructions would've been a lot simpler.

'Where?' Angel said.

'The docks.'

'And what happened at this meeting?'

Broz was shaking his head even before the question was out.

'He didn't show. We wait one hour. Then go home.'

They both recognised the truth when they heard it. That didn't mean they had to let him know that.

'Then what?' Angel said. 'You went with Gavin—'

'*No!* I went home. Ask my wife. I don't know where he went.' He put both large hands flat on the table. 'Are we finished now?'

Angel and Kincade exchanged a look. There wasn't any point in antagonising him, continuing for the sake of it in the hope that something might come of it.

They could piece it together for themselves.

The killers had pretended to lure Gavin to a meeting. He'd seen through it, taken Broz with him. Except it had been a ploy. Get Gavin out of the house so that they could call his wife, send her some damning photographs in the hope that she locked him out. Which she did. They took a gamble on him going to his father's house instead of his girlfriend's. That also paid off.

Sounded to Angel like somebody upstairs liked handing down Old Testament-style justice.

'Yeah, we're done,' he said. 'Thanks for coming in, Mr Broz.'

THE INQUEST REPORT INTO JESSICA CAMERON'S DEATH WAS waiting for Kincade when they got back to their shared office. They'd briefly discussed the implications of what Broz had told them as they picked up coffee on the way.

The idea of Janis Lynch being behind the killings was still feasible. Broz could simply have been caught up in the ploy to get Gavin out of the house. After they'd given up waiting, he could then have gone to Roy Lynch's house to wait, while Gavin went home to find himself locked out.

Except nobody's heart was behind the idea. It had the feel of something that needed to be explored but which nobody expected to lead anywhere—similar to ninety-five per cent of everything they did.

They were hoping the inquest report on Kincade's desk would be different.

And it was.

She kept her face deadpan after skimming it.

'What do you think?'

There was no point trying to read her face, but he tried anyway for a couple of beats.

'I'm going with, no, the baby didn't die.'

'Based on?'

'The fact that Aiden Cameron has lied about a number of things. No reason why he shouldn't lie about that, too.'

She handed him the report to read for himself.

'You're right. The baby survived. It wasn't raised by Jessica's mother, so it presumably went into care.' They both knew she could have phrased it differently—into a black hole.

Angel continued to read, then looked up sharply.

'What?' Kincade said.

He handed the report back, his finger on the section he'd just read.

'Evelyn Walker gave evidence. Jessica collapsed whilst she was living with her.'

'She lied, too, when she said she cut her sister off and had nothing to do with the children as a result.'

'Not necessarily. She gave us the impression she disowned her sister as soon as she hooked up with Roy Lynch, but it could have been later, after Jessica died.'

'I suppose. It's a bit harsh to cut her off completely because she didn't approve of her choice in men. They could still meet for lunch, just the two of them. But when her sister failed to protect her daughter...'

He saw the connection she made to her own situation

register in her eyes. Anyone she felt was responsible for harming one of her daughters would be straight off the Christmas card list.

They kicked it around for a while longer, the implications.

Tessa Walker, currently AWOL, had lived with her cousin Jessica for the thirty-seven weeks before she collapsed and was rushed to hospital where she later died. They would have become close. And then to have Jessica taken from her life in such a brutal, abrupt way. Was it sufficient to provoke a killing spree thirty years later?

Or was Jessica's child avenging her dead mother?

Who had the greater claim to a desire for vengeance? A child at an impressionable age such as Tessa living through losing a friend? Or a woman hearing years later about how the mother she'd never known had died?

It was impossible to say, dependent on the personalities and subsequent lives of each woman.

They needed to find them both.

49

'You drive,' Angel said as they headed off to talk to Evelyn Walker in the light of what they'd learned from the inquest report.

Kincade was reminded of the previous day. The feeling she'd experienced that he'd been about to tell her something important just as Craig Gulliver came barrelling in with the news of Gavin Lynch's body having been found.

That wasn't all. Whatever the big secret was behind DS Stuart Beckford's absence, there wasn't ever going to be a good time to ask about it.

In a quiet pub after work with a drink in their hands was arguably more appropriate than in the front seat of the car as they set off to confront a witness who'd lied. Against that, there are some things that go better without alcohol. Trouble is, there's no way of knowing in advance—what might help can also aggravate.

'You want me to drive?' he said when she'd stayed sitting in the driver's seat for thirty seconds without starting the engine.

She took a deep breath, went for it.

'No. I want to know what changed yesterday. Before that, you acted like you didn't trust me behind the wheel. Then you had dinner with Isabel Durand. The next thing I know, I'm driving everywhere. What happened at that dinner?'

'Apart from being served murder victims' organs, you mean?'

She shook her head. *Oh, no, you don't.*

'Don't avoid the question . . . sir.'

Angel had felt this moment coming ever since that dinner when Durand had delivered her inescapable verdict.

It's not fair on Kincade to keep her in the dark.

He couldn't disagree. Getting the actual words out past your front teeth was a different matter.

'It might put you off your stride when we're interviewing Evelyn Walker.'

'That's a risk I'm prepared to take.'

He looked away out of the side window. She was convinced he was about to get out the bloody mouth organ, try to distract her that way.

She was wrong.

But the way he started surprised the hell out of her.

'Do you read *The Telegraph*?'

Momentarily, she thought he was about to tell her to call up the online version on her phone. Direct her to a particular article to read later rather than have to tell her himself. She answered the question when he didn't.

'No, I don't read *The Telegraph*. I'm going to try not to take the question as an insult.'

Now who's trying to cause a distraction? she thought as the words rolled out. *Am I scared to know, now that he's about to tell me?*

'A fascist rag?' he said, not bothering to hide the mocking smile on his face.

'I wouldn't go that far.'

'It's the only paper my father's ever read.'

'Is he a fascist?'

Angel rocked his hand, his voice equally ambivalent.

'Sometimes I think he'd like to be. Like Idi Amin, he's certainly had the training for it. Anyway, pretty much everything that comes out of his mouth originates from *The Telegraph*. He told me about an article he read in it one time. About how the different social classes behave in certain situations. The example they gave was when you've got two couples going out together in one car.'

Angel couldn't blame her for the look she was giving him. Curiosity was there, but it was outweighed by a creeping dread about what she'd got herself into provoking this conversation.

Fate was also having its fun, as ever. Prompting her to ask the question as they were sitting here in the car, the necessary props for his story easily to hand.

'That sounds interesting,' she said, sounding the exact opposite.

'According to this article, if the two couples are working class, the men sit in the front, the women in the back. If you're middle class, the owners of the car both sit in the front. What do you think the upper classes do?'

'Is this some kind of a test? Secretly assessing my social background without me realising it?'

If only, he thought.

'No test.'

She thought about it, came out with the only remaining permutation.

'They mix it up. The owner driving and the other man's wife next to him in the front. Like mixing people up at a dinner party.'

'Exactly.'

He paused, wondering too late if it had been fair leading into the story in the way he had. Lulling her into a false sense of security with its apparent banality. But he was committed now, the thundering of his heart in his chest testament to that.

'I'm good friends with Stuart Beckford.' He ignored the sudden hitch in her breathing the name provoked. It was only going to get worse. 'We used to go out as a foursome on a regular basis. Stu and his wife, Catherine, myself and my wife, Claire. She was a doctor.'

Kincade didn't miss the use of the past tense. She *was*. Not, she *is*. But then she was listening for it. Somehow, she didn't think it was early retirement. She made an irrelevant remark, the knot tightening in her stomach.

'That's why you were so good at remembering the medicalese about Jessica Cameron and her baby.'

'Maybe. Anyway, we took it in turns who drove. It was Stu's turn the last time we went out. I'd told him about the article I've just told you about. Naturally, he says, let's act like we're upper class twats for once, forget about being a pair of working-class coppers. So Stu drove, Claire beside him in the front.'

The curiosity or even boredom at the *Telegraph* anecdote that had been on Kincade's face a minute earlier had been replaced by a look of growing horror as the inevitability of the story dawned on her.

Angel then reached towards his left shoulder with his right hand, took hold of the seat belt.

And Kincade felt sick.

'I was playing my role as an upper-class twat, sitting in the back chatting to Stu's wife. I'm sure it's the same when you go out with friends, but the men talk to the men, the women to the women. There was a lull in the conversation. I pulled out my harmonica, played a couple of notes to get everyone going. You and Gulliver and Jardine aren't the only ones who like to give me a hard time about it. Claire was the worst. She twisted in her seat, gave me a look. *Don't you dare*. I carried on. She tried to grab it. I leaned away, played a few more notes. By now she's leaning all the way through the gap between the front seats. And she still can't reach. Her seat belt was holding her back. So she unclipped it.'

He'd pulled the seat belt out as he talked. Now, he let go of it, allowed it to snap back.

Silence filled the car as his throat thickened, the words refusing to come. Hearing again the despair in Stuart Beckford's voice as a nervous but now relieved doctor walked away from them in Southampton General Hospital, the job of delivering the tragic news behind him.

I'd seen the warning light and ignored it.

And his own response.

I should've let her grab the bloody harmonica, throw it out of the window, whatever.

And in the midst of the self-recrimination as they each tried to claim responsibility in the vain hope that it would bring the other man some small measure of peace, the words that would never be said.

There was ultimately only one person responsible. And she'd paid the price for her foolishness, her sense of fun.

Does St. Peter let you into heaven with a face like a patchwork quilt, Padre?

'You had a crash?' Kincade said, her voice barely above a whisper.

'A Romanian lorry driver called Bogdan Florescu fell asleep at the wheel after driving twelve hours without a break. One second, he was in his own lane, the next, he was in ours. Stu was distracted by everything that was going on in the car. There was nothing he could do. Or Claire. Stu tried to swerve into the lane the lorry should've been in. The passenger-side front wing took the brunt of it. Claire turned towards the front as the car swerved, got thrown into the A pillar. She died in hospital a few hours later. A combination of massive head trauma and major internal haemorrhaging—'

'What about the airbag?'

'It didn't activate. A faulty sensor. Stu had seen the warning light a couple of days before. Forgot all about it. He suffered a fractured clavicle. Catherine got away with concussion, whiplash and a broken wrist.' He raised both arms above his head, forearms pressed together against his forehead. 'I adopted the brace position everyone's heard a million times and hopes they never have to use. I had a stiff neck for a week, but that was it. And whilst Stu's collarbone will heal with time, nobody's sure whether his mind ever will. Survivor's guilt on steroids.'

He saw what passed back behind her eyes, didn't need to spell it out.

You too. You should never have told the stupid story about car seating etiquette.

And she was right. He and Stuart had always sat in the front before that. As is the men's right the women mockingly joked from the back.

He should've been in that front passenger seat. Then nobody would've died. Or at least if some spiteful twist of fate had caused his seat belt to fail at the same time, a veritable clusterfuck of tragic coincidence, it would've been him.

She didn't know what to say.

Didn't know whether she was pleased she'd asked, pushed him into a corner, or not. She hadn't known him long enough to put her hand on his arm, let human contact say what words could never express.

So many questions she wanted to ask but didn't dare.

Instead, she hid behind the factual ones. Because that's what they're there for. When you don't want to go to the place where emotions live, waiting to ambush you when you least expect it.

Like on the way to interviewing a lying witness who'll come out with more of the same until you just don't care anymore.

'How long ago?'

'Thirteen weeks.' Thinking how some days it felt like thirteen minutes, other days thirteen years. Hoping that nobody ever asked him which of those were the good days, which of them the bad. 'I had to wait for the inquest before I could arrange the funeral. Then I spent six weeks on a walking holiday. The Camino Frances. The catharsis of physical exertion. And the Cameron-Lynch saga has been occupying my mind ever since I got back.'

Until some nosy cow started asking questions, she thought bitterly.

'What happened to the lorry driver?'

'He was unhurt.' He shrugged, resignation in the gesture and his voice. 'They always are, up there in their cab. He did a bunk afterwards. He's safely back in Romania by now.'

He shifted position in his seat suddenly feeling more exhausted than at any time on the four hundred and ninety-two miles of the Camino Frances. He slotted the seat belt into place, the sharp click like an accusation in the quiet of the car. But if it was, it was at him, not her.

'I haven't spoken to Stu since the funeral. I know that I should. I just can't seem to make it happen.'

She saw the opportunity to come out with a platitude—almost as good as facts for covering up real feelings—and jumped at it.

'It's still raw. Give it time.'

'And sorry it took so long getting around to telling you. I hate to think what you've been imagining has been kept from you.'

And you don't know the half of it, he thought as she started the engine, told him not to worry about it.

50

EVELYN WALKER WASN'T SURPRISED TO SEE THEM, NOT EVEN AT what were obviously the big guns being rolled out after she'd spun a yarn for Gulliver and Jardine.

If anything, she looked relieved. That something that had been weighing on her conscience was coming to an end, whatever form that end might take.

Angel got the impression that Kincade was looking for an opportunity to vent the pent-up frustration that he'd felt coming off her in the car at all the questions she'd wanted to ask but hadn't felt comfortable doing so. He was happy to let her take the lead, feeling a little detached from reality at present.

'You told our colleagues that you cut your sister Marianne off, had nothing to do with her or her children—'

Evelyn was quick to interrupt, taking the line that Angel had predicted.

'And I did. *After* Jessica's death.'

'But you allowed them to believe it was as a result of your sister meeting Roy Lynch. Why?'

If she was expecting Evelyn to crumple under the weight of

the accusation, she was very wrong. Evelyn came right back at her.

'Because I had no intention of helping you catch a person who did to Roy and Gavin Lynch what should have been done a very long time ago.'

'You realise that's perverting the course of justice?'

Evelyn looked as concerned as if she'd been told it was one step down from littering. She smiled tightly.

'Okay, I got confused. Charge me with being a forgetful old woman. What did you say your name was, constable?'

Angel took a moment to inspect his shoes, thinking that was one up to Evelyn. She was still talking, sounding as if she'd made it to the top of the high moral ground.

'Anyway, it depends on the sort of justice you're talking about.'

Kincade saw the remark as an invitation to work a broomstick up her backside before replying.

'We have to limit ourselves to the legal form.'

'Then I pity you.'

Angel stepped in at that point, put a stop to what was turning into a pointless exchange.

'Our colleagues didn't share everything with you, either, when they asked you whether you knew if your sister had been visited by anyone else in the hospice. Marianne did have another visitor. A youngish woman who despised her enough to whisper, *I hope you burn in hell.*'

Kincade didn't miss the way Angel had described her as young*ish*. The distinction was lost on Evelyn.

Angel ploughed on in the face of her silence.

'Do you know any women who harbour such strong feelings that they feel the need to send an old woman to her maker in the knowledge that she was hated?'

He waited. Kincade could've told him not to hold his breath.

'I can think of two,' he said. 'Jessica's baby. And your own daughter, Tessa. Was she close to Jessica?'

Evelyn so desperately wanted to tell them to shove their questions about her family's tragedy where the sun don't shine. She couldn't do it, the power of a simple question that underscored all of her fears overwhelming her, compelling her to answer truthfully.

'Very.' She consulted with her hands resting in her lap a long moment, then gave a fuller answer. 'She was devastated when Jessica died. Why do you think she became an obstetrician, for Christ's sake?'

'Has she got it in her to kill three men because of what happened?'

Evelyn looked utterly wretched, the feisty comeback of a minute ago already a distant memory. It was an impossible question to ask a parent. Does your child have it in them to become a mass murderer? She answered in the only way she could.

'I honestly don't know.'

'Does Tessa know Matt Cameron?'

On the sofa opposite them, the rapidly deflating shell that used to be Evelyn Walker nodded unhappily.

'They stayed in touch, even after he ran away. She was happy to. He was her connection to Jessica. I think he wanted it to be more than that. She wasn't interested in him that way.'

'What about Jessica's baby?'

'She was put into care.'

'It was a girl?'

'Yes, Rachel.'

'You didn't think to take her in yourself?' Angel said.

It struck Kincade that there was too much of the incredulous in his tone. Evelyn agreed. Looking at him as if he'd been placed on the earth by a spiteful God for the sole purpose of tormenting her.

'No.'

Still Angel probed, Kincade's discomfort intensifying.

'Why not?'

Both expecting her to tell him to mind his own business.

'I couldn't risk her growing up and seeing Gavin Lynch in her and not Jessica. You can't blame the child for how they came into the world, but you have to trust that you've got the strength of character to overcome your own prejudices. I'm not sure I would have.'

The damning personal admission put a dent in the flow of Angel's relentless questioning. His voice was softer when he resumed.

'Do you know if Tessa is in contact with Rachel?'

'I've got no idea.'

'Do you know where Tessa is?' He paused, and Kincade knew he was about to leverage the admission Evelyn had just made. 'Don't worry, we won't prosecute you for obstruction if you don't tell us. You'll do far worse to yourself if you don't help put a stop to this now.'

Five minutes later and Angel was on the phone calling for back-up as they set off for the Sandy Hills Holiday Park at Fordingbridge on the western edge of The New Forest. Kincade was at the wheel, driving like she'd found a new, heavier right foot.

51

'Give me a caravan over a house any day of the week,' Angel said as they pulled up outside Tessa Walker's Swift Bordeaux static caravan.

'Not with two young girls,' Kincade said.

'I don't mean to live in. One door, limited number of rooms all on one level. It makes our job a lot easier.'

They went up a short flight of steps onto a wood composite deck that ran the length of the long side of the caravan, a glass-topped table and two folding chairs arranged beside the railing.

The door opened before they got to it and Tessa Walker stepped out, leaving the door open behind her. Like her mother, she didn't look in the least surprised to see them. Angel sat her on one of the chairs, a uniformed officer standing over her, as he went inside with Kincade. Tessa called after them, a *waste your time if you like* note in her voice.

'There's nobody else here.'

They checked for themselves, nonetheless—both bedrooms, two bathrooms, kitchen and living room—didn't find Matt Cameron or his dead sister's daughter Rachel anywhere inside.

Nor any evidence of them having been there. The spare bed

didn't look as if it had been slept in. No rucksack stashed in a corner, not even two different sets of phone charging leads. Tessa's phone was plugged into a double socket it shared with the kettle. Angel left it where it was for now.

They had a general poke around. An Ikea shelf unit at the side of the gas fire contained local guide books, as well as a number of Ordnance Survey maps of the surrounding area. There were also a number of well-worn paperback crime novels, a coffee table book entitled simply *The New Forest* as if the author couldn't be bothered to think of a snappier title, and another book that made Angel pull a pair of latex gloves from his pocket and work them onto his hands.

He lifted it off the shelf, the answer to something that had puzzled him from the beginning in his mind as he read the title.

In Search of Sir Thomas Browne – The Life and Afterlife of the Seventeenth Century`s Most Inquiring Mind.

'What's that?' Kincade said.

He showed it to her. From her reaction, he might as well have shown her a pretty shot of wild flowers in the early-morning sunlight he'd found in the New Forest book.

'You remember the suicide note supposedly written by Roy Lynch?'

She thought back, couldn't remember it exactly.

'Something very high-brow. Something not very Roy Lynch, from what I remember.'

He opened the book, quoting from memory.

'*We are in the power of no calamity, while death is in our own.* Nothing can hurt you if you're prepared to kill yourself, basically.'

She didn't waste any time dwelling on the seventeenth-century wisdom as he flicked through the book, hooked her thumb in the direction of Tessa Walker waiting outside.

'She came up with it?'

'Maybe.'

He held the book out to her, open at the inside front cover. She read the hand-written inscription out aloud.

'*To Doctor Tessa, Congratulations!* It must have been when she qualified as a doctor. Doesn't say who it's from. Pretty stupid thing to do, if you ask me, using a quote from it, whoever gave it to her.'

That depends, he thought and kept to himself.

They went outside to where Tessa was waiting. A number of rubberneckers had come out of the surrounding caravans, sitting on chairs and leaning on railings as they watched the excitement of a real, live police raid. One woman brought out a cup of tea and a piece of cake for her husband as Angel looked across.

Ought to get out more, he thought as he spoiled their fun, ushering Tessa back inside and closing the door behind them. She saw the book on the table where he'd left it, didn't say anything about it. If anything, she looked puzzled rather than worried—*uh-oh, they're onto me.*

Angel sat down opposite her at the small table while Kincade leaned her butt against the kitchen counter. The three of them around the small table would've felt as if they were planning tomorrow's hiking trip together, not interviewing her about three murders.

Angel went right back to the beginning.

'Did you visit Marianne Lynch in St. Joseph's Hospice shortly before she died?'

Tessa didn't hesitate, no apology in her voice, no inability to meet his eyes.

'I did.'

'Why?'

'To tell her what I thought of her.'

The apple doesn't fall far from the tree, he thought to himself, remembering what Gulliver and Jardine had said about Tessa's mother giving Roy Lynch a piece of her mind at his wife's funeral. He didn't need to ask his next question, but did so for completeness.

'Which was?'

'That she was an evil, uncaring bitch who was every bit as responsible for her daughter's death as the man who raped her, Gavin Lynch, was. And that I hoped she burned in hell for it.'

'Did Jessica tell you that Gavin Lynch raped her? Or is that your assessment of what happened?'

Tessa nodded, her eyes misty and out of focus, adrift in a faraway place that only she could see.

'She told me. I was the only one. There was no point telling her mother. She wouldn't hear anything bad said about Roy Lynch. Or his sons. And she knew better than to accuse them directly. I told her to go to the police, but she refused.' She glared at Angel, hatred and resentment burning off any mistiness in her eyes. 'You lot never believe the woman.'

Now was not the time to get into an argument about the police's response to rape accusations. Angel got the impression Dr Tessa Walker had a large store of bitter anecdotes backed up by extensive case notes proving just how far short of the mark they fell.

'Did it make you want to punish Gavin and Roy Lynch yourself?'

'What do you think?'

He stared at her without answering until she accepted that it wasn't his place to answer his own questions—particularly those like the one he'd just asked.

'Yes, it made me want to kill them,' she said. 'I used to fantasize about it all the time. All the different ways I was going to do it. Making it as painful as possible. Make them beg for their pathetic lives. Then kill them anyway—'

'And Guy Yardley?'

The sudden interruption completely threw her. The question *who?* was on her face if not her lips.

It was very evident that although they were talking to the woman who'd sent Marianne Lynch on her way with a spiteful curse in her ear, they were not in the presence of a murderer.

'He was a friend of Roy Lynch.'

Tessa's face made it clear that she couldn't see the connection. How could a friend of Roy Lynch's have anything to do with the death of her cousin, Jessica? The only crime she cared about.

Angel didn't waste time explaining, stated the obvious instead.

'It all stayed as fantasies in your head, didn't it? You didn't actually kill anyone.'

'Of course, I didn't. I'm a doctor.'

That was a non sequitur that nobody wanted to get into. Kincade moved them on.

'Why did you come here and hide?'

Tessa looked at her, head cocked, then said something nobody was expecting.

'You're a woman. How's your relationship with your mother?' She didn't give her a chance to answer. 'I can see in your face that it's ... difficult. Or maybe you prefer *complex*.'

Angel leaned back, on the face of it to allow the two women to see each other better. But more than that, because he felt like a spectator to some bizarre gladiatorial combat that was about to take place.

In the event, it fizzled out before it began. Kincade shrugged. It is what it is.

Tessa took it as conclusive proof of her point.

'I didn't want my mother to know what I'd done. It's stupid, I know. It'll all come out now. And she'll want to rake it all over again. Dig up what needs to be left buried in the past. Fan the flame of all that old hurt and warm ourselves in the glow of our self-righteous pain. *I'm hurting more than you're hurting.* Better than daytime TV. In fact, it *is* daytime TV, but living it for real, not watching it. The thought of it makes me want to give myself an epidural in my head.' She smiled suddenly, as malicious an expression as Angel had ever seen. 'That's how I would've done it if I'd killed them. Give them an epidural. Cut them open and leave them to slowly come around after they've watched me doing it. You see anyone killed like that, Inspector, you know where to come.'

Angel got the impression that now she'd started, she wasn't about to stop. He headed her off.

'What's your relationship with Matt Cameron?'

'We're cousins. And friends.'

'Just friends?'

'I just told you, we're cousins.'

'Or you'd be more?'

She rocked her hand, her voice reflecting something he guessed she'd thought about before.

'Ignoring the morally and socially ambiguous aspects, as a doctor I'm aware of the dangers posed by a limited gene pool. Besides, I think he might be gay.'

'Do you know where he is at the moment?'

'Were you thinking that he'd be here with me? And that we were hiding out? Taking a well-earned break after our killing spree?'

Kincade thought Angel did very well with his answer in the face of her sarcasm.

'I thought the first of those suggestions might be a possibility, yes. Do you know where he is, seeing as he's obviously not here?'

'No idea. I haven't spoken to him for some weeks.' She

pointed at her phone charging on the kitchen counter. 'Take a look at my phone if you like. See when the last time we had any contact was. Unless you think I've also got a secret burner phone —that's what they're called, isn't it?'

He could've pointed at her collection of crime novels. *You should know, given your reading preferences.*

'When was the last time you were in contact with Jessica's daughter, Rachel?'

'That's easy. I've never met her.'

She hadn't answered the question. He knew she wasn't playing word games even as he asked for clarification.

'Have you ever spoken on the phone?'

'No, never. As far as I was aware, she was swallowed up by the care system at birth and hasn't been seen since. Your line of questioning suggests that Matt has been in contact with her.'

'It's a possibility that we're looking into.'

'I'll take that as a *yes*.' She tapped the book on Thomas Browne still sitting on the far edge of the table where he'd pushed it when he sat down. 'What made you look through this? Is it evidence? I can't see how, if it is.'

'A quote by Browne was left at a crime scene.'

Given the reason for their presence in her caravan, the deaths they'd been discussing including a staged suicide, it wasn't difficult for her to work out which one.

'*We are in the power of no calamity, while death is in our own.* I find that strangely comforting. To know that there's always a way out of anything. Well, almost anything. Not if you're in a persistent vegetative state, I suppose.'

He got the impression she was talking for the sake of it. Anything that came into her head to prevent him from saying what she knew was coming. The book had been given to her as a gift. A quote from it had been used as a final farewell to the world from a man she had every reason to hate.

'Somebody is trying to frame you,' he said. 'I'd be interested to know who. And why.'

'Me too, Inspector, me too. But I'm not going to hold my breath. I suggest you don't, either.'

'W<small>HAT DID YOU THINK OF HER SPEECH ABOUT HATING</small> G<small>AVIN AND</small> Roy and dreaming of killing them?' Angel said as they walked back to the car.

'Same as you must be thinking. A bit over the top. A bit pointless. If she was a deranged killer off her medication, I'd say she was taunting us. *Look how much I hated them. And you still can't touch me.* Except she isn't. And the fact that she's not in handcuffs in the back of the car tells her we don't think she did it, anyway.'

'True. But is it because she actually didn't hate Gavin? And she doesn't want us to know that?'

It gave them both something to think about as they drove away. He put into words what was on both their minds.

'I wonder if we'll find her number in Gavin's call log?'

52

CRAIG GULLIVER STUCK HIS HEAD AROUND THE DOOR OF ANGEL and Kincade's office the next morning looking as if what he was about to say was a direct result of tireless hard work put in by himself and not something that had landed in his lap because his phone happened to ring and not Jardine's.

'Just had a call from the control room at Netley. They took a 999 call from a chap called Russell Stanford. He's the owner of the Big Meadow campsite at Brockenhurst.'

Angel came out of his seat at the words *campsite at Brockenhurst* as if Gulliver had lit a fire under it, pulling his jacket on as he crossed the room in a couple of strides, blowing past Gulliver in the doorway, Kincade not far behind.

'He said there's a young woman sitting outside her tent,' Gulliver went on as the group half-walked, half-ran for the lifts like a single multi-limbed investigative android designed by a madman. 'She's drunk. Apparently, she's been there all night in the rain. Sitting staring into space with a vacant look like something out of a horror movie and an empty whiskey bottle in her hand. Control have already despatched a couple of uniforms from Lymington.'

'Is she alone?'

'We don't know for sure. She claims her uncle is dead inside the tent. The owner didn't want to risk going near her to check. She's wearing a coat, but it looks to him like she's got blood on her clothes underneath.'

It took them twenty minutes to cover the fifteen miles to the campsite. By the time they got there the two uniformed PCs out of Lymington had cordoned off the immediate area around the tent and placed the young woman who had remained mute the whole time in the back of a liveried patrol car. One of the officers had checked inside the tent she'd silently guarded to confirm that there was a man inside. He was indeed very dead, as she'd claimed, the nylon groundsheet as sodden as her clothes with his blood.

His external carotid artery on the left side had been severed immediately below the jaw, a wound consistent with an attack by a right-handed person with whom he was face to face. The long, slim filleting knife that had sliced through it lay on the ground nearby where it had been dropped by the woman who'd wielded it, a lonely flash of silver adrift in the sea of darkening red.

The site owner, Russell Stanford, had also been right. The young woman in the back of the car looked like a reject from a low-budget horror movie. Like some pitiful medieval wretch accused of witchcraft dunked repeatedly in the river. Jeans and bright blue Puffa jacket soaked through from sitting in the rain all night, her matted unkempt hair plastered to her pale skin as it dried in the morning sun. The once-white T-shirt visible poking out of the bottom of her jacket was drenched with blood that was not her own.

Angel opened the door and squatted down as she stared silently ahead.

'Rachel?'

She ignored him, along with the rest of the world around her as far as he could make out. His second attempt was louder, the sort of imperious bark the men who'd served under his father would recognise.

'Rachel!'

She turned her head slowly towards him. Gave him a look he didn't think he'd ever see again—not in his waking hours, nor since he traded his dog collar for a warrant card, turned his back on the dusty heat and relentless suffering of the Iraqi and Afghan wars.

SHE WAS INTERVIEWED UNDER CAUTION THE FOLLOWING DAY BY Angel and Kincade, a duty solicitor, Dinesh Khan, in attendance.

Her full name was Rachel Pascoe. She was twenty-nine years old. Six months previously, she'd begun the process of piecing together her family history-cum-tragedy when the psychiatrist treating her for attachment issues had suggested it.

Everyone concerned hoped for the sake of his conscience that he'd been lax in his attitude to following up on his patient's progress or lack thereof. And that he didn't read a newspaper.

Rachel claimed she had nothing to do with the killing of Roy Lynch. Her statement that she'd never been in Lynch's garage was consistent with the lack of forensic evidence linking her to the scene. The woman's hair found on Lynch's trousers was not hers.

She was shown a video that had been taken on a burner phone found lying on the floor of Matt Cameron's tent. It showed Roy Lynch's last moments thrashing on the end of a blue clothesline suspended from a rafter in his garage. Despite her fingerprints being all over the phone, she claimed it was the first time she'd seen the video.

Yeah right, Angel thought as he watched her swallow thickly, a moist sheen to her eyes.

She admitted to being present at the killing of Guy Yardley. She claimed that she had no idea that Matt Cameron had planned to kill him—let alone cut out his tongue. She believed that blackmail was the reason behind luring him to the industrial unit. She was aware that Matt felt he'd been cheated out of his inheritance. It made sense to her that the plan was to extort money from him. A monetary righting of a monetary wrong.

She'd been appalled when Matt cut out Yardley's tongue. And scared. She realised that with a man like Matt Cameron, you were either with him or you were against him. And she'd just watched what he did to people he believed were in the latter camp.

Angel thought she was a very clever young woman.

She had a lot more to say about the death of her biological father, Gavin Lynch. She gave them a detailed account of what had happened on that night. Her appointed legal representative, Mr Khan, crossed his arms and thought about the fee he was earning for doing nothing. He wasn't paid enough to try to stop a young woman hell-bent on destroying herself.

MATT CAMERON STEPPED BACK FROM THE SITTING-ROOM WINDOW AS A *car turned off the road and into Roy Lynch's drive, its headlights sweeping ahead of it. The poker from the fireplace was already in his hand.*

He put his finger to his lips as the car crunched across the gravel outside the window, the unnecessary gesture annoying the hell out of her—but not as much as when he pointed at her as if she was a disobedient dog.

'Stay there.'

He went out into the hallway, stood to the side of the front door in the darkness. Raised the poker as they both heard the key in the lock. From the sitting room, Rachel heard the man she'd never met but who she'd learned to despise come in, then shut the door behind him.

And for reasons she didn't fully understand, she stepped into the sitting room doorway.

'Hello, Dad.'

The word in her mouth making her feel unclean. As if the open and voluntary acknowledgement of their relationship damned her more unashamedly than the blood ties that bound them the one to the other ever could.

Matt surged out of the shadows. The look on his face illuminated by the porch light coming through the door glass made her shrink backwards, as if it was her he wanted to brain. Instead, he brought the poker down onto the back of Gavin's head before he could respond to his daughter's greeting. A vicious, murderous blow, legs crumpling as he pitched forward onto his face under the force of the attack, unconscious before he hit the floor.

They turned him over, dragged him up the stairs by his arms. Grunting and swearing at each other, the narrow staircase making the job twice as difficult.

Except Rachel felt a burning righteous anger filling her. As if she could've thrown him over her shoulder, carried him up herself.

She used her hip to push open the door to the small fourth bedroom that opened directly off a half-landing, three-quarters of the way up the stairs.

Knowing without asking that this was the room where it had happened.

Where the crime that had resulted in her very existence had been committed.

And the stairs they'd hauled Gavin Lynch's dead weight up were the same ones he'd pushed her uncle down all those years ago when he'd tried to intervene. Prevent Gavin from going into Jessica's room while their mother and his father were out on the town, oblivious to the life-changing events unfolding at home.

'Come on,' he hissed. 'What are you waiting for?'

They dragged him into the bedroom, starting to come around now. Not so unresisting in their hands, a low moan on his lips. Heaved him up onto the bed. She tried not to think of her mother lying on that same bed, her mind tormenting her, filling her head with infected thoughts.

Face down, pushed into the pillow?

Or face up, looking into his eyes as he clamped her mouth shut with his big hand?

Fighting?

Or accepting a small piece of the evil that lives in this world, and hating herself for it?

They went to work on his wrists and ankles, tying them to the bedposts. Matt took the wrists, her the ankles. Good and tight, because he was a big, strong man and very soon he was going to wake up with a sore head in all meanings of the phrase.

Not a minute too soon.

'What the fuck?'

Writhing uselessly on the bed like his father had thrashed on the end of a clothesline in the video she'd watched so many times, the small bed banging into the wall.

And the thoughts she couldn't ever stop, so why even try, just let them come.

Did it bang against the wall when you raped her?

Did the bedsprings creak as you humped away?

Did the earth move as you spilled your tainted seed?

They tuned him out, the threats he spat at them bouncing impotently off the walls as his rage and frustration grew.

They didn't know what pain was.

He'd pay them back a thousand times over.

They'd wish they'd never been born.

Matt slapped him hard, silenced him. Wrapped a strip of duct tape all the way around his head and over his nose, squashing it flat. No air getting in or out of that nose, not ever again. Hand in his pocket, the anticipation of what was to come causing it to shake. He frowned, tried the other pocket.

'Shit!'

'What?'

'I've lost the fucking tongue.'

A giggle burst from her mouth, the sound of sanity suspended.

'It must have fallen out.'

He gave her a look as if he'd caught her eating it. Phone out, scanning the floor with the flashlight. Then out onto the landing, his footsteps receding as he went slowly down the stairs.

Behind her, the man they'd dragged up them spoke, startled her.

'I didn't rape your mother.'

She spun around. Slapped him hard across the face, sufficient to make her hand ache. Spitting words into his face.

'Shut the fuck up, you lying bastard.'

'I'm not lying. I didn't rape her. I loved her. And she loved me.'

She clamped her small hand over the black hole spewing lies that was his mouth. He shook his head out from under it, back arching, his whole body lifting off the creaking bed.

'It's true. You have to believe me. It was an accident, but it wasn't rape. That's why she didn't have an abortion like everyone tried to force her to. We wanted to have you.'

Both her hands over his filthy mouth now. Slapping him again as he tried to bite her, her hand throbbing with pain.

And still he wouldn't shut up. On and on and on about how much they'd loved each other, had wanted her, their daughter.

She was screaming at him now, tears stinging her eyes, the word daughter cutting through her anger and hatred like bleach through fat and grease in a blocked drain.

'Don't you dare use that word to me, you piece of lying shit.'

Behind her, the door almost came off its hinges. Matt crashed into the room, the Ziploc bag with its bloody contents in his hand.

'You'll wake up the neighbours, for Christ's sake.'

She was beyond caring. A single thought consumed her. Made her question everything she thought she believed on her long journey to this moment.

'He says it wasn't rape.'

Matt looked at her, then at Gavin Lynch. Pity for her, loathing for him. She didn't want to be asked which was worse.

'Of course he says it wasn't rape. What's he going to say? Ha, ha, I raped your mother as she begged me to stop, but I kept on going? Don't get flaky on me, Rachel, not now.'

She didn't know what to do, what to think. And from the bed her father's pleading voice making her want to scream.

'It's not true. We loved each other.'

She turned on him, ripped the pillow out from under his head and over his face, smothering him, anything to shut him up.

'Will you stop saying that!'

An inhuman wail from the bottom of her lungs filled with frustration. Except Matt heard something else. The doubt creeping into her voice. Taking hold in her mind, a delicate unbalanced organ at the best of times.

He did something about it.

Stepped up behind her, wrapped his arms around her in a bear hug. Lifted her off the ground, feet kicking in vain, the pillow still in her hands. Carried her to the door and out. Dumped her on the small half-landing and slammed the door in her face, the key turning a moment later.

She hammered against it with her fists until her hands ached. Put the pillow on the top of her head and clamped it over her ears. It didn't stop her from hearing her father's last words coming through the door that had muffled her mother's screams thirty years before.

Please. I didn't rape her.

. . .

ANGEL LOOKED AT RACHEL A LONG WHILE AFTER SHE STOPPED talking. The duty solicitor, Dinesh Khan, cleared his throat. Angel stopped him with a raised hand as he addressed Rachel.

'You're saying you weren't in the room when Matt Cameron forced Guy Yardley's tongue into Gavin Lynch's mouth, then put his hands over his mouth so that he couldn't breathe until he was dead?'

Rachel shook her head looking utterly dejected. As if by telling the story she'd come to realise too late the truth in her father's words.

'No. He knew I was having second thoughts. That's why he threw me out.'

Forensic analysis would reveal whether fibres from Rachel's clothes were found on Matt Cameron. The act of holding a person tightly enough to carry them bodily across a room would ensure that there would be a transfer, if there had been any contact at all. Those results were not yet available.

'Tell me again about the friend of Jessica's that you talked to . . .' He sorted through the papers in front of him, found the one he was after. 'Nicole Johnston.'

In finding Nicole Johnston, Rachel had demonstrated initiative and tenacity that would've had Angel offering her a job as a civilian researcher had circumstances been different. Unlike everyone else in her family, she'd requested a copy of her mother's inquest report. Background information contained in it had given her the school her mother had attended. She'd then found the school's Facebook page—obviously not in existence at the time. She'd performed a search for *Jessica Cameron* and got lucky. In what she later admitted was a red-wine-fuelled moment of sentimentality, Nicole Johnston had scanned and posted an old photograph of herself with Jessica and two other girls with a mawkish comment about *old friends never forgotten* that included a specific reference to Jessica. Rachel had then contacted Nicole directly.

Nicole had told a very different version of the story. She'd been Jessica Cameron's closest friend before and during her pregnancy, privy to what had occurred during the period when Jessica was staying with her aunt, Evelyn Walker, and her cousin, Tessa.

'She said Gavin Lynch kept coming to the house, trying to see my mother,' Rachel said. 'He wanted to apologise.'

It was clear from her face that the possibility had now crossed Rachel's mind that he wasn't coming to apologise at all. He was trying to see the girl he loved, the girl who was carrying their child.

'They wouldn't let him see her. But he got sneaky. He tried to get to her through Tessa. Asked her to let him know when her parents weren't around so that he could sneak in. But Nicole reckoned Tessa had a crush on him. When my mother collapsed, her aunt wasn't at home. Tessa was. And Nicole thinks she deliberately delayed calling the ambulance. Because she wanted my mother to lose the baby, lose me, or even die herself.'

Nobody needed to say that her prayer had been answered.

'She was just a kid,' Rachel went on. 'Nobody blamed her. Her pregnant cousin had collapsed. She panicked. It's understandable. But Nicole said there was a look in her eye when she told the story afterwards. Like she was trying hard not to laugh at her own cleverness.'

It was all supposition based on schoolgirl gossip—not the most reliable of sources. However, it had one unforeseen and serious consequence.

Rachel had told the story to Matt Cameron.

Suddenly, the cousin he'd been so close to, Tessa, was cast in a very different light. A jealous, vindictive bitch who contributed to his sister's death as a result of putting her feelings for the person he despised most in the world above all else. He responded with an equally-vindictive attempt to frame her, using a quote from the book on Thomas Browne he'd given her as Roy Lynch's suicide note.

That killing had been made to look like a suicide so as not to spook the other victims. But he'd known the deception would eventually be discovered. And he'd done his best to point the finger at Tessa when it was.

'And Nicole didn't say anything about it being consensual?' Angel said. 'She knew everything else that was going on in that house, but she never once said Jessica confided in her that it wasn't rape?'

Rachel shook her head solemnly.

'Never. Nicole insisted Gavin just wanted to see her to apologise for raping her.'

Angel and Kincade were planning on speaking to Nicole Johnston at the earliest opportunity. At present, it was impossible to say whether she would back Rachel up or not. It would hinge on whether she wanted her long-dead friend painted as an innocent victim or a promiscuous minx who opened her legs for every boy who told her he loved her.

'What happened after Matt came out of the bedroom?' Angel said. 'Did you go back in?'

'He wouldn't let me. I'm not stupid. I knew he'd killed him. I'd heard all the noise and then suddenly it went quiet. And he was sweating like a pig when he came out. He grabbed me by the arm and marched me down the stairs. Said we didn't have time to hang around. Not after all the noise I'd made screaming. Like it was my fault. I knew he was right. About not hanging around, I mean. I didn't know what to think about . . .' She struggled deciding on a way to describe her father, then didn't bother to finish the sentence. 'So I went with him.'

'To the campsite?'

'Yeah.'

'What happened when you got there?'

'We had a massive argument. He had a bottle of whisky in the tent. Things started to get nasty as we drank it. I said he didn't care about my mother. His sister. All he cared about was his broken ankle and not being a professional footballer and earning millions. He called me a stupid bitch for believing anything Gavin said when he was trying to save his skin. He started taking the piss, putting on these silly voices. *I love you, Gavin. I love you, too, Jessica. Let's make a baby.* And I'm getting more and more wound up.'

She paused, took a sip of water from the paper cup she'd been toying with as she spoke.

'Then he said I was exactly like my mother who'd been a stupid cow for believing Gavin when he said he loved her, just so she wouldn't cry rape. That's when I slapped him. I thought it would snap us both out of it. But he slapped me back, knocked me to the ground. He sat on top of me and grabbed me by the neck. Started strangling me.' She'd already been examined by a doctor, the bruising to her neck noted. Despite that, she held her chin up so that they could see it for themselves. 'I thought he was going to kill me. I started to black out. There was a knife on a plate on the ground from when he'd been preparing food for a barbeque earlier. I grabbed it and slashed at him to try to get him to let go of my throat. And suddenly there's blood spraying out of his neck and all over me. That's when I passed out. He was already dead when I came to. I know I should've called the police, but I was in shock.'

The decision wasn't Angel's to make, but it was likely she would be charged as an accessory to the murder of Gavin Lynch.

Even if it were true that she wasn't in the room at the time, she'd helped carry him upstairs and tie him to the bed. After Roy Lynch and Guy Yardley had already been murdered, she wasn't stupid enough to claim she thought it was only to scare him. The *mens rea*, the criminal intent, was present.

It would be for the Crown Prosecution Service, in conjunction with police officers a number of pay grades above Angel and Kincade's, to assess the reasonableness of Rachel's actions in acting in self-defence as Matt Cameron sat astride her and strangled her. Given that he'd already murdered Roy Lynch and Guy Yardley by similar means, it was likely she would be viewed as justified in believing that her life was at risk.

That was all before they spoke to Nicole Johnston.

53

Nicole Johnston looked as if she wished she'd said a final goodbye to her friend Jessica thirty years previously and had never given her another thought, not posted the picture of her on Facebook that had led Rachel to her door.

The presence of Angel and Kincade at that same door told her nothing good had come from the secrets she'd shared with her.

But it was Angel and Kincade who were in for the biggest shock.

It started well enough.

'We'd like you to take us through exactly what you told Rachel,' Angel said.

Nicole shook her head. Angel and Kincade shared a look. She didn't look as if she had it in her to refuse to cooperate with the police in a murder enquiry. Except it wasn't that at all.

'It's what I didn't tell her that's important . . .'

Angel stopped her there.

'We'll get to that in a minute. We need to confirm what you did tell her first.'

Nicole looked as if she was about to argue, then decided it

was easier and quicker to simply comply. She confirmed everything they'd already been told by Rachel.

Jessica had never once said anything to Nicole other than she'd been raped by Gavin Lynch. She was fifteen at the time.

She'd refused to tell anyone else who the father was, let alone accuse him of rape, because she was scared of both Gavin and his father, Roy—even after she moved in with her aunt.

Her refusal to have an abortion was a private decision based on her own beliefs.

Gavin had repeatedly tried to see Jessica whilst she was living with her aunt, claiming he wanted to apologise. Nicole believed his aim was to threaten her. He was aware that Jessica could accuse him at any time, DNA from the baby she carried proving his guilt.

Nicole believed Jessica's cousin, Tessa, had a crush on Gavin. As a result, she deliberately delayed calling an ambulance when Jessica collapsed.

'I don't want to think about whether Tessa thought the consequences through,' Nicole said. 'That would make her a monster. Now can we get on to what I didn't tell Rachel?'

Angel extended his hand towards her, please do.

'I didn't think it was important at the time,' Nicole began. 'Rachel's life was screwed up enough as it was. I didn't want to add to that for no good reason. Her mother, Jessica, wasn't Lucas Cameron's daughter...'

'Aiden Cameron,' Angel said, feeling the crushing weight of inescapable inevitability descend on him.

Nicole nodded unhappily as if she'd been the one to broker the liaison.

'Lucas Cameron was a workaholic. His wife was a party girl. That's how she ended up with Roy Lynch. But she had a one-night stand years before that with Lucas's brother, Aiden. And she got pregnant. That's why Aiden went to America.'

'Jessica told you this?' Angel said.

'Yeah.'

'How did she know?'

'Her mother told her.' She held up her hand as if to ward off their misunderstanding. 'Not sat her down and told her. Her mother was drunk. They were arguing. Jessica had found out about the affair with Roy Lynch. She said to her, *how can you do that to Dad?* And her mother said something like, *Dad? He's not your real father, so what do you care?* Then it all came out. Jessica never told anyone apart from me. And she thought her mother had forgotten in the morning.'

Angel came away thinking he wasn't so sure money was the root of all evil. A lot of the blame should be laid at alcohol's door. It had no doubt played a part in Marianne and Aiden's one-night stand. It had caused Marianne to blurt the truth out to her daughter. And, as they would find out, it had shaped a lot of what had really happened in Matt Cameron's tent on the night he died.

ANGEL PUT IT TO RACHEL THAT EVERYTHING SHE'D SAID IN THE previous interview concerning the deaths of Roy Lynch, Guy Yardley and Gavin Lynch should remain exactly as she'd told them, apart from the simple but crucial substitution of the name Aiden for Matt in every case.

Having been informed that Aiden Cameron was in a cell waiting to be interviewed immediately after her, Rachel found herself in a classic prisoner's dilemma. She chose to tell the truth, pointing the finger squarely at Aiden Cameron.

She also told them the true version of what had happened in Matt Cameron's tent in the aftermath of Gavin Lynch's murder.

'Aiden knew Matt was camping in The New Forest. I called him as we were leaving the house. Told him I was in trouble and needed his help. Aiden dropped me at the campsite and drove home. He hasn't got a problem driving after his operation. It was his left leg and his car's an automatic.'

Nobody needed to say that the fact that he'd have been uninsured so soon after his operation was the least of Aiden Cameron's worries.

'I told Matt all about it. He'd already been drinking. It was like I'd made his day, telling him Gavin Lynch was dead. He was toasting Gavin's death. I joined in, wanting to get on the right side of him. Then I asked him to give me an alibi, say I'd been with him the whole time. And he said, you bet, if I couldn't kill the bastard, it's the least I can do.'

She began to chew intently at a fingernail. They were all bitten to the quick, some raw and bloody. They hadn't been like that in the last interview.

'Matt was getting more and more carried away as he kept drinking. But the more he went on about how much he'd hated Gavin, what a bastard he was who'd ruined all their lives, the more the doubts grew in my mind about whether Gavin had raped my mother. Like for some subconscious reason I had to balance everything bad he was saying with something good.'

She fell silent as she contemplated the stupid admission she'd made that changed everything. She closed her eyes, took herself back to the tent where her search for her identity had reached its horrific climax, her voice coming from a long way away when she spoke again.

'I'm not sure Gavin raped my mum.'

Matt Cameron choked on the mouthful of whisky he'd just swigged from the half-empty bottle.

'What?'

'He said he loved her. And she loved him.'

All of the good humour the news of Gavin Lynch's death had produced went out of him. Now looking at her as if not only had it been a brutal rape, but that the result of that hate-filled assault, the child it had spawned, herself, Rachel, was tainted with the evil that lay behind it, that evil manifesting itself in contemptible stupidity and naïve sentimentality.

'*If you believe anything Gavin said just to save his skin, you're as stupid as your mother was for believing him when he said he loved her, just so she wouldn't cry rape. Jesus wept. I can't believe women are so stupid.*'

'What do you know about women, you fucking queer?'

'No wonder your family didn't want you and gave you away, you poisonous little bitch.'

Angel had long ago ceased being surprised at fate's unerring ability to make people somehow pick on the absolute worst thing to say in any situation.

The argument hadn't been so different to the one Rachel had first described. But the devil is in the detail. Rachel had touched the raw nerve of Matt's unacknowledged homosexuality. And he'd responded in kind with a spiteful remark that went to the core of the problem that defined her life.

She blew the air from her cheeks, looked at Angel and Kincade as if surprised that they were there.

'That was when I slapped him. Everything else happened exactly like I told it to you yesterday.'

Aiden Cameron confessed to all three murders. It all made sense once he had. He'd lost the most. His brother, Lucas. And his daughter, Jessica. Fate hadn't even been satisfied with that, striking him down with an illness that prevented him from coming home to attend her funeral.

He didn't even get to say goodbye.

Thirty years of dormant anger and hatred were rudely awakened by his granddaughter, Rachel, turning up at his door.

He'd known that she'd survived, but had not tried to stop her from being put into care, the family ramifications too complex and damaging for all concerned. Rachel herself might have disagreed—not quite *all* concerned.

The hardest part to pull off had been the initial approach to Roy Lynch. Like all the best lies, Aiden worked a lot of truth into the story he told when he called him. Rachel had approached him demanding money. He didn't have any. He knew that Roy did. DNA would prove that Roy's son Gavin was her father—and there was no statute of limitations on sexual assault. Surely Roy wanted to protect his son, make the problem go away? One way or the other. He had a picture of Rachel and an address for her. Would Roy be interested in seeing them? Roy told him to come to the house. Nobody wants a digital footprint of evidence like that floating around in the ether.

Before calling Lynch, Aiden had taken a saw to the stock and barrel of the Armsan Paragon Grande semi-auto shotgun that he used for wildfowling in order to conceal it under his coat. At the house, he'd mixed GHB into a glass of water and forced Lynch to drink it at gunpoint.

During Lynch's and the other murders, he'd found that the adrenaline rush and spiteful satisfaction of long-overdue justice having its day was better than any pills the doctors might prescribe following his hip operation.

His confession was in part inspired by his guilt over causing Matt's death. He was well aware that Rachel was unstable, and that she was having a crisis of conscience over the killing of her father. He also knew that Matt Cameron was a heavy drinker prone to argumentative bouts of self-pity when drunk. And he'd been the one to tell Rachel that Matt struggled with his closet homosexuality.

He should never have put them together in a small tent with a bottle of whisky—a facilitator, if not the actual root, of all evil.

54

'I WANT TO GO TO CONFESSION,' SIX-YEAR-OLD DAISY KINCADE yelled after she and her sister, Isla, opened the door to Angel, their mother behind them, wineglass in hand.

She had the girls down for the weekend and had quickly concluded that she wouldn't get a minute's peace until she invited the strange man she worked with to an early dinner for that strangeness to be demonstrated to their satisfaction.

He squatted down to Daisy's level.

'Have you committed any sins, Daisy?'

Daisy inspected her shoes as she thought about it, then looked at her sister.

'Isla brushes Arthur with Hannah's toothbrush. He's our hamster.'

Isla came right back at her.

'You do, too.'

The stifled snort from Kincade reminded him who Hannah was—her husband's new partner, variously described as a bunny boiler and a gold digger. He went back to Daisy as her mother shook her head, hiding her smile behind her glass.

'Does Arthur look smart afterwards?'

Daisy nodded happily.

'Then I'm not sure it's a sin.' He glanced at Kincade who widened her eyes at him. 'You'll have to try harder.'

As with all children and a lot of adults, information goes in, but it doesn't stay in for long. Daisy now demonstrated the phenomenon.

'Mummy says you love the lady who cuts up the dead bodies.'

Angel bit down hard to stop himself from laughing, saw Kincade doing the same.

'Really? Then I think it's Mummy who should go to confession. Telling lies is a very bad sin.'

'So is beating up prisoners in the cells,' Isla said. 'That's what Daddy says she did.'

Out of the mouths of babes, Angel couldn't help but wonder.

'Well, yes. It looks like we'll have to book Mummy in for a double session.'

They made their way through to the kitchen. Kincade handed him a glass of red wine, refilled hers at the same time.

'Play something on your mouth organ,' Daisy demanded.

Angel wasn't sure he liked the logical progression that flowed so easily in the uncluttered mind of a child. Sins to confession to the implied penance to him playing the harmonica.

'Maybe later.'

'*No!* Now.' Two small pairs of lungs bellowing in unison.

'Not with me in the room,' Kincade said with no less heartfelt emotion.

Angel suddenly found a small girl clamped onto each of his hands, tugging him.

'In our bedroom,' said Isla, sounding like a hanging judge passing sentence.

'You can see the sea,' Daisy added.

Angel allowed himself to be dragged.

'Maybe I forgot to bring it with me.'

'What was that you said about lying being a sin?' Kincade called after him as he was led away. She followed slowly behind the small cortège, the girls' bedroom door shut firmly in her face as soon as they had their captive inside.

'Don't you dare play something sad,' she said quietly to herself.

Too late, the sounds of something haunting and poignant already coming through the door. Life's too short, she thought as she recognised *Green, Green, Grass Of Home* a moment later, the familiar lyrics running through her head.

She hoped nobody on the other side noticed when she put her ear against the door.

ALSO BY THE AUTHOR

The Angel & Kincade Mysteries

THE REVENANT

When ex-drug dealer Roy Lynch is found hanged in his garage, a supposed routine suicide soon becomes more insidious. As the body count rises, DI Max Angel and DS Catalina Kincade are forced to look to the past, cutting through thirty years of deceit and betrayal and lies to reveal the family secrets buried below. The tragedy they unearth makes it horrifically clear that in a world filled with hatred and pain, nothing comes close to what families do to one another.

The Evan Buckley Thrillers

BAD TO THE BONES

When Evan Buckley's latest client ends up swinging on a rope, he's ready to call it a day. But he's an awkward cuss with a soft spot for a sad story and he takes on one last job—a child and husband who disappeared ten years ago. It's a long-dead investigation that everybody wants to stay that way, but he vows to uncover the truth—and in the process, kick into touch the demons who come to torment him every night.

KENTUCKY VICE

Maverick private investigator Evan Buckley is no stranger to self-induced mayhem—but even he's mystified by the jam college buddy Jesse Springer has got himself into. When Jesse shows up with a wad of explicit photographs that arrived in the mail, Evan finds himself caught up in the most bizarre case of blackmail he's ever encountered—Jesse swears blind he can't remember a thing about it.

SINS OF THE FATHER

Fifty years ago, Frank Hanna made a mistake. He's never forgiven himself. Nor has anybody else for that matter. Now the time has come to atone for his sins, and he hires maverick PI Evan Buckley to peel back fifty years of lies and deceit to uncover the tragic story hidden underneath. Trouble is, not everybody likes a happy ending and some very nasty people are out to make sure he doesn't succeed.

NO REST FOR THE WICKED

When an armed gang on the run from a botched robbery that left a man dead invade an exclusive luxury hotel buried in the mountains of upstate New York, maverick P.I. Evan Buckley has got his work cut out. He just won a trip for two and was hoping for a well-earned rest. But when the gang takes Evan's partner Gina hostage along with the other guests and their spirited seven-year-old daughter, he can forget any kind of rest.

RESURRECTION BLUES

After Levi Stone shows private-eye Evan Buckley a picture of his wife Lauren in the arms of another man, Evan quickly finds himself caught up in Lauren's shadowy past. The things he unearths force Levi to face the bitter truth—that he never knew his wife at all—or any of the dark secrets that surround her mother's death and the disappearance of her father, and soon Evan's caught in the middle of a lethal vendetta.

HUNTING DIXIE

Haunted by the unsolved disappearance of his wife Sarah, PI Evan Buckley loses himself in other people's problems. But when Sarah's scheming and treacherous friend Carly shows up promising new information, the past and present collide violently for Evan. He knows he can't trust her, but he hasn't got a choice when she confesses what she's done, leaving Sarah prey to a vicious gang with Old Testament ideas about crime and punishment.

THE ROAD TO DELIVERANCE

Evan Buckley's wife Sarah went to work one day and didn't come home. He's been looking for her ever since. As he digs deeper into the unsolved death of a man killed by the side of the road, the last known person to see Sarah alive, he's forced to re-trace the footsteps of her torturous journey, unearthing a dark secret from her past that drove her desperate attempts to make amends for the guilt she can never leave behind.

SACRIFICE

When PI Evan Buckley's mentor asks him to check up on an old friend, neither of them are prepared for the litany of death and destruction that he unearths down in the Florida Keys. Meanwhile Kate Guillory battles with her own demons in her search for salvation and sanity. As their paths converge, each of them must make an impossible choice that stretches conscience and tests courage, and in the end demands sacrifice—what would you give to get what you want?

ROUGH JUSTICE

After a woman last seen alive twenty years ago turns up dead, PI Evan Buckley heads off to a small town on the Maine coast where he unearths a series of brutal unsolved murders. The more he digs, lifting the lid on old grievances and buried injustices that have festered for half a lifetime, the more the evidence points to a far worse crime, leaving him facing an impossible dilemma – disclose the terrible secrets he's uncovered or assume the role of hanging judge and dispense a rough justice of his own.

TOUCHING DARKNESS

When PI Evan Buckley stops for a young girl huddled at the side of the road on a deserted stretch of highway, it's clear she's running away from someone or something—however vehemently she denies it. At times angry and hostile, at others scared and vulnerable, he's almost relieved when she runs out on him in the middle of the night. Except he has a nasty premonition that he hasn't heard the last of her. Nor does it take long before he's proved horribly right, the consequences dire for himself and Detective Kate Guillory.

A LONG TIME COMING

Five years ago, PI Evan Buckley's wife Sarah committed suicide in a mental asylum. Or so they told him. Now there's a different woman in her grave and he's got a stolen psychiatric report in his hand and a tormented scream running through his head.

Someone is lying to him. With his own sanity at stake, he joins forces with a disgraced ex-CIA agent on a journey to confront the past that leads him to the jungles of Central America and the aftermath of a forgotten war, where memories are long and grievances still raw.

LEGACY OF LIES

Twenty years ago, Detective Kate Guillory's father committed suicide. Nobody has ever told her why. Now a man is stalking her. When PI Evan Buckley takes on the case, his search takes him to the coal mining mountains of West Virginia and the hostile aftermath of a malignant cult abandoned decades earlier. As he digs deeper into the unsolved crimes committed there and discovers the stalker's bitter grudge against Kate, one thing becomes horrifyingly clear – what started back then isn't over yet.

DIG TWO GRAVES

Boston heiress Arabella Carlson has been in hiding for thirty years. Now she's trying to make it back home. But after PI Evan Buckley saves her from being stabbed to death, she disappears again. Hired by her dying father to find her and bring her home safe before the killers hunting her get lucky, he finds there's more than money at stake as he opens up old wounds, peeling back a lifetime of lies and deceit. Someone's about to learn a painful lesson the hard way: Before you embark on a journey of revenge, dig two graves.

ATONEMENT

When PI Evan Buckley delves into an unsolved bank robbery from forty years ago that everyone wants to forget, he soon learns it's anything but what it seems to be. From the otherworldly beauty of Caddo Lake and the East Texas swamps to the bright lights and cheap thrills of Rehoboth Beach, he follows the trail of a nameless killer. Always one step behind, he discovers that there are no limits to the horrific crimes men's greed drives them to commit, not constrained by law or human decency.

THE JUDAS GATE

When a young boy's remains are found in a shallow grave on land belonging to PI Evan Buckley's avowed enemy, the monster Carl Hendricks, the police are desperate for Evan's help in solving a case that's been dead in the water for the past thirteen years. Hendricks is dying, and Evan is the only person he'll share his deathbed confession with. Except Evan knows Hendricks of old. Did he really kill the boy? And if so, why does he want to confess to Evan?

OLD SCORES

When upcoming country music star Taylor Harris hires a private investigator to catch her cheating husband, she gets a lot more than she bargained for. He's found a secret in her past that even she's not aware of - a curse on her life, a blood feud hanging over her for thirty years. But when he disappears, it's down to PI Evan Buckley to pick up the pieces. Was the threat real? And if so, did it disappear along with the crooked investigator? Or did it just get worse?

ONCE BITTEN

When PI Evan Buckley's mentor, Elwood Crow, asks a simple favor of him – to review a twenty-year-old autopsy report – there's only one thing Evan can be sure of: simple is the one thing it won't be. As he heads off to Cape Ann on the Massachusetts coast Evan soon finds himself on the trail of a female serial killer, and the more he digs, the more two questions align themselves. Why has the connection not been made before? And is Crow's interest in finding the truth or in saving his own skin?

NEVER GO BACK

When the heir to a billion-dollar business empire goes missing in the medieval city of Cambridge in England, PI Evan Buckley heads across the Atlantic on what promises to be a routine assignment. But as Evan tracks Barrett Bradlee from the narrow cobbled streets of the city to the windswept watery expanses of the East Anglian fens, it soon becomes clear that the secretive family who hired him to find the missing heir haven't told him the whole truth.

SEE NO EVIL

When Ava Hart's boyfriend, Daryl Pierce, is shot to death in his home on the same night he witnessed a man being abducted, the police are quick to write it off as a case of wrong place, wrong time. Ava disagrees. She's convinced they killed him. And she's hired PI Evan Buckley to unearth the truth. Trouble is, as Evan discovers all too soon, Ava wouldn't recognize the truth if it jumped up and bit her on the ass.

DO UNTO OTHERS

Five years ago, a light aircraft owned by Mexican drug baron and people trafficker Esteban Aguilar went down in the middle of the Louisiana swamps. The pilot and another man were found dead inside, both shot to death. The prisoner who'd been handcuffed in the back was nowhere to be found. And now it's down to PI Evan Buckley to find crime boss Stan Fraser's son Arlo who's gone missing trying to get to the bottom of what the hell happened.

Exclusive books for my Readers' Group
FALLEN ANGEL

When Jessica Henderson falls to her death from the window of her fifteenth-floor apartment, the police are quick to write it off as an open and shut case of suicide. The room was locked from the inside, after all. But Jessica's sister doesn't buy it and hires Evan Buckley to investigate. The deeper Evan digs, the more he discovers the dead girl had fallen in more ways than one.

A ROCK AND A HARD PLACE

Private-eye Evan Buckley's not used to getting something for nothing. So when an unexpected windfall lands in his lap, he's intrigued. Not least because he can't think what he's done to deserve it. Written off by the police as one more sad example of mindless street crime, Evan feels honor-bound to investigate, driven by his need to give satisfaction to a murdered woman he never knew.

Join my mailing list at www.jamesharperbooks.com and get your FREE copies of Fallen Angel and A Rock And A Hard Place.

Printed in Great Britain
by Amazon